"Are You Offended?"

Travis's voice behind her was like the brush of velvet. Jessica turned and looked helplessly at the lips that had just touched her skin. She couldn't quite believe it, but he was bending slowly, his mouth coming toward hers. She felt breathless, dizzy. He was going to kiss her, but she might well faint before it happened. The accursed corset strings were pulled so tight. Had her mother done it as a precaution, thus ensuring Jessica would never know what it was like to be kissed by Travis Parnell?

Then his lips were against hers, his breath warm, and she didn't faint. He encircled her waist with his hands and pulled her forward. Jessica was floating, tingling waves of warmth radiating from every point of contact between them. His hands at her waist tightened; his kiss deepened. But then abruptly it was over.

Other Leisure Books by Elizabeth Chadwick:

Wanton Angel
Widow's Fire

Virgin Fire

Elizabeth Chadwick

LEISURE BOOKS  NEW YORK CITY

For my wonderful parents,
who taught me to love books.

Special thanks to Alicia Condon, my editor,
whose advice is always excellent; to Joann Cole-
man, who so patiently reads my manuscripts; to
James Stowe, whose writing workshops are an
inspiration to every writer who has taken them;
and to Margaret Burlingame and Pat
Worthington, who can always recommend the
perfect book when I'm doing research.

A LEISURE BOOK®

August 1991

Published by

Dorchester Publishing Co., Inc.
276 Fifth Avenue
New York, NY 10001

Prologue

Fort Worth, Texas
November, 1883

Travis Parnell was eight years old the morning he rode into Fort Worth with his father. They'd been several days on the road from Jack County, stopping over at night with Pa's friends. "First the bankers, then the birthday present!" Will Parnell promised, his smile so enthusiastic that Travis felt the excitement rising like bubbles in a hot spring.

Folks in Jack County liked to say that Will Parnell had a smile could make a corpse rise up and dance at his own wake and that when Will laughed, everyone laughed with him for the pure joy of it. Of course, they didn't know that sometimes, instead of laughing, Pa fell into sadness. Sometimes he sat by the fire staring at Mama's picture and drinking whiskey until the bottles piled up by his chair. Sometimes he never said a word for a whole day, or even a week, but that wasn't often. Mostly, since Mama died, Travis and his father spent all their time together, and Pa made life seem like a wonderful adventure.

Just before they left for Fort Worth, Pa had said, "You're a big boy now, pardner. Think I'll take you along an' show you off to the bankers, let 'em take a look at my son an' heir."

So for the first time Travis got to see the trains puffing into the Texas and Pacific station and the streetcars rocking on their tracks between the depot and the courthouse, where more horses and buggies and wagons were herded together than folks saw in a whole year out in Jack County. And people—there were people everywhere—cowboys staggering out of the saloons, drunk and happy; ranchers lounging on the corners talking drought and fence cutting and tick fever just like everybody did back home; and ladies in fancy clothes buying things in the shops, where you could find just about anything you wanted, including a brand-new birthday saddle for a boy just eight years old. And finally the Cattleman's Bank, a three-story stone fort of a building with slitted windows looking out over all the sights.

Travis held on tight to his father's hand, staring wide-eyed at everything and listening carefully while Pa told him about bankers—which was an important subject because Travis and his father were partners in the cattle business, and Pa said a cattleman needed a good banker to carry him over the lean years.

"Texas ranchers never had a better friend than Hugh Gresham." His father was pushing open the heavy door to the bank. "Back in '79 when the state started sellin' land for fifty cents an acre, Hugh said, 'Will, buy all you can while we got money to lend,' so that's what I did. Then he said I ought to borrow enough to fence it, an' I did that too."

Travis nodded as he looked at the marble floors and the men standing behind metal grills shuffling money like cards in a bunkhouse poker game. He knew about the land-buying and the fencing, but he never got tired of hearing his father's stories, especially the ones about how they were on their way to owning the biggest ranch in Texas.

"So I bought our land, instead of dependin' on open range like so many did, an' then I fenced it," said Will Parnell. "Cost a pretty penny, but we're gonna put a million acres under barbed wire before we're through, boy, an' when we have an occasional bad year, Hugh Gresham an' Cattleman's will tide us over."

Travis believed it. He could tell, when a prune-faced man with round spectacles showed them into the banker's office, that Mr. Gresham was very rich. He had a carpet with flowers all over it such as Travis had never seen before and a big desk made of shiny wood that was as smooth as an oiled leather saddle. Mr. Gresham sat on a brown leather chair behind his desk. Travis's father took the one in front of the desk, and Mrs. Gresham, who was a very beautiful lady—although not as beautiful as Travis's mother had been—perched on the arm of Mr. Gresham's chair like a pretty bird on a live oak branch.

She looked rich too. She was wearing a sort of purply dress with so many ruffles all over her bottom that Travis wondered how she could ever sit down properly and so much lace on the front that he bet it got into her beans when she ate supper. But pretty as she was, Mrs. Gresham didn't seem to like little boys, because when he was introduced, she didn't say hello; she said, "Your boots are dirty!" which surprised Travis. Dirty boots didn't upset anyone at home. Then she pointed her finger and said, "You'll have to sit on the floor, and don't you get mud on Mr. Gresham's carpet!"

11

Because his father nodded to him, Travis walked carefully around the edge and sat down on the hardwood floor to play with his lead soldiers that he'd got for his fifth birthday just before his mother died. He didn't think Mrs. Gresham was a very nice lady, but Pa evidently did. He said, "Well, Penelope, you're lookin' as beautiful as ever." Pa had a way with the ladies; everybody said so. Since nobody was looking at him, Travis rolled up a corner of the carpet to make a fort for his soldiers.

"Our talkin' business will surely bore you, Penelope," said Pa in the voice he used when he was being polite but really wished the person would leave. He sounded like that when the traveling preacher stopped over. Travis untied his cowhide pouch and spilled the soldiers onto the carpet.

"Why, you know I'm always interested in how you're doing, William Henry," said Mrs. Gresham. "That's why I'm here." And she took off her big feathery hat and dropped it on her husband's desk as if she intended to stay all day. On the floor side of his fort, Travis lined up the lead soldiers with the red coats.

"Well." Pa cleared his throat. "I haven't come with the best news, Hugh. Been a bad year for ranchers because of the tick fever, as I'm sure you know, an' then there's the drought."

"Now, Will," said Mr. Gresham, "I hope you're not going to tell me you won't be making a payment on your loan."

The fort Travis had made unrolled, so he lay down on his stomach and pushed the carpet into a hump with his elbow. Then he lined the red-coated soldiers up again on the floor. He was pretending they were the Mexican army.

"A payment this year?" Pa chuckled. "Glad to know

your sense of humor hasn't failed you, Hugh."

Travis arranged the blue soldiers on the flowery carpet. They were the Texans and the carpet hump the Alamo, a fort where his granddaddy had died. Travis had been named after Colonel William Travis, the commander at the Alamo, who had died too. Everyone had—except the Mexicans.

"Now about my gettin' another loan—" said Pa.

Mr. Gresham frowned. "Will, you owe the bank a lot of money."

"I know that, Hugh, but like I said, it's been a bad year. The open range boys been cuttin' my new fences an' drivin' their stock in to drink out of my water holes."

"I've heard about the wire cutting," said Mr. Gresham.

Travis's father shifted his big body on the leather chair. He'd stopped smiling. "Just last week I took a shot at Manse Rayburn. Never thought I'd shoot a man over land, but it's mine; I paid for it."

"Hugh paid for it," said Mrs. Gresham.

Travis's father laughed again, but he didn't sound much amused. Travis wasn't either. He'd have taken a shot at Mr. Rayburn too if he'd been old enough, but he was only allowed to shoot at rabbits and such. His mother hadn't liked guns at all.

"When *do* you expect to repay your notes, Will?" asked Mr. Gresham.

"Well, times are bound to get better," said Pa. "With a new loan to tide me over, I ought to see the turnaround in a year's time, maybe two."

Travis mounted his cannons on the Alamo hump in the carpet and blew over half the Mexican soldiers on the floor. He wished they had a carpet at home. It was better than dirt for playing soldiers.

"I'm not a rich man, Will," said Mr. Gresham. "It's

not as if I can give you the money myself."

"I wouldn't expect it, Hugh," said Pa, "but like you're always tellin' me, the bank's in business to lend money."

"Not when we don't get it back," said Mr. Gresham. "The fact is, Will, I'm going to have to call your notes."

There was a long silence while Travis set the Mexican soldiers back up. He wasn't sure what "calling a note" meant unless it was like "calling a square dance." Pa had been a wonderful dancer before Mama died, the best in Jack County. Everyone said so.

"You can't do that," said Pa. His face had got very white. "I'd lose everything."

Travis sat up because he knew something had gone wrong.

"What did you expect, William Henry?" asked Mrs. Gresham. "Borrowing all that money the way you did!"

Because Travis had taken his elbow off the carpet, the Alamo flattened out, and the cannons fell off and knocked over all the Texas soldiers.

"Hugh, you're the one who convinced me to take out those loans," said Will Parnell. "You can't—"

"I have no choice, Will," interrupted Mr. Gresham. "There's my shareholders to consider."

"And Justin Harte's one of them. He'll never let you get away with this." Pa sounded to Travis just the way he'd sounded when the doctor told him Mama wasn't going to make it. "We've been friends for years, Justin and me. We rode together in Cureton's Rangers during the war."

Then Mrs. Gresham smiled and said, "Why, William Henry, Justin's not in town; he's not even in the state, so you can't count on him to save you." She gave Travis's father another smile, a really mean one. "By the time Justin Harte gets back, you won't have an acre left to call your own."

Mrs. Gresham scared Travis. When his own mother had smiled, you knew she really liked you, but when Mrs. Gresham smiled, she looked as if she expected something awful to happen and could hardly wait to see it, although Travis didn't know why she'd want anything bad to happen to Pa. Everyone liked William Henry Parnell. Travis decided she must be a bad lady—like the witches in the bedtime stories Mama used to tell. He didn't like Mrs. Gresham at all.

Pa shouted at Mr. Gresham when the banker said something else about his shareholders, but shouting didn't do any good. Then they went back to the hotel.

When they got to their room, Travis tried to cheer his father up. He tugged at Pa's hand and said, "We don't need their money. We can get rich all by our own selves."

His father smiled. "That's right, pardner," he agreed, but his smile wasn't the happy kind; it reminded Travis of Mama's when she was so sick and trying to pretend she wasn't.

Then his father sat in a big chair by the bed and drank a lot of whiskey, just the way he did at home. After an hour or two, Travis asked hopefully if they were going out to supper. His father gave him a handful of money and said to buy himself something to eat, but Travis didn't want to do that. He and his father always ate together, and Travis didn't know where to get supper or how you went about it.

Still, he didn't want Pa thinking he was scared to go out by himself, so he put his soldiers away, went downstairs, and wandered around until he noticed a candy store. Travis didn't see much candy in Jack County, so he bought some, and it tasted wonderful and cost hardly any money. That was a good thing since the banker wouldn't give them any more and even wanted some back.

Then Travis watched the mule cars coming and going between the courthouse and the station, and after that he stood at the window of the gunsmith's, looking at the guns and deciding which ones he'd have when he was a big boy and he and Pa were rich and owned a million acres, like Pa was always saying. By that time he figured he'd stayed away long enough to have had supper if he'd known how to get it, so he headed back toward the hotel. He didn't think his father would notice that he hadn't spent all the money. Pa didn't notice much of anything after he stopped talking and started drinking.

Travis climbed the stairs again and turned left down the hall just like he had before, but when he opened the door, something was wrong. His father was still sitting in the chair, but his head had tipped over, and the front of his shirt hung red and wet with blood. On the floor an old Colt revolver lay among the broken whiskey bottles.

"Daddy?" Travis didn't usually call him Daddy because Will Parnell said that eight years old was too old for baby names, but this time Travis forgot because he was so scared. Someone had shot his father!

He took one last, frightened look and ran downstairs to tell the man at the desk that Pa needed a doctor.

"Likely he just needs a night to sleep it off," said the man. "He's had two bottles sent up this afternoon."

"He's bleeding," said Travis. "He needs a doctor."

The man took the steps two at a time and threw open the door without knocking.

"The bad lady shot him," said Travis.

"What lady?"

"Mrs. Gresham. She lives over at the Cattleman's Bank."

"Well, that's one for the books."

Which books? Travis wondered.

The man leaned over and put his hand on William Henry Parnell's neck. Then he straightened, shaking his head. "He don't need a doctor, boy. He's dead."

"No, he isn't!" Travis knew what dead meant. His mother was dead. If his father were dead too, they'd put him in the ground and throw dirt on him, and he'd never come back. "He's not dead," said Travis. "The bad lady shot him, but—"

"Stop sayin' that, boy. You'll get yourself in a heap of trouble tellin' lies about important people like Mrs. Gresham. Grand ladies don't go 'round shootin' folks."

"But—"

"Now, you come along with me. I gotta send for the police."

People in the lobby got pretty excited when the man told them Will Parnell had shot himself, although Travis knew it wasn't true. Pa wouldn't have done that. But no one would listen to Travis or even let him go back upstairs. They said things like, "Go away, little boy," and, "Stop pullin' on my sleeve, kid."

While Travis waited, huddled on a chair in the corner, the police arrived, and the man who'd called them went home. Then a new desk clerk came over and ordered Travis out the door. The new man said the hotel didn't allow loitering in the lobby and Travis should go home, but Travis didn't know how he could do that without his father. He didn't even know what *loitering* meant.

Because they wouldn't let him in at the front door,

he slipped up the back stairs. It was dark by then, and he had to find his father, but when he got to the room, Pa was gone. So were all their things—almost as if they'd never been there.

Travis closed the door behind him and walked slowly down the front stairs. They must have taken his father to a doctor. Since Travis knew how to read— even after Mama died, he'd kept up with his lessons 'cause Pa said that's what she would have wanted— he walked up and down the streets looking for a doctor sign, but he didn't find any. Finally, he asked a boy in front of the livery stable if he knew where the doctor lived.

"You got money for a doctor?" the boy asked.

When Travis nodded, the boy pulled him into the alley and knocked him against a big pile of packing boxes and trash. Travis tried to get up and hit back the way the cowboys at home had taught him, but the boy knocked him down again and said, "Stubborn little bastard, ain't ya?" After the third time, Travis didn't get up again. He didn't even *wake* up for a while, and then his head hurt. His supper money and his sheepskin jacket were gone. Feeling sick to his stomach and dizzy, and hoping the big boy wouldn't come back and hit him again, he crawled into a wooden box to wait for Pa. He was cold and hungry, but he knew his father would come looking as soon as the doctor'd sewed him up.

It was only the next morning that Travis realized he'd fallen asleep. The gray November light filtering into his box woke him up. Pa must be awfully worried by now, he thought, an unformed dread beginning to grow in his heart. Not knowing where else to go, Travis returned to the hotel and asked again for his father.

"Don't know him," said the desk clerk.

"The man who was shot last night," Travis persisted.

"The suicide? He's dead, what else? But nobody said he had a kid along, an' if he did, it wouldn't be no dirty little beggar like you. Now git on outa here before I call the police."

Travis knew he was dirty, but he didn't have any place to wash—not here and maybe not in Jack County either. He'd begun to realize that his father really must be dead; otherwise, he'd have come to find Travis. Pa would never have let Travis sleep in a box without any dinner.

Outside, he looked at the strange town, which just yesterday had been so exciting, and he wondered what to do. Go home? Jack County seemed a million miles away, and he didn't know how to get there. Even if he managed to find his way, Mama and Daddy wouldn't be waiting. And although his father had always said that he and Travis were partners, Travis knew the cowboys wouldn't see it that way. They'd want a grown-up to give them orders and pay their wages.

Bewildered and frightened, he trudged down the street past stores that sold birthday saddles he'd never own and restaurants from which came the smell of bacon he couldn't buy. Finally, he got to the Cattleman's Bank. Travis stared at it a long time, rubbing his eyes because he was crying, although he knew he was too old for crying. His father had said so.

That bad lady had killed his father. She'd been happy because they'd had a hard year in Jack County and because her husband wouldn't give Pa any more money. She was probably happy that William Henry Parnell was dead.

Travis wiped away more tears. He was always going

to remember that lady and her husband and their bank. When he got to be a grown-up man, he'd make them sorry they'd killed his daddy. "We're gonna be rich, Daddy," he whispered, "an' we'll get 'em. They'll be sorry."

"Move on, boy," said a man in a leather apron who had come out of the Barnaby Saddle and Harness shop.

Eight years old, hungry, cold, and very frightened, William Travis Parnell moved on.

Book I

Parker County, Texas
August, 1900

Chapter One

"And here's our sister Jessica," said Ned Harte.

So this was Penelope Gresham's daughter. Travis Parnell looked her over while responding courteously to the introduction. Plain little thing, wasn't she? Miss Jessica Harte obviously didn't take after either parent—at least, physically. Penelope Gresham's face was as distinct in his mind today as it had been seventeen years ago when he first saw her at her husband's bank; she had been a great beauty. Harte, Jessica's father, was a handsome man still, as was the girl's stepmother, Anne, a woman with curling red hair and a ready smile. Travis had had an uneasy stirring of memory when he'd been introduced to the father. The name somehow—oh, well, it wasn't the father who interested him; it was the daughter.

And if he were lucky, she wouldn't take after Penelope in temperament. He planned to marry Jessica Harte and didn't relish the idea of saddling himself with a selfish, vicious woman. Still, if that's what he got, it would be worth it, because through Jessica he'd gain access to Penelope Gresham and her husband Hugh, and then he'd make them rue the day they ever heard the name Parnell.

"We call her Jessica the Genius," said Ned, "'cause she's smarter an' got more education than any of us."

"That's enough, Ned," said Anne Harte, glancing at the girl, whose cheeks had flushed with embarrassment.

Genius? Travis suppressed a frown. The last thing he needed was a girl too smart to succumb to a whirlwind courtship conducted for the least romantic of reasons. Then, looking at her again, at that pale hair, severely styled—and hadn't she been wearing spectacles when she entered the parlor?—he decided she'd be vulnerable. Likely as not, even with her rich father, Miss Jessica Harte hadn't had all that many beaus, and now she was going to get herself not just a beau but a husband. If she turned out to be a malicious bitch like her mother, he could divorce her—as Justin Harte had divorced Penelope—but there'd be no divorce until he'd had his revenge on the Greshams.

With those cheerful prospects in mind, Travis smiled warmly at his future wife, and the girl's lips parted in surprise. Hadn't a man ever smiled at her before? he wondered, feeling a little sorry for her. Well, sorry wouldn't avenge his father. Travis's heart clenched as it did every time he thought of William Henry Parnell, his joyous, laughing father whom he'd loved so much, a suicide at thirty-seven, the gun that killed him on the floor beside him, the people that killed him still alive and richer than ever.

Then Jessica Harte smiled back, raising her eyes for the first time, and Travis felt a jolt of pleasure. The smile was as sweet and shy as wild honey, and the eyes—blue, deep blue, wide, and slightly tilted. She never got those eyes from Penelope Gresham. There wasn't a gleam of malice in them, nor an iota of calculation. And when you really looked, she wasn't that plain. Her skin was smooth and clear, her features delicate with a lovely, full mouth. Maybe he'd keep her, he thought wryly. A rich father-in-law never hurt anyone, not that Travis needed Harte's money. He had enough money and enough hate to destroy the Greshams without any financial help. All he needed was to plant himself in their midst, and Miss Jessica would accomplish that for him.

"And this is our sister Frannie, the scamp," said Ned. "Pay no attention to anything she does or says, unless you find a toad in your soup. If you do, Frannie put it there."

"Ned," said Anne Harte reprovingly.

"But, Ma," protested Ned, all injured innocence, "that's just what she did to Henry Barnett last time he came to talk legal business with Pa."

Frannie the scamp, far from being embarrassed, was giggling, a girl of fourteen with her mother's curly red hair. She was going to be a beauty in a few years, Travis thought absently, but she was too young for his purposes, and, more important, she wasn't Penelope's daughter. When he got through with Penelope and Hugh, they'd be poorer and more miserable than William Henry Parnell had been when he killed himself. Travis would do to them what they'd done to his father.

"May I sit next to you, Miss Jessica?" Travis asked when Anne Harte announced dinner. "With your permission, of course, Mrs. Harte."

"Why certainly," said Anne, giving him an approving smile. Poor Jessie had been a bit sad and bored since she got back from school in Washington City, thought Anne. The attention of a handsome young man would be just the thing to cheer her up.

Travis wondered if Anne Harte would be so pleased when she discovered how fast he planned to marry her stepdaughter. He didn't have the time for a long courtship, as he had other business besides the destruction of the Greshams, which money, power, and cunning would bring about. Money was important. Lack of it had destroyed his father. Lots of it would help Travis ruin Gresham, and a man didn't make and keep lots of money by ignoring his livelihood.

As he seated Jessica Harte at the long oak dining table, he rested his hand just briefly on her shoulder. Because he was watching closely, he saw her swallow and duck her head. Good, she wasn't too much an intellectual to be unaware of him in a physical way, which always helped when you were pursuing a woman. This one, although twenty-two and reportedly intelligent, was no sophisticate. Twenty-two and unmarried—he couldn't ask for a more promising situation.

As he took his own seat, strange sounds were floating into the dining room, chopping and swearing, as if some irate lumberjack were in the kitchen dismantling a particularly difficult tree.

"I do hope Mab remembers to take the food out of the can as soon as she gets it open," murmured Anne, looking anxious. "If she doesn't, we'll all surely be poisoned."

Travis knew the theory that canned food turned bad as soon as you opened it, but the theory was nonsense, and he wouldn't have thought a family as rich as the Hartes would be eating their dinner out of a can. "I don't think you need worry, ma'am," he said

26

politely. "In cattle camps, I've eaten canned beans many a time with no ill effects—sometimes as much as a day after opening."

Anne Harte looked horrified. Justin said, "Are you a cattleman, Mr. Parnell? I knew a cattleman once named Parnell."

"There are a heap of Parnells in Texas," said Travis quickly, for he didn't want his father remembered so early on. "Even one in Corsicana, Howard Parnell; no relation of mine, though."

"Don't think I know him," said Justin, sidetracked.

"Travis is an oilman," Ned explained.

"Oil, eh?" A particularly loud thud issued from the kitchen.

"She's missed the can and hit the table again," said Anne.

"With what?" Travis asked, glad to get further away from the subject of his family and truly curious as to what might be going on in the kitchen.

"An axe," said Ned. "She opens cans with an axe, but Mab can't see much beyond her nose. She misses more than she hits."

"Does she?" Travis didn't hold out much hope for a good dinner.

"I don't know anyone in oil," said Justin Harte. "Is it profitable?"

"Very," Travis replied, glad for a chance to impress his future father-in-law, "and should become more so," he predicted, thinking of the information he received periodically about a hill south of Beaumont.

"How'd you get into oil?"

"Well, I was ranching out in Lubbock and Crosby County on my guardian's place—Joe Ray Brock, maybe you know him." Travis was concocting a hastily edited version of his life. Best leave out those four years when he was homeless and hungry in Fort

27

Worth; they might ask why. He'd let them think he'd been with Joe Ray all through his childhood.

"Brock," Justin mused. "Think I've met him. Choleric man, isn't he?"

"That's him," said Travis. "Anyway when I was eighteen or so, I built up a water well drilling business on the side." A business that Travis had established when the rancher refused to let him attend the university at Austin. "Seemed natural to go into oil when it was discovered in Corsicana."

That decision had arisen from the last of many acrimonious skirmishes with Joe Ray, who wanted Travis tending the land and cattle, not out on his own, drilling wells and building windmills. Travis had found his guardian's opposition ironic, since Joe Ray had been one of the first to engage in those activities when he settled on the arid South Plains.

"Besides, I never cared much for the cattle business." As soon as Travis said it, he wished he hadn't because that would hardly sit well with Justin Harte, one of the most powerful cattlemen in the state. Still, it was the truth; Travis hated ranching; dreams of a cattle empire had killed his father, dreams and the greedy machinations of Hugh and Penelope Gresham. According to Joe Ray, they'd confiscated everything his father had left, more than the debts amounted to, and they had never mentioned there was a son to be considered, although he'd been sitting right there by their fancy carpet, playing with his soldiers, never realizing that his childhood was about to end.

To his surprise, Jessica Harte looked up from the soup plate, newly plopped down before her by a stocky, grumpy-looking woman in rough homespun, and gave Travis a sympathetic smile when he said he didn't like ranching.

28

Justin Harte, instead of taking offense, shouted, "Mab, you've used salt instead of flour again to thicken the soup."

"Did not," said Mab.

"It's inedible."

"Then don't eat it," she retorted, not the least intimidated, and snatched it from his place.

Travis watched the byplay with amazement. He knew for a fact the Hartes were rich, but they sure didn't live like it. Oh, they had this big frame house in Weatherford with turrets and verandas and God knows how many rooms, with fancy scrolled woodwork and gardens and trees and a drive to the front door so long no sensible man would want to walk it, but you'd think they'd hire a better cook. Justin Harte was right; the soup was awful. Fortunately, the grumpy woman took his away too and plopped a huge roast down at the head of the table.

Justin began to carve immediately. Travis turned to smile at Jessica, who smiled shyly back and said, "You must be very pleased with the Supreme Court ruling that breaks the Rockefeller monopoly in Corsicana."

Travis blinked. How the hell did she know about that? Waters, Pierce, which was a Rockefeller front, although not everyone in Texas knew or cared, had the Corsicana drillers in a stranglehold because the company controlled all the distribution facilities. "Well, we were pleased when the legislature passed the antitrust laws and the Supreme Court upheld them," Travis agreed, "but I don't think we're out of the woods yet. Word is that they're in bed with Senator Bailey—" Lord, what a way to put it! Hardly the language to use when talking to the young lady he hoped to lure into marriage. "—er—we're afraid he may find a way to get them—Waters, Pierce—back into Texas."

29

"Senator Bailey?" Those wonderful blue eyes widened in astonishment. "Oh, I'm sure he'd do nothing to contravene the court's ruling. Senator Bailey's a friend of Papa's."

"Is he? Well, no doubt you're right," said Travis hastily. "I don't know him myself." But he knew enough about the man to know he was taking bribes from Waters, Pierce. "Now tell me about this education of yours, Miss Jessica."

She didn't look too eager but mumbled, "I went to the Mount Vernon Seminary for Ladies in Washington City."

"Say, Pa, did you know Travis wouldn't volunteer to fight the Spanish?" interrupted David. "Said he'd rather make money drilling for oil in Corsicana than go catch dysentery an' malaria in Florida."

"It wasn't that bad in Florida," Ned protested. "An' we'd a had a lotta fun if we'd ever actually got to Cuba."

"Seems that there's one sensible young man at my table," Justin Harte observed, "and it's not you, Ned. That fool war didn't do a thing but give us a few islands we've no use for and set the Texas economy back twenty years."

"Oh, Pa," protested David, "you fought Indians in the Civil War. Surely you didn't expect us to stay home when our turn came."

Again Travis felt that uneasy prick of memory. Did David mean his father had fought on the frontier during the War Between the States? But that meant—

"I expected you to stay home instead of go chasing after a fool-headed romantic like Teddy Roosevelt," Justin Harte declared. "Mab, why are you taking away Jessica's plate?"

"She wasn't eating so I—"

"The girl hasn't half finished."

"Mab can't see that," said David.

"Then let her get spectacles," said Justin.

"Don't need 'em," said Mab.

What an eccentric household, thought Travis and turned determinedly back to Jessica. "So you're just home from the ladies' seminary?"

"No," said Jessica reluctantly, "I went on to Columbian College for my baccalaureate degree after I finished at Mount Vernon."

Travis was impressed and envious. He'd managed to get some education after his father's death, but a lot of it was from reading on his own. He wondered what his learned wife-to-be would say to the fact that he'd read Tom Paine from a coffee-stained edition he'd plucked from a trash heap in a Fort Worth alley.

"And then she went to the law school at Columbian where all the professors were famous judges," said Justin. "I had to cash in a few favors for that since they don't ordinarily take girls."

"You have a law degree?" Travis asked, taken aback.

"No, I just did the course work. Even Papa couldn't get them to let me graduate."

"Damn fools," muttered Justin. "I'm glad your grandmother didn't live to see that."

Jessica nodded. Cassandra Harte, her beloved grandmother, had always supported her academic aspirations. In many ways she'd been closer to her grandmother than to any other member of the family, and alone among the Harte grandchildren, Jessica had inherited a share of Cassandra's estate, the rest of which went to her sons.

Grandmother Harte had even sympathized with Jessica's aversion to ranch life, her fear of horses, and her embarrassing attacks of sneezing when she got anywhere near cattle. Jessica wondered if cattle affected Mr. Parnell that way, since he disliked ranching. She didn't suppose he was afraid of horses. He didn't look as if he'd be afraid of anything. He also didn't look as if he approved of women studying law. Well, she thought with resignation, experience had hardly led her to expect anything different. He turned to smile at her again—pure politeness, she supposed. "No doubt, you disapprove of higher education for women," she observed, firmly setting aside any romantic flutterings she might have had during their brief acquaintance. "Most men do."

"Why would you say that?" Travis exclaimed. "I think education is invaluable to either sex, and in a woman, it certainly improves her conversation." Jessica Harte looked so astonished that he added, "You're the only woman I know who's talked intelligently—hell, who's talked at all—" Then he realized that he'd used rough language and reflected wryly that his social graces were hardly up to this project; he'd had to watch Jessica constantly out of the corner of his eye just to make sure he used the right eating utensils. "—who's even heard of Waters, Pierce and the antitrust laws. It's a welcome change, I can tell you, to find a woman who can talk about something beside clothes and babies."

"It is?"

Travis could tell by the soft, surprised pleasure on her face that he'd said the right thing. And he hadn't lied. It was going to be unusual to pursue a girl who expected intelligent conversation instead of pretty compliments, but once he'd got her and if he decided to keep her after he'd finished with the Greshams, she'd be very useful to him. A man could get love anywhere, but how many had wives who knew the law? The oil fields spawned more lawsuits than a Texas steer had ticks.

The meal ended with Mab's favorite dessert, unadorned canned peaches. Ned, who sat on the other side of Travis, confided that sometimes they ate really well—when his mother cooked, for she, among other things, made the best apple pie in the world.

"Sh-sh-sh, Ned," said Anne Harte. "You'll hurt Mab's feelings."

Not wanting to overstay his welcome, Travis rose to go after another forty-five minutes of the strange camaraderie of the Harte family, but as he collected his hat, he murmured to Jessica, "Maybe you'd accompany me to the door, Miss Jessica." Again, she looked nonplussed. Hadn't the girl ever had a suitor? She stammered her agreement and followed him out to the steps of the veranda.

"That boy's moving a little fast, isn't he?" asked Justin. "Maybe we ought to find out something about him."

"Oh, for goodness sake, dear," Anne laughed, "it's not as if they're about to elope. Let the girl have a gentleman caller if she likes him."

"Where'd you meet Parnell?" Justin asked Ned.

"We were tryin' out Bag Moster's new filly, you know the one that's so fast? An' Gussie Bannerman was there with the same idea—to get a good horse to ride in the race next month. Well, I made Bag an offer, 'cause b'lieve me, Pa, that horse runs like greased lightnin', an' Gussie made a better, an' I upped 'im, but then seems like I didn't have enough money on me—hadn't figured to pay that much, so Bag, he was gonna sell the filly to Gussie until Travis, who'd been watchin' us ride—he said to me, 'I'll loan you the extra,' an' he did right then an' there, so I bought the filly.''

"Why would he do that for a stranger?" asked Justin suspiciously.

"Travis said she was a fine horse an' oughta win a lotta races with a good rider. Said he liked my style, an' maybe he'd bet on me'n the filly if he was here in Weatherford come race time. So one thing leadin' to another, him an' me and David went off for a drink, an' we ended up invitin' him home. Nice fella, didn't you think?"

"Seemed all right to me," Justin agreed.

Out on the veranda, Travis was saying, "Your family certainly has a variety of hair and eye colors." He wasn't just making idle conversation.

"What you mean," Jessica replied sadly, "is that I don't look like any of them. That's because I'm not their daughter."

"Oh?" said Travis encouragingly. He was sorry to pursue this because she looked so miserable as she said it, but he wanted to know how much she knew about her mother, Penelope Gresham.

"I don't know who my parents are."

Travis frowned. That wasn't the reply he'd expected. "Haven't you asked?"

"Oh yes, but Mother always says, 'You're our daughter.' Unfortunately, that's impossible. The twins and I are only a month apart in age, and Mama couldn't have had three children in two months. Papa won't talk about it at all."

"I see," said Travis, confused. If he had been able to find out that Jessica was the daughter of Justin Harte and Penelope Gresham, who had been married until just after the child's birth, it couldn't be that

34

much of a secret. How had they managed to keep it from Jessica? And why?

Her contention that the twins were her age was certainly a surprise and perhaps explained the family reticence on the whole subject. Anne, who was obviously the boys' mother, couldn't have been married to Harte when she'd had them. Interesting, but irrelevant as far as he was concerned.

"I suppose that I'm a foundling they took in out of kindness," she added. Jessica had noted his bemused expression and assumed that he had been interested in her because she was the daughter of a wealthy cattleman. That had certainly happened before. Now that he knew she wasn't, he would disappear. Jessica felt a sharp stab of regret at the thought. "Well, good night, Mr. Parnell," she said. "It was very pleasant to meet you."

Her quiet farewell jolted Travis out of his calculations and back to his purpose in striking up an acquaintance with the Harte boys. "May I call on you, Miss Jessica?" he asked.

Again the flash of surprise and pleasure in her blue eyes. "Why—why, yes, certainly." Then she seemed to think better of her moment of vulnerable enthusiasm. "We'd be glad to have you visit any time you're in Weatherford, Mr. Parnell."

"Thank you," said Travis. She might be surprised at just how soon he planned to accept that invitation and which member of the family he'd be calling on.

Jessica Harte floated into the house, her previous disappointment dispersed like summer mist by warm sunlight. What a lovely man, she thought, and he seemed to really like her, not her father's money, not her mother's cooking—her, Jessica. He hadn't even minded that she was smart—and educated. He didn't think taking law courses made her a freak.

She remembered with a shiver of pleasure the touch of his hand on her shoulder as he seated her at the dinner table. At that time she hadn't known how nice and how interesting he was, just how handsome. That thick, dark hair, sort of like Papa's but darker and not so curly, and his eyes—they were so intense. Sometimes she almost thought he looked sad, as if there'd been some tragedy in his life, although she was probably being silly and romantic. Drilling for oil didn't sound tragic, just intriguing and unusual.

And he was very well built. She had to compare him with various young men she had known in Washington, young men who took up boxing and other manly sports to develop their physiques, young men who admired cowboys without ever having seen a real one. He made them seem effete in retrospect, for he was overpoweringly male. And this handsome, dashing man had asked to call.

She smiled dreamily, speculating on how soon he'd come. Next week maybe? Certainly not earlier than three or four days.

"Has Mr. Parnell gone, Jessie?" her mother asked when Jessica reentered the parlor.

"Yes, Mama, but he's asked to call again."

"That's nice," said Anne. "He seems a personable young man." Actually, when she thought about it, Travis Parnell reminded her of Justin, with whom she'd fallen so hopelessly in love years ago. It was that aura of power some men had, and, of course, Parnell was handsome.

The combination could make him a heartbreaker, and Anne wondered if Jessie, who was so unsure of her own attractions, could handle the attentions of such a man, because Parnell *was* interested; Anne knew the signs. She had no fears that her daughter would get herself into trouble; Jessie was too sensible for that, too intelligent, but she could be hurt.

Anne sighed. There was a point past which you couldn't protect your children, she decided; you had to let them live their own lives, else they'd have none worth living. Jessie was twenty-two. It would be a shame if she never loved a man, as Anne had loved her father all these years, a shame if she never married.

Chapter Two

Returning from an afternoon visit with an elderly family friend, Jessica trudged up the long drive to her parents' house. She wished with all her heart that she still had her bicycle. It had been stolen from the stable just before she left Washington, and although she'd asked her father to buy her another, he'd objected to purchasing the Overman drop frame she had her eye on.

Jessica had never understood why, but Papa seemed to think she was always in danger of becoming a spendthrift, whereas Jessica knew herself to be quite thrifty and sensible. The machine she coveted was a case in point; it had a chain guard and a twine-laced rear fender to protect the rider's skirt from damage, a very practical bicycle but not particularly expensive because the model had been on the market ten years. She'd chosen it for just those reasons.

Papa had said, when she brought the subject up, that he expected his children to take better care of their property. She might have considered his point of view more reasonable had it not been so hard to protect one's property in a big city like Washington. All kinds of things were stolen there. Perhaps Papa didn't realize that.

Still, his flashes of disapproval hurt and reminded Jessica that she wasn't a part of the family in the same way that her red-headed brothers and sister were. Had she been left on Mama and Papa's doorstep, a mysterious foundling? Mysterious foundlings might be very intriguing in novels, but Jessica didn't want to be one. She wanted to be an ordinary Harte daughter, although she supposed that could never happen. Because she sneezed around cattle and was afraid of horses, she couldn't even be an ordinary ranch daughter the way her sister Frannie was.

Papa, seeing how disappointed she'd been about the bicycle, had suggested that she try again to overcome her fear of horses, which were a more practical mode of transportation in the West. He'd offered to teach her to ride himself. Much as Jessica yearned to spend time with her father, whom she adored and thought the handsomest, bravest, smartest man in the world, she couldn't face getting up on a horse. She knew exactly what would happen. The horse would realize immediately that she was terrified and run off with her or toss her out of the saddle or scrape her off on a fence, if one were handy. No, even for Papa she couldn't face riding.

Thinking of Papa reminded her of Mr. Parnell, who was also very handsome. Would he really come to call again? she wondered. Last night she had been sure he would and so excited at the prospect that she'd found it hard to fall asleep. She'd sat for hours in the window of her tower room listening to the sound of leaves rustling in the old tree beside the house and thinking of Mr. Parnell.

Jessica stopped to pat Frannie's dog Bobble, who had bounded across the lawn to greet her. Then she resumed her walk. Had she liked Mr. Parnell so much because he treated her like a real person instead of a brainless social ornament? Jessica knew that she wasn't particularly ornamental and that men preferred to marry pretty women rather than intelligent ones. Not that she thought Mr. Parnell wanted to marry her. Goodness, they'd only met once, and she was being very silly, although silliness was not ordinarily a part of her nature.

After all, she'd been to law school and persevered in the face of her disapproving professors—Supreme Court justices, renowned legal scholars and very formidable men. She'd ignored the snickers and the resentment of her fellow students, all of whom were male as well. And she'd distinguished herself academically even if they wouldn't let her graduate. Much good it had done her.

Here she was at home, where she couldn't practice law because, to become licensed, you had to have the approval of a judge and a committee of lawyers, something a woman was unlikely to win. No doubt she should have encouraged one of the young men who had come to call in Washington, but she hadn't wanted to marry a Northerner and be separated from her family for the rest of her life. She'd missed them terribly all those years away at school.

On the other hand, now that she *was* home, she had nothing to do. It would be nice, very nice, to have a handsome beau like Mr. Parnell, even if only for a little while, and she did hope he'd come to call as he had promised. If he did, when would it be? Tomorrow? The next day?

She climbed the steps to the veranda, Bobble at her heels, and closed her ruffled parasol, relieved to be out of the hot August sun. She was wearing her prettiest afternoon dress, a blue dimity that matched her eyes, but the high choker collar brushing her chin was uncomfortable on a day like this, and she was sure she looked rumpled and wilted. She should have taken the carriage as Mama had suggested when she asked Jessica to visit old Mrs. Artemis Culp.

In the front hall Jessica noticed a strange hat on the big oak hat rack and wondered who was visiting. As she unpinned her own hat, she peeked into one of the mirrored sides and groaned to herself. Her hair, which had at least been neat when she set out, was now coming down in little strands around her face and neck. Messy, she thought with a grimace. Outside, Bobble, who was not allowed in the house because he devoured small decorative objects, had stopped howling mournfully at the door and tumbled down the steps to chase butterflies. Jessica always felt guilty about closing the door in his face.

"Jessie, look who's come to call."

Jessica looked up to see her sister emerging from the commode room and after her—oh heavens! It was Mr. Parnell. What were they doing in there—and Jessica with her hair in disarray and her dress damp and rumpled.

"I've been taking him on the commode tour," announced Frannie.

Commodes? Frannie was showing him the commodes! Jessica felt a wave of horror roll over her. "H-hello, Mr. Parnell," she stammered.

"Good afternoon, Miss Jessica," he replied.

41

"Goodness, Jessie, don't look so embarrassed," said Frannie cheerfully. "Everyone wants to see our mechanical commodes. Hardly anyone in Weatherford has them."

"Frannie—"

"Why, if I've shown one visitor, I've shown a hundred since we got them."

"Frannie," said Jessica weakly, "I'm sure Mr. Parnell has seen—"

"Oh no, he hasn't. He said he doesn't know a soul in Corsicana with a mechanical commode. He said outhouses are more the fashion there."

Jessica wanted to sink through the floor. No one mentioned commodes! Certainly not in mixed company. Could Frannie be up to one of her pranks—like the time she'd put the cow pattie between two pieces of bread in Ned's lunch bucket, and he'd taken a big bite at school and—Jessica didn't even want to think about that, any more than she wanted to think about Mr. Parnell being dragged around the house to view the new mechanical commodes. Once he got loose, he'd run for his life and never come back.

"Come along, Mr. Parnell," said Frannie, taking his hand and tugging him toward the staircase. "Wait till you see the one on the second floor. We call it the throne because it's built on a platform."

Miserably Jessica watched them disappearing up the stairs.

"Oh, darling, you're home." Anne came down the hall from the back of the house, removing her gardening gloves and wide-brimmed hat. "How was Mrs. Culp?"

"Mother, Frannie is—"

"I hope you had a nice visit."

"Yes, fine, but Frannie's—"

"Poor old woman. Do tell me all about her."

42

Jessica sighed. It was too late to stop her little sister from showing Mr. Parnell the upstairs commode, and obviously her mother wouldn't let her get a word in until the affairs of Mrs. Artemis Culp had been discussed. "Mrs. Culp thinks the servants are trying to steal her spectacles," said Jessica, "so she hides them at night. Unfortunately, this morning she couldn't remember where she'd put them, and since she can't see a thing, she was in a bad way. Does Frannie always—"

Anne, shaking her head over the problems of Mrs. Artemis Culp, interrupted to ask if Jessica hadn't offered to help look for the missing spectacles.

"I spent the whole two hours of my visit searching," Jessica replied. "Now could we discuss—"

"Poor old thing," cried Anne. "Whatever will she do until she gets a new pair?"

"I found them!" said Jessica. Then she spotted her sister and Mr. Parnell descending the stairs and groaned.

". . . and because of the commodes, Papa had to have a cesspool dug," Frannie was explaining enthusiastically.

I can't believe she's saying that, thought Jessica.

"Did he?" murmured Travis Parnell with solemn courtesy.

"Frances Harte, are you showing off those commodes again?" her mother demanded.

"Of course I am, Mama, and Mr. Parnell is ever so interested, aren't you?"

"It was very instructive," said Travis politely.

Jessica knew her cheeks were pink with embarrassment.

"You're looking blooming, Miss Jessica. I dropped by to ask if you'd care to attend the Molly A. Bailey circus parade with me this afternoon."

43

"You did?" Jessica had been sure he would never want to see any member of her family after such an embarrassing incident.

"With your mother's permission, of course." He smiled at Anne.

"Oh, goodie!" cried Frannie. "Do say yes, Mama. I want to go too."

Jessica glared at her.

"Absolutely not, young lady," said Anne. "You go straight into the parlor. I want a word with you." Then she turned to Jessica. "Don't forget your hat, dear, and don't get near the elephants. I'm always afraid they'll step on someone."

"Yes, Mama," said Jessica gratefully.

"And it's a hot day. Try to walk on the shady side of the street and not get overheated."

"We'll stop for a cold drink," Travis promised.

"Good idea," said Anne. "Now, have a nice time, children." Then she turned and marched into the parlor, saying, "Frances, how many times have I told you . . ."

Grinning, Travis whisked Jessica out the front door.

"M-Mr. Parnell," she stammered, "I'm so sorry—"

She stopped because he was leaning against the veranda column, laughing helplessly. When he saw how astounded she looked, he said, "I hope you'll excuse me for laughing, Miss Jessica, but your sister is the funniest little girl I've ever met."

"She is?" He'd thought it was funny? And he thought of Frannie as a "little girl"? Frannie, who was so pretty with her red-gold curls that boys were already starting to follow her around, cow-eyed, although she was only fourteen?

"You mustn't be embarrassed. She's a sweet child, and no one could take offense just because she's

44

excited about the new—er—plumbing." Travis was thinking how pretty Jessica looked with her face all flushed and her hair loosened from its customary severity.

Jessica knew better. Plenty of people would have taken offense, but she was certainly glad Mr. Parnell hadn't, and he was giving her that wonderful, warm smile that made her stomach flutter disconcertingly.

By the time they returned, Jessica knew that it had been the happiest afternoon of her life. They watched the parade, which was delightful, and then had tea in the wagon of Molly A. Bailey herself, whom Mr. Parnell knew personally. Mrs. Bailey told them tales of her life in the circus, a life that stretched over more years than Jessica had been alive. Then Jessica was able to offer Mrs. Bailey legal advice.

"The man claims my elephant spooks his cattle," said Mrs. Bailey indignantly. "What I want to know is why he didn't think of that before he signed the contract to rent me land for winter quarters."

"If you have a contract, he'll have to honor it sooner or later," said Jessica.

"Oh, sure," grumbled Mrs. Bailey. "So my lawyer says, but going to court could take years, and in the meantime I've got a circus to quarter."

"Maybe there's another way," said Jessica thoughtfully.

"Miss Jessica's a lawyer herself," Travis explained.

"Is she?" Mrs. Bailey perked up. "Well, suggest away, girl. I reckon I need a miracle."

"Not a miracle," said Jessica, her eyes beginning to twinkle, "just an interim solution. I imagine this gentleman has a yard at his home?"

"Of course, he does. Bastard's as rich as a crooked politician."

45

Jessica was somewhat taken aback at the language but went on with her train of thought. "And he probably has no cattle in his yard."

"That's true," agreed Mrs. Bailey, looking intrigued.

"So he could honor his contract by quartering your elephant and any other animals that need space right there in front of his house," said Jessica, "at least, until the courts can settle the matter. I'm sure the county sheriff would agree to that as a fair interim solution, and once the animals are settled in, the gentleman might even decide to honor his contract without going to court."

"Reckon I'd come to terms after a couple of days with an elephant in my front yard," said Travis, and the three of them howled with laughter at the surprise coming to Mrs. Bailey's prospective winter landlord.

"I'll swear, girl," exclaimed Mrs. Bailey, wiping her eyes, "I wish I could take you along with me when I leave town."

Jessica thought wistfully of how much fun it would be to run away with the circus.

"Now, how much do I owe you, child? You're a lot cannier than my lawyer, I can tell you."

Of course, Jessica refused to accept payment, and although Mr. Parnell said nothing at the time, later, over lemonade, he pointed out that her advice was valuable and *should* be paid for, which had made her feel wonderful.

After that he had asked if they might go riding the next afternoon, and Jessica's brief balloon of happiness deflated, for she just couldn't and had to explain that she was afraid of horses and only rode a bicycle.

"A bicycle?" echoed Mr. Parnell dubiously. "Can't say I've ever been on one."

"It doesn't matter," Jessica replied sadly. "Mine's been stolen anyway."

Somehow or other she found herself telling him about her father's refusal to buy her a new one, which proved to be embarrassing because Mr. Parnell said, rather disapprovingly, that her father had money enough to replace her stolen bicycle and should have done so. Naturally Jessica had to defend her father. She and Mr. Parnell even got into a little argument about it, although the last thing she wanted to do was argue with Mr. Parnell. Jessica decided unhappily that he must think them a very peculiar family. No doubt, he wouldn't want to see her again.

However, once they reached the house, he invited her to the theater, and she was so pleased that she accepted without even asking her mother's permission. Fortunately, when she floated in with the news, Anne said, "How nice, Jessica. Is something interesting playing?"

"I forgot to ask," Jessica replied.

"Justin, look at this." Anne waved her hand at the bicycle sitting in their hall beside the hat rack, resplendently nickel- and gold-plated with elaborate carving on the metal parts, semiprecious stones embedded, ivory handlebars, laminated wood trim, and a leather seat. The instruction booklet that accompanied it announced importantly that it was the top-of-the-line Columbia Model 41 Woman's Safety Bicycle.

Justin viewed the machine and scowled. "I *told* her she—"

"—couldn't have a new bicycle," Anne finished for him. "Well, Mr. Parnell obviously thought she should."

"Parnell sent her that?" asked Justin, astonished.

"The thing must have cost a fortune."

"Of course it did," said Anne, "and she'll have to give it back. It's hardly proper for her to accept such an expensive gift. But I can tell you, it will break her heart. The girl's starry-eyed over him."

"She is? After just one dinner? And why's the fellow sending her expensive presents? If he thinks—"

"Justin, no matter how smitten Jessica may be, she's an extremely intelligent girl. If he's a fortune hunter, she'll realize it."

"I suppose you're right," said Justin. "Has she seen it yet?"

"No, she hasn't, and this wouldn't have happened if you hadn't refused to replace the one that was stolen."

"People can't expect to have every damn thing they take a fancy to," said Justin defensively.

"Jessica doesn't take a fancy to that many things, Justin. She's not Penelope. I wish you'd remember that."

He sighed and slumped into a chair in the parlor. "No, of course she isn't," he agreed. "She's a good girl. It's just that every time she asks for something, I hear Calliope telling me that my first wife—that bitch—" his voice went gravelly with bitterness "—was spoiled by her father's indulgence. I'm so damned afraid of turning Jessica into her mother that I—"

"That won't happen, Justin," said Anne earnestly. "Jessica's nothing like Penelope. If anything, she takes after your mother, and your mother's father. She's of that same pragmatic, scholarly turn of mind that Cassandra was."

"Well, if she's like my mother, why the hell can't she ride horses instead of bicycles? You'd never have caught Cassandra Harte riding a damn fool bicycle wearing bloomers and a straw hat."

"Now, Justin," said Anne, laughing, "they're not bloomers; they're knickers, and they're what fashionable girls wear to ride bicycles, which are all the rage. Heavens, they have bicycle *races*—where is it?—Dallas, I think."

"Who'd want to see a bicycle race?" muttered Justin.

Anne shrugged, then sobering, added, "As for horses, she'll never be a horsewoman. If you'll remember, the poor child had nightmares for months when that ill-tempered roan scraped her off on the fence and broke her arm. I've never come closer to taking a whip to a child of mine than I did the day Ned dared her to get up on that horse."

"She was a brave little thing at the time. Hardly shed a tear."

"It might have been better if she had," said Anne. "I rather imagine she was trying to win your approval."

"She's always had my approval," said Justin. "I just can't understand why she hasn't got over her fear of horses."

"Well, she hasn't and won't, so please, please stop expecting her to show signs of turning into Penelope. She's not going to do that either. You've got to go easier on the child, Justin. Be more generous with her."

"It's not that I don't love her," Justin muttered.

"*I* know that, but I'm not sure Jessica does."

"Of course she does!" he exclaimed, shocked.

"Just show her more often," Anne advised. "As for the bicycle, I want you to go out and buy her one. In the meantime I'm going to send the one in the hall back myself. I'll just write a little note to Mr. Parnell, telling him how kind it was of him to send it and explaining that I didn't want to disappoint her by letting her see it when it's only proper that she send it back. In the meantime, you'll—"

"—get her a bicycle," he agreed.

"Good." Anne smiled. "Do you know what I thought of when I saw that machine in the hall? I thought of the time you brought me the saddle, and I imagine you remember what happened after that."

Justin did. They'd gone out riding to test the saddle and ended up making love in the first grove of trees they came to.

"I've a mind to march right over to Mr. Parnell's rooms and ask if he was married."

Justin flushed. It was a question Anne hadn't asked him until too late, and the misunderstanding had led them into scandal and heartbreak because Justin, who was married to Penelope at the time, had taken it for granted that Anne knew.

"Fortunately, Jessica has more sense than I did."

"Do you regret what happened between us?" Justin asked.

"Of course not," said Anne. "I adored you then, and I still do. Now go out and get your daughter that bicycle."

Justin Harte smiled at his wife and temporized, "Later, sweetheart. Thinking about that afternoon I brought you the Goodnight saddle, it's put me of a mind to go upstairs."

Laughing fondly, Anne said, "Justin, you're an irresponsible father."

"Maybe," he replied, "but I'm a fair to middling husband."

Travis read Anne Harte's note, glanced at the bicycle that had just been returned, and decided he must have made a social error of some kind in sending the gift. Well, he thought philosophically, you didn't grow up on the streets of Fort Worth, the plains of Texas with Joe Ray Brock, and finish off your education in the oil fields and then expect to turn out a perfect gentleman, but he'd have to watch his step. He didn't want to offend the girl.

Still, they could have bought her a bicycle themselves. They had the money, and she was as nice a young woman as you'd expect to meet. A hell of a lot nicer than her natural mother. Was that the problem? Did Justin Harte dislike Jessica because she was Penelope's child?

Chapter Three

Jessica and Travis made their way up the stairs and across the splintered floor to their seats, where they had twenty minutes to wait before the performance of *East Lynne* began. Her father had declared before they left that anyone who set foot in the Haynes Opera House was a fool because the theater was bound to collapse and dump them into the grocery housed below it. Travis had taken that warning in good part, and Jessica would have gone with him had her father said the sheriff was planning to shoot down the cast and jail the audience.

"I love melodramas, don't you?" she asked enthusiastically once they were seated.

"Not particularly," Travis admitted. "They seem pretty unrealistic to me. In real life the hero and heroine don't always marry and live happily ever after, and the villains don't always get what they deserve." Then he added broodingly, "Although sometimes they do."

Jessica felt somewhat confused. "If you don't like melodrama, why did you want to see *East Lynne*?"

Realizing that his remarks about marriage and happy endings weren't particularly well timed for a man involved in a whirlwind courtship, he replied, "I wanted to spend the evening with you."

His answer so enchanted Jessica that she couldn't think of anything else to say and stared happily at the painted theater curtain as if she had a life-and-death interest in its mist-shrouded temple and its three rather awkward muses.

Travis, however, curious about the outcome of his gift, asked if her father had ever relented and bought her a bicycle.

"Why, yes, he did," said Jessica. "I was so surprised, because Papa doesn't usually change his mind, but he got just the one I asked for, the Overman drop frame. It's so cunningly designed that my skirts can't get caught and torn in the chain or the rear wheel," she explained.

Travis had seen that model and considered it greatly inferior to the one he'd got her. He was sorely tempted to say so, but at that moment the management decided that enough theatergoers had taken their seats to warrant displaying the *pièce de résistance* of the Haynes Opera House, a second painted curtain with a view of trees tastelessly engirdled with the advertisements of local merchants. Travis stared at it with amazement.

Jessica put her hand over her mouth to hide a grin, for it really was a dreadful sight. However, she couldn't say anything, for beside her sat old Mr. Hans Steinbrunner, who had an advertisement on the curtain. Well, actually she noticed that his announce-ment was not visible. The curtain was too long for the space it occupied, and Steinbrunner Mercantile, along with several other businesses, lay on the floor out of sight.

Mr. Steinbrunner noticed this too, for he stood up and bellowed, "You show mein notice, Haynes, or I get mein money back."

Management promptly rolled the curtain from the top, and Mr. Steinbrunner's section came into view. For the next five minutes the curtain shifted erratical-ly so that the audience could appreciate the messages of all the local businesses represented. Jessica and Travis, peeking at one another like mischievous chil-dren, tried to stifle their laughter. Mr. Parnell was so much fun! Jessica thought happily.

Finally *East Lynne* replaced the advertisements, and Jessica enjoyed the play thoroughly. In fact, no matter what had been on stage, she would have enjoyed it, for on her right the girth of Mr. Steinbrunner filled his chair and overlapped hers, forcing her to the left edge of her seat and into contact with Travis's properly suited but amazingly hard upper arm. Since she could do nothing about the situation, Jessica simply settled down to enjoy the excitement of this extended physical contact. As they shared chocolates, which melted deliciously on her tongue, and watched the drama, she savored the rough texture of his sleeve against her bare arm and speculated on how those hard muscles would look if she were to see them without their usual covering of shirt and coat sleeve. That was a highly improper speculation, as she well knew, but Jessica didn't care at all, she decided with unrepentant glee.

In the darkness she thought she could smell him, a hint of shaving soap perhaps and some nice masculine fragrance that might be peculiar to Travis himself. Did men have their own aromas, aside from sweat? The cowboys often smelled sweaty, although she seldom noticed it. She was usually sneezing as a result of proximity to the cattle.

She glanced up at Travis from beneath her lashes. He had a very determined chin, slightly shadowed with beard; wonderful high, hard cheekbones; and thick, glossy black hair. Her fingers tingled with the desire to touch it. How strange. She'd never thought of touching a man. She glanced at him again, and this time he caught her eye and smiled. Embarrassed, Jessica glanced away, but she could see in her mind that mouth, long and beautifully shaped, and, God help her, she wanted to look again. He was really so handsome, although handsomeness was not something Jessica had given much thought to before.

Then her pleasantly simmering excitement dampened when she asked herself why a man who looked like Travis Parnell would devote time to Jessica Harte. Was she setting herself up for a painful disappointment? Chastened, she focused her wandering attention on the play, which had reached its height of pathos accompanied by a tragic swelling of piano and violins and a few loud sniffs from Mr. Steinbrunner, who muttered, "Ist zo sad," to his daughter Gretchen Bannerman, who was sitting next to him. Then he blew his nose loudly.

Jessica clapped her hand over her mouth, horror-stricken because she had giggled. Had Mr. Steinbrunner noticed? Had Travis? Mr. Steinbrunner hadn't; he was too busy wiping away a tear or two. Travis had and was grinning widely. Staring into his laughter-filled eyes, Jessica had to stifle a whole new attack of giggles, which were hardly suitable to the poor heroine's plight.

"You didn't explain," remarked Travis later as they walked home, "that you liked melodramas because they're funny."

"They're very edifying," said Jessica primly and started to laugh all over again, Travis following suit and giving her an astonishing, if fleeting, hug. Her heart rate accelerated alarmingly.

Then as they approached the lights of the railroad depot, several men came reeling out, one of them shouting to another, "Can't get a drink in this town, but maybe we can find a woman."

Travis pulled her abruptly into the shadows of a large tree at the edge of someone's yard. "Drunks," he said tersely in answer to her question. "Weatherford's dry, but Fort Worth isn't. The train must have got in."

"But it comes in the afternoon," stammered Jessica, acutely conscious of his forearm across her waist and his body pressed to hers from behind. A wave of heated response swept over her.

"It was late today," said Travis calmly. "Some trouble down the track."

Jessica was trembling. She'd never been pressed against a man's body, and she was frightened by her own reaction, by her extreme sensitivity to the feel of his upper arm against the side of her bosom. The tips of her breasts were contracting, tingling, and she felt both breathless at the new sensation and embarrassed. What if he knew it? What if . . .

"There's no reason to be afraid, Jess," he said reassuringly. "We'll just stand here quietly while they go their way."

He might expect to stand here quietly, she thought, panic-stricken, but she felt that she would fall down if he weren't holding her with that forceful arm. Her stomach was fluttering madly, and he had called her

Jess. No one called her Jess; certainly no young man had ever thought to be so familiar. Did that mean Mr. Parnell thought of her as some—some loose woman? As well he might, considering the embarrassing fashion in which her wayward body had betrayed her.

"All clear," said Travis, freeing her waist as the men lurched around a corner. Jessica blinked because he was offering his arm to resume the walk home as if nothing untoward had happened. On the veranda, he took her hand and asked if he might see her again.

Jessica shivered with excitement because her mother had given permission to invite him to the pre-roundup ball at their house on the weekend. Now that she knew he wanted to see her again, she felt that it would be quite proper to invite him. She had a lovely gown that her mother had bought her the year before in Washington for a reception at the White House, and Frannie had offered to do her hair, although Jessica was somewhat dubious about that, fearing one of Frannie's practical jokes.

No matter how understanding Mr. Parnell had been about it, Jessica had not forgotten the commode tour. In fact, Frannie's offer had been in the nature of a peace offering, so Jessica supposed the hair styling might be all right. Any change was bound to be an improvement, and Frannie proposed to give her the Gibson Girl look. Jessica issued the invitation, and he promptly asked for first choice on her dance card.

She nodded happily. She'd have given him every dance had it been proper.

With a critical eye Jessica studied herself in the pier glass. She did want to impress Mr. Parnell—a little, at least—and was pleased that her hair looked better than usual. She had never known what to do with it once she was too old to wear it in plaits or straight down her back. With fearful reservations Jessica had accepted Frannie's offer, but Frannie's hair looked fetching no matter how she pinned it up because it was all glowing red highlights and curls. What would Frannie do with straight, fine, pale, brown-blonde hair like Jessica's? What could anyone do with it?

Fortunately, the upswept pompadour devised by her sister looked attractive with its straying curls around the face, the work of a curling iron bought for the purpose. Jessica wondered if her father knew about the purchase. After his generosity in buying her the bicycle, he wouldn't appreciate this latest frivolous expenditure. It was a blessing that she already had a suitable gown and hadn't had to ask for a new one.

But was the gown too daring? She smoothed the fitted waist nervously. It had been perfect for an evening out in Washington and was, in fact, a beautiful dress—pale green tulle over taffeta with appliquéd, pearl-studded velvet leaves and flowers outlining the train and a décolleté neckline that exposed the upper curves of her breasts and the smooth line of her shoulders.

Her face felt warm at the thought of Mr. Parnell seeing her in this gown. She knew that evening dresses of similar cut were worn in Fort Worth; she had seen them, but on older, married women. Still, at twenty-two she wasn't so young herself, and she liked Travis Parnell. She wanted to see more of him, so tonight he was going to see more of her, she thought, feeling decidedly naughty.

"Ready, dear?" A smiling Anne Harte studied her eldest daughter. "You look lovely, Jessie. What marvelous taste I have!" Anne herself had chosen as well as paid for the gown. Mother and daughter laughed companionably and strolled downstairs to join the men of the family.

"Where the devil did you get that dress, Jessica?" her father demanded as soon as he saw her.

"I bought it for her when I was in Washington last year," said Anne with a warning frown.

"Isn't it a little low-cut for a young girl?" he muttered defensively.

"Papa, I'm not a young girl. I'm twenty-two years old," Jessica protested, "and I've seen respectable women here in Texas wearing dresses more revealing than this."

"Who?" snorted her father.

"Well—" Jessica thought back. "Two years ago I noticed a particularly beautiful blonde woman at the theater in Fort Worth. Her name was Mrs. Gresham."

Much to Jessica's surprise, both her mother and father turned pale, and her father, his face tightening with angry disapproval, seemed about to speak until Anne took his arm and whisked him out into the hall to receive the first of the guests.

What could be wrong with Mrs. Gresham? Jessica wondered as she followed her parents. She had been told that the woman was a banker's wife, which seemed eminently respectable.

She had been dancing all evening. Mr. Parnell's interest had inspired that of other young men, particularly a neighbor named Gavrell Pickering, whom she had found tedious when she was in pigtails and still did. Not only had he insisted on claiming two spaces on her dance card, but he had cut in while she was dancing with Mr. Parnell, who had been telling her fascinating things about the oil-drilling business.

Elizabeth Chadwick

Gavrell, on the other hand, talked about some bull he'd just bought and shipped in from Kentucky. What a dreary young man!

Mr. Parnell had four dances, the most her mother considered allowable to one partner, and he escorted her in to dinner. One curious thing she noticed about Mr. Parnell was that he had little to say about his early boyhood. Jessica had told him all about her own childhood, even about Frannie slipping the snake into the church offering plate, causing Mrs. Artemis Culp to scream and faint, although it was just a tiny garter snake; and about the time her brothers had chloroformed the skunk and left it in the headmaster's parlor; and about how jealous she'd been when Papa had sent her off to school in Washington and Frannie had taken her place with Ned and David. "They're all wonderful riders," said Jessica wistfully. "And good with stock. I'm the one who's left out now."

But when she asked about his early life, he said brusquely, "My mother died when I was five, my father when I was eight."

"And that's when you went to live with your guardian?" she asked, wanting to know everything about him.

"No," he replied, "Joe Ray picked me up off the streets four years later." Momentarily prodded into indiscretion by anger when he compared his childhood, for which he held Jessica's mother responsible, with the opportunities and the love she had had, Travis gave her a window into the worst years of his life. "I fended for myself in Fort Worth from the time I was eight until I was twelve—sleeping in packing cases, wearing rags I got out of church barrels, cleaning out stables and shining shoes for pennies."

He stared bleakly down at his plate and added, "Stealing if I had to." There he managed to stop himself before he told too much and frightened her off.

Her eyes were wide and shocked. "I even got some schooling," he added, "although my fellow students weren't very friendly to homeless, unwashed boys turning up in their midst. I pretty much had to fight off all comers."

"Travis, that's—that's—"

"Pathetic," he suggested, resenting both her inquisitiveness and her sympathy. He did notice that she had slipped and called him *Travis* rather than her usual, formal *Mr. Parnell*.

"No," she said slowly. "It's admirable. You survived, and look how far you've come. It makes me wonder how I could possibly feel sorry for myself. I had every advantage, and I certainly haven't done much with my life."

Disarmed by the fact that her assessment of their comparative opportunities and achievements matched his, he muttered, "Women aren't expected to do much with their lives."

"Maybe not, but I hoped to do something with mine," snapped Jessica.

Repenting his own surliness, Travis said, "You've lots of time." Couples were then beginning to drift back to the dance floor, and he asked, "Do you really have to dance again with Pickering?"

"Not if he can't find me," she replied, feeling daring and breathless at what she was about to propose, but then the breathlessness might be due to the fact that her mother had laced her so tightly, which for once she hadn't protested. "If we went out to the veranda, I doubt Gavrell would think of looking for me there." She didn't want Travis to think for a minute that she preferred Gavrell Pickering because he was wealthy while Travis had just confessed to such a poor, sad childhood.

Travis accepted her offer by grinning and whisking her into the hall so quickly that no one noticed they hadn't returned to the room cleared for dancing.

"Shall we sit down?" he asked, gesturing toward two wicker chairs by a small table.

Jessica shook her head decisively. "Wicker," she explained.

"I reckon you'd look even prettier sitting in a white wicker chair in your beautiful green dress."

Jessica felt a little quiver of pleasure. He thought she looked pretty! Still, she couldn't provide the picture he evidently had in his head. "As soon as I got up, I'd lose about ten yards of fabric from my skirt, and Papa would be very disappointed in me for such carelessness. Wicker's famous for tearing up ladies' skirts," she added, leaning her head dreamily against the support column of the veranda as she looked out at the shifting patterns made by moonlight shining through the oak leaves. Then she went quite still, for she had felt just the briefest touch on the sensitive skin where her neck met her shoulder. His fingers? No, there had been a whisper of warm breath just before. His mouth?

"Are you offended?" Travis's voice behind her was like the brush of velvet. Jessica turned and looked helplessly at the lips that had just touched her skin. She couldn't quite believe it, but he was bending slowly, very, very slowly, his mouth coming toward hers. She felt breathless, dizzy. He was going to kiss her, but she might well faint before it happened. The accursed corset strings were pulled so tight. Had her mother done it as a precaution, thus ensuring that

Jessica would never know what it was like to be kissed by Travis Parnell?

Then his lips were against hers, his breath warm, and she didn't faint. He encircled her waist with his hands and pulled her forward just far enough that she rested lightly against him as he tipped his mouth and fitted their lips even more closely.

Jessica was floating, her heart beating in a slow, powerful thud in her breast, tingling waves of warmth radiating from every point of contact between them. His hands at her waist tightened; his kiss deepened. But then abruptly it was all over.

"Jessica, are you out here? Gavrell's looking—" Anne Harte came to an abrupt halt. "Oh, dear," she murmured, her voice distressed.

Her mother's words wrenched Jessica back to reality. At the same time Travis's hands fell from her waist, and he turned to Anne Harte. "Mrs. Harte," he began earnestly, "I hope you don't think—"

"I don't know quite what to think, Mr. Parnell," she interrupted, "beyond the fact that my daughter should not be out here on the veranda kissing you."

"Believe me, ma'am—"

"Mr. Parnell, perhaps you wouldn't mind leaving now, and Jessica, I'll see you in your room shortly." Anne glided calmly back into her house, leaving the couple staring at one another with dismay.

"I guess I have to go, Jessica," he said regretfully, taking both her hands in his, "but I hope you won't let this keep us from seeing one another again."

"Oh no," said Jessica breathlessly. "It's been such a wonderful evening—at least, until Mother came looking for me."

Travis squeezed her hands and then turned to walk down the veranda to the steps. Jessica thought sadly that she'd rather he'd kissed her again—no matter what her mother thought about kissing on the veranda.

"Jessica," said Anne, "it's so easy for a young woman to lose her reputation. If anyone had seen you—"

"Mother, I think I'm in love with him," Jessica interrupted impulsively.

"It's too soon," cried Anne, alarmed and shocked at how fast her sensible daughter had fallen victim to infatuation, but then she remembered how she'd felt about Justin in every bit as short a time. Maybe Jessie *was* in love. "Do you think Mr. Parnell returns your affection?" she asked, the worry showing on her face.

"I don't know, Mother, but if he asked me, I'd marry him today," said Jessica passionately.

"Oh, my dear—no. That's absolutely out of the question. We know nothing about him. He could be—" She hesitated, reluctant to bring up something that now had to be considered. "Jessie, he could be a fortune hunter."

"You just say that because you think I'm not pretty enough to attract someone like Mr. Parnell," cried Jessica, tears filling her eyes because her mother had voiced the very fear that always hovered at the edge of Jessica's consciousness when young men came to call.

"Jessica, you're a handsome young woman," said Anne reprovingly. "Why, you look absolutely lovely tonight."

"Oh, Mother, we both know I'm as plain as paste," said Jessica sadly, "but if Mr. Parnell should want me—"

"We'd certainly consider an engagement," said Anne quickly. "A long engagement. A year, at least." She regretted having said anything to undermine her daughter's fragile confidence, but on the other hand, she would not let some stranger take advantage of the girl.

A year? That sounded horrible, but on reflection Jessica realized that the whole conversation was ridiculous. Mr. Parnell hadn't asked for her hand and probably had no intention of doing so.

Travis Parnell walked his horse slowly along the street toward his hotel thinking of the young woman he'd just kissed. Jessica Harte had a sweet, warm mouth—and an enticing body. And her figure was *not* the result of the tight lacing and the chest full of starched ruffles which gave so many modern ladies their fashionable, top-heavy look. In that low-cut green gown, Jessica had looked very pretty. No, actually she had looked beautiful. Marrying her might not be such a hardship after all, he decided cheerfully.

Chapter Four

"Justin, I'm awfully worried," said Anne the next morning.

"You mean about Jessica mentioning Penelope; I've been thinking about that too." He put down the stockman's journal he'd been reading. "It gave me a shock, I'll have to admit, but I don't think it necessarily means Jessica's heard anything."

"Actually, I'd forgotten all about that." She ran distracted fingers into her red curls. "Oh, Justin, I've always worried that we did the wrong thing in not telling her about Penelope. I'm afraid it was just cowardice on my part; I couldn't face explaining everything that went on back then."

"She hasn't asked lately, has she?"

"Not in years, but you know she has to realize that she's not my daughter—my natural daughter. God knows, I couldn't love her more if she were."

"Well, if she's not pushing for explanations, we can

put that problem off a little longer. What is it that's worrying you right now?"

"She's in love with Travis Parnell."

"Nonsense. It's probably just infatuation." Then he squinted at his wife. "How do you know?"

"She told me, and I'm afraid that she really is in love, Justin."

"But she hardly knows the fellow, and *we* don't know a thing about him."

"I realize that, which is exactly why I'm so worried. He wouldn't be the first fortune hunter to go after her. You remember that cattle broker when she was eighteen? Oh, and that boy in D.C. with all the gambling debts."

"I remember," said Justin grimly. He closed his eyes and tipped his head back. His wife waited. At last he brought both hands down decisively on the table and said, "We'll send her to Sissie's." Anne looked surprised but was willing to hear him out. "Your sister's pregnant again, isn't she? What is it? Number eleven? Well, with ten children in the house and another on the way, Sissie obviously needs help, and it wouldn't be the first time she got it from Jessica. We'll send her off to the Bar-M. That'll keep her out of Parnell's way while I find out something about the man." Pleased with his solution, Justin added, "Who knows? Maybe he's a legitimate suitor. He seemed a sensible enough fellow to me."

"How soon would we send her?" asked Anne.

"Today."

She looked troubled and admitted, "I hate to tell her. Jessica's going to know what we're up to."

"I'll tell her," said Justin firmly. "After all, we can't have some stranger breaking our Jessie's heart."

* * *

"So you're sending me away again?" asked Jessica. "Just like you did before."

"I don't know what you mean by that, Jessie," said her father, startled at the accusing look on her face. "Your aunt needs—"

"Papa, you don't care two figs about Aunt Sissie. I've only been back a couple of weeks, and you can hardly wait to get me out of the house." She looked as if she might burst into tears. "You sent me away to school as soon as you possibly could, and now—"

"Jessie, what are you talking about? We sent you to Washington because your teachers said a girl as intelligent as you should have the opportunity of—"

"You just used that as an excuse to get rid of me, and it broke my heart, being kept away from home all those years. None of the others had to go away to school. I was so lonely and homesick."

"But you never liked the ranch," said her father, his eyes shocked and troubled.

"I loved this house and all of you. *I* never treated *you* like some greedy interloper."

"Jessie—" Her father looked stricken.

"Well, at least Aunt Sissie loves me, even if she is a bit scatty." Jessica turned to leave. "I'll be out of the house by nightfall," she mumbled as the door closed behind her.

Dear heaven, thought Justin. *Anne's right. The child thinks I don't love her.* Somehow he'd have to make it up to Jessica when she got back. In the meantime, he'd investigate this Travis Parnell. If the man was suitable and Jessie wanted him, by God, she'd have him.

Upstairs, throwing clothes carelessly into her railroad trunk, Jessica suddenly realized that in agreeing to go to Aunt Sissie's, she was agreeing to leave Travis Parnell behind. By the time she got back, he'd probably have finished his business in Weatherford, whatever it was, and returned to Corsicana. Was that what her parents had planned? Jessica sat down and cried.

Jessica was pedaling disconsolately down a rough cattle path on her cousin Martha's bicycle, her first break in a week from the rigors of life in Aunt Sissie and Uncle David's chaotic household. She paid no attention to the rider cantering up behind her, taking him to be a Bar-M cowboy on his way to repair a fence or rescue a cow or some such thing. Only when he pulled up beside her and said, "Jess?" did she realize, with a fearsome welling of joy, that the man she'd been missing so terribly had tracked her down.

"Your aunt told me where to look for you," Travis explained as he dismounted. "Can we sit and talk for a minute?" He nodded toward the shade provided by an old oak tree beside the path. Silently she climbed off Martha's bicycle and followed him, barely able to conceal her delight.

"I had to find out if you'd left Weatherford without sending me word because you wanted to get away from me."

"No!" cried Jessica, shocked that he could think such a thing. "My parents asked me to go to Aunt Sissie's one day and shipped me off the next. I didn't have time to contact you. And I didn't know where you were staying so I couldn't write." She glanced away from him self-consciously. "Of course, it wouldn't be proper for me to write first anyway," she added.

"I don't want letters from you," Travis replied to her unspoken question.

Her heart sank.

"I want you to marry me, Jessica."

"You do?" She couldn't believe he'd actually said it. Oh, she'd fantasized that he might; she'd thought of nothing else for a week but never believed it would happen. Then she remembered her mother's reaction when Jessica had impulsively declared her love for Travis. "My parents would expect us to have a long engagement. A year at least," she warned, hoping he wouldn't ask how she knew that.

"I don't want to wait a year," said Travis. "Do you?"

Jessica shook her head.

"We could elope."

She looked up at him unhappily, knowing there was something she had to find out. As much as she yearned to be his wife, she had to know *why* he wanted to marry her. "If we did that, my parents would be very angry. I imagine they'd cut me off."

"You mean disinherit you?" She nodded, and Travis laughed. "Jessica, I don't want your father's money. I've plenty of my own. What I want is your father's daughter, and I don't want to wait a year or even a month to marry you."

She felt almost faint with relief. He wanted her for herself! She basked in the joy of that thought before forcing herself to consider how upset her parents would be if she eloped. Then she thought about Travis, and how much she wanted to marry him, and how afraid she was that, if she asked him to wait a year, he'd change his mind. And it wasn't as if she were that happy at home, or even that they really wanted her there. She was the outsider in the family. "When would—would we do it?" she asked hesitantly.

"Today," he said without a moment's hesitation. "There's a siding on the Bannerman ranch. We can ride over and flag down the train to Fort Worth."

"Ride what?" asked Jessica, alarmed.

"My horse, but you'll ride in front of me, so there's nothing to be afraid of." He smiled encouragingly. "I'll have my arms around you the whole way. And you're wearing those—what are they called?"

"Knickerbockers." The idea of having Travis's arms around her all the way to the Triangle siding sounded wonderful, even if she did have to sit on a horse to enjoy it. "There's Aunt Sissie—she'll be terrified if I don't come back."

"I'll pay someone getting off at Weatherford to take her a message—about where you've gone and where to pick up your cousin's bicycle." He laughed exuberantly and asked, "Does that take care of all your objections?"

She nodded, her eyes beginning to shine with excitement.

"Then you'll marry me?"

She nodded again, such a radiant smile lighting her face that Travis caught his breath in wonder.

Book II

Fort Worth, Texas
August, 1900, to
March, 1901

Chapter Five

As he strode along West Seventh Street past the ranks of elegant houses inhabited by Fort Worth's wealthiest families, Travis considered what he had got himself into. Jessica Harte might be captivated by his charms, he thought wryly, but she had a mind of her own. She had insisted, until the marriage was actually performed, on staying with a Mr. Henry Barnett, her father's lawyer and her godfather.

Convinced that Barnett would contact Justin Harte, who would doubtless try to stop the overhasty marriage, Travis advanced his timetable. His errand on West Seventh Street was designed to reunite Jessica immediately with her natural mother, Penelope Gresham.

And here was the house, an Italianate place, rather out of keeping with the Fort Worth climate and style, he'd have said. His knock was answered by a maid in a black uniform with a ruffled white apron and cap. The contrast to Harte's Mab with her hatchet and country-woman clothes was telling. The maid ushered him into a room graced by, among other things, a pastel flowered carpet, a marble fireplace, a crystal chandelier, a platoon of heavily carved chairs, sofas, and tables, and two walls of mirrors, placed there, no doubt, to provide the mistress of the house with a number of pleasing reflections of herself. Penelope Gresham was almost as beautiful now as she had been seventeen years ago. She wore a lavender dress, all flowing lines and flounces. He thought it was called a tea gown; one or two wealthy matrons in Corsicana had them. Penelope, ensconced in a velvet armchair, inspected him as closely as he had her.

"Have we met before?" she asked, her glance flirtatious rather than suspicious.

Because Travis did not want her to remember the frightened child in Hugh Gresham's office and perceive him as an enemy, at least not until it was too late for her to take precautions, he answered her question with another. "Have you ever been to Lubbock County—or Corsicana?"

"Goodness no," she replied.

"Well, those are my stamping grounds," he announced, projecting for her benefit the reassuring image of a simple man stunned by her beauty and sophistication. "And you can be sure I wouldn't forget you, Mrs. Gresham." He watched her preen. This one could be manipulated without too much trouble, he decided with a secret grin.

"Will you have tea?" Her delicate hands fluttered over the china tea service.

"No, thank you, ma'am." Travis wasn't drinking tea for any woman, even if it meant he could have slipped arsenic into her cup and poisoned her on the spot. "I've come to ask a favor, Mrs. Gresham, and to do you one, I wouldn't be surprised."

She raised finely etched eyebrows.

"I've eloped with your daughter." Shock spread a brief flush over her cheeks; then her face went blank. "Jessica, the daughter of your first marriage," he added, so that she couldn't act as if she had no child.

Her mouth settled into a dangerous, ugly line.

"The Hartes are against the marriage," said Travis, "but then Justin's a hard man, as you know. Anyone who'd separate a mother from her baby would have to be."

Travis judged that he had just provided her an easy excuse by holding Justin Harte responsible for the separation. In truth, he had no idea whether Penelope had wanted her child or not. She didn't seem the motherly sort. He didn't even know why the couple had divorced, although in Harte's place, he'd certainly have divorced Penelope for the prospect of marrying Anne.

"I was hoping that you might—how shall I say?— take Jessica under your wing. Unless, of course, you're afraid of your ex-husband. I could sure understand—"

"I am not afraid of Justin Harte!" she snapped.

"Yes, ma'am. But since Mr. Harte has kept her from you all these years, I suppose he'd be mighty upset to find her in your house." Travis watched the malice bloom in her violet eyes and knew he had her. She loved to cause pain; he'd seen that in her treatment of his father, and he saw it now. She wanted to cause Justin Harte anguish and thought she could be espousing her daughter's cause.

"You're married to my daughter, then?"

"Not yet," Travis replied. "She's staying with Mr. Henry Barnett." Barnett's name evidently touched another sensitive chord. The violet eyes once more turned black with hatred. "For propriety's sake. Until we can be married," Travis explained, as if he had not noticed the reaction.

"That won't do at all," said Penelope sharply. "Barnett is a widower." Then she smiled that smile of sugared venom and added, "The perfect solution is for Jessica to come here. In fact, I'll make the wedding arrangements myself; I'd love to. What a lucky girl she is to have found a smart young man to reunite her with her mother, who'll give her a truly lovely wedding, better than anything her *father* would have provided." Penelope drummed long nails on the arm of her chair. "Justin always was a cruel man, and miserly."

"I've noticed that," said Travis.

"What did you say you did for a living, Mr. Parnell?"

"I'm an oil man from Corsicana."

"Oh? Is that a lucrative profession?"

"Very," Travis replied.

"Lovely. Now you must bring Jessica here immediately. Pay no mind to what Justin may think—or Henry Barnett either. Tell me, how does her stepmother feel about all this?" The violet eyes narrowed.

"I'm afraid that I am not Mrs. Harte's favorite person," said Travis, which was probably true since the last time Anne Harte had seen him, he'd come close to tarnishing her daughter's reputation.

"Indeed. Well, don't let it bother you. Anne Harte's is not an opinion worth cultivating. She was a woman of poor taste and poor reputation years ago, and I doubt that she's changed."

Travis smiled cheerfully. Spite had won the day—Penelope's against Anne and Justin—and perhaps spite would win another day now that Travis had secured the approval of his future mother-in-law. In fact, a little judicious flirting might well convince Penelope that she wanted the newlyweds living in her very house, which would make Travis's opportunities for revenge that much more numerous.

His father's stricken face flashed before his eyes, and he gave Penelope his warmest smile, which came from a heart as filled with malice as her own.

"For God's sake," cried Justin, "couldn't Sissie have kept an eye on the girl?"

"Sissie had no way of knowing that Jessica would go off for a bicycle ride and elope."

"Bicycles," muttered Justin.

"It wasn't the one you gave her," said Anne. "It was Martha's. Oh dear, I hope she's all right. I know she loves him, but does he love her?"

"Well, he didn't do it for the money," said Justin. "He's made a fortune in Corsicana, so why else *would* he marry her? He must love her. Unless—we don't know that they're married."

"Just put that thought out of your mind, Justin. She's a very proper and sensible young woman. She'd never let anything happen until after the wedding." Anne realized that she was whistling in the dark. Travis Parnell had reminded her of Justin, and twenty-five years ago she too had been a proper and sensible young woman.

"She might at least have said where they were going," Justin muttered.

"That's my fault," Anne admitted, sighing. "When she told me she'd marry him that very day if he asked,

I said we'd expect an engagement of at least a year." Her brow furrowed with worry and regret, she added, "I only said it because we knew nothing about him, but I suppose they thought if we knew where they were going, we'd try to bring them back."

Justin groaned. "Well, let's hope he makes her happy. She made it pretty clear to me before she went to Sissie's that I hadn't."

Anne put her arms consolingly around her husband's waist. "None of us ever realized how left out she felt, poor child."

"Jessica," Travis said, taking her hands into his, "do you remember wondering about your natural parents?"

Jessica shivered. Had he found out something that had changed his mind about marrying her? She didn't think she could stand such a disappointment after the joy of his proposal and the excitement of running away with him.

"I could see how unhappy it made you, thinking you were a foundling, so I looked into it."

When? she wondered. This morning? Oh, Lord, if she hadn't insisted on staying with Henry Barnett, Travis wouldn't have—

"Justin Harte *is* your father."

Jessica's panic changed to confusion. How could that be if Anne wasn't her mother, and she knew— well, Travis had to be wrong about that. "It's not possible. I told you about David and Ned."

"I know," he said soothingly, "but think about it, Jessie. Your eyes are very distinctive, and they're just like your father's."

She supposed that was true, but—

"He was married to another woman when you

were born, and that woman's your mother."

"But—but—David and Ned—they're a month older than me. How—"

"We mustn't judge," said Travis, knowing how much she loved Anne. "It was a long time ago, and we have no idea what happened. The important thing is that your natural mother is alive. She and your father were divorced soon after your birth."

"She's alive?"

"Her name is Penelope Gresham."

Jessica drew in an awed breath, remembering the stunning woman she had once seen at the opera house.

"Do you know her?" he asked, puzzled.

"I've seen her, but we've never—" Jessica faltered into a confused silence. "I don't suppose she'd want to see me."

"She does want to, Jess. In fact, she's invited you to live in her house until we're married. She even wants to provide the wedding and reception."

"She does?" Jessica's eyes widened with pleasure, and Travis, remembering what Penelope was like, felt a prick of remorse. Still, he could protect Jessica, should that prove necessary. Probably it wouldn't. In order to infuriate Justin, Penelope would, no doubt, treat her daughter very lovingly.

Jessica sank down on the satin coverlet of her canopy bed. Her mother wanted to be called Penelope. She had explained that calling her *Mother* might remind people of those scandalous old days. To Jessica it seemed that being introduced as Penelope's daughter would do that anyway. After the first explanation, Penelope had said, with a trilling laugh, "After all, dear, we do look more like sisters than mother and daughter, now don't we?" However, Penelope had also made it clear that she didn't think they looked alike at all. In fact, she had said more than once that it was a shame poor Jessica hadn't inherited the Duplessis beauty. Of course, Jessica knew that was true, but it hurt to be reminded.

On the other hand, Penelope had whisked her from one dressmaker to another, buying not only a beautiful wedding gown, but a lovely trousseau, and remarking lightly but frequently that she supposed poor Jessica was unaccustomed to expensive clothes and furnishings, having lived in Justin Harte's house all these years. She never did explain *why* Jessica had stayed with her father after the divorce, and somehow Jessica couldn't ask. Despite Penelope's lavish display of generosity, which must mean she felt some affection, Jessica remained uneasy with her. She was so changeable, so suddenly and inexplicably cutting, although usually the things that hurt were said with smiles and laughter.

Henry Barnett had strongly opposed the move to West Seventh Street. Hugh Gresham had also seemed unenthusiastic about Jessica's introduction into his household, and he was certainly uncomfortable in her company, although he adored his wife and seemed to do everything she wanted, even to providing this trousseau and wedding, which must be costing a fortune.

Jessica was awed by the amounts of money her mother spent, and she knew that she should be grateful. Instead she felt like weeping. She missed Anne, whose love she had always trusted. And she missed her brothers and sister—and her father, for all she had never been sure of his affection. She shouldn't have eloped. When they realized how much she cared for Travis, they might have relented about the long engagement. But that was what it all came down to—she loved Travis.

"Yes, sir," said Hugh Gresham expansively, "when I bring in one of the big northern packinghouses, the value of my shares in the Fort Worth Dressed Beef and Packing Company will skyrocket." He helped himself to a second slice of the roast and poured himself a third glass of wine. "You're probably not aware, Parnell, being an oil man, but the Texas rancher is being strangled because of the quarantine lines against tick fever."

Travis found it ironic that Hugh Gresham should be telling him about the very disaster Hugh had capitalized on to take William Henry Parnell's ranch.

"What we need is a *successful* packinghouse. Fort Worth Dressed Beef has always been a losing proposition, but when Armour or Swift come in with us, all that will change." He spooned more potatoes and gravy onto his plate.

Travis noted with dry satisfaction that high living hadn't improved Hugh Gresham's looks over the last seventeen years. His waistline had expanded, and his face had developed a ruddy, alcohol-induced color. Travis wondered how Penelope felt about the physical deterioration of her husband. He glanced over at her and decided that as long as she had her own looks and Hugh's money, she probably didn't care.

"As I was saying," Hugh continued, recatching Travis's attention, "with the new packinghouse, the ranchers can avoid the quarantine lines by sending their beef to Fort Worth for processing, which will enrich them, the city, and the bank, and I'll make a tidy fortune on my stock."

"Sounds ideal," said Travis.

"It is," Hugh agreed smugly. "The Armour people are already in town for preliminary discussions."

"Are they?" murmured Travis. He smiled across the table at his fiancée, who was toying with her meat and looking pale. Probably exhausted from the endless rounds of shopping with Penelope. He was surprised at how generous the woman was proving to be but chalked it up to a combination of spite against her first husband and irresponsibility about money.

"We've had word from Henry," said Anne, looking distraught. "Jessie was staying with him, but now she's moved—oh, Justin, I can hardly bear to tell you where she is." Anne's eyes filled with tears. "If only I hadn't panicked when she said she'd marry him that very day."

"What is it, Anne?"

"She's at Penelope's."

Justin looked stunned.

"You've got to get her out of there, Justin."

"I'd like to know how that happened," he muttered.

"It doesn't matter. Penelope will do her harm, and Jessica has no idea. We never warned her."

"Jessica's not a helpless baby any longer," said Justin, but his face was white with dismay.

"Penelope's vicious and cruel. At best, she'll destroy the child with that malicious tongue of hers."

"I don't understand how this could have happened," said Justin, "unless Parnell—" He frowned. "Do you think Parnell could have engineered the marriage because he wants something from Hugh, maybe the banking connection? It must be expensive to drill an oil well—especially when they've no idea whether they'll hit oil or come up dry. Maybe he's looking for financing. From Hugh, from me—"

"Which would mean he did marry her for money. Oh, poor Jessie."

"Well, whatever he married her for, we've got to get her away from Penelope. I'll have to go to Fort Worth and have a talk with Parnell."

"But then you'd have to tell him what actually happened when Jessica was a baby, and he'd tell her, and Justin—the poor child—"

"You're right, of course," he agreed, frowning. "All right, I'll pressure Hugh. He may run that bank, but I own a big block of his shares."

Travis paid for the drinks and lifted his glass to his new acquaintance from Chicago. "I'm surprised Armour's interested in a partnership with local bankers and cattlemen," he remarked.

"I didn't say we were," Groiner responded evasively, "and I sure as hell wouldn't want to be the one to come down here and run the place—not that Fort Worth isn't a fine town," he added hastily.

"I'm from Corsicana." Travis grinned and tossed back his shot of whiskey. "You don't have to love Fort Worth on my account."

The Armour man grinned in return and admitted that Fort Worth would be hard to love on anyone's account. "Oil, you said? Think there's going to be any money in it here in Texas?"

"Already has been," said Travis, "and I reckon there'll be more." He thought of additional information he'd received about a hill called Sour Springs Mound outside of Beaumont. Yes, there would be more money in Texas oil, probably lots more, although not too many people believed it yet.

"I'm interested in your comment about going in with local businessmen—not that there's any deal been made. We're just in the talking stage."

Travis nodded but didn't pursue the opening lest he appear too anxious to warn Groiner off.

"What did you mean?" the man asked, pressing for an explanation.

Travis shrugged. "Just that their big interest'll be in how good a price the beef brings, not how much profit the packinghouse makes."

The Armour man frowned and turned his glass around and around on the bar, tracing and dispersing circles of moisture. Finally he said, "Many of the thirty stockholders are bankers and businessmen here in Fort Worth, not cattlemen."

"Of course," Travis agreed. "This is a cattle town. Everyone here profits or loses on the price of beef."

"Ah." The packinghouse representative frowned again.

"Jessica, I do not want to hear another word about feathers," said Penelope sharply. "The wedding is tomorrow, and the headdress *will* be decorated with feathers and flowers. It's absolutely lovely and very fashionable."

"You probably don't realize it," said Jessica, determined to have one last try at changing her mother's mind, "but the American Ornithologists' Union, of which I'm a member, estimates that five million birds a year are killed—five million!—just so ladies can—"

"I not only don't realize it," interrupted Penelope firmly. "I don't *care*. What an irritating girl you are!" She plied her feather fan vigorously.

Jessica felt a little queasy at the thought of the poor

birds that must have died to make it.

"You've upset me no end, Jessica," said Penelope. "Where is my medicine?"

Jessica went to a burlwood cabinet and fetched the bottle. Penelope's disposition improved substantially after a dose of the medicine, which made Jessica wonder what could be in it.

"I have something of importance to discuss with you, and I want you to pay close attention." Penelope had already stopped tapping her fingers impatiently. "Tomorrow you'll become a married woman, and there are some things I should warn you about— things about men."

Jessica felt the color flood her cheeks and wanted to assure her mother that she did know more or less what to expect, even if she was a bit nervous about it. Still, she didn't want Penelope to think her unmaidenly just because she was well educated.

"When you go to bed tomorrow night, Travis will want to do something that is—well, painful and disgusting."

Jessica's eyes snapped open.

"Still, it's expected of you, and you must put up with it. I wish my mother had been foresighted enough to warn me," Penelope added bitterly. "Be that as it may, since you are my daughter, I know you'll hate it. Most women do, decent women, although there are a few—well, the less said about *that sort*, the better."

Jessica remembered her excitement when Travis had kissed or touched her and cringed to think of how Penelope would react if she knew.

"My advice is to concentrate on clothing."

Clothing? Did her mother mean the nightdress made especially for her wedding night? It was very pretty, to be sure, with a high-necked, lacy collar, lace at the cuffs, and pearl buttons nestled amid swaths of delicate embroidery down the front. Still, it was of a sheer, fine linen, and she did not find the thought of its near transparency particularly calming.

"At those times, I picture all my favorite dresses and decide on which new styles I shall have my dressmaker run up. That way it's over in no time at all, and I hardly notice. Of course, the first time, you can't help but notice, but it *does* get less painful . . ."

Jessica felt stunned. Even if what Penelope was saying proved to be true, this didn't seem a very reassuring conversation for a mother to have with her daughter. Jessica doubted that Anne would have approached the subject so negatively. She didn't even think Anne felt that way about Justin, but then Anne must have been—well, intimate with Justin while he was still married to Penelope. Anne must be one of those *other* women Penelope had mentioned, and yet Anne had always been so kind. And Jessica missed her mother so much—not her *mother*, she reminded herself, her stepmother. Her mother was sitting across from her, sipping that medicine for her nerves and saying things about men that Jessica was sure, at least she hoped, didn't apply to Travis.

All through the interminable dinner Hugh had grumbled about the failure of his packinghouse negotiations. The Armour people had left town, uninterested in a merger with local interests, after all. Travis had been very sympathetic.

"Well," said Hugh Gresham as they settled down for an after-dinner cigar in Hugh's study, "I presume the ladies are having a cozy chat."

Travis couldn't imagine anyone having a cozy chat with Penelope Gresham, who was not a cozy person. Still, he wasn't averse to a chat with Hugh. He'd be particularly interested in discussing where the man got all the money it cost him to indulge his wife's whims—her house, her furnishings, her wardrobe, her vindictive spending on the wedding of a daughter she cared nothing about. Did Jessica realize how shallow and evil a woman Penelope was? Probably not, and with luck she wouldn't find out before he'd dealt with Penelope and Hugh as they deserved.

"I thought perhaps I should have a talk with you about—er—the married state."

Travis raised his eyebrows inquiringly. Was this to be a fatherly chat? How ironic that Hugh, having destroyed Travis's father, should decide to stand in his stead, at least for this evening. Hugh cleared his throat, looking embarrassed. Travis, concealing a rush of hatred, continued to look pleasant but uninformed.

"Being a young man—with—ah—little experience of virtuous women . . ." Hugh looked at him questioningly. Travis stared back. "Well. Ah— perhaps you are unaware that your bride will not be—not be very—ah—enthusiastic, as it were, about the—ah—marriage bed."

Travis tried to look properly enlightened, but he thought that if Jess proved to be unenthusiastic, which he doubted, he'd damned well change her mind for her.

"So you want to be—er—understanding, and— ah—not expect too much."

"I see." Travis nodded respectfully.

"Good." Hugh beamed. "Well, I have a little gift for you, my boy. A wedding gift." He went over to the sideboard and removed a package, which he handed to Travis. "Ladies do *not* like nudity," he confided as Travis opened the box to discover a nightshirt and a paisley dressing gown.

Poor Hugh, thought Travis wryly. *Married life with Penelope must be hell.* Perhaps over the years Penelope had gone a long way toward exacting Travis's revenge against the banker, but then again, exacting his own revenge was sweeter, and he'd already begun. The cost of this wedding was one small blow in memory of William Henry Parnell, and when he discovered where the money was coming from, the information might give him more ammunition.

"This is most kind of you, sir," said Travis, pretending to admire the dressing gown. *And the failure of the packinghouse negotiations is my wedding gift to you*, he added silently.

The wedding was held on a hot day in late August at the Trinity Protestant Episcopal Church, which, Penelope explained, was the most socially acceptable church in town. It was known for its wealthy parishioners and fashionable charities, like the All Saints Hospital for the indigent, a cause for which Penelope had been an important fund raiser, although she personally made it a point to avoid the indigent patients. She did not like sick people, especially poor sick people.

Trinity Church overflowed with well-dressed strangers, and Jessica's bridal party was made up of acquaintances so new that she couldn't remember all their names, which might have bothered her if she'd had eyes for anyone but Travis. She floated through the ceremony in a sort of astonished dream, her eyes on Travis's, her vows made with a soft, happy solemnity. Even the talk with her mother the night before failed to dim her euphoria.

The reception was to be held in her mother's beautiful round glass conservatory with its host of exotic potted plants, which Penelope, for all she loved to talk about her green thumb, had nothing to do with. The maids took care of the plants. Just before the wedding there had been a tantrum. On her last tour of inspection, Penelope discovered some brown leaves on a bush tucked unobtrusively in a corner. The mistress's shrieks were quieted with a dose of medicine, but not before she had fired an unfortunate maid, dismissal to go into effect after the wedding.

By the time they returned from the church, Penelope was all gracious smiles again, telling her guests how much they were going to enjoy a reception among the flowers, which were so much lovelier in their natural state than cut and poked into vases. Then the disaster occurred, for half the plants in the conservatory had withered. "What have you done?" Penelope screamed at the maids, some of whom were looking terrified, while one looked smugly bland.

"You're the person who does all the work, ma'am," said the maid who had been fired. "Could you have made a mistake, like in some of them things to pour on the plants that you're always tellin' folks about?"

Jessica knew what mistake had been made, for she remembered a time when Frannie, as one of her well-meant experiments, had poured salt water on some of Anne's plants. Anne had not screamed at the child, nor had Anne fainted over a few withered plants, as Penelope did.

91

A terrible commotion ensued, with doctors sent for and the reception called off. Jessica thought wistfully of the reception there might have been at home in Weatherford, all the friends and family present. Still, Penelope had tried hard to make it a beautiful wedding. The sight of her dead plants must have been a terrible shock.

"Think we could sneak out to the kitchen and have something to eat?" Travis whispered in her ear as the guests departed and Hugh stood in the hall wringing his hands while the doctor tried to reassure him that his wife would survive the destruction of her greenery, even live to plant again.

"Seems a shame to starve the bride and bridegroom just because the mother-in-law's having the vapors," he added.

Jessica had to stifle a giggle; she could just imagine how Penelope would react to such a casual description of the tragedy.

"Come along, Jess. Hugh will take care of her. He's probably used to this sort of thing." Travis edged her back toward the kitchen, and in moments the bridal couple were seated at the large wooden table being offered samples of a feast that would now go largely uneaten. Travis managed to overcome the cook's ill humor with fulsome compliments on her food. Soon he had the whole household staff laughing, even the maid who had been fired, and Jessica began to enjoy her wedding reception. They all adored him, she thought wistfully, just as she did.

"Stop looking solemn, love," he admonished her, "and have one of these sticky green things. What did you say they were, Cook? Grasshopper livers? We ate grasshoppers out in Lubbock County, not willingly, mind you, but because the blasted things would hop in your mouth if you didn't keep it closed."

"Oh, Mr. Travis, get on with you," laughed the cook.

He called me *love*, thought Jessica.

Chapter Six

"Are you afraid?" he asked.

"No, of course n—well, maybe a little," she admitted.

"I imagine everyone is the first time."

"Even men?" she asked with interest.

"Especially men," Travis assured her. "After all, if the woman wants it that way, all she has to do is lie there. It's a shame for her not to take part, but—"

"Take part?" Jessica interrupted anxiously.

"We'll get to that later, and don't look so upset. We'll get to that a *lot* later—when you're comfortable with the basics. But the thing is, Jess, the man *can't* just lie there, so the first time he's scared to death—that he won't do it right or even that he won't be able to do anything at all and make a complete jackass of himself."

As he talked, Travis had been patiently unbraiding the hair Jessica had so carefully braided after she put on her pretty nightdress. She had been very relieved to see, when he entered the room, that he too was well covered in a handsome robe, although she'd have been happier to catch a glimpse of a nightshirt under it. Still, he was probably wearing one.

"But since it's not my first time, you don't have to worry that I'll do things all wrong. Now do you feel better?" He smiled at her and added, "I'll be very gentle."

"Penelope said it would hurt," Jessica admitted tentatively.

"It might, but probably not. I expect the women who get hurt are those who don't want to be in bed with their husbands in the first place. You're not one of those, are you?" he asked as if sure she wasn't.

Jessica had begun to feel somewhat confused. Travis's expectations and Penelope's seemed to be so far apart that Jessica didn't know how to reconcile them. If she said she did want to be in his bed, he'd think her one of those *other* women Penelope had mentioned. He wouldn't respect her. Could this conversation be some kind of test? Rather than fail the test, she said nothing. She wasn't sure what would have constituted an honest answer anyway. Because she was so nervous and embarrassed, Jessica almost wished she'd stayed home in Weatherford, a safe old maid with law books to read and no emotional upheavals.

Travis ran his hand down the long length of her hair. "Just like silk," he murmured.

Jessica felt the most astonishing warm weakness in her thighs when his hand, running through her hair, brushed her buttocks.

"I think the next thing to do is get out of our nightclothes. Hugh provided mine. I suppose Penelope chose yours."

Swallowing nervously, Jessica nodded.

"I've a feeling those two don't know a thing about making love. It really is easier without all the encumbrances."

Jessica supposed that must be true, and when he left the room so that she could disrobe and get under the sheet, his absence would give her a moment's respite, which at this point she needed.

"Shall I help you?" he asked.

"You mean—you mean you want me to take my nightdress off right *now*?"

"No, sweetheart. I'll be glad to do it for you."

"But—" He'd called her sweetheart; even as she went into shock at the thought of being naked where he could *see* her, she'd noticed the endearment.

"Would you rather I go first?" His fingers rested on the knot at the waist of his robe.

Did he or didn't he have a nightshirt on under there? she wondered desperately. "The light's on," she quavered.

"That's all right," said Travis soothingly. "We're going to be married a long time, so you'll have to get used to me sooner or later, and I'm looking forward to seeing you."

"You are?"

"Of course. Did you think I hadn't noticed what a lovely body you have?"

Jessica had never thought of herself as having a lovely body. She never thought much about bodies at all—well, about his once.

"I was overcome with admiration the night of the ball, and I didn't see that much of you."

Already undoing the pearl buttons at her throat, he leaned forward and kissed her neck, causing the pulse to race alarmingly. After that he began to lift the skirt of her nightdress, very slowly and carefully, but still nakedness would be the end result, and Jessica was so scared and embarrassed that she couldn't protest.

"Lift your arms, love." Numbly, Jessica lifted her arms, and he whisked the nightdress over her head and tossed it casually onto a chair by the bed. Then he looked at her, at her naked person. She couldn't believe this was happening.

"My Lord, Jess, you are just beautiful."

Beautiful? Could she believe him? Even hearing it brought a flush of pleasure, which she hoped he took to be embarrassment. She wouldn't want him to think her vain, not when she had so little to be vain about. Obviously he was being kind. He was also discarding his robe, and her eyes, humiliatingly, went straight to his thighs. Well, now she knew how the act was managed, but she felt a little terrified to think he was going to . . .

"Now, now, Jess. Don't look as if you're about to be murdered. What you're seeing is only the evidence that I want very much to make love to you."

She pulled her eyes away. It was bad enough that she had looked, ten times worse that he had caught her.

"We'll go to bed now," he said quietly, "before you die of fright."

"I—I'm sorry I—"

"No apologies needed, love." And he swept her up into his arms, taking her completely by surprise and making her tremblingly aware of all the warm, bare flesh that was touching between them. "Although the truth is, you've a lot more to fear from falling out of this ridiculous bed than you have from me." He laid her down on the high canopy bed and, grinning, suggested that he might need her help to get up there himself.

How could he be so cheerful and joking at a time like this? she wondered miserably. But then Travis jumped up beside her and stretched out, and Jessica knew that it was absolutely too late to get out of this. "M-maybe we should p-pull up the sh-sheets," she stammered.

"It's a little hot for that," he replied patiently.

"Th-then we sh-should p-put out the lamp."

"Would that make you feel better?"

"Yes."

Travis sighed and reached for the lamp, plunging them into moonlit darkness. Jessica looked quickly toward the balcony doors which stood open, sheer curtains stirring in a lazy breeze.

"I can't turn off the moon," he said soothingly. "Just close your eyes if the light bothers you." Propped beside her on one elbow, he bent over and brushed a soft kiss against the side of her neck.

Jessica shivered. She hadn't thought she'd be so frightened. If only Penelope hadn't had that talk with her. Travis was moving his mouth with excruciating slowness along the line of her jaw, sending little pinpricks of sensation over her neck and across her scalp. Then, while she was wondering if he had any idea how that felt and if he expected her to do the same thing to him, his mouth closed over hers, and his palm curved ever so gently over her breast. Jessica gasped, but she didn't think Travis heard because he had made a sort of humming sound of appreciation, like the sound a child might make on first tasting something new and delightful.

That sound touched Jessica. Did he really find her new and delightful? His hand, open-fingered now, was circling, hardly touching, against her breast, making her nipple contract and quiver, sending tremors of sweet, hot aching into her stomach and then lower, deep inside her. Jessica murmured helplessly against his kiss, her body restless with confused expectations.

"Shall I hold you close?" he whispered. "Would you like that?" When she failed to answer, mostly because she felt a vague reluctance to have him take that circling palm away from her breast, he slid both arms around her and tightened them slowly until she and he were body to body on top of the smooth sheets.

Jessica thought she must be in contact with every inch of him. She could feel the roughness of hair on his chest and thighs, the intimidating pressure of his manhood, and under her hesitant fingers, the hot, silken skin and smooth musculature of his back. It was like touching a beautiful Greek statue, except that she had never touched one, of course, and a statue wouldn't be this warm, or holding her so closely.

Her fingers trembled against his skin, and he put his mouth to her ear and whispered, "I like that."

Jessica liked his warm breath stirring invisible nerve endings in her ear and the sound of pleasure he made when she ran her fingertips over his shoulder.

"Ah, Jessica," he said softly, and he did the same thing to her, except that his fingers ran from her shoulder all the way to her waist where he had her pinioned against him with a powerful forearm. He stroked every inch of her skin from her neck to her waist until she felt languid and dazed. Then he loosed his hold on her and closed both hands over her buttocks to press her firmly against him, hip to hip. Before she could panic, his hands ran up to her shoulders, and he turned her gently onto her back to begin a light fingertip stroking over her arms and shoulders, then, when she had relaxed to that, over her breasts, circling lower each time until his fingers brushed tantalizingly over her belly and she felt the inner trembling again on the rise, as it had been when he was rubbing his palm over her breast.

"Beautiful legs," he murmured, his hands moving to her knees and stroking up the front of her thighs. "Feels good, doesn't it?"

Jessica didn't know. A powerful, deep throbbing had started inside of her and threatened to swallow up every thought in her head. Again the hand stroked up, now on her inner thigh, on skin so sensitive that she pressed her knees together in reflex, both to hold off the burgeoning sensation and to retain it. Travis stroked up again, into the silky hair where her thighs were pressed together, making her buttocks clench and flex. He smiled into her eyes, now wide open, and flicked his tongue across the joining of her lips as his hand moved down to curve gently around her knee and nudge it out and up so that he could lie between her legs. Her whole body clenched in last-minute rejection.

"Don't be afraid now, love," he murmured reassuringly, even as he moved carefully and she felt the pressure start. "What follows—"

It wasn't going to work, she thought desperately. He was pressing harder into her, and there was no . . .

"—is going to feel as good—" he whispered.

He was going to hurt her. She felt something— Penelope had been—

"—as what went before."

Jessica's eyes flew open as, astonished, she felt him push deep into her body. And it didn't hurt, not after the first brief moment.

"All right?" he asked as he lay still, his body over hers and in full possession.

She nodded, thinking that next time she'd believe him. It wasn't terrible at all, and the first part had been—well, very nice. And she didn't think she'd disgraced herself by enjoying it, because he couldn't have known what she was feeling. Jessica wondered when he'd get off her. Although the sensation of him inside her was pleasant, even causing some of those little quivers she'd felt before, still he was heavy. Ah, there. He was drawing back. She began to edge her knee in.

"Don't do that, love." He balanced above her on an elbow and used his free hand to lift the other knee aside.

Then he slid up into her again, and Jessica gasped. That was—he did the same thing again. And kept doing it. Jessica's hands closed urgently over his shoulders. Her whole world was tilting off its axis. He was winding her up like a music box. Tight. Too tight. He was going to break her spring, she thought in desperate incoherence as sensation built on sensation inside her and she had to dig her nails into his back to hold on, to keep from disintegrating.

His breathing was rough against her ear now, and from her own throat tiny, pleading sounds came. "Soon, love," he promised, and then her body turned from flesh to a million tiny glittering points of rapture. A moment later Travis shuddered deep inside her and gasped, "Ah, Jess." He held her some moments longer as their breathing returned to normal. Then he rolled to the side and pulled her close in the circle of his arm.

"Still frightened?" he asked, a smile warming his voice. Jessica shook her head. "Go to sleep," he murmured, his arm tightening in a brief hug. He did.

His breathing evened out almost immediately. Jessica took longer. Although she was drowsy, she stayed awake long enough to feel the sweat drying on her skin and his as the slight breeze brushed across their bodies, to slant her eyes curiously at his powerful nudity, outlined by the moonlight, to pull a sheet up lest a maid enter in the morning and find them without their nightclothes. Then she drifted off, too content to really give much thought to the momentous thing that had happened.

As he had every morning of his life, Travis awoke before the first light of day. The difference this morning was that his wife lay beside him, sleeping. He looked down at Jessica and thought what a dark horse she was, so much more passionate than he could have expected, so much more loving than he deserved. Maybe Penelope Gresham, without meaning to, had already begun to pay him back for what he had lost seventeen years ago. She'd given him her daughter. Smiling at the thought, he bent to kiss his wife, and Jessica awakened to the touch of his lips on her shoulder.

Even while the ripples of delight were still radiating out from that touch, he smiled into her sleepy eyes and said, "I have a wedding gift for you," and he sprang out of bed, still quite nude, and strode to the curved-front walnut dresser with its heavy mirror.

Jessica, because of the glass, could see both front and back of her husband and veiled her eyes. His privates looked much less intimidating this morning, but the rest of his body was corded with long, powerful muscles, rough with curling black hair, smooth with satiny brown skin. Even in the cool of early morning, the sight of Travis, with whom she had been so intimately entwined the night before, brought a flush of excitement over her and, as if in self-defense, her fingers closed in a tight fist on the edge of the sheet and drew it up modestly to her neck.

"Hold out your hand," he commanded, now back beside her on the bed. "Not that one."

Jessica swallowed hard. He wanted the one holding the sheet. She changed hands while Travis laughed softly, and then she felt like a fool, for he had opened a blue leather box lined in cream silk and taken out a bracelet set with deep blue stones, sapphires she decided. The box held many jewels; her mother had such a set, which was called a *parure*. Travis lifted her hand and kissed the inside of her wrist, sending shivers all the way up the inside of her arm. Then he clasped the bracelet over the fine bones.

"It's beautiful," she gasped. She had never had a piece of jewelry so lovely, not even the pearls her mother and father had given her on her eighteenth birthday before she was sent away for yet another year.

"Now the other hand," he instructed. Jessica stopped staring at the bracelet and self-consciously changed hands on the sheet. Travis took the freed right hand and, under her wide-eyed gaze, carefully kissed each fingertip. Then he slid a magnificent sapphire ring onto her finger and pulled her close to him, breaking her hold on the sheet so that her breasts came bare against his chest as he bent to flick his tongue against the lobe of her ear. Jessica's breath whisked in sharply, but Travis was already threading a sapphire earring into the lobe he had kissed, then kissing and decorating the second.

"Now the piece for your hair," he murmured, reaching once more into the jewelry box. He took out an intricately wired gold and sapphire comb and laid it on the sheet where the fabric covered her thigh. Then he slid long fingers into the hair at the nape of her neck and tilted her head for a soft kiss before fanning the pale silk onto her shoulders and catching it up in the comb.

"And now the best," he whispered, taking up the necklace and fastening it carefully around her neck so that the heavy medallion fell between her breasts, which he cupped and lifted to his lips.

At the touch of his mouth, Jessica trembled violently and let herself be borne back onto the sheets, only to find that he wanted to look at her. The sun was coming up in the window, streaming in soft buttercup light across their bed, and Travis, holding her wrists against the sheet, studied his handiwork. She twisted, embarrassed to be inspected.

"Hold still, love," he commanded. "I just need a moment to congratulate myself."

She stilled in confusion.

"I've got the color of your eyes exactly." Then he bent over her, still holding her wrists to the bed, and murmured, "Now I'll have the rest of you," as he began again to kiss her breasts, closer and closer to the tightened rose nipples, but too slowly.

She wanted to moan with frustration and had to bite her lip to keep quiet, only to have her whole body jerk revealingly when at last his lips closed on her. Then she did moan, and toss, as he drew on the nipple, as he seemed to draw the very soul out of her. Every inch of her skin burned. Inside, the pulsing drumbeat restarted, even more overwhelmingly potent than it had been the night before, and she knew in a brief moment of panic that she had no control left over her body. Travis controlled her and was already moving to take his prize.

"Wrap your legs around me," he instructed, his voice low and urgent as he completed his first thrust.

She did it, and Travis made a low, pleased growling sound in his throat and thrust again, his hands under her to lift her closer, kneading her, thrusting until she gave herself over, mind and body, to the rocketing excitement, the bursting glory at the end.

When he had released her and turned onto his back, breath rolling deeply from his chest, Jessica stared at the ceiling. She didn't think she could keep doing this. She felt as if she might never move again, never get up and take part in ordinary pastimes. His jewelry, cool and heavy, weighed her down as, hot and hard, his body had done a few minutes earlier. A wedding gift. She had one for him and had to shake off this lethargy, which, embarrassingly, she wanted to indulge. She had to offer her gift.

"I have a present for you as well," she said shyly. "It's not nearly so grand, but—"

"Jessie," he interrupted lazily, as he rolled onto his side and looked at her, "you've already given me a wonderful gift."

"I have?"

"Yes." He brushed his thumb lazily across her lips. "You enjoyed my lovemaking."

Stricken, all of Penelope's admonishments repeating ominously in her mind, Jessica burst into tears.

"Jess, for heaven's sake." He swept her up tight against his chest. "What in the world?"

"My—my behavior has been—has been—"

"What?" he prompted.

"Unseemly." She rarely cried and hated it that she couldn't seem to stop.

"In what way?" Travis demanded.

"In—because I—last night—and this morning—"

"Ah." He rubbed his hand comfortingly over the back of her neck. "Jess, who put such ideas in your—no, you don't have to tell me. Penelope."

She nodded against his chest.

"My lovely wife," he said gently over the top of her bowed head, "don't you know that you're every man's dream?"

"I guess you mean that men dream of—of unseemly women, but they never—never respect them."

Travis laughed and said firmly, "Any man who wants a cold wife is a fool. It means he has to go elsewhere for warmth."

"Elsewhere?" Jessica's tear-stained face came up from its hiding place against his chest.

"Elsewhere," he assured her.

Jessica didn't like that thought at all. Travis was *hers*.

"I'm glad to see the idea doesn't please you. It probably would your mother, and you're to pay no attention in the future to any of her nonsense, Jessie. Do you remember your promise yesterday in church? You promised to obey me. Well, that's an order; ignore Penelope. Now, let's see my present."

"Of course," Jessica mumbled, wondering whether he really felt the way he'd said. She had to stretch for her nightgown and then wiggle into it under his eyes, a miserably awkward maneuver while she was trying to keep herself covered with the sheet. She knew he was watching her with great amusement, but she didn't care; she could never, as he had, walk across the room in front of him without a stitch on.

"Here," she said, thrusting the leather case into his hands a minute later. Travis pulled her down beside him on the edge of the bed and opened his present, which contained, nestled in separate maroon silk-lined compartments, a set of razors with silver and mother-of-pearl handles, a glass shaving mug in a silver holder, and various brushes with mahogany handles decorated in silver. Travis lifted out each item and inspected it, looked at himself in the diamond-shaped mirror that was set into the lid, ran his thumb over the razors after unfolding them from their beautiful handles.

"It's a travel grooming set," said Jessica anxiously. She was still wearing the jewelry he had given her and, for once in her life, wished that she had had lots of money to spend on a gift for him.

Travis smiled at her and said, "This is the nicest present I've ever been given."

Because there was such sincere pleasure in his face, she was flooded with happiness and mumbled impulsively, "You're the nicest gift I've ever been given."

"Why, Jessica."

She flushed and tried to turn away, but Travis wouldn't allow it. He held her face still and gave her a long kiss, which she finally broke off herself, saying nervously, "I'm afraid the hour is scandalously late."

"In that case," Travis replied, laughing, "I think we should do something scandalous to celebrate the hour," and he tumbled her backward onto the rumpled sheets. "Now off with that nightgown," he ordered, grinning. "It doesn't show off your jewelry at all."

"Travis," Jessica protested breathlessly.

"I know you're in a hurry, love," he replied, laughing so heartily that she had the sinking feeling he could be heard all over the second floor, "but you'll not get so much as another kiss until you've taken off your shift." He nuzzled her ear, then murmured into it, "But I *am* willing to help."

Jessica wondered dizzily if other brides spent more time out of their nightclothes than in. Then she stopped thinking at all and gave herself up to the pleasures of the morning.

Chapter Seven

"It's a nice little company," said Hugh expansively. "Their formula for cattle dip is, I'm told, the best on the market, and they have a salesman who could sell whiskey to a Baptist." Hugh poured himself another brandy and raised his eyebrows inquiringly to Travis, who declined. "Not that cattle dip takes much selling. Because of tick fever, every rancher in Texas needs it. The best part is that I can sell that company to a northern buyer for an immense profit and earn a commission besides for seeing that it goes on the market."

"I thought the owner didn't want to sell," said Travis, who often found himself on the receiving end of Hugh's confidences over the after-dinner brandy bottle. The man had no one else to brag to about his business triumphs since his wife was interested only in the money they produced.

"He doesn't," Hugh agreed. "Dead set against it. Loves that company."

"Then I don't see how—"

"Oh, everything's possible when you know how to go about it," said Hugh with a crafty smile. "He wants to expand but doesn't have the money. I have the money, and I'm willing to lend."

"And?" Travis felt a cold prickling up his spine as he remembered how willing Hugh Gresham had once been to lend money to Travis's father.

"In fact, I'll lend him more than he asks for. Within six months he'll be in trouble, so I'll have to call the notes." Hugh smiled and raised his glass to the absent owner of the cattle dip company. "A banker has to think of his shareholders."

"Yes," said Travis. That was just what Hugh had done to William Henry Parnell. The bastard! How many good men had he ruined since he pulled that same trick seventeen years ago?

"I can't afford to do it too often," Hugh confided, "only when I see a particularly profitable opportunity."

"Remind me not to borrow money from you," said Travis, and the two of them laughed easily.

"Justin." Hugh Gresham looked nervous. "I'm surprised to see you in town with roundup so close."

"Jessica's been living in your house," said Justin, scowling.

"Why, yes," Hugh stuttered. "Nice girl. We've—"

"I want her out of there. More accurately, I don't want her anywhere near Penelope."

Hugh flushed. "Jessica's a grown woman," he said defensively. "And they came to *us*. Of course, Penelope was delighted to help."

"I find *that* hard to believe," snapped Justin. "Penelope never made a helpful move in her life unless she expected to get something in return. In this case, I'd guess it's to even an old score with me, but I'm not letting her use Jessica to accomplish that."

"You do Penelope an injustice," said Hugh. "She has a genuine affection for the girl."

"Nonsense." Justin stared broodingly across the desk at a man who had once been his friend. "I understand she's already married Parnell."

"Several days ago."

"Why are they still in your house?"

"Because that's what Penelope wants," said Hugh resentfully. "You needn't think it was my idea. The wedding cost me a fortune, and the trousseau was worse."

"I'll reimburse you if you make sure that Penelope never sees her again."

"She won't agree." Hugh sounded as if he wished she would.

"On the other hand, I'll pull out of the bank if you don't."

Alarm flashed into the banker's eyes. "That would hurt you as much as it would me," he pointed out quickly.

Justin shrugged. "I can absorb the loss; I doubt that you can—especially if the sale of my shares triggers a run on the bank." He smiled coldly and added, "Think how Penelope would react if you had to curtail her extravagant spending."

"This is ridiculous, Justin. What harm can it do for Penelope to spend some time with her daughter?"

Justin was glad to see that he had managed to frighten the banker. "Penelope tried to kill Jessica when she was a baby," he revealed bluntly. "God

111

knows what she'll try when she gets tired of having a daughter around this time."

Hugh had gone pale. "That's a lie. Penelope wouldn't—she'd never—" Then his face cleared. "You're still angry because she was unfaithful to you, because she fell in love with me."

"You really think Penelope committed adultery because she was overcome by passion for you?" Justin asked sarcastically. "You must have found out in twenty years of marriage that Penelope is never overcome by passion."

Hugh flushed and suggested stiffly that Justin leave.

"She's never motivated by anything but greed and vanity. Penelope hated ranch life and was looking for a second husband richer than me. You were it."

"She loved me."

"She loved money. The only reason she backed off demanding half my assets when we divorced was that she knew I could send her to jail for attempted murder."

"I won't listen to this."

"I'm at the Worth Hotel. I'll expect to hear from you tomorrow." Justin rose. "I'm not making idle threats, Hugh. You loose that woman's grip on Jessica, or I'll sell, and then I'll find some other way to protect my daughter."

"Mr. Calloway, I understand you're thinking of borrowing money from Cattleman's Bank."

"Why, yes." The man looked surprised. "Hugh Gresham's been very encouraging."

"That's because he's going to call your notes when he's sure you can't pay up and then sell your company to Branch, Hubbard."

Oscar Calloway went pale. Branch, Hubbard was the northern company that had been so anxious to buy him out. "How do you know this?" Calloway asked.

"Because he was bragging about it, and because that's what he did to my father seventeen years ago. It's a little game he likes to play from time to time. If you don't believe me, check with these men." Travis handed him a piece of paper on which he'd written the names of five other people who'd been tricked by Hugh Gresham in recent years. Then he turned to go.

"What's your name?" the owner called after Travis.

"Doesn't matter," said Travis over his shoulder. "Just be sure you check into what I've told you before you borrow money from him."

"I will," said a bewildered Oscar Calloway, who had thought Hugh Gresham the most sympathetic banker he'd ever met.

"If you decide against Gresham, maybe I can find you an honest investor," Travis offered as a last incentive.

"Justin must have been absolutely furious to threaten you like that," cried Penelope, her eyes sparkling.

"But the bank, Penelope," Hugh reminded her anxiously.

"Jessica has to stay. There's no question about that now, even though she's—well, you can't imagine what tedious opinions the girl has. About feathers and things."

Hugh began to look hopeful.

"Still, she's my daughter," Penelope continued, glancing at him slyly. "I can hardly be expected to give up my own child now that we've finally been reunited."

"I told him how fond you were of each other."

"Did you see the jewels Travis gave her? What a

shame her looks don't do them justice."

"She's a handsome enough girl," said Hugh, but without enthusiasm.

"Oh, my dear." Penelope laughed. "You don't have to stick up for Jessica, not when it's just between us. We both know how plain she is—too much Harte blood, poor girl."

"Yes, well, we've got to think of the bank. If Justin offers his shares, it could cause a panic."

"Not if you buy them."

"But Penelope, that would be very costly. Especially after the expense of the wedding. I'm not sure you realize how much you spent."

"Well, Travis must be very rich. His deposits will—"

"He doesn't bank at Cattleman's."

"Then insist that he do so, Hugh. And as for Justin's shares, you'll find the money." She rose and patted him on the cheek. "You always do."

"Even if I could get the money, I'd have to buy the shares through intermediaries. Justin *wants* to cause a run on the bank, Penelope. He wants to ruin us."

"Then you'll just have to outsmart him, won't you? Think of how angry that will make him!" she murmured triumphantly. "We'll have his precious daughter *and* his shares in the bank."

Gliding to the mirrored wall, she smoothed her hair into a more flattering wave, then turned to admire herself in profile. "You'll never believe where they've gone for the evening." Penelope was studying the line of her chin, testing its firmness with a dissatisfied fingertip. "To hear some minstrel show provided by the streetcar company. It's at the park out by the water plant." She give a little trill of laughter. "I'm afraid my daughter has rather plebeian tastes."

"She strikes me as being unusually well educated."

"Goodness, Hugh, education is *not* what makes a woman of refinement." She ran an assessing palm over the flow of her skirt, then turned to view the back. "Not at all."

Hugh wasn't much interested in what made a woman of refinement. He'd had two shocks in as many days. First, Justin Harte's threat, then the business of Calloway, who had decided, for no good reason, that he didn't want to expand his facilities, which meant a substantial loss in income that Hugh had been counting on. He couldn't understand it and wondered what ill luck would next come his way, over and above the continuing pressure of his wife's unbridled spending.

They fell laughing onto the bed, having managed to evade Hugh and Penelope on returning from the park. "Hush," whispered Jessica.

"You hush," Travis whispered back. "I'm not the one doing all the giggling."

To stop him from tickling her, Jessica hugged his arms against his body and rolled toward the head of the bed.

"I knew it," said Travis. "You want to ravish me."

"Tra-vis!"

"And it's only fair. After all, it's your turn." He broke her hold on his arms to fling them wide on the bed. "Go ahead," he invited.

Jessica sat up, breathless, and pushed back her loosened hair. "What are you talking about?"

"First, I suppose you're going to take off my clothes."

"I am not!"

"Why aren't you? I did it for you last night."

Jessica blushed and looked away. It had taken him

115

a long time, and she had been helpless with desire by the end of the disrobing.

"Don't you think I'd like to have the favor returned once in a while?" He gave her a wistful smile, comically exaggerated, and Jessica forgot her embarrassment as she started to giggle again. "I'm serious, Jessica. You can start right here." He pulled his tie loose, having already discarded his jacket, and pointed to the top button of his shirt. "Or here, if you're in a hurry." He caught her hand and brought it to rest against his trousers. Jessica drew back as if burned. "Or here." He swept an arm across her waist and pulled her on top of him, then wrapped both arms around her shoulders as he kissed her. "Your hands are free. What are you going to take off me first?" She tried to wiggle away.

"Don't be a sissy," he teased. "You're one of the new women—intelligent, athletic—I'll bet you played basketball at school, didn't you?"

She nodded. "I did until they brought in women's rules in '96. They were so afraid our delicate female systems might be damaged," she explained scornfully, "that they took all the fun out of it."

"There, you see. Tonight's your chance to get even. I'm not worried about your delicate female system. I just want to be taken advantage of in the most shocking ways you can think of."

Jessica looked thoroughly confused. "Travis, I can't think of any—any . . ."

Travis laughed. "Sweetheart, start with my clothes —accompanied by kisses and so forth. After that, if you really put your heart into it, I'm sure you'll think of something else."

Jessica looked at him curiously, then glanced at all the buttons that stood between Travis and nakedness. She didn't feel very confident that she knew how to play this new game, but she tucked her feet under her skirt and leaned forward to begin unbuttoning his shirt.

"Jess, I'm not one of Sissie's grubby kids that you're undressing to plunk into a tub of hot water."

She had just freed the button over his diaphragm and glanced up at him from beneath her lashes. Then she leaned forward and dropped a kiss on the skin where her hand had been, hoping that wasn't an unacceptable thing to do. There was a narrowing line of hair that disappeared into his trousers and tickled her lips.

"Use your tongue," he said softly.

Jessica touched the skin hesitantly with her tongue. What a curious sensation. She shivered with excitement.

"Now kiss my navel."

He had done that to her once, and she'd thought she might jump right out of her skin. Would he feel the same way? She moved her mouth to the small hair-swirled indentation and, without being asked, flicked her tongue into it. Travis groaned, the sound of which she found electrifying.

"Get the trousers, sweetheart."

Oh, God, Jessica didn't want to do that. Why had she let him nudge her into this? Why—he tumbled her thoughts into disarray by putting her fingers against the top button. The next one told her that he was fully aroused, and she was unable to avoid touching his erection, which she had never done, wouldn't have dreamed of doing.

"Ah, Jessie," he sighed, and she glanced up at the taut pleasure in his face, the arched lines of his neck, which gave her a dizzying sense of power and set her trembling with arousal herself. After that, she stripped him eagerly and then stopped because she couldn't quite think of what else to do.

She looked up into his face hopefully, and smiling, he said, "Now you. I don't want to be the only naked, excited person in this room." Jessica nodded and reached for the lamp, but he covered her hand with his. "If we can make love in the morning by sunlight, we can make love in the evening by lamplight."

Hands trembling, she began to deal with her own buttons. "Slowly," he advised her. "Let me enjoy it." And he began to coach her in the order of removal: first the beige silk dress with its high lace collar and mantle of tucks, then the silk petticoat, layered V's of ruffles decorating the bottom. When she was down to her camisole and drawers, and feeling increasingly uncomfortable, Travis sat up. "I'll take over now," he announced and relieved her of the drawers, then ran his lips over her legs as he rolled her stockings down. "You'd make a wonderful can-can girl," he murmured.

"What's that?" Jessica asked suspiciously.

"A girl who dances around on the stage in a ruffled petticoat showing her garters." Travis was kissing her toes when she pushed him over. For a moment he was too surprised to react. Then grinning, he grabbed her foot and pulled her down on top of him where he lay on the flowered carpet beside the bed. "Now, sweetheart, I've got you just where I wanted you in the first place."

"On the floor?" she asked, giggling.

"No, on top of me. We're going to try it a new way."

"What new way?" she asked, alarmed.

"You'll like it," he assured her, lifting her astride his hips. She did.

Travis strode along Houston Street feeling very pleased with himself. He had left his wife in bed

118

looking sleepy, tousled, and slightly embarrassed with herself, but Travis was delighted. Once he overcame her inhibitions, she was a wonderful bed partner, full of laughter and passion. It would be better for the marriage, he admitted to himself, if they could move out of Penelope Gresham's house, but he had goals to achieve other than the pleasures of the body, so he and Jessica would have to stay where they were for the time being. His success so far in undermining his stepfather-in-law had been phenomenal, and it was so easy. The Armour people were long gone, and Calloway had decided that he didn't need a loan after all.

Hugh was obviously feeling the pressure, for he had urged Travis to transfer his money to the Cattleman's Bank. Interesting. Was Hugh dipping into depositors' funds? Of course, Travis had no intention of putting a penny in Cattleman's, not when he hoped to bring the bank down and Gresham with it. However, Hugh's air of desperation told Travis that his stepfather-in-law had problems, as would any man with a wife who spent money the way Penelope did. As for Penelope, there were so many things that were important to her, things that he might be able to take away from her—beginning with money and social position.

Yes, he'd get the Greshams, and in the meantime his own fortunes were improving. His oil business in Corsicana was thriving without too much attention from him. He'd heard that Captain Anthony Lucas in Beaumont, whose oil exploration he'd been keeping track of, had run out of money and was seeking eastern financing. Travis found that encouraging. The sooner Lucas got hold of the money to bring in a well, the sooner Travis's land investments in the area would begin to pay off. Maybe he'd move his drilling company there after the first well came in. He'd have to see. But that was in the future. For now he'd keep his information lines open and let someone else spend the initial development money.

Today he had a more important errand—a present for Jessie, his increasingly delightful wife. Travis chuckled and headed across the square toward a ladies' wear store. Jessica's birthday was coming up, and he had to find a suitable present. Now what would catch her fancy?

"Parnell."

Travis groaned to himself, anticipating that he was about to have a strip torn off his hide.

"We need to have a talk." Justin Harte, glancing at his pocket watch, nodded toward a restaurant beside the shop. Reluctantly, Travis followed him to a table. "How's Jessica?"

"Wonderful," said Travis enthusiastically.

Justin's eyebrows went up. Parnell hadn't said that like a man who'd married to secure financing from one or both sides of his wife's family. Maybe they'd misjudged him. "Couldn't you have married her in the ordinary way? Eloping seems a little drastic." Justin, trying hard not to lose his temper, signaled a waiter, and both men ordered coffee.

"We didn't want to wait," said Travis, "and your wife had evidently said something to Jessica about favoring long engagements."

Justin sighed. It was as Anne had feared. She'd triggered the hasty marriage herself, and Justin knew that, given the opportunity, he'd have supported her. "And Penelope—why did you have to bring her into it?"

Travis considered the question. Obviously, he couldn't tell the whole truth, although he thought that, under other circumstances, Justin Harte might have sympathized with the vendetta against the Greshams. "You may not realize it," he began slowly, "but Jessie has known for a long time that she's not a—not a real member of your family."

"She damn well is!" said Justin. His coffee had arrived, and he stirred it vigorously although he'd put neither sugar nor cream in his cup.

"Well, she didn't feel like it. She didn't even know she was *your* daughter."

Justin winced.

"She thought she was a foundling—that's the way she put it—and no one would answer her questions." Travis sipped his own coffee and, finding it bitter, reached for the sugar bowl. "Because not knowing was hurting her so much, I wanted to find out who her real parents were if I could, and it wasn't too hard once I set my mind to it."

"I don't suppose it was," said Justin. "People have long memories, but you should have left well enough alone."

"I don't see that," said Travis. "It made her happy to know that she was your blood daughter, and it's made her happy to know her real mother."

"That won't last long," Justin muttered, "as you'd realize if you knew Penelope."

I do know Penelope, thought Travis, but he said nothing.

"The woman's not to be trusted. She'll do Jessica harm."

"Don't you think you're overreacting?" asked Travis mildly.

"No, I'm not, and I'm going to tell you something very few people know, something we never wanted Jessica to know and still don't if it can be helped."

More and more curious, thought Travis. Was Justin going to explain how Anne Harte happened to have

121

borne him two sons before his wife gave birth to his daughter?

"Penelope tried to kill Jessica when she was just a few months old, tried to smother her with a pillow. That's one of the reasons I divorced her and took the baby with me."

Travis felt cold fingers crawling up his spine. Kill Jessica? How could that be? He'd known Penelope to be vicious. He'd seen it in her attitude toward his father, but murder? He didn't believe it. She was too self-protective for that. "Did you see this?" he asked Justin.

"No, Jessica's nurse saw it. A woman named Calliope."

Travis felt a wave of relief. He knew how his mother-in-law treated servants—very badly. The nurse had probably hated her and made up the story in a bid for revenge, and Justin, with good reason to want to divest himself of his wife, had chosen to accept this Calliope's story.

"If you don't believe me, talk to Calliope," said Justin. "She's still alive. You'll find her out on Anne's ranch, the Rocking T in Parker County."

Travis shrugged. What could he say to a man who obviously hated his ex-wife enough to believe anything of her? "Why didn't you do something about it then?"

"I wish I had," said Justin broodingly. "At the time, I wanted to avoid scandal. As long as Jessica stayed with me, I thought she'd be all right."

"She's still all right," said Travis. "Penelope treats her like a princess."

Justin looked surprised, then muttered again, "It won't last." He stared narrowly at his son-in-law. "You're not going to get her out of there, are you?"

"I think Jessica deserves a chance to get to know

her real mother," he replied.

"Anne is her real mother!" Then Justin sighed. "A better parent to her than I was, unfortunately. Well, if you won't take care of it, I will. I've already told Hugh that if he doesn't separate them, I'll sell my shares in Cattleman's and cause a run on the bank."

Travis felt an exultant flash of triumph. Unwittingly, Justin was going to help him destroy Hugh. "Look, Mr. Harte, why don't I bring Jessie to the Worth tonight, and we'll all have dinner together. She'd be very happy to know you don't hate her for running off."

"Hate her?" said Justin sadly. "Is that what she thinks? I wish I *could* meet you, but I've got to catch the train to Galveston in just about twenty minutes."

"That's too bad," said Travis, but he wasn't, on reflection, particularly disappointed. He didn't want Justin Harte frightening Jessica with wild tales about Penelope. His mother-in-law *had* been treating Jessie like a princess, and the girl deserved the generosity she was receiving after so many years of being treated with stingy suspicion. Justin Harte might love his daughter—Travis believed he did—but the man had hurt her.

"Give her our love, Anne's and mine," Justin was saying. "Anne will be sending her things and would be grateful to hear from her."

"I'll tell Jess," Travis agreed, and the two of them walked together from the restaurant, Justin Harte turning toward the Texas and Pacific Station, Travis heading again for the ladies' wear shop.

So Justin was going to attack the bank? Travis thought of his father, coming to Cattleman's, so optimistic, although he was desperate for help. Soon the bank would be gone and Gresham as desperate as Will Parnell had been. As for that story about Penelope, it was obviously the tale of a disgruntled servant, like the maid who'd killed off Penelope's plants. Travis felt another stab of uneasiness, but he shook it off. Penelope was too canny to have done anything that would have endangered herself.

And now for Jessie's present. He'd get her something delightful, something to bring that smile of surprised pleasure to her solemn mouth. He'd never realized how much fun it was to give pleasure to another human being, but then Jessie was special. He imagined that giving a present to someone like Penelope would be about as much fun as tossing it into a deep well. Surprisingly, Jessie didn't seem to recognize her mother's true nature, but then Penelope was obviously on her best behavior, just the way Travis wanted to keep her for his wife's sake.

Later that night, when he told Jessica of his talk with her father, omitting, of course, that wild story about Penelope, Jessica was beside herself with happiness and sat down immediately to write to Anne.

Chapter Eight

As Travis and Jessica walked home from the Labor Day festivities, the streets were still thronged with people, many of them wearing the badges of their trades. That morning there had been a huge parade led by uniformed police and firemen, followed by city officials waving from carriages. Then came the body of the parade, a noisy union band and various trade delegations on floats and in marching units—tinkers wearing tin hats and carrying tin canes, mill workers in white, brewers round-bellied from sampling their own product, cigar makers, railroad men, printers, carpenters—all marching, often with the businessmen who employed them. Their destination was the park north of the river bridge and a day of contests and picnicking.

After Travis won the lean man's race, he and Jessica were made honorary firemen, there being no contingent of oil-field workers for them to associate with, and they ate their midday meal in the shade of the aerial hook and ladder truck while the men and their wives told stories of fires and firemen. Jessica described the funeral procession of Long-Haired Jim Courtright, who had been a famous marshal of Fort Worth, a friend of her mother's, and a member of the M. T. Johnson Hook and Ladder Company before the department became professional. She recalled, as one of her most vivid childhood memories, the fire bells tolling in the afternoon and the black-draped horses and wagons that escorted Courtright to his grave.

"Why, I was there," exclaimed one of the men. "I remember it as if it was yesterday, though 'twas twelve years or more since he died. Jim was gunned down by Luke Short in the door of a shooting gallery." The fireman knuckled away a sentimental tear with a large, freckled fist. "How did your mother happen to know Long-Haired Jim, child?"

Jessica grinned. "Marshal Courtright once stopped her from shooting a driver who'd left her on a runaway streetcar. Mother did shoot the mule before it could drag the car, with her in it, into the Trinity." The firemen were so tickled with her story that they invited her to visit the new stone fire station on Throckmorton and Monroe.

Then she and Travis moved on to share cake and lemonade with the police in their navy blue uniforms and blue helmets and listen to reminiscences about Old Charlie who had pulled the first patrol wagon. Travis seemed quite friendly with one of the officers, a handsome lieutenant wearing the slouch hat of his rank. As Jessica cuddled the infant who had won the baby contest, she could hear them talking about a man named Jim Lowe and a woman called Fannie Porter. She felt a twinge of unease. Who was Fannie

Porter? She'd have to find out, for she remembered Travis saying that a man who was unsatisfied at home went elsewhere. Was he unsatisfied? Or disappointed because she still felt wary of responding too ardently in bed?

She returned the prize-winning baby, and they moved on to a gathering of men who ran the electric cars. During this stop, they listened to the complaints of the night driver on the Arlington Heights Line who kept a rifle by his side for protection. He hated the sound of howling wolves as he made the trip across the prairie to the Lake Como Pavilion. The drivers for the electric car company had to hear Jessica's story about Anne and the streetcar mule too.

"I recall that," exclaimed one of the men. "Tad Boynton it was that she pulled a gun on, followed him into a saloon. Red-headed woman. Like to scared him to death, took his day's pay, and then he got a lecture from the marshal besides." The driver thought Tad Boynton had drunk himself to death long since, leaving a widow and children.

Jessica, thinking over the day and the reminiscing, felt blue as they walked home. How she missed her mother—no, stepmother. Penelope would never hold a gun on an errant mule-car driver. Penelope would never ride the cars at all. "Penelope mentioned that my grandfather will be at dinner tonight," she said to Travis.

Jessica had never met Oliver Duplessis, who had not attended the wedding, having been out of town on business. She was nervous at the prospect because he was reputed to be a formidable man, a wealthy and powerful merchant with widespread lumber and hardware interests. Had he ever seen her? When she was a baby, for instance? Would he be prepared to like her? Perhaps he already disliked her because her father had divorced Penelope to marry Anne.

"Stop worrying," Travis advised. "You're his only grandchild; he's bound to be predisposed in your favor." Travis hoped so. It had occurred to him that he could damage Penelope by promoting a close relationship between Oliver Duplessis and his grand-daughter. The man was old and rich. He had to leave his money to someone. Undoubtedly Penelope had already managed to get more than her share. She'd not be happy to see her daughter inherit the rest. Then it occurred to Travis that Jessie would not want to profit at her mother's expense and would be horrified if she thought her husband had any such plans.

"Just be yourself, Jess. He'll be enchanted." Actually, he didn't have to *do* anything; Duplessis was bound to find his granddaughter preferable to his daughter. He glanced at Jessica and noted her glow of happiness. Just because he'd said she was enchanting? Didn't she know that? He'd have to tell her more often.

In the meantime, he had picked up interesting rumors about Hugh Gresham, who was scrambling for money to buy out Justin Harte. A man with money troubles was a vulnerable man, one who might be tempted to go outside the law. Why else would Hugh be making contacts down in Hell's Half Acre? as Travis's friend on the police force had said.

Jessica lay back in the warm water and closed her eyes as the rigors of the day floated away from her, taking along her niggling worries about meeting her grandfather. The one problem she couldn't forget was how much she missed her Weatherford family, from whom she had had no word. Could Travis have been mistaken? Were they actually angry with her?

She lifted a toe from the water and stared at it gloomily, estimating that she had somewhere between fifteen and thirty minutes before she had to get out of the huge nickel-plated tub. Penelope and Hugh were paying late-afternoon holiday calls on friends and wouldn't be back before time to dress for dinner, but when that time came, her mother would blow through the house like a cyclone, finding fault everywhere. She would harass the cook about dinner, although she had probably left the woman without instructions; she would scream at the maids for minor or imagined housekeeping infractions—dust discovered on the ornate handle of a prized Minton vase, chandelier prisms without the requisite sparkle, or Jessica taking an inordinate amount of time in the tub. Penelope considered the tub her private preserve, only and reluctantly lent to others, a privilege not to be overused. Lazily Jessica rubbed some of her mother's scented soap on one shoulder.

"Ha! Usurping the bathing facilities again."

Her head swiveled as she slid protectively into the water. It was not her mother; it was Travis. "I didn't know you—if you'll just leave, I'll . . ."

"Have I asked you to hurry?" he demanded, laughing. "I came to join you."

"Travis!" she protested.

"What? There's no one in the house."

"The—the servants."

"They're supposed to mind their own business." He had stripped out of his paisley wedding robe and was lifting a hairy, muscular leg to get in with her.

Jessica cowered at the far end of the tub, knees drawn up, arms hugging them. "You can't—"

He splashed down opposite her, proving that he could. "Now, shall I soap you, or will you soap me?" He picked up the perfumed oval of Penelope's French

129

soap and sniffed it. "H-m-m. Your mother's, I presume. I'm going to smell like pansies."

"Violets," quavered Jessica. "I'll get out, so you can bathe in private."

"No, you won't, sweetheart." He leaned forward, taking her wrists in his hands, and pulled her steadily forward until she fell on top of him in a wave of warm water that rolled over the edge of the tub and onto the floor.

"Penelope will be terribly upset about the puddles," Jessica gasped.

"She'll get over it," he murmured, more interested in the soft pressure of Jessica's body against his in the scented water. He inserted his knees between hers. "I've been thinking about doing this all afternoon," he murmured.

She could feel the roll of his hips as he pressed up.

"You wouldn't think a man drinking lemonade and eating chicken legs with a crowd of police and firemen would be having lascivious thoughts," he muttered against the wet skin of her neck. He ran both hands up into her hair and moved his hips seekingly again between her thighs.

Remembering the overheard name Fannie Porter, Jessica wondered just whom his lascivious thoughts had been about. Then she forgot about Fannie Porter and the water being splashed on the floor and even the possibility of being caught in the tub with her husband by a disapproving mother. When he moved against her again, she closed her eyes and thrust her hips forward. Travis groaned with satisfaction and, catching her buttocks in his hands, rolled her hard against his penetration until she forgot everything but the swelling, tightening, wonderful feeling that exploded inside her. In seconds she had collapsed against his chest, her long hair trailing into the water, clinging in wet tendrils to both of them.

"My hair's all wet," she murmured against his chest.

Travis's head rested against the high curve of the tub. "I'll wash it for you," he offered, although he made no move to do so for some time. Then he reached one long arm toward a table beside the tub and scooped up a bottle embellished with the picture of a woman whose curly hair flowed to her ankles. "'Hall's Vegetable Sicilian Hair Renewer,'" he read, holding it up over Jessica's head. "'Thickens growth, prevents baldness, cures dandruff, restores gray to original color and beauty.' This yours, love? Do you have trouble with baldness? Gray? Dandruff?"

Jessica, smiling into the wet curls on his chest, shook her head.

"Must be Penelope's. I'll have to ask her about it."

Jessica laughed helplessly as Travis returned the bottle to the table.

"How about Glosteria? It says here it will leave your hair glossy and easy to manage after shampooing."

"I always used soap and rainwater at home," Jessica murmured, feeling drowsy and content in the warm water.

"Penelope doesn't seem to have those."

Jessica knew it was going to be a bad evening as soon as she entered the parlor—late. Her mother began to complain immediately about puddles of water found beside the tub. When Jessica, guiltily flushed, opened her mouth to apologize, Travis entered the room and, laughing cheerfully, asked Penelope if her maids were so poorly trained as to be incapable of mopping up a bit of water. Penelope backed off as she always did when Travis could hear.

This exchange occurred before Jessica and Travis had been introduced to the old man sitting stiffly by the hearth. The introduction earned Jessica a hooded glance and a curt grunt of acknowledgment from Oliver Duplessis. She felt saddened and disappointed. If only her mother hadn't launched into that tirade, Grandfather Duplessis might have had a better initial impression.

The introduction was followed by Penelope's advice to Jessica on her hair. "You're going to have to do something about it, dear," said Penelope sweetly. "The style is—well, not very fashionable, and the color—" She shook her head.

Jessica bit her lip. What could she do about the color? Not dye it, surely. Was that what her mother meant? And as for the style, well, she didn't have Fannie here to play hairdresser, and Penelope never offered to share her maid, who was the expert in hair style.

Travis didn't help matters by assuring his mother-in-law that Jessica's hair felt just like silk. Penelope gave him a look of amused tolerance, but when he turned to speak to Hugh, she cast Jessica a disapproving glance as if she knew Travis had been running his fingers through Jessica's hair as they lay entwined under the canopy of their bed. As they went in to dinner, Jessica considered pleading illness in order to escape upstairs.

"Jessica," said Penelope over soup, "I found a book in my sitting room." Her voice was gentle but disapproving. "I seem to find them everywhere since you moved in. You must stop reading all the time, dear. It's bad for your eyes, and it's so unfeminine."

"But, Penelope," said Jessica helplessly, "you're a member of the Fort Worth Library Association. You told me yourself that you've raised hundreds of

Virgin Fire

dollars and that the city is to have a Carnegie Library by next year."

"Certainly, but I don't *read*. The library association is a social activity—teas, dances, dinners, cakewalks. We entertain in order to raise money to *buy* books; we don't *read* them. Why, I'm sure Mrs. Teagarten was horrified the other day to hear you talking about some author named Hearty."

"Hardy," said Jessica. "Thomas Hardy."

"If you must read, you really should try to find more suitable books. Mrs. Teagarten told me that the man's novels were not proper for a young woman, that they contain very unpleasant subject matter."

The woman's an idiot, thought Travis. He couldn't imagine how Jessica could stand being around her so much, but he supposed there must be some mother-daughter bond there that a man wouldn't understand.

"I really must insist, Jessica, that you take care not to discuss books of an unsuitable nature with my friends. I'm sure Travis will agree with me that he doesn't want his wife—"

"Betty, get Mrs. Gresham her medicine," interrupted Oliver Duplessis.

Penelope gave her father an astonished look.

"Leave the girl alone, Penelope," he commanded testily, "and let me eat my dinner in peace."

"Really, Papa, I think at my own table I can talk to my own daughter just as I—"

"Now, now, Penelope," soothed Hugh, glancing anxiously at his father-in-law.

Travis watched this interplay with interest. Rumor had it that Oliver Duplessis had spoiled his daughter shamelessly when she was a girl, that he had thought she could do no wrong. If so, he no longer seemed prone to put up with her silly conversation. Also,

Duplessis evidently realized that she was addicted to that medicine but didn't much care as long as it kept her quiet.

Travis suspected the stuff of being mostly alcohol or liberally laced with an opiate, possibly both. If he wanted to cause Penelope anguish, all he had to do was throw out the medicine. Again he felt guilty when he thought of how shocked Jess would be if she could read his mind. He watched his mother-in-law daintily sipping from the small glass brought to her by Betty and wondered how soon the stuff would take effect. Not yet, obviously, for she was glaring at her father.

"Papa," she said sharply, "I do hope you've done something about your commode. With all your money, you can surely afford to have it put inside the house instead of outside on the back veranda."

"Commodes are just a passing fad," snapped Oliver. "When they fall out of fashion, I'll be able to get rid of mine without being inconvenienced. You, on the other hand, will have your house at sixes and sevens while they take yours out."

"Really, Papa—"

"That's enough, Penelope," said Hugh sharply.

Penelope gave him a murderous look that promised later retaliation. Why would Hugh suddenly risk his wife's easily aroused anger? Travis wondered. Was he afraid she might alienate her father or, more important, her father's money? Interesting. Did Hugh need help from his father-in-law?

"Where were you and Travis all day, Jessica?" Penelope asked. "We expected you to visit the Caldwells with us."

"As I told you, we went to the Labor Day parade," Jessica replied.

"Of course. I guess I was hoping you'd change your mind about spending the day among a noisy, uncultured mob of workingmen."

Travis grinned. "Jessica's been a union sympathizer for years," he remarked. "Her brother told me a story about her joining a crowd of strikers' wives and children here in Fort Worth when she was just nine. They all stood on the T & P tracks and kept the engines from leaving the railroad yards and breaking the strike. Isn't that right, Jess?"

Jessica flushed and mumbled, "They were going to run over the women and babies."

"Jim Courtright, who was working for the railroad as head of the guard force, had to rescue Jessie from danger."

"Really, Jessica!" cried Penelope with exaggerated surprise. "I'm surprised Anne Harte would allow such behavior."

"Unions are ruining the country," muttered Oliver.

"True," Gresham agreed hastily. "I hope you won't give any further encouragement to the union movement, Jessica."

"I'd have thought a sympathetic interest in the welfare of hungry mothers and babies was a virtue to be expected of the feminine sex," said Travis dryly.

"*I* would have thought my daughter could restrain such unladylike impulses to associate with the lower classes. You and I have a lot to discuss, dear, about the proper conduct for a lady here in Fort Worth."

"Leave the girl alone, Penelope," ordered Oliver Duplessis. "Maybe you need another dose of that elixir."

"I don't know what you mean, Papa. It's my duty to instruct my daughter in proper social conduct, since no one has seen fit to do so while she was growing up." She reached across the table and patted Jessica's hand.

Travis wished she wouldn't take her motherly duty so much to heart; it made him uneasy, although Jess didn't seem to mind. She probably appreciated the attention after years of being ignored or viewed with suspicion by her father.

Penelope expected her to attend a tea that afternoon, but Jessica doubted that she'd make it home in time. Frannie's note was the first direct communication she'd had from the family except for a trunk of clothing sent by Anne, and although she had never seen such rain in September, Jessica intended to meet her sister.

Tucking the precious letter into a pocket, Jessica ran upstairs, changed her sweeping taffeta skirt for one so short it brushed the tops of her oldest high-buttoned boots, snatched up a shawl and umbrella, and sped back down. As she slipped through the hall, she could hear Penelope screaming, "What do you mean, Mr. Gresham said we can't afford my favorite English tea? I demand . . ."

Jessica drew the front door softly shut behind her and hurried across the street toward town. It was no day to be out on foot, but she hadn't dared ask for the carriage. Penelope's carriage could only be used with Penelope's permission, and Jessica was on a secret errand.

"It's closed," lamented Frannie as Jessica entered the first floor of the Wheat Building, dripping water, her feet and skirt hem wet. They had planned to meet at the Roof Garden with its potted rubber plants, spindly tables and chairs, and delicious offerings of lemonade and sarsaparilla concocted under the gaily striped canopy of the soda fountain.

"They could hardly keep it open in this kind of weather," said Jessica, giving her sister a consoling hug.

"Why don't we go back to your mother's?"

Jessica could see how curious Frannie was about both Penelope and her house, but she dared not take her sister home. She hated to think how Penelope might treat Justin and Anne's daughter, since she made no bones about hating both of them. On the other hand, how could Jessica explain her new mother's difficult temperament without seeming disloyal?

"I guess she wouldn't want me in her house," said Frannie. "Mother warned me. Well, we can go back to my hotel room."

"Who's with you?" asked Jessica eagerly, knowing that her sister would not have come to Fort Worth unchaperoned.

"Papa was, but he had to go to Galveston." The two young women launched themselves out into the storm again. "They've had a terrible hurricane there. Mr. Barnett said probably thousands of people were drowned and much property lost. You know Papa owns something or other in Galveston, so he's gone to see about it." Frannie giggled. "I'm to move to Mr. Barnett's house this evening as soon as he gets out of court and then take the train back to Weatherford tomorrow."

"I wish I could invite you to stay with me," said Jessica sadly.

"Send tea and cakes up to my room," Frannie called to the desk clerk at the Worth as they trailed water through the lobby and toward the stairs. "Mama was so happy to get your letter. She gave me the money to take you to tea, but I thought the Roof Garden would be more fun. Isn't it lovely? I'll bet you go there all the time now that you're married and live in Fort Worth."

"Actually, I haven't been at all," said Jessica absently. "Was Mama very upset when she found we'd eloped?"

"She was sad. So was Papa." Frannie opened the door to her room, saying, "When they really got upset was when they heard that you'd gone to stay with your real mother." She hung her wet cape over a chair and reached for Jessica's. "Goodness, it's all so romantic!" Frannie exclaimed, grinning. "When Mama heard you'd gone to Mrs. Gresham's, she became frantic. Papa too. You'd think they expected Mrs. Gresham to murder you in your sleep or something. Is she really as mean as they say?"

"They said she's mean?" asked Jessica slowly.

"Well . . ." Frannie looked embarrassed. "Well, it seemed that way to me."

"She's been . . . she's been very . . . generous to me," said Jessica, choosing her words carefully. She still didn't know what to make of her mother; perhaps Penelope's illness, whatever it was, caused her uncertain disposition.

"Anyway—oh, here's our tea." Frannie admitted the waiter with his tray and, when he had gone, set about sloshing tea into the cups and plopping cakes onto Jessica's plate. "Anyway, Mama says to tell you she loves you, and you can come home anytime you want."

"What does Papa say?" asked Jessica.

"He just goes around looking gloomy. Do you want to come home?" asked Frannie.

Jessica shook her head and then bent over her cup

so that her sister could not see the wistfulness in her eyes.

"Are you madly in love with Travis?"

Jessica sighed. She *was* madly in love with Travis, but she hoped her sister wouldn't ask if he was madly in love with her. In truth, he never said. How did a man madly in love act? Jessica wondered.

"Also, Mama said you were to have all your clothes and books and such. She's already sent some, and there'll be more coming. Mama said she didn't want any daughter of hers dependent on Penelope Gresham—isn't that funny, because really you're Mrs. Gresham's daughter, not Mama's—but Mama said you were to have your own clothes and to tell you she'd send them."

Jessica nodded. In a way it made her feel that she was being cut off from them, although she knew that her mother—stepmother—had meant it kindly.

"Oh, Jessie, it's so good to see you." Frannie threw her arms around Jessica. "I miss you so. I thought once you got back from Washington, you'd be home forever and ever, and we'd be such good friends, now that I'm grown up too, and then you had to go fall in love with Travis—although he's very handsome. If I were old enough, I'd have fallen in love with him too, but I'm never going to fall in love with anyone." She scraped frosting from one of the cakes and popped it into her mouth, blissfully unaware of the contradictions she had just uttered.

"And guess what I did to dumb old Gavrell Pickering? If he'd found you for that last dance, you wouldn't have been out there kissing Travis, and then—well, anyway, I got even with Gavrell. I baked up these cookies with Mama's loosening tonic in them when I heard he was coming to call, and then I fluttered my eyelashes at him every chance I got till he didn't know what to do. He ate every single cookie." Frannie burst into more giggles. "I'll bet he hasn't left the outhouse yet. They don't have a commode, you know, so he has to . . ."

Jessica smiled fondly at her sister. This was the girl who was *all grown up*? Dear Frannie.

"What is that garment you're wearing?" demanded Penelope.

"It's called a rainy-day skirt," mumbled Jessica.

"It's disgusting. Your boots show."

"It's English," said Jessica. "English ladies wear them on rainy days, so their skirts aren't ruined."

"Yours is. It's soaking and muddy. So are your boots. And how dare you fail to appear at my tea? Where were you?"

Jessica had hoped to return in time for at least part of the tea but, in her delight at seeing Frannie, had forgotten. Then she'd hoped to slip into the house unnoticed, but Penelope had been waiting for her in a rage. Well, there was nothing for it; she confessed to meeting Frannie.

"Your sister? Anne Harte's daughter? I forbid you to associate with those people."

"But, Penelope—"

"You're not to see Justin Harte or any of his family. Do you understand me? Do you realize how much taking you in has cost me? The wedding, the trousseau. Then the bank. Oh, no one's told you about that? *Your father*—" her voice dripped venom "—was so furious with you that he threatened to cause a run on the bank unless we threw you out in the street— *out in the street*, young lady. We'll have to buy him out to keep him from ruining Cattleman's. So I think you might show a little gratitude. And don't you tell him who's buying those shares either. And do something about your appearance, for heaven's sake. You look like some common little seamstress in your muddy boots and skinned-back hair. How any daughter of mine could have so little sense of style . . ."

Chapter Nine

"Jess, wake up, honey."

Jessica dragged herself out of the frightening coils of her dream. Penelope had been pursuing her, face twisted with rage and hate.

"Jess, what is it?" Travis lit the bedside lamp. "You were crying."

Because Travis had awakened her so abruptly, Jessica could remember her dream in all its ugly detail, and she knew what had caused it—the afternoon confrontation with Penelope, when her mother's contempt and dislike had been so disturbingly evident. But how could she tell Travis about it when he had gone to so much trouble to find Penelope for her? How could she admit that her own mother hated her?

"I must have had a bad dream," said Jessica vaguely. "Too much excitement, I suppose."

"At Penelope's tea?" he asked, astonished that a

woman of Jessica's intelligence could enjoy such a stultifying afternoon.

"Actually, I didn't go. Frannie was in town, and we had tea at the Worth." Her face warmed at the memory. "She gave me all the news. Papa's gone to Galveston because of the hurricane, and Mama sent her love. She's having my things sent to me—books and clothes and so forth. We had a wonderful time." Jessica felt more cheerful already. "Frannie's so funny. You wouldn't believe what she did to Gavrell Pickering."

"Gave him the commode tour?" asked Travis, grinning.

"Worse," said Jessica and told him about Frannie's cookie recipe.

"Serves him right," said Travis, "cutting in on me when I was dancing with my future wife. Seriously, though, Jess, I'm glad you had such a fine visit with Frannie. I know how you've missed them."

He's so kind, thought Jessica. He'd never believe how awful Penelope could be, especially since Penelope inevitably behaved better in Travis's presence. Oh, Jessica realized that her mother was ill, but sometimes the mood changes were hard to tolerate. Jessica had lived so many years doubting her father's love, and now to discover that her mother didn't like her either! Even at her sweetest, Penelope was critical. Why did Travis never notice that?

"Why are you still wearing nightshifts to bed?" Travis asked teasingly as he captured her attention by untying the pale blue ribbons at the throat of the garment and moving his lips to the tempting valley between her breasts.

Jessica didn't feel like making love. With her heart as heavy as lead in her breast, she wanted to sleep and escape the ugly memories of that appalling scene with her mother. "Travis, I don't—"

"Hush," he cut her off, already lifting the long skirt of the nightdress.

"Travis." Jessica had never asked him to leave her alone and couldn't believe that he was ignoring her. "Travis!" He had pushed the soft batiste gown up around her waist and moved above her. "Don't!" she said sharply. "You're hurting me!"

Shocked, he drew back. She had never refused him, and he didn't like it. One of the wonderful things about their marriage was her responsiveness, but perhaps she had a point. He hadn't prepared her. Angry with himself, Travis sat up to blow out the lamp, the conviction growing in his mind that Jessica's wonderful afternoon with her sister couldn't be at the root of her bad dream and subsequent depression.

No, more likely it was Penelope. Now, *that* made sense. Jessica had skipped Penelope's tea to spend the afternoon with her sister, and Penelope hated to be thwarted every bit as much as she hated the Hartes. Given the combination of events, it stood to reason that she'd said something hurtful to Jess and precipitated all this.

"Sweetheart, did your mother have anything to do with that bad dream you had?"

"What would m-make you think that?" Jessica stammered.

What a poor liar she was, he thought. Penelope had to be at the bottom of this, and if he backed off now, he'd be ceding a round to his mother-in-law, the bitch; Travis was beginning to feel a great deal of sympathy for Justin Harte, who'd actually been married to the woman.

In the meantime his wife had pulled her nightshift

back into place, which wouldn't do at all. "Let's try something new," he murmured, promising himself that this time she'd be eager. She might be in shock, but she'd be eager. He smiled into the darkness as he removed the garment entirely.

"Travis, I really don't—" She stopped because he had put his lips against her breast, which was something she loved, even if her own reaction embarrassed her. Then as he continued to kiss her breasts, he rubbed the palm of his hand in circles on her stomach, very lightly, wider and wider circles until he was brushing her thighs and the soft triangle of down at their apex. Trembling, Jessica's mind skipped to the times he had touched her between the legs, causing a wonderful rush of heat and the overpowering drumbeat of passion inside her. As if he could read her mind, he stroked her thighs until her whole body craved a more intimate touch, until her legs weakened and parted of their own accord and his hand stroked higher, rewarding her, but not high enough.

Now she ached for the touch, and, little by little, stroking her legs, kissing her now around the waist and navel, Travis enticed her into the invitation he wanted, which, when she had opened to him sufficiently, he took with his mouth rather than his fingers.

She cried, "No!" and tried to heave him away, clutched his thick black hair to drag his head from her, but even as her fingers clenched, her protest changed to dazed, electrified passion. She writhed against the sheets as the intimacy of what he was doing overtook her.

She had once seen a man, sprinting beside a streetcar through standing water, grasp the hand rail to board. He had gone rigid with electric shock. That happened to her. First, shudders wracked her body and she cried out. Then the wonderful, unbearable tension peaked, and her body arced like lightning across a midnight sky until she collapsed, spent and trembling. Travis covered her, fitted himself to her, and his easy movement within felt almost like peace after a cataclysm.

"Not hurting anymore?" he murmured against her throat.

She shook her head. His persistent rocking felt wonderful, but she was floating, drowned after the storm he had subjected her to. She could only accept passively as the ripples spread and spread through her body and she murmured with pleasure, her head thrown back against the pillow, arms limp against the fine, smooth linen.

Later when she lay asleep, Travis smiled and thought, *To hell with you, Penelope. You'll never come between me and mine again*. Or would she? Travis suddenly had a picture of what would happen if Jessica ever found out why he had courted and married her. He turned on his side to look at his sleeping wife. She'd be heartbroken—sweet, sensitive Jessica, who couldn't even see the evil in Penelope. How would she feel if she found out that her husband was eaten up with hate and had used her to appease it? He turned onto his back again, staring bleakly into the darkness. Was he willing to risk hurting Jessica in order to avenge his father's death? He didn't know.

Abraham Hartwig laid his slouch hat with its silver cords of office on the table of the private room they'd commandeered in the saloon. "Mr. Arleigh here's a

Pinkerton agent, one of the best. He's tryin' to head off Butch Cassidy an' that bunch, catch 'em next time they take on a train or bank."

Travis studied Hamlet Arleigh, a small, slender fellow wearing an impeccable derby above a pinched face and round steel-rimmed spectacles. He looked more like a bookkeeper than a detective.

"Ever since I looked into the Greshams for you, I been interested in your new father-in-law," continued Lieutenant Hartwig. "An' like I told you Labor Day, suddenly Hugh Gresham's got connections down in Hell's Half Acre with Cassidy, who's taken to callin' himself Jim Lowe an' hangin' 'round Fort Worth between jobs. Cassidy turned up here two years ago an' spends his time over to Fannie Porter's when he's in town." Hartwig stopped talking until their beers had been delivered and they were alone again.

"They say his partner, the Sundance Kid, is in love with a new girl at Fannie's named Etta Place. Anyway, they're real popular fellas, do lots of hell raisin', an' lots of outlaws visit them from time to time. Lotsa outlaws an' your father-in-law—they've met three times in the last six weeks. Me an' Arleigh here are real interested in what them two got in common."

"Any ideas?" asked Travis, his own curiosity piqued.

"On a big robbery, Cassidy and his gang sometimes pick up nonnegotiable securities," said Hamlet Arleigh. "If that happens, they either have to throw them away or forge signatures—bank presidents' and cashiers'. Then they have to find someone to take them. We figure that, for a price, someone like Gresham might be willing to let that sort of paper pass through his bank and into circulation. If he were

147

desperate, he might even sign some himself." Arleigh stared at Travis. "Is there any reason to think your father-in-law might be willing to participate in such a scheme?"

"Perhaps," said Travis, excitement beginning to bubble in his head. If Hamlet Arleigh was right, and with both Pinkerton's and the Fort Worth police on the alert, disaster was already stalking Hugh and the Cattleman's Bank. Travis could sit back and watch it happen, savor Gresham's downfall without lifting a hand, without risking any hurt to Jessica. "Yes, Hugh might be that desperate."

"Why?"

"Several reasons," murmured Travis. "First, he's got a wife who spends money like she was coining it. Then just recently one of the bank's directors threatened to sell off his stock. Hugh panicked. He's trying to get enough money together to buy the shares himself so there'll be no loss of confidence among the depositors."

"Then he's afraid of a run on the bank?"

"Right," Travis agreed. "So he's strapped for money and cutting back on expenses, which gets him a lot of recriminations from his wife."

Hartwig grinned. "Good. Real good. In that case, we got a favor to collect from you, Travis."

"Oh?" Travis shifted uneasily in his chair.

"Yep. No one's going to invite me to dinner at Gresham's or give me a chance to look through his papers, but you—you're livin' right in his house."

"Look, Abe, I—"

"Hear me out. 'Sides that, I can't go down to Fannie Porter's an' get friendly with Cassidy an' them without causin' comment, an' if Hamlet here went an' anyone at Fannie's found out he was with

148

Pinkerton's—hell, they'd probably hustle him out back and shoot him. But you, Travis, you can go down there." Hartwig grinned and slapped Travis on the shoulder. "Cassidy's bound to like you, amigo, a fine fellow like you. You can get us all kinds of information."

"Abe, Gresham's my father-in-law now," Travis protested.

"I know. That's why I dug up all that dirt on him an' his wife—so you could marry the daughter an' do a job on them. Well, now we're gonna do it."

Travis sighed. How was he going to explain this to Abe Hartwig, who knew exactly why he wanted revenge? "If I take an active part in this scheme, Abe, my wife's going to get hurt, and I don't—"

"You owe me, Parnell," said Hartwig. "You weren't worried about the girl's feelin's when you married her."

"Mr. Parnell," said Hamlet Arleigh, "I think your new wife would be greatly distressed were *I* to tell her why you married her, something I might feel constrained to do."

Travis looked into those cold eyes, glittering behind the steel-rimmed spectacles, and he shuddered at the thought of Arleigh talking to Jess. "She'd never believe you," he muttered.

"Of course she would, especially when I tell her about the Armour deal you ruined as soon as you'd used her to worm your way into Gresham's confidence."

"That was before we were married."

"And then there's the matter of the cattle dip factory," said Hamlet Arleigh. "That was *after* you were married." He stared at Travis with expressionless eyes. "We're only asking you to do what you planned to do in the first place, Mr. Parnell, and your wife need know nothing about any of this."

Travis returned home in a black humor to find Jessica close to tears. "What is it now, Jess?" he asked, irritated to find yet another problem facing him.

Jessica glanced at him, clenched her fingers in her lap, and mumbled, "Nothing."

"It's not nothing when you look like that," he insisted.

"She heard us last night," Jessica burst out, then dropped a crimson face into her hands.

"Heard what?"

"Heard us in—in the bedroom."

"Did she have her ear pressed to the door?" he asked sarcastically.

"We were noisy," said Jessica. "She said if we were going to act like animals—"

"God damn it!" Travis exploded.

Jessica gave him a startled look, shocked for the first time since the humiliating talk with her mother into thinking of something other than her own misery.

"I'm sorry, Jessica," he said more gently. "We'll be—we'll be more—circumspect in the future. I know this must have embarrassed you."

"We—you—can't ever do what—what you—what happened last night."

"We'll do whatever we damned well please," said Travis through gritted teeth, determined that Penelope wasn't going to put a crimp in his sex life. "Just ignore her."

"I can't ignore her!" cried Jessica. "I don't even want to go down to dinner."

"I'll have it sent up."

"You mean for both of us?"

"No, I have to go out tonight." Both Hartwig and Arleigh had insisted that he make contact in Hell's Half Acre immediately.

"What if Hugh sees me there?" he'd asked.

"He'll be more embarrassed than you," Hamlet Arleigh had replied.

Travis gritted his teeth in rage. Damned and double damned Hugh Gresham had better keep his nose clean, because Travis could just imagine how Jessica would react if her husband had to go to court and testify against her stepfather. She wouldn't *need* to be told anything by that cold bastard, Hamlet Arleigh. Travis didn't know what to hope for. He wanted to see Hugh and Penelope ruined; every time he looked at them, he saw his father, the despair shining like death in his eyes. But Travis didn't want to cause Jessica pain.

Well, he'd have to play along with Arleigh and Hartwig until he could think of a way out of this mess, which meant he'd best get dressed and go. A bunch of high-spirited outlaws awaited him at Fort Worth's most notorious whorehouse.

Thinking that he was leaving because she had irritated him, Jessica watched with unhappy eyes as he changed his clothes. She wanted to ask where he was going but didn't dare. Still, she wasn't going to placate him by eating downstairs. If Penelope said anything in front of Hugh, Jessica thought she'd die of embarrassment. She'd stay up here and write a letter to Anne. She didn't care what any of them thought—Travis or Penelope. She'd write to her mother, who loved her.

"Don't forget to have my dinner sent up," she said

to Travis as he strode toward the door. She didn't bother to keep the anger out of her voice; it was his fault she found herself in this position, he and his shocking ideas of what was acceptable conduct between husbands and wives. She should have pushed him off the bed. She should have—

Travis suddenly was looming up beside her, having come back from the door when she snapped at him. "I'm glad to see you've got your spirit back, love," he said and kissed her soundly. "I'll try not to be too late."

He left and took the stairs two at a time, musing on how to handle his mother-in-law and her seeming desire to wreck his love life. Then, struck by an amusing idea, he stopped in mid-stride and headed back up the stairs to knock sharply at her door. "I believe you've got something to say to me," Travis declared and walked right in when she answered.

For once, Penelope looked confused. "I—I don't know what you mean," she stammered.

"You had a talk with Jessica. I reckon you'll want to talk to me as well."

"No!" Penelope turned white. "I mean Jessica and I understand each other. A mother, you understand, has to—has a duty—"

"Very admirable," interrupted Travis softly. He didn't want to alienate her; he just wanted to make sure that she never, ever, brought up such a subject with Jessica again. "But, Penelope, Jessica's a young bride, whereas you and I are, shall we say, experienced adults." He could see that his mother-in-law wasn't pleased to be described as experienced in the realm around which they were tiptoeing so circumspectly. "In the future if you want to discuss this particular subject, you come to me."

"I hardly think . . ." Her face was now flushed.

"I insist," said Travis. "Any advice you want to give can be given to me. That way Jessica won't be embarrassed. Agreed? Oh, and I'll be out tonight. I'd appreciate your having a plate sent up to Jessica. On the other hand, maybe I'll just tell the cook myself. We don't want to inconvenience you, Penelope." He smiled at her. "By the way, you're looking particularly lovely." His smile turning grim, he excused himself and went off to solicit an introduction to a man calling himself Jim Lowe.

The cook brought up Jessica's dinner and fussed over her, having decided that she must be ill since she never gave anyone "a bit of grief, like some folks." The cook frowned as she muttered *some folks*; then she fluffed Jessica's pillows and plunked a tray of tasty food onto her lap.

Cook was really a nice enough woman, but she wasn't Mab, thought Jessica wistfully. Cook never snatched your plate away because she couldn't see that you hadn't finished, and Cook never served canned peaches with hatchet cuts in them for dessert. Cook never made you take your wet clothes off in the kitchen so that she could hang them on the stove and feed you Mama's good tonic to keep you from taking cold, and Cook, if you still had a doll, probably wouldn't offer to sew its foot on if David and Ned had torn it off playing Indian captive. Mab had done all those things.

Jessica sniffed her excellent dinner, which Mab couldn't have produced in a hundred years. Then Jessica put the tray aside and went to the little ladies' desk to write her mother—stepmother. She wouldn't tell Anne any of the bad things; she didn't want to worry her. Sighing, she bit the end of her pen and began a long, long letter, sifting through her days for the happy events.

It was very late when Travis came in; Jessica had been asleep. He smelled of whiskey, cigar smoke and—perfume? Her heart speeded up in fear as she remembered him saying that a man who was satisfied at home didn't have to go elsewhere. Had he been so angry when she told him about Penelope's lecture that he—that he—should she ask him?

Before she could decide, he put his arms around her and whispered, "Are you awake, Jessie? God, you smell sweet. Like pansies."

"Violets," she corrected automatically, thus losing her chance to feign sleep.

Travis chuckled. "Violets then. I know I must smell like the devil. I hope you're not going to push me out of bed."

If the devil smelled like whiskey and cigars and nasty perfume, Travis did, Jessica decided resentfully, but he obviously had no intention of allowing her to push him out of bed. In fact, his hand was at her breast, his mouth covering hers. If he'd been to another woman, he wouldn't want her as well. Would he? Now, all she had to do was keep quiet so her mother wouldn't hear. Ah-h, it was hard. If only they lived somewhere else.

"Touch me," he whispered. After that, Jessica forgot, for a time, to think of her mother, and even later she fell into a deep sleep.

"What do you want for your birthday?" he asked the next morning.

Rubbing her eyes, Jessica mumbled, "I didn't think

anyone was going to remember it this year."

"Hasn't your mother said anything?" he asked, frowning.

She shook her head.

"Probably has some surprise planned," he muttered. He'd have to remember to drop some hints. He doubted that Penelope remembered anyone's birthday but her own. "Now what do you want? How about a piano?"

"Are we going to get our own house?" she asked eagerly.

"No, Jessica." If his wife insisted on moving, he'd be in a bad spot; likely Hamlet Arleigh would pay her a call before they could get their trunks out the door. "Penelope has plenty of room for another piano, and I remember your saying hers wasn't very—very something."

"Well tuned," said Jessica, sighing. "And I don't want a piano. Goodness, I don't even play well."

"You don't? But she asks you to play every time she has guests."

"I know," said Jessica dejectedly. "It's embarrassing."

Damn, Travis thought. Being no expert on music, he hadn't realized what Penelope had been up to. She'd seemed to be treating Jessica pretty well. Had he been wrong? Then his mind returned to the birthday present. Jessica did like music, even if she didn't want a piano. "How about a phonograph?" he suggested.

Her eyes lit up.

"A phonograph and lots of those things with the music on them. I saw one in a store the other day with a horn that looked like a giant red flower."

"Travis, you don't have to buy me anything so

expensive. Any little thing would do," said Jessica earnestly, and she meant it. If he saved his money, maybe they could move out.

"That's all right, love. I'll get you some little things too."

Jessica sighed. "Well, if we have a phonograph, we can hear some good performances instead of mine."

Chapter Ten

"David!" Jessica launched herself into her brother's arms, laughing delightedly.

"Guess I found the right house." He stuck his head out the door and signaled to a cowboy seated on a wagon loaded with boxes. "Brought your things," he told Jessica as the man began to unload. "Ned's gonna meet us at the Worth, an' we're gonna buy you about a hundred a them little chocolate cakes an' catch up on the news."

"Those," said Jessica, giving him another hug. "Those cakes."

"Well, I guess marriage hasn't changed you. You're still correctin' my grammar. I swear, Jessie—"

"Are you going to introduce me to your friend, dear?"

Jessica turned to face her mother and, swallowing hard, said, "Penelope, this is my brother David."

"Harte?" Penelope's gracious expression disappeared as she stared intently at David. "Of course. I should have recognized that slut's red hair."

"Penelope!" cried Jessica, horrified. She looked anxiously at her brother, whose face had gone cold and white.

"Well, ma'am," said David slowly, "my mother, the lady you've just insulted, brought me up to be polite to my elders, but maybe that don't apply to you."

He took a step forward, and Penelope, looking alarmed, backed away. For the first time, Jessica recognized how much like Justin her brother was. Before, she had seen it only in the blue of David's eyes; now she saw it in the expression and the hard power and threat that emanated from him. David was no longer a carefree boy, and had she been Penelope, she'd have backed away too.

"I've heard you were an ugly an' vicious woman, Miz Gresham. All I had to do was ask around Fort Worth to find out what folks thought about you, so let me say, ma'am, that you better watch yourself with my sister. I don't like her livin' here—none of us at home do—an' if I hear you've been treatin' her bad, I might have to do somethin' about it."

Having retreated to the foot of the stairs, a distance from which she evidently considered it safe to counterattack, Penelope turned on Jessica and said, her voice high with anger, "I want him out of my house."

"He's come from Weatherford with my things," said Jessica quickly, hoping to calm her mother before the tension and ugliness escalated.

"I don't care what he's come for. You're never, never to bring another Harte into my house. Do you understand? Now, get him out of here. I won't have a son of that red-headed whore in my—"

David, scowling, took another step forward, and

Penelope screamed, "I'll get help. I'll have him jailed. I'll . . ." She fled up the stair, skirts clutched in both hands, her threats trailing over her shoulder until she disappeared into the upper hall.

"Whew," said David. "I'm sure glad you don't take after her. How can you stand to live here?"

"She's—she's not well," said Jessica.

"If you mean she's crazy, I'd say that's right. Now how are we supposed to carry this stuff in if I'm going to get thrown in jail for bein' here?"

"Beau can take everything up to my room," said Jessica, inclining her head toward the cowboy who was standing in the doorway with a large parcel in his arms and his eyes as round as pie plates.

"I don't want to go up there, Miss Jessie," said Beau.

"I'll go with you," Jessica assured him.

Galey and Guffey. Travis couldn't have been more pleased. He knew them both; they were the men who had financed the Corsicana field. If they thought Lucas's efforts at Spindletop promising enough to warrant their backing, Travis knew his investment in the Beaumont area would be a winner. In fact, he'd leave as soon as he could to buy up more land on the hill—and anywhere else in the area where he found oil seepage from the ground or the odor of gas, anywhere he could get such land at reasonable prices. That way he could maximize his future profits and at the same time avoid Hamlet Arleigh and the spying missions he insisted that Travis undertake.

Travis's sources said the financiers expected to start drilling anew within a month, sometime in October. He considered offering his services but decided against it. Better to lie low so that he could buy land without attracting notice. When the field came in, his drilling crews would be in demand. Then he could take his wife and leave Fort Worth, where Hartwig and Arleigh kept pressing him for information about Hugh Gresham.

He hadn't found out much, although he'd managed to strike up a friendship with Jim Lowe, also known as Butch Cassidy. The outlaw was an interesting man, though, Lord, Travis had to do a lot of drinking to keep up with that bunch. He had an aching head the morning after a session at Fannie's, not to mention an unhappy wife. Jessica couldn't know where he'd been, so evidently she just didn't like him going out nights. Still, diverting her when he got home was a pleasure.

It was about the only pleasure he got these days, torn as he was between loyalty to his father's memory and worry about his wife. He wished Hugh would do something blatantly illegal, get caught at it by someone else, and earn himself a nice long jail term, which he richly deserved, leaving his bitch of a wife poverty-stricken, which she richly deserved. Penelope would probably rather be dead than poor.

Then Travis could spirit Jessie away to Beaumont without risking Hamlet Arleigh's threatened retaliation. Jess would enjoy Beaumont. The legal complications to the lease and ownership of land around there were already horrendous and could only get worse when prices skyrocketed. Indications were that Spindletop, as they'd taken to calling the hill, would be every bit as lucrative a field as Corsicana. Jess could stay busy from morning till night protecting his interests. In fact, maybe he should ask her to study Texas land law. He remembered Justin's lawyer, Henry Barnett, suggesting it during her brief stay at his house. Barnett had offered the use of his books, but Travis decided to buy the books for her himself.

Reading law would give her something to keep her mind off his nighttime and out-of-town absences. He didn't have to tell her about Beaumont; he wasn't telling anyone about Beaumont. He'd say he had title problems in Corsicana.

Travis stopped beside a ladies' apparel shop, a parasol in the window having caught his eye. He couldn't believe it was out in plain view, not with that carved ivory handle, the figure of a woman who looked, for all the world, to be nude, and whose body looked like Jess's. Grinning, Travis pushed the door open.

Jessica returned home from a wonderful afternoon with her brothers during which they had laughed and talked and eaten thirty-three tiny chocolate cakes between them, drunk ten cups of coffee, and exchanged all their news. She could hardly bear to leave them at her door, but on the other hand, she couldn't invite them in, not after that scene with Penelope.

Jessica's lips compressed. Her mother's behavior had been inexcusable. No matter how ill used Penelope might have felt herself to be by Justin and Anne in the past, the things she had said to David were not to be forgiven. Angrily Jessica decided to stop making excuses for her mother. It was one thing to say the things she said to Jessica, but what Penelope had said to David about Anne exceeded the bounds of decency.

Resolutely, Jessica turned her mind back to her brothers. They had come for her birthday, bringing not only her belongings but presents from all the family as well. She skipped up the stairs, thinking that she would open the gifts right now, while she could enjoy them in private. Of course, she'd show them to

Travis later, but she was under no obligation to show them to her mother, who had obviously forgotten Jessica's birthday.

As she sped down the hall, she saw that her door was open. Could Travis be home already? The scene that confronted her in the bedroom brought her to an abrupt halt. Her mother was there. She had opened all the boxes and parcels, and strewn the contents everywhere. At that moment she was holding up the green evening gown Jessica had worn to the pre-rodeo ball and muttering over it. Jessica stood stunned in the doorway and gasped, "What have you done?"

Penelope looked up. "This is your wardrobe?" she asked disdainfully. "It's pathetic. Everything will have to be thrown out. Everything. I can't have a daughter of mine wearing such ridiculous garments." She took the gown in both hands as if to rip it down the front, the gown Jessica had worn when Travis first kissed her.

Jessica snatched it from her mother. "These are my things, Penelope," she cried. "You have no right to do anything with them."

"And this is my house. I can do what I want. Look over here." She waved a hand toward another box. "Books. Huge, dusty books."

"My law books!" exclaimed Jessica, delighted.

"Law books?"

"I went to law school for three years in Washington."

"Good heavens, don't you dare tell anyone. My friends would never stop laughing. A woman lawyer? That's—that's ludicrous. You must throw them out immediately. I won't have you reading such things in my house."

"Up until now, it's been almost impossible to read anything in your house. You have no books," snapped Jessica, not bothering to hide her contempt.

"Don't you talk to me that way, young lady. Emily!" she shouted. "I'll have her carry all this debris away."

"No, Penelope, you won't," said Jessica, determined that not one item of her property would be discarded to satisfy Penelope's warped ideas.

Then Jessica discovered the most distressing thing of all. "You've opened my gifts." She looked around wildly, recognizing the gift wrappings that had gone upstairs covering those birthday presents she had so looked forward to opening. Now she couldn't tell what, in the heaps of things strewn everywhere, had been given her or by whom. "How could you?"

"What gifts? If someone sent you gifts, you can be sure there was nothing of interest. I'd have noticed."

"Been shopping, ladies?" asked Travis who had just entered, carrying a huge box crowned with a blue satin bow.

"My goodness," murmured Penelope. She gave him a flirtatious glance. "Another gift? What's the occasion? Is this one for me?"

"Surely you haven't forgotten, Penelope," he said, cursing himself because he had neglected to make sure that his mother-in-law remembered his wife's birthday. Poor Jessica! He'd have to move fast to repair the damage before she noticed. "It's Jessica's birthday, but of course you're teasing, Penelope. I'm sure you've got her something wonderful."

"She not only forgot," said Jessica, "but she came in here and opened all my gifts from home. Now I don't know—I can't tell . . ."

Jessica's eyes shone with angry tears, and Travis could have strangled Penelope. He could see that

163

Jessica's belongings, along with the birthday presents, had been opened and dumped, unidentified, around the room. "Well, honey, we can figure it out. Look over here. This must be the bicycle your father got you." Travis pointed to a blue bicycle with bronzed handlebars, partially hidden by a muslin petticoat and leaning against the hearth.

"You ride a bicycle?" Penelope demanded.

Since she looked as if she were on the verge of a tirade, Travis said, "Now that we're opening Jessica's presents, you'll want to go get yours, Penelope." The woman closed her mouth, confused, and he thought, *The bitch, she's half drunk.* "We'll wait for you." That ought to get rid of her; it was obvious she had no gift for Jessica.

"It's being made up," said Penelope, a sly look on her face. "I'm giving her a lorgnette, very lovely, to replace those spectacles she wears. I really had no choice, did I, since she insists on reading books, looking exceedingly frumpy in those—"

"I'm sure the lorgnette will be beautiful," interrupted Travis before Jessica could voice the protest that had been hovering on her lips and before Penelope could come up with any more malicious gibes. How could he have thought she was treating Jessica well? The woman was incapable of treating anyone well.

"Of course it will be beautiful," said Penelope, smiling at him and smoothing a slender hand over her hair, which had begun to come loose during her raid on Jessica's belongings. "Everything I buy is of the best quality and in the best taste—unlike these things." She waved a disdainful hand at the havoc she had wreaked. "Now, I want all this trash carted away. Jessica simply cannot wear these clothes. I'll buy new ones to replace them." She smiled sweetly at Travis, evidently having thought better of her earlier unpleasantness. "You know how generous I am where Jessica's concerned."

"Penelope." Hugh was standing in the door, attracted by the commotion when he arrived home from the bank. His voice held a world of alarm and warning. Travis was pleased to note that the prospect of providing yet another wardrobe was more than Hugh could face, even though his wife was now glaring at him. "Penelope, if these are Jessica's clothes, I'm sure they'll do very well. She doesn't need you to—"

"Do you realize who bought these clothes?" Penelope demanded. "I won't—"

"Come along, darling," said Hugh, grasping her arm firmly and propelling her to the door.

"Well," said Travis, trying to look cheerful in the face of Jessica's anger, "we'll need a maid to hang all these things up, but first the presents. There's this one." He waved to the huge box he had set down on the bed. "You take off the ribbon, and I'll open it for you."

Reluctantly, glancing at her things tossed so carelessly everywhere, Jessica went to the bed. Travis crossed to the door and locked it. He didn't want his mother-in-law escaping from her husband's lecture on financial responsibility and coming back to do further damage to Jessica's birthday. Jessica removed the ribbon; then Travis cut the box open to reveal an Edison Home Phonograph, which he lifted out and placed on a table to better display the huge red horn with painted blue flowers disappearing into the throat and the carved oak cabinet, which actually contained a hundred two-minute cylinders. "Let's see. How about a Sousa march?" he suggested, selecting the music and then demonstrating the procedure for working the mechanism.

Jessica watched with a sinking heart. He'd bought a hundred cylinders? At this rate they'd never be able to afford a house of their own, and she wanted to get out of here! The music came miraculously out of the horn as Travis presented her with another gift. "Oh, Travis," she said, "you shouldn't have."

"Open it," he commanded, laughing. "You're going to be surprised."

Jessica unwrapped the long narrow package. "A parasol?" Why was she supposed to be surprised at a parasol? It was very pretty, to be sure, cream silk overlaid with fine black lace, daintily ruffled both at the tip and the edges.

"Look at the handle."

Jessica examined it, and her mouth fell open. "She's—she—"

"—looks just like you."

"She does not!" cried Jessica. "She doesn't have any clothes on!"

"I got the same impression," he agreed. "But with or without clothes, I'd recognize that body anywhere."

"Travis Parnell!"

"Happy birthday, love." He caught her waist and leaned forward to kiss her, a light, warm kiss that changed suddenly when he slid his tongue between her lips, something he did occasionally, something that always took her by surprise. "If you don't believe me about the parasol lady, I think we should make a comparison."

Jessica drew back, eyes wide. "We're expected down to dinner."

Virgin Fire

"It can wait." He sat her on the bed and removed her shoes and stockings. "Now, come over here." Travis drew her to the pier glass, where he stood behind her and began to unbutton the back of her shirtwaist.

"It's a formal dinner," Jessica protested, watching the shirtwaist as it slid to the floor, after which her dark skirt followed. "For twelve."

"So they'll only have ten for a few courses." Travis bent his head to kiss the curve of her shoulder, then busied himself with the tapes that held her petticoat to her waist.

Jessica swallowed. She had never watched herself being disrobed by her husband. The sight in the mirror of her petticoats sliding to the carpet, followed by her corset cover, made her stomach flutter. "She—Penelope will be very angry if we're late." She heard her own voice as if from a distance, high and a little unsteady.

Travis unlaced the strings at the back of her corset, then, dropping it at her feet, lifted her chemise over her head and looked into the mirror at his own brown fingers against the white skin of her breasts. He raised his eyes to hers and asked, "Aren't you angry with her?"

"Y-yes," she admitted reluctantly as she watched, mesmerized, while he loosened the ties of her drawers and dropped them around her ankles, leaving her quite naked.

"Step out of them," he said softly as he reached for the parasol. "That's you," he murmured, looking from the sensuously carved handle to Jessica's reflection in the mirror. Then he turned her and pulled her tight against him. "We *are* going to be a bit late for dinner."

Jessica glanced over her shoulder at the mirror which now reflected her pale body pressed against the dark power of his, fully clothed. "Very late," she agreed, shivering.

Travis swung her up into his arms and carried her to the bed, sweeping aside the things Penelope had thrown so spitefully across the satin counterpane. Minutes later, when he had thrust himself deep into her, he told Jessica to look into the glass. She turned her head to see their joined bodies reflected there, never having realized that every time they had made love by daylight, or lamplight, or even moonlight, she could have looked and seen herself there with Travis. She found the sight and the thought both embarrassing and very exciting. Then he flexed his hips, and Jessica closed her eyes.

"Don't you want to watch?" he asked.

She shook her head. It was hard enough to maintain any kind of control with him. She didn't need added stimulation.

"Another time," he murmured, flexing again. "Maybe we'll get a mirror to put above the bed." He was driving her, with slow, sure strokes, toward ecstasy. "Hide the mirror under the canopy."

"Travis," she gasped.

"H-m-m?"

"Stop—talking." Jessica felt as if she were beginning to come apart, every inner particle of her body separating from every other, driven apart by a whirling rush of wet warmth. By talking, he was distracting her from that sensation. "Just . . ."

"Whatever you want, love." Gasping himself, he had begun to hasten toward mutual rapture. "Better?" he asked.

Jessica couldn't answer. She had found disintegra-

168

tion. They were very late to dinner, and Penelope treated Travis with a saccharine flirtatiousness; Jessica she ignored.

Jessica stared gloomily out the window. It seemed to her that they had had nothing but rain in Fort Worth since the hurricane that devastated Galveston. For the remaining weeks in September she had worked as a volunteer in various church and civic relief projects for the storm victims. Her efforts were appreciated by the organizers, and she had made some friends. However, Penelope disapproved of anyone she didn't already know and refused to let Jessica invite new acquaintances to the house. If they were friends or relatives of Penelope's own circle, she accused Jessica of trying to make her look hard-hearted because she refused to participate in charitable activities unaccompanied by social events.

Jessica had given up hoping that she could please or even understand her mother. She no longer cared. Penelope's mood seemed to depend entirely on how recently she had taken her medicine, and either way she was difficult to bear, whether wildly abusive or sweetly malicious. Jessica avoided her mother whenever she could.

The worst times were those when Travis went off to Corsicana on business. Then Penelope became especially critical, almost as if she governed her behavior by a desire to keep Travis's good opinion. Why she should care what he thought, Jessica couldn't imagine. Although still beautiful, Penelope was old enough to be his mother; she certainly wasn't cultivating him out of any concern for Jessica; and although both Penelope and Hugh hinted often enough, Travis didn't bank at Cattleman's and thus afford them any financial advantage. Jessica almost wished he would—as a sort of recompense for their hospitality. She disliked feeling indebted.

After watching the rain pour across the window for another few minutes, she turned back to the ladies' sitting room, which, being somewhat plain and cold, Penelope seldom visited. Jessica was bored. She had spent the morning reading law in her room, but with no prospect of using her studies, she tired of the effort. If she read anything else, anywhere else in the house, it had to be something her mother approved of, and Penelope looked at nothing but fashion magazines. Restlessly, Jessica swept up a copy of *Vogue* from a pile on the table. At least it had interesting articles.

How she wished Travis would let her go with him to Corsicana. However, he never did; he said she wouldn't like it. She'd suggested that they move there; Travis had shrugged and said he had business in Fort Worth as well, and here she had family.

Some family, thought Jessica grimly. Her *real* family lived in Weatherford, and in Parker and Palo Pinto counties. She wrote to them regularly; she'd have written every day, but then they might have guessed at her loneliness. Not that she wasn't happy with Travis. She adored him, but he spent so much time out of town. Even when he was in Fort Worth, he went out at all hours of the day and night, excusing himself, when she asked, with vague references to his business affairs. He'd once actually said she wouldn't be interested. Travis had never made any remark so insulting before.

She flipped through the magazine looking for something not too silly to read and found the most astounding article. Some college professor had stated that the only romantic love men felt for women was "sex attraction." Jessica blinked. Could that be true of her husband? When she examined their relationship, she decided that it could.

Many ladies were very upset, even incensed, at the professor's opinion, according to *Vogue*. Jessica sighed. She would have been upset too if she hadn't had the disheartening conviction that the professor might know what he was talking about. *Vogue* advised its female readers to have no illusions about men. The magazine writer, in fact, advised ladies to do the sensible thing and make a scientific study of sex.

How depressing, thought Jessica. Where was she to find any scientific information on sex, a subject no one ever talked about, except Penelope when she was being horrid and Travis when he was having it with Jessica. And was that really all their marriage meant to him? Sex attraction? It didn't sound like a very lasting emotion. Did that mean he'd leave her eventually? Her father had left her mother. But then the more she saw of Penelope, the more sympathy and understanding she felt for her father. If she were a man, she'd have preferred Anne, who was loving, to Penelope, who was not. Could sex attraction be all that her father felt for Anne?

Jessica's mind jumped back to her birthday when Travis had brought her that parasol, the handle of which she had to keep covered with her hand so that no one could see it. He had undressed her in front of the mirror and made such wild love to her that they had missed the first two courses of Penelope's dinner. Sex attraction, she decided. It had to be. She felt more than that for him. But Travis—Travis had never said he loved her. When he found someone more attractive, and that wouldn't be hard to do, what would happen? And how was a scientific study of the subject going to help her? She tossed the copy of *Vogue* across the room and vowed that she'd read nothing but her law books in the future. *They* didn't cast doubts on the longevity of her marriage.

Chapter Eleven

"Travis, you really can't come to the corset shop with me," said Jessica. Penelope had said much the same thing when Travis caught her complaining about Jessica's waist size.

"I'll take her out for new corsets myself," Travis had offered gaily. Horrified at the idea of a man in a corset shop, Penelope told him she wouldn't think of asking such a thing.

"Not at all," Travis insisted. "My dear mother-in-law, I shall make the sacrifice for you."

Penelope evidently took his *sacrifice* at face value and only her due. Jessica, knowing Travis, realized that he was teasing. He had been in remarkably good spirits since his latest return from Corsicana. Perhaps now was the time to suggest that they move to a house of their own. Travis may have seen Penelope's lecture on corsets as amusing; Jessica knew it to be one more attack in a long line of them.

"Travis," she said, "I have something I must talk to you about."

"Something more pressing than corsets?" he asked, laughing, for they were on their way to the corset shop.

"This is a serious matter."

"Well, in that case, you need sustenance. Into the tearoom with you, love."

Jessica sighed, hoping he'd still be calling her *love* when she brought up moving from her mother's house. She waited for her tea, his coffee, and a plate of chocolate cookies to be served, then said, "I'm very unhappy living at Penelope's."

His smile immediately disappeared.

"Because—because of *her*," Jessica faltered. "Not—"

"Jessica," said Travis, equally serious, "you have to have some tolerance for your mother." And *he* had to do some fast talking. Hamlet Arleigh would never let them leave.

"She has little tolerance for me," Jessica muttered.

"I know, love, but Penelope is—the truth is that your mother has a serious problem. That medicine she takes—"

"I understand, Travis, but it doesn't make the way she treats me any—any easier to withstand. Even when she's had the medicine and is feeling cheerful, she says—really—really ugly things to me."

"Can't you just overlook them, knowing that—"

"No, I can't. It's not as if she needs me. She has lots of servants and—and Hugh to look after her. I don't see why we can't live somewhere else and visit them occasionally."

Travis frowned. He had come back from Corsicana with very good news. The Hamils, three hometown brothers who owned a drilling outfit, had been hired by Lucas to drill the Galey and Guffey–financed well outside Beaumont, drilling to start the end of October. Al had said it was going to be a bitch—hard rock and quicksand—but they were excited, as was Travis.

In addition, his sources of information at Fannie Porter's place had been productive. Hugh did have a deal to help the Wild Bunch handle any nonnegotiable securities they might take in their next robbery. Hugh had already received money, although as yet he'd done nothing to get himself arrested, nothing that Hartwig could prove. Until that happened, neither Hartwig nor Arleigh was going to turn Travis loose, and Jessica's desire to leave had to be circumvented. Not for much longer, but still . . .

"Sweetheart, it's very expensive to set up a household. You may not realize how much it would cost us."

"You seem to have lots of money, Travis. If you'd just stop spending it on presents that I don't need . . ."

"The things I buy you are nothing compared to what we'd have to spend to furnish our own home. I'm not saying we won't do that, Jess, or that I can't afford it, but it would be an extravagance here in Fort Worth when we'll be moving."

"Oh?" Jessica studied him eagerly. "To Corsicana?"

"Or wherever the next oil strike is."

"But you've said you had business here as well."

Damn. She was so logical. "I do, but oil is my main interest. When I get things running here, we'll be off. It won't be that long." He could see that she wanted to ask how long and forestalled her by saying, "Surely you can put up with Penelope another month or two—for my sake."

Defeated, Jessica nodded.

"Wonderful, love." How he hated to do this to her. "Now off to the corset shop."

"Really, Travis . . ." But he wasn't listening. In minutes he'd paid the bill and hustled her across the square where he announced enthusiastically to the astounded proprietress that he was a married man come to supervise the purchase of a superior corset for his wife.

"But, sir," said the woman, "husbands never—"

"Good heavens," interrupted Travis, eyeing all the armless, headless mannequins laced into their corsets, "do your garments make ladies' arms and heads fall off, madam? If that's the case . . ."

The sales clerk began to giggle. Jessica would have done the same had she not been so embarrassed, and the proprietress, looking quite horrified, said stiffly, "Sir, I assure you that our garments will have no untoward effects on your wife."

"Is that true, madam? I would be devastated, I assure you, were my bride to lose an arm, or even a leg—I notice that your models have no limbs of any sort."

Jessica had to turn away to hide her laughter. He was so endearing, and she knew he wanted to erase from her mind that unpleasant scene with Penelope that he had walked in on. It was amazing that anyone could be so critical over the size of a set of corsets, but Penelope seemed to consider Jessica's waistline a matter of grave importance. As the proprietress, red-faced, scurried off to fetch her most expensive model, which was what Travis had demanded to see, Jessica murmured, "Actually, people who advocate rational clothing for women—"

"Like those knickerbockers you wore to ride your bicycle?"

"They are called rationals," Jessica agreed. "At any

rate, the rational clothing societies do not really approve of corsets, and they say that no woman should wear undergarments totaling more than seven pounds in weight."

"Seven pounds!" exclaimed Travis. "Good lord! Madam, how much does that corset weigh?"

"Why, I don't know, sir," the woman stammered, and there followed a half hour during which Travis examined and discussed stays and laces and whalebone amid the giggles of the salesgirls, the frowns of the proprietress, and Jessica's efforts to maintain a sober demeanor.

After that she chose a corset, and they went home, where Penelope refused to hear a description of their visit to the corset shop and declared that she would have to take her custom elsewhere since Jessica had been so improper as to allow her husband to accompany her. Travis said he had thoroughly enjoyed the mission and hoped to be informed when Penelope needed to go so that he could accompany her as well. Jessica decided that it was a shame her mother had no sense of humor.

Penelope was giving another of her interminable dinners, which had been preceded by the usual family squabbling. First, Penelope had complained about Jessica's choice of gown, an unusual robelike garment patterned on medieval lines that flowed without a waistline from beneath her breasts to the floor and was topped by an open, floor-length coat with full, flowing sleeves.

Penelope had never seen anything like it and demanded that Jessica take it off. She said loudly and not for the first time that she intended to throw out and replace every tasteless item in Jessica's wardrobe, an announcement that brought Hugh scurrying from his dressing room and caused an argument about money between Hugh and Penelope that Jessica could hear all the way down the hall.

Grim-faced, she continued to dress, knowing that whatever she wore, her mother would criticize it. Furthermore, Travis had not yet returned, and the idea of facing her mother's friends and her mother's gibes without his protection was really more than she could bear. When they congregated in the drawing room, he was still absent, and Penelope took the opportunity to point out to the guests the entirely unsuitable gown her daughter had chosen to wear, against advice.

"Have you ever seen the like, Blanche?" asked Penelope.

"It's in the aesthetic style, Mrs. Holloman," Jessica explained politely to Blanche. "All the rage in London. This fashion was popularized by the Pre-Raphaelite painters and is espoused in artistic and intellectual circles."

"Did you buy it in London?" asked Mrs. Holloman, impressed. All the ladies were now inspecting the gown with interest while their hostess fumed.

"Yes, ma'am. I also have a lovely Worth gown given to me by my stepmother. I don't wear it because Penelope—" she gave her mother a cool look "—doesn't care for that either."

The magic word *Worth* was whispered reverently among the ladies, causing Penelope's face to flush with anger. Jessica ignored her. She had come to the conclusion that nothing could mitigate her mother's hostility, so she might as well fight back.

"It's a bit plain," suggested another of the ladies, but hesitantly. She obviously didn't want to denigrate a gown that might well be the latest thing in places more knowledgeable than Fort Worth.

"Yes," Jessica agreed, beginning to enjoy herself. "Ladies in the centers of fashion are beginning to feel foolish about cluttering their wardrobes with tasteless frills. For instance, feathers."

She watched her mother draw a sharp, angry breath, but the circle of women was too fascinated for Penelope to feel comfortable in contradicting Jessica.

"Women of sensitivity, realizing how many unfortunate birds are killed—and the deaths number in the millions—such women are turning their backs on feathers as a fashion accessory. Did you realize that feathers are actually plucked from living ostriches, causing the poor birds great pain?"

The ladies, not wanting to be thought insensitive, looked suitably shocked.

"And the case of the even more popular egret is sadder," exclaimed Jessica, warming to her subject. "Because the feathers are more beautiful during the mating and nesting season, the birds are killed during that time."

Penelope cut in with an announcement of dinner, although the cook had not indicated that it was ready and Travis had yet to appear.

"—leaving the poor baby birds to die for lack of parental care," Jessica finished. "I fear there will be no egrets left in future years."

On that note they trooped into the dining room, and Jessica astonished the guests by explaining Darwin's theory of evolution as espoused by Professor Henry Drummond, a noted New York divine and speaker on the Chautauqua circuit.

"From apes?" echoed Mrs. Holloman weakly, as if she could not believe that any man would accuse her of being descended from a large monkey when everyone knew that on her mother's side she traced her lineage to settlers of Boston, Massachusetts. "I can't believe a man of the cloth said that."

"Yes, indeed," Jessica insisted. "Many churchmen are quite forward-looking. Why, not three years ago Dr. Lyman Abbott gave a very interesting lecture series on the Bible as literature. For instance, Dr. Abbott disbelieves the story of Jonah and the whale, which, when you think about it, does seem unlikely."

"But it's in the Bible," stammered Mrs. Bettina Manrich.

"Durn Easterners," muttered Mr. Manrich, the milled flour king of Fort Worth. "Always coming up with some foolish idea. Parnell, you'd best watch what your little lady here reads and listens to. She's just told us some of the durn fooledest things I ever heard."

Travis dropped a "sorry to be late" and a kiss on Penelope's cheek, causing her to jump, then took his seat by Jessica with a warm smile. "You're looking beautiful," he murmured. "Lovely dress."

"Penelope hates it," said Jessica, still on the attack.

"Well." Travis glanced around the table at the embarrassed guests. "I just heard an interesting rumor. They're saying Senator Bailey got himself a real big loan from Pierce, Waters. A sort of thank you for helping them to get their greedy forks back in the Texas pie, and of course, helping Pierce, Waters means helping Standard Oil."

In the uproar of anger and denial following that statement, Jessica's shocking choices of conversational subject matter were forgotten, just as Travis expected they would be.

What had gotten into the girl? More hard words from Penelope, he reckoned, wishing the woman would control her tongue. He supposed he himself would come in for some of Penelope's malice since he'd been late for her dinner party, but it would be worth it. He'd just heard that the Hamil brothers, hired by Lucas and backed by Galey and Guffey, had at last started drilling. Galey had chosen the spot—right next to a hog wallow on Spindletop mound.

"I heard an interesting rumor," said Penelope, "about a place owned by a woman named Fannie Porter."

Travis stopped chuckling over the hog-wallow oil well as he watched Hugh shift uneasily. Did Penelope realize she was cutting close to her husband's illegal activities? Travis wondered, amused.

Jessica kept her eyes fixed on her plate. She had heard that name before in a conversation between her husband and a police officer at the Labor Day picnic; the conversation had made her uneasy and a bit jealous.

"It's a house of ill repute," said Penelope.

Shocked gasps went around the room. Such things were never discussed in polite company, certainly not by or in front of ladies. Jessica had stiffened as she made the connection between Travis and such a place—but no, he wouldn't; probably the policeman had been telling him about some—some illegal activities there.

"It seems that not only do scarlet women and famous outlaws—"

Travis had felt his wife stiffen, shocked no doubt by the subject; now he watched Hugh turn white.

"—frequent the place," Penelope announced with relish, "but rumor has it that some gentlemen—previously assumed to be respectable and happily married—have been seen there as well."

"That's enough, Penelope," said Hugh in a hard

voice that took everyone at the table by surprise, especially his wife, who was unused to being interrupted.

Travis was hard put to keep from laughing at the reaction to Penelope's bombshell. Wives were frowning, husbands glancing at them anxiously. Could all the men here be frequenting Fannie Porter's? If they were unfortunate enough to be married to women like Penelope, they probably needed to. Travis gave his wife a warm smile, thinking that he wouldn't have to go near the place himself if it weren't to protect her. Conversation languished for the rest of the meal, after which Penelope led the ladies out so that the men could enjoy their cigars.

Jessica hated this part of the evening most of all because she knew her mother would say something awful to her. The remarks might be blatantly hostile or covert, but they would come, especially since Jessica had gone out of her way to be displeasing, instead of being just unintentionally irritating as she usually was.

"Do bring me my medicine, Jessica," said Penelope, opening the attack once the ladies were all seated. "After your very unsuitable topics of conversation this evening, my nerves are quite frayed."

As she went to the cabinet, Jessica wondered whether her mother considered rumors about sporting houses more socially acceptable.

"One of the men who has been seen at Fannie Porter's is your husband, Jessica." Penelope had her hand stretched casually in front of her so that she could admire a ring Hugh had just given her. "So surprising. Young bridegrooms don't usually stray that quickly. Goodness, you've only been married two months."

Jessica felt sick. Travis—patronizing a haunt of loose women?

"Perhaps that should be a lesson to you, Jessica. Men do not admire women who are always flaunting their knowledge and expressing antisocial ideas. Your husband might stay closer to home if you paid more attention to your clothes—and, I might add, my advice—and less attention to books and competing in such an unfeminine way with men."

In the face of these cruel words, Jessica froze in her place. She'd heard such opinions before, but never coupled with the sentiment that her husband found her—unattractive and—and unlovable. She swallowed hard, knowing she had to say something—for pride's sake, if for no other reason. Therefore she loosened her death grip on the medicine bottle and continued toward her mother's chair. "If what you say is true—"

"Oh, I assure you it is, Jessica," said Penelope smugly.

"*If* what you say is true, I'd have thought good manners would keep you from repeating it, Penelope."

"How dare you question my actions?" snapped Penelope, then smiled through her anger and added, "Though, of course, we must make allowances, I suppose, as this evidence of your husband's—ah—straying from the marriage bed must come as quite a shock to you, new bride that you are."

Jessica placed the bottle softly on the velvet-skirted table beside her mother's chair. "Perhaps you should take a larger dose of medicine," she suggested.

Penelope's eyes narrowed, but she let the challenge pass and moved on to other matters. Jessica hardly listened, so miserable had Penelope's attack made her. Even when the gentlemen returned, she paid no attention. For the moment, she didn't want to look at Travis, only to remain inconspicuous until she could escape from this stifling company.

"Now," said Penelope, "I think we'd all love to hear Jessica play. My daughter is so talented, isn't she?"

There were unenthusiastic murmurs of assent, and Penelope smiled expectantly at Jessica, who said firmly, "You either have a terrible ear for music, Penelope, or you're bearing some grudge against your guests. Even people who love me think my piano playing singularly uninspired. I do myself."

Penelope, for once, was silenced.

"If you want to hear music, Travis can bring down the phonograph." With that and without looking at her husband, Jessica sat back to endure the rest of the evening.

Before the door had hardly closed behind them and before Travis could ask her what the devil was the matter, Jessica turned on him and asked, "Do you patronize Fannie Porter's sporting house?"

His eyes narrowed. "Who told you that?"

"Penelope."

"When?"

"What difference does it make?"

"Just a matter of interest. I'm curious as to what occasion a mother would choose to inform her daughter that the daughter's husband had been seen in the company of whores."

Jessica colored at his blunt language. "When the ladies retired," she mumbled.

"So Penelope accused me of whoremongering over the coffee cups, did she, or did you just take some remark of hers the wrong way?"

"She said that any woman who paid no attention to fashion and spent her time reading unsuitable books and talking about them to men could expect her husband, even her bridegroom, to stray, and you obviously had."

Travis swore. His mother-in-law was really out for blood. "All right, Jess, I've been to Fannie Porter's, but not for the reason Penelope was intimating."

Jessica turned away, feeling as if her heart would break.

"No, don't turn your back. Look at me. Men go to places like that to meet, drink, talk, and hold business discussions, not always to consort with the women. I don't patronize the women at Fannie's."

"Oh, Travis," said Jessica sadly, unbelievingly.

"Jess, do you really think I'd be interested in some unintelligent, disreputable, half-dressed slut?" He looked at her keenly and saw that he wasn't making the impression he had hoped for. "I'm very happy with you, Jessica. I have no desire for other women."

Now she did raise her eyes to his, and he smiled.

"You satisfy all my wants, some I never expected a woman *could* satisfy." He took both of her hands in his and added firmly, "Believe it, Jess." Seeing the self-doubt that still shadowed her eyes, he cupped her face and leaned forward to kiss her. "You're the only woman I want, and it will stay that way as long as you want me too." He shifted his mouth to deepen the kiss. "Don't let your mother hurt what we have together. She will if she can, you know."

"I wish we could leave here," Jessica whispered unhappily.

"You have to learn to trust me," he replied. "Now, come to bed. I do like this gown." He had begun to look for ways to get her out of it. "But I don't know how to take it off." He gave up for the moment and pulled her hard against him.

Jessica reached for the ties that were hidden under the flowing outer robe. Even with the doubts still lingering in her mind, his urgency had catalyzed hers.

Chapter Twelve

As the weather turned chilly in November, Jessica began to think of Christmas and how wonderful it had been at home. In contrast, she could imagine what it would be like at Penelope's—expensive presents, tedious socializing, and cruel gossip. Perhaps if she were very economical, she could convince Travis to move to their own place before the holidays. But on the other hand, she had Christmas presents to buy for so many people. Frowning, she puzzled over the problem and decided that she could make her gifts this year.

Penelope would probably appreciate a handmade gift. She was always bragging about the quality of the hand embroidery on her undergarments. Fired with enthusiasm, Jessica decided to acquire Royal Society packages, which had pamphlets with marvelous diagrams full of numbers, arrows, and dotted lines that showed how to produce an amazing array of things.

Perhaps she'd make Penelope a set of tea napkins embroidered in flowers with scalloped edges. And she could construct a pretty boudoir cap for Anne, who always complained that her hair curled up tighter than ever overnight if she didn't wear one. And Frannie—let's see, maybe a dresser scarf for her new bird's-eye maple dresser. If she had time, she might make cuddly dolls for Aunt Sissie's younger children, and—Jessica reined in her runaway enthusiasm, remembering that she wasn't that skillful a needlewoman; she had never been as talented as Anne, but then Anne was her stepmother, not her mother; Jessica wouldn't have inherited Anne's talents.

Sighing, she went to get a cloak. Before she embarked on these Christmas projects, she had to get the Royal Society packets, only a few at a time so as not to spend money on something she wouldn't have time to finish.

What should she make for Travis? A shirt! If only she were at home. Anne could have shown her how. But still, if she managed it, she could embroider his initials on the pocket, and she certainly wouldn't have to worry about him catching her at work. He was almost always away from home, often out of town. Enthusiasm somewhat undermined, Jessica started down the stairs.

"My goodness, Jessica, what are you up to? If it's mending, just have one of the maids do it."

"I'm working on a Christmas gift for my sister." Jessica had managed to hide the tea napkins and whip out the dresser scarf when Penelope walked into her room unannounced.

"Oh, my dear, what a quaint idea. I hope your sister won't be disappointed."

"Why should she be disappointed?"

"That she's getting a Christmas gift so—well, modest. If I were you, I'd just go out and buy her something *nice*. But then, knowing your father, I suppose you're all accustomed to rather limited Christmases. And why aren't you using the lorgnette I gave you for your birthday? You're wearing those dreadful spectacles again."

"For one thing, I can't sew and hold a lorgnette at the same time, and for another, as I told you, it's very handsome, but the lenses don't improve my vision."

"Well, goodness, Jessica, it's not what you can see; it's how you look, and the lorgnette I chose is really lovely. Gold, inlaid mother-of-pearl—why, I was almost tempted to keep it for myself—but of course, I don't need spectacles."

"Since the lenses are clear glass, you can certainly use it if you like. Shall I get it for you?"

"Of course not. I don't want to cover up *my* eyes, but then mine are such an unusual color. What a shame you inherited your father's. Now what did I come in here for? Oh yes, I wish you'd stop by the dressmaker for me this afternoon to pick up a gown she's made alterations on."

"Shouldn't you go yourself to see if the alterations are acceptable?"

"If they're not, you can take the dress back," said Penelope sharply.

Jessica stared down at the dresser scarf on her lap. In her workbag were the tea napkins, which she now realized Penelope was not going to appreciate. And she wouldn't be able to finish any presents if Penelope planned to send her on an endless round of time-wasting errands.

As she stared bleakly ahead of her, her eyes fell on the law books piled up on her desk. She'd been reading them again at Travis's suggestion. Although he said that a time would come when he could use any expertise in land law she could accumulate, Jessica suspected that he encouraged her reading to distract her from his frequent absences. Of course, if he did eventually call on her expertise, he wouldn't pay for it—but somebody might.

It would be a lot more effective if she were to *earn* money instead of just trying to save it, as she had been doing the last few weeks. Travis might be more amenable to spending whatever was necessary to establish a temporary household if she were contributing. Her relationship with Penelope might even improve if she and Travis moved out. No doubt, both Penelope and Hugh resented the drain on their income that two extra people in the house represented.

Stuffing the dresser scarf into the bag, she hurried to her wardrobe for a waist-length mantle with a hood and silk tassels. She had a second errand to run; she was going to see Henry Barnett.

"Do you need money?" Henry asked when she had begged him for a job.

"Travis is very generous to me," she said stiffly. She couldn't tell Henry that she wanted money in order to get out of her mother's house, not when he had been so strongly opposed to her moving there in the first place. "But I—I have nothing to do."

Henry smiled whimsically. "A young bride with nothing to do?" Then he frowned. "Is all well with you and young Parnell?"

"We're very happy, but he's busy, you know, with all his business interests, and I—well, I'd so like to put my education to work. It seems such a waste. If you could use someone, I don't see why—unless it's that I'm a woman. Would your colleagues think the worse of you for employing a woman?"

"They might," said Henry, "but that's not the problem. Under other circumstances, I'd be delighted to hire you, Jessica, but as it is, I can't."

"Why?" Jessica felt so discouraged. He had just confirmed what she suspected, that her godfather might be the only lawyer in town who would consider her as a prospective employee, and he didn't want to.

"Jessica, your father is one of my most important clients. He has been for years, and you are now living in the house of a woman who would go out of her way to do him ill. I simply cannot make you privy to his affairs under those circumstances."

"But—but, Henry, I would never reveal Papa's business to anyone."

"No doubt that's so, Jessica, but Justin would have cause to complain at the mere suggestion of such a conflict of interest, especially when he has severed important and lucrative ties with Hugh, presumably because you are living there."

"He has?" Jessica felt stunned. Conversations began to come back to her—her father saying how important it was for ranchers to have their own banking sources, Penelope complaining that they had had to buy Justin out because they refused to evict Jessica. She'd completely forgotten about that. The private buy-out, which Hugh had accomplished through an intermediary, had been the price for preventing the open sale of her father's shares and a possible run on the bank.

Had Justin sold out because, as Penelope said, he was angry with Jessica or because, as Henry intimated, he hated and distrusted Penelope? Travis had seen her father in September and said he wasn't angry, but Papa had never come to call or written, thought Jessica unhappily. Whatever the truth, she had evidently caused both her parents financial reverses. Justin no longer had access to the bank or its profits. Hugh and Penelope had lost money buying him out.

"I—I won't bother you further about this, Henry," she said, conscience-stricken. "Thank you for seeing me."

"My dear child, you're my goddaughter. I'm always happy to see you. I hope you'll come to visit me more often, and feel free to call upon me should you need anything. Do you understand, Jessica? I'm always at your disposal."

"Thank you, Henry." He seemed so intense. What did he expect her to need, besides a job? He probably thought job hunting was just a whim on her part, not at all in the nature of a necessity. Should she try other law offices? Travis might be upset if he discovered that she was soliciting employment all over town. He would probably have understood her going to work for Henry Barnett but not for some stranger, not when he considered himself quite able to support her.

So if she couldn't work for a lawyer, what could she do? Jessica looked anxiously down the street before crossing, and her eye fell on a skinny little newsboy selling the *Gazette*, as Travis had had to do when he was a child. Was this lad an orphan living in a packing case? Jessica shivered in the cold air and purchased a paper, giving the child several pennies extra, for which she received a huge, gap-toothed smile and a "Thank you, miss."

With the paper tucked under her arm, she began to walk home. How nice it would have been to ride her bicycle, which would have got her home and out of the cold so much faster, but Penelope had made such a fuss that Jessica gave bicycle riding up rather than listen to her mother's carping. Glancing at the paper as she shifted it to the other arm, she lifted her skirt to cross the street. The editor, she noticed, advised his readers in large letters that today's edition had a new short story and a ladies' article on Christmas decorations for the home.

I could write things like that, thought Jessica. *I always got good marks in composition.* She wondered what the newspaper paid for such articles. Instead of going to the dressmaker's, she turned around and headed for the offices of the *Gazette*, where the editor told her he'd be willing to look at a contribution from her, even pay for it if it was any good.

Elated, Jessica hurried home to begin her new career. What should she write? A short story? An historical piece? That was a good idea. Everyone at the Labor Day picnic had been so interested in her stories about the late marshal. She could call it "Reminiscences About Long-Haired Jim Courtright." If that sold, she'd try a short story, maybe something with a Christmas theme. She read fiction; a short story shouldn't be too hard to write. And she had read that novel by Theodore Dreiser that so shocked people, even in Washington, D.C. Perhaps the editor would be interested in a review of a shocking novel. Brimming with enthusiasm, Jessica bounced into the hall of her mother's house.

"Where's my dress?" Penelope demanded.

"I forgot it." Good heavens, had her mother been looking out the window, hoping to discover just that omission? A flood of recriminations followed her up the stairs, but Jessica had better things to do. If her mother really wanted to go on and on about the gown, she'd have to wait till dinner. Jessica closed her door firmly, locked it, and went straight to her desk.

Now let's see, should she start with the railroad

workers' strike from which the marshal had rescued her when she was nine? Would her readers be interested in tales of ranch life? Maybe she could submit things to the Weatherford paper as well, or a paper in Washington, D.C. "Reminiscences of a Student at Mount Vernon Seminary" or "A Lone Female at the Columbian School of Law." She whisked her writing paper from the drawer and began: "When I was nine and on a visit to Fort Worth . . ."

Travis let himself into the darkened house and went to Hugh's study to pour a whiskey and relax for a few minutes before going upstairs. Jessica had been busy and cheerful for several weeks now, and he hadn't questioned it. Whatever kept her occupied and happy met with his approval as long as she didn't pressure him about moving or question him about where he was on the nights when Hamlet Arleigh's threats forced yet another visit to Fannie Porter's.

Idly Travis thumbed through the papers on Hugh's desk. Much to the Pinkerton agent's disgust, there was never anything relating to the bank, just piles of bills. Penelope had evidently nagged Hugh into abandoning the frugality campaign. These were all her expenditures, and they were mind-boggling.

Travis decided that Hugh must need money; he was behind on the bills, so it stood to reason that he'd get careless as he got desperate. Travis wanted that to happen—but *after* he and Jess left town so he wouldn't be involved in the collapse of Hugh's fortunes. At this point he didn't think Jessica would be devastated should financial disaster befall Hugh and Penelope. She just wanted to get away from her mother. And that could happen soon.

Word had come that Al Hamil out near Beaumont had found oil in the sludge pit on December ninth, which meant they'd bring in the well—probably in January. Travis's sources said Galey had told the crew to drill three hundred feet deeper; they were at eight eighty when they hit the oil. Evidently Galey thought there would be even more oil at a deeper level. In fact, Galey wanted the rig closed down over Christmas while Lucas bought up more land and leases in the area. Travis chuckled; they wouldn't get his. He'd been out buying himself in early December, but he doubted he'd acquire any more, not at a good price.

He was going to be richer than Croesus as long as he left for Beaumont when the Lucas well came in. His only worries were that Hamlet Arleigh, deprived of his spy, would follow and have that talk with Jess, or that Hugh would get caught before they could leave town and Hartwig would expect Travis to testify at the trial.

Travis picked up a copy of the *Gazette* lying on the leather sofa and sprawled out to thumb through it. Jess would be happy to move to Beaumont; at least she'd expect to be happy about it. Corsicana had been a cesspool when oil was discovered—hordes of strangers moving into town with no place to stay, rigs, derricks, and oil everywhere. Beaumont could be worse. Still, he'd keep her busy enough that she might not notice the unpleasantness of her surroundings. Just the fact that Penelope was hundreds of miles away ought to make Jessica euphoric.

He turned a page and saw his wife's name. "Should Women Have the Franchise?" He scanned the article, which told him that as early as 1892 the English Parliament had failed by only twenty-three votes to give women the vote. So that's why she'd been so cheerful and busy; she'd been hired by the newspaper as a female rabble-rouser. The little devil! Why hadn't she told him? Did she think he'd object? If all women were as smart as Jess, the country might be better off with the females voting and the men disenfranchised. Unfortunately, all women weren't like Jess. He wondered if Penelope had seen the article. If she had, she wouldn't take it well at all.

Travis sailed the newspaper across the room, threw back the last swallow of whiskey, and headed for the stairs. Too bad if Penelope didn't like her daughter's new outlet. He slipped quietly into the room and over to the bed, where he leaned down to kiss his sleeping wife. "Is this the noted lady author and suffragette?" he whispered when she stirred and opened her eyes.

"You saw the article?" she mumbled.

"Um-m." Travis licked her ear. "How many have you published while I've been slaving away in Corsicana?"

"Two others," she whispered. "Are you angry?"

"Of course not. I'm struck down with awe at the many talents of my wife. May I touch you? How about here?"

Jessica gasped and moved restlessly beneath his seeking fingers.

"And here?"

"Get undressed," she whispered urgently. "You've been away so long."

"Too long," Travis agreed. "We have all those nights to make up for."

As he rose to strip rapidly out of his clothes, it occurred to him that he now knew what he'd get his wife for Christmas. If she was going to take up writing, he'd buy her one of those typewriters, which he'd heard were a lot faster and neater than handwriting. Some typists, so they said, could run the apparatus without even looking for the letter keys, literally with their eyes closed. The typewriter was as amazing, when you thought about it, as the rotary drill, which was making it possible to drill for oil on the swampy land near Beaumont, or the horseless carriage, which might one day provide another market for oil men. Of course, the contraptions had to catch on first. He climbed into bed and took Jessie into his arms. Lord, it was good to hold her again.

Wearily, Jessica took a seat in the parlor. They were about to have another horrid family dinner. Because her grandfather was to be in attendance, Jessica had come down for the pre-dinner gathering, something she usually tried to avoid. With her hand on the doorknob, she had heard another of Hugh's pleas to Penelope to watch her spending. As Jessica entered, Penelope retaliated by staring pointedly at her husband's head and telling him that he should purchase a toupee.

Hugh flushed and sputtered.

"I'm serious, Hugh," said Penelope. "If you don't do something about your hair, people will think you're my *father* instead of my husband. I saw an ad in the newspaper just the other day. You cut a piece of paper to the size of your bald spot, snip some of your own hair or at least describe it so that the toupee will blend with what you have left, and then send the whole thing in with the money; I've forgotten how much."

"Penelope, I am not going to wear a toupee."

"I really must insist, Hugh."

"Oh, leave the poor man alone, Penelope," snapped Oliver Duplessis, who had come into the room in time to hear the end of the conversation.

"I don't see what business it is of yours, Father," said Penelope.

"Enough!" snapped Oliver. "I'm too old to listen to such foolishness."

Jessica couldn't believe her mother had spoken so disrespectfully to Grandfather Duplessis. If Jessica had spoken like that to Justin, he'd probably have taken her across his knee, no matter what her age.

"And speaking of the newspaper—" Penelope glared at Jessica "—a friend of mine said she saw an article in the *Gazette* written by you, Jessica. I told her that it couldn't be so, that you'd never do such a thing without first consulting me. However, when she mentioned the subject—feathers, ridiculous opinions on feathers—I knew, to my horror, that it was true."

"Why are you horrified, Penelope?" asked Travis. "I'm very proud of Jessica." He ignored the ugly look his mother-in-law gave him, although he knew that each time he disagreed with her, he risked her enmity. In this case, he couldn't resist. "It's not every woman who can get published in the newspaper regularly."

"Regularly? You've had more than one article in the paper?" Penelope's voice rose with an edge of hysteria. "This is really too much, Jessica. I don't know what could have motivated you to take up such an unsuitable pastime."

"For one thing, I find it pleasant to get paid." Jessica noticed her grandfather looking at her sharply and wondered if he was shocked to hear such an unladylike sentiment.

"Women are supposed to spend money, not earn it," said Penelope disdainfully.

"Nonsense," said Oliver. "A desire to earn money is a healthy attitude." He turned his heavily jowled face with its shining dome in Jessica's direction and said, over Penelope's sputtering, "Good for you, girl."

"Thank you, Grandfather," Jessica replied, pleased

to have attracted favorable notice from the old man, who had pretty much ignored her at previous dinners.

"My congratulations, Jessica," Hugh added. "I haven't read your work, or even noticed it, I must admit, but I shall certainly look for it in the future. I too admire a woman who understands the value of money." He slanted his wife a resentful look.

Jessica was doubly astonished. It was the first complimentary thing Hugh had ever said to her.

"Come over and visit me, if you've a mind to, girl," said Oliver.

"I will," said Jessica, thinking that she'd love to visit someone other than her mother's gossiping friends.

"She won't have time, Father," snapped Penelope. "She has to help me with my yearly holiday preparations."

"I hope you're not planning a lot of expensive entertainments, Penelope," said Hugh anxiously.

"We shall have certain affairs, just as we always have, Hugh, and I'm tired of hearing about money. If you need money, why don't you talk to Father about putting his in your bank?"

"I don't bank with relatives," said Oliver in a voice that brooked no argument. "And it strikes me, Penelope, that you have little understanding of your husband's business after all these years. Even if I did put my money in Cattleman's National, it would not be there for Hugh to spend on any whims of yours," he added dryly.

Travis watched with sharp interest as Hugh turned white. For the second time he wondered if the man could be appropriating the funds of bank depositors. He was tempted to pass the thought on to Hartwig.

"You are so irritating, Father," said Penelope. "Well, if you won't bank with Hugh, Travis certainly should."

Travis smiled blandly. "Why, Penelope, I'm like your father. I don't bank with relatives, especially relatives with free-spending wives." He laughed jovially and clapped his father-in-law on the shoulder, noting as he did so that Hugh did not look amused.

"Since we're speaking of money, a subject my daughter doesn't much care for unless she's discussing how she intends to spend some, I have a question for you, Parnell," said Oliver. "A Captain Anthony Lucas came by to see me, offering to buy some land I own around Beaumont."

"Where around Beaumont?" asked Travis.

"Section called Spindletop Heights. Not much profit in it so far. I picked it up in a trade. Then there's some other parcels spread around that general area, swampy I'm told."

Travis was thinking hard as the old man talked. What he knew about oil activities in Beaumont he had intended to keep to himself. He certainly didn't want to get Hugh interested in anything that might prove immensely profitable. On the other hand, he wouldn't mind cultivating Oliver Duplessis. Jessica's grandfather could do a lot for her, and anything Oliver Duplessis did for Jessica might accrue to Penelope's disadvantage and could hardly be held against Travis—at least by Jessica. He could tell by the wistful look on her face when Duplessis came to dinner that she'd like her grandfather's approval.

"I put him off," Oliver was saying. "Asked around about him. Word is he's in oil, which is why I'm asking you. Oil—that's your business, isn't it?"

"I wouldn't sell," said Travis, not with any urgency. He didn't want to alert Hugh. "Let me make some

200

inquiries, then give you a more informed opinion."

Oliver looked at him with wise, ancient eyes under shaggy brows and nodded. "Don't be too long about it."

"I won't," Travis assured him. In fact, he would go to see the old man the next day. Oliver Duplessis would understand that land investments of the sort they both had in Beaumont would be worth more if their potential were kept quiet.

The dinner dragged to an unpleasant close because Penelope had been bored by a topic that didn't concern her. She said to her husband over dessert, "I've decided, Hugh, that if you won't get yourself a toupee, I'll give you one for your birthday."

Hugh scowled at her, Oliver Duplessis called for his carriage, and Travis whisked Jessica upstairs before her mother could detain them.

"When is *your* birthday, Travis?" Jessica asked as she began to remove an earring. "You've never told me, although I remember asking several times." She gave him a sparkling smile and added, "If you'll share the date, I promise not to buy you a toupee."

Travis didn't want his birthday remembered. He tried to forget it himself because it was the day his father had died.

"Please," Jessica wheedled.

"November," he muttered.

"November!" she cried unhappily. "You let it go by without telling me."

"I never celebrate it. Now, what Christmas festivities are these Penelope needs your help with?" he asked.

"I have no idea," said Jessica moodily, "but you can be sure they won't be much fun, nothing like we had at home in Weatherford," she added wistfully. "Travis, I can't believe you wouldn't tell me—"

"Don't worry about it, Jess!" Then he moderated his tone. "What was Christmas like in Weatherford?"

"Oh, we used to have a huge, lovely tree with candles, and we always hung our stockings and found them full of oranges and almonds and a gold piece in the toe on Christmas morning." She sat down at her dressing table and began to brush her loosened hair, smiling reminiscently.

"One holiday out on the Rocking T my mother's foreman, Last Cauley, even played Santa Claus. We were so excited. We never guessed it was he until his stomach pillow fell out onto the hearth. Frannie started to cry because Santa's tummy had caught fire, and the cowboys poured the Christmas whiskey punch on it and nearly burned the house down, while we children all giggled like crazy and Mama rushed us out into the yard. The whole family had to sleep in the bunkhouse with the hands while the house aired out, and I sneezed all night and kept everyone awake, and . . ."

Jessica had been laughing over her memories until she noticed that her husband was scowling. Then she realized how insensitive she had been. Poor Travis had no wonderful family Christmases to remember and no birthday celebrations. Repentantly, she rose and threw her arms around his neck. "We'll have a lovely Christmas, Travis," she cried, "in spite of Penelope."

She couldn't have said anything to make him feel worse. He hadn't been thinking about what he'd missed; he had been thinking about what she would miss because he had dragged her away from her family, whom she evidently yearned for more than he had realized. His desire to avenge his father's death was proving to be Jessica's misery.

In the spirit of irritation caused by his guilty

conscience, he muttered, "I wouldn't have thought you'd be so nostalgic. Weren't they always shipping you off to school instead of including you in the family circle?"

Jessica looked taken aback and said, "I didn't realize I'd made them seem unkind. Actually, they were very good to me." She turned away, frowning thoughtfully, and added, "I'm even beginning to understand the way my father treated me. He was probably afraid I'd turn into a spendthrift like Penelope."

Travis too turned away. How long before she started to resent him for separating her from the people she loved? he wondered uneasily. Then he thought about his father's death, of which Jessica had inadvertently reminded him. God, how he wanted to have revenge. He wanted to see Hugh and Penelope as miserable as Pa had been, as frightened and hungry and alone as Travis had been. But he didn't want to hurt Jess, and, God help him, he was being torn apart by the irreconcilable demands of the past and the present.

Chapter Thirteen

Jessica stood before the cabinet in which the medicine was kept. Penelope's behavior had become more erratic and spiteful as she resorted to larger doses of her elixirs, one a patent medicine, the other a concoction mixed up by the family doctor. Jessica's well-meant suggestion that the potions might be doing Penelope harm, that perhaps she should give them up or at least change doctors, had resulted in a stream of abuse and accusations, the last of which was that Jessica wanted to destroy her mother's health because she coveted Hugh, having lost the interest of her own husband.

On that note, Penelope had swept from the room, leaving Jessica to wonder what could be in the bottles. Tentatively she stretched a hand to the one whose elaborate label announced that it contained Huffhouser's Bitters, a specific for digestive upsets, liver complaints, female trouble, and a host of other ailments. Jessica took off the top and sniffed. She recognized the odor, having smelled it on Travis when he came home late.

She quickly closed that bottle and reached for the other, the one the doctor provided. It too was a liquid but with no odor that Jessica could identify. Penelope had said it soothed her nerves. After that ugly scene with her mother, Jessica's nerves were certainly in need of soothing. Perhaps she should find out why Penelope took it. For a change, no social events had been scheduled, so if the potion made her sick, she could go to bed.

With a trembling hand, Jessica poured a little out and drank it down in one nervous gulp, then hurriedly recapped and replaced the bottle before going to her room to await the results. She sat down at her desk to look at an article on Christmas customs, which she had researched by questioning Penelope's friends about their childhood memories. Surprisingly, women she had never cared for became warm and nostalgic on the subject, their husbands chimed in with reminiscences, and Penelope finally put a stop to the interviews, complaining that Jessica was monopolizing conversation.

Jessica leaned her head on her hand. Silly Penelope, always wanting to be the center of attention. It was really a bit pathetic. Jessica wasn't sure now why she had been so upset about her mother's little gibes. Foolish, spendthrift Penelope. No wonder Justin had divorced her. Maybe Hugh should too. Maybe Jessica should suggest that at dinner tonight. Maybe she should tell everyone at the table about the night she had seen her mother rolling a string of little balls from her neck to her lower lip. Jessica giggled.

Penelope had looked so foolish, trying to roll away her incipient double chin.

Grandfather Duplessis had big rolls of fat under his chin. He even had rolls on his forehead. Maybe he'd like some little balls on a string for his forehead. Maybe Penelope was afraid she was going to look like her father, who had no hair. The idea of a bald Penelope struck Jessica as hilarious. In the bathtub room Travis had found a shampoo for bald ladies. Maybe that shampoo was all that stood between Penelope and the need for a toupee of her own. Still giggling, Jessica rose with the idea of going to pour out the shampoo for bald people. She wanted to see her mother without any—without any—whoops! Jessica grabbed the back of the desk chair. Goodness gracious, maybe a little nap was in order.

"Where can I hide this, Penelope?" Travis asked as he came into the house on a gust of cold wind. He carried a large Remington typewriter elaborately wrapped.

"Put it in there." She waved toward the hat rack, which had a wide seat hinged for storage below. "And now I have the most interesting surprise for you."

"Oh." Travis didn't want any surprises from Penelope. "Where's Jessica?"

"Upstairs, I presume. Betty, go tell Miss Jessica to get herself down here. I won't tolerate tardiness, especially when we have an unexpected guest." Penelope turned back to Travis. "Your guardian is here, Travis."

"He is?" Travis shifted uneasily. "Joe Ray?" What the hell was Joe Ray Brock doing here? Dear Lord, he had to get to his foster father before the man said anything irretrievably damaging in front of the

Greshams or, worse, Jessica. Travis had written to Joe Ray to announce the marriage, but he hadn't mentioned his bride's name. Since Joe Ray had been a good friend of Will Parnell's, he'd be furious to find Travis married to the daughter of his father's worst enemies.

"We've been having quite a chat," said Penelope.

That sounded ominous. "Well, where is he?" Travis asked. "I've all sorts of business to talk over with him, so I'm sure you'll excuse us if we get right to it."

"Your business will have to wait, Travis. I've invited Mr. Brock to dinner, and we're about to sit down."

"Miz Gresham, I cain't hardly wake Miz Jessica up atall," said Betty, the maid.

"Nonsense," snapped Penelope. "Mr. Travis's foster father is here, and I expect—"

"Let her sleep, Betty," Travis interrupted. Why would Jess be sleeping at this time of day? Well, no matter. He wasn't going to argue with this one small piece of luck. "She's probably coming down with a cold."

Then a second idea occurred to him. Could she be with child? Travis felt a stab of joy at the thought of Jessica carrying his child. His baby and Jessica's. They'd give it so much love—more than either of them had had as children.

"She'll have to put it off," snapped Penelope.

"What?" asked Travis, confused.

"The cold. Get her dressed and down here immediately, Betty. Come along, Travis."

"Red ants in vinegar," Joe Ray was saying as they entered the drawing room. "I was just tellin' your husband here, Miz Gresham, that there's nothin' for rheumatism like red ants an' vinegar." Joe Ray rose from the delicate sofa, all two hundred and fifty pounds of him, and made an old-fashioned bow to Penelope. "Travis, boy, imagine my surprise to find you livin' here at the Greshams'." He gave Travis a narrow look. "Had to do a lot of askin' to find out where you was."

Evidently Joe Ray had yet to mention Will Parnell, for the couple looked superciliously amused rather than upset. Travis shook Joe Ray's hand and said, "Reckon we got a lot to talk about, Joe Ray. I know you'll excuse us, Penelope, if we skip—"

"I won't. Pleasure before business." She laughed that trilling laugh he hated.

Did she sense that he was desperate to get Joe Ray out of the house? He'd have sworn she wouldn't ordinarily allow Joe Ray Brock through the front door. If the evening ahead weren't so potentially disastrous, Travis would have laughed aloud. Joe Ray looked dusty and unkempt and smelled strongly of cattle; he was going to make an unlikely dinner guest among the expensive china and fine linens.

"Mr. Brock," said Penelope, extending slender fingers in his direction, "you may escort me in to dinner."

Travis noticed that those fingers hovered above Joe Ray's arm rather than resting on it. Joe Ray continued to talk after they were seated. They had embarked on the main course before Jessica made an appearance, looking dazed and slightly mussed. *Was* she pregnant? Travis wondered with another stab of pleased anticipation.

"Have to tie strings around your pants to keep 'em from crawlin' up your legs," Joe Ray was saying, for he had been telling grasshopper stories. "Why, I recall a horse race we had to cancel 'cause them Rocky Mountain locusts was so thick on the course, the horses couldn't wade through, much less run. Same year they et a woman's washin' right off the line."

"This is my daughter, Jessica," Penelope interrupted, "who seems to think she has no obligation to arrive at the dinner table at an appropriate hour. Jessica, Mr. Joe Ray Brock, your husband's foster father. You owe him an apology."

"Had any experience of grasshoppers, young lady?" Joe Ray asked by way of greeting.

Jessica dropped into her chair and fumbled for her napkin. "They ate the tops of my mother's onions once," she recalled. "And then they kept eating right down into the ground and finished off the bulbs too."

"Do tell?" Joe Ray guffawed. "Ain't heard that one." Then he studied Penelope. "I wouldn't a thought you'd be an onion grower, ma'am."

"I guess I meant my stepmother," Jessica added, looking confused.

"'Pears you got lotsa relatives, young lady— mothers, stepmothers, foster fathers-in-law, like me. On the other hand, you ain't got no mother or father-in-law, bein' as Travis here—"

"No use to bring up old sorrows, Joe Ray," Travis interrupted, giving the rancher a sharp look and hoping that Joe Ray would catch on and cooperate.

"Now, you'd think," resumed Joe Ray, "what with all the grasshopper plagues and droughts we done had out there, them farmers woulda give up, but you'll be interested, Travis, to know they're still tryin' to buy an' farm land that God meant for cattle."

"Well, you got it cheap in '87 when the state declared it grazing land. Now you can sell it dear to folks dumb enough to want to use it for something else," Travis replied. "You always were a hand for making money on land deals."

"Ain't that the truth," crowed Joe Ray. "Why, I had me a lotta land right here in Fort Worth," he explained to Hugh. "Bought it back in 1870 for three dollars an acre."

Hugh's eyes lit up at the thought of the profit that purchase could have entailed.

"Yep, three dollars an acre, an' I sold it for a thousand an acre in '87 an' bought cheap in Lubbock an' Crosby. Now, like the boy says, I could make me another killin' sellin' it off to them fool farmers if I'd a mind to."

"My goodness, Mr. Brock," said Penelope, giving him a demure, fluttering smile, "you'll need to talk to my husband about investments, won't you?"

"Cattleman's would, of course, be delighted to be of service, Mr. Brock," said Hugh solemnly.

"Would they now? Well, I'll just have to give that some thought. You puttin' your money in with Mr. Gresham, Travis boy?"

"I bank in Corsicana where my business is, Joe Ray," said Travis.

"But you're livin' right in this here house with Mr. an' Miz Gresham. Must be quite a treat for you, son."

"We certainly do our best to make our young couple feel at home," said Penelope sweetly.

Travis spotted his wife giving her mother a comically astonished look. What was the matter with the girl? This was a touchy enough evening; he certainly didn't need Jessica renewing her feud with Penelope. At least, Penelope seemed to be on her best behavior.

"Speakin' a farmers," said Joe Ray, "some jackass out home done put in a crop a cotton. Can you b'lieve that, Travis? Course, the cowboys, soon as they heard, they come along an' made the fella plow it up. Tole him where you got cotton, you got colored folks, an'

Lubbock County was white man's territory an' gonna stay that way."

"I can certainly sympathize with that sentiment," said Penelope. "They are not to be trusted. I wouldn't have one in my house."

Jessica had been looking from Joe Ray to Penelope with wide, slightly befuddled eyes. "I don't understand that at all," she said. "Some of the finest men and women I know are colored. We had a wonderful nurse named Calliope, and we all love her dearly. She still lives out at the Rocking T."

"Don't you mention her at my table," hissed Penelope. "I won't have it. You said that just to spite me, and you can be sure that I'll make you very, very—"

"Here now, Miz Gresham," Joe Ray intervened, "I didn't mean to cause no to-do between you an' your daughter, no sir."

Jessica had drawn back, white-faced.

Before Travis, feeling protective once more, could intervene on Jessica's behalf, Joe Ray continued. "My, you are a feisty lady, ain't you, Miz Gresham, an' fer a fact, I've heard that about you. We'll just change the subject. I ain't had a chance to tell you, Travis, how good it's worked out 'tween me an' that Calloway fella you sent my way."

"Glad you were pleased, Joe Ray," said Travis quickly. "How much land you figure to sell to the sodbusters?"

"None. Why would I want to sell good land when I'm gonna make me a fortune in the cattle dip business?"

Hugh Gresham paused in the act of pouring himself more wine. "Calloway?" he asked.

"Yep, Travis was bein' a good Samaritan like the Good Book tells us to."

"Joe Ray," murmured Travis, trying to keep his

voice casual and still get the warning across.

"I didn't realize my son-in-law was given to philanthropy in business matters," said Hugh grimly. "I'd like to hear about it."

"Oh, 'twarn't nothin' that important, but it sure turned out good for me."

Travis groaned to himself, knowing that there was no stopping Joe Ray at this point. Did the man realize what he was doing?

"Seems Travis knew someone was tryin' to cheat this Calloway outa his business. Some fellas won't stop at nothin'," Joe Ray added, giving Hugh a bland smile. "You've prob'ly run into that sort your own self, Gresham." Joe Ray put down his knife and fork and patted his stomach. "Mighty fine grub, Miz Gresham."

"Why, thank you, Mr. Brock," Penelope replied, smiling graciously.

Penelope had no idea what was going on, but Jessica seemed to have come out of her dream; she was listening with a puzzled frown. Had she heard his conversation with Hugh about Oscar Calloway? Travis wondered. He couldn't remember if she'd been in the room. One thing he was sure of; he couldn't let her hear any more of this. "Well, since you're through eating, Joe Ray, we need to—"

"I haven't heard the rest of the story," Hugh interrupted.

"Not much to tell," said Joe Ray. "Travis sent him to me, an' I put up the money for this Calloway fella to expand. Man's come up with the best cattle dip in the country. Him an' me is gonna make us a gol-danged fortune. Why, orders is already up a hunnerd percent 'cause, a course, I been spreadin' the word in the cattlemen's associations. Took up the distribution on the South Plains my own self, an'—"

Hugh was no longer listening. Face white, lips trembling with fury, he had turned to Travis. "That was my deal! You used what I'd told you in confidence."

"I'll be damned," said Joe Ray. "You was the fella gonna cheat ole Calloway?"

"Don't be naïve!" snapped Hugh. "It was a perfectly legal business deal."

"Oh, sure it was, Gresham. Jus' like the one that drove Will Parnell to his grave," said Joe Ray.

"Will Parnell?" Looking as if he'd seen a ghost, Hugh turned to Travis. "You're related to Will Parnell?" The man's voice was trembling.

"Course he is. Didn't you never remember what you done to Will, Gresham? Didn't you remember he had a boy heard the whole thing an' found the body? You mus' kill a lotta ranchers an' cheat a lotta orphans to forgit a thang like that 'cause it ain't been so many years. Fifteen, sixteen."

"Seventeen," said Travis. "Seventeen years and one month."

Joe Ray nodded. "Glad to know you ain't forgot, boy. I was wonderin' why you'd marry Gresham's daughter. Seemed like a disloyal thing to me, but I guess you got more meanness in you than I thought. Maybe I done taught you something after all."

"Are you saying, Mr. Brock, that Travis married Jessica out of a desire for revenge against my husband?" asked Penelope, having finally begun to understand the conversation.

"I ain't sayin' nothin' 'bout why he married her," said Joe Ray. "I wasn't here when he done it." He glanced uneasily at Jessica, who seemed turned to stone.

"How dreadful!" cried Penelope, but her tone said she didn't find it dreadful at all. "It would seem that Travis wasn't madly in love with you, after all, Jessica. In fact, didn't you wonder *why* he married you? I certainly did."

"Yes," said Jessica. She was staring at her husband, pale and stunned.

"How very embarrassing for you, dear."

"Yes." Jessica rose, folding her napkin and placing it carefully beside her plate.

"Jessica certainly seems to be taking this calmly," said Penelope, sounding disappointed. "But then I don't suppose she'd want to burst into tears here in company." She watched her daughter leaving the room, then turned to Travis.

"So you were that grubby little boy. Heavens, I haven't thought of Will Parnell in years," she declared, her laughter tinkling around the table. "He courted me when I was just a child, and then he married that chit Rose Anne—what was her name?—Bascomb. Rose Anne Bascomb. Not that I'd have had him." Penelope tossed her head disdainfully.

What a despicable woman! Travis thought. Had she treated his father so maliciously because Will had preferred another woman to her? "Yes," he said coldly, "I was the boy."

"I had my duty to the bank," said Hugh. "It was a perfectly justifiable move from a financial point of view."

"You suckered him, just like you tried to do Calloway," said Travis.

"It served Will right," said Penelope complacently.

"Shut up!" Hugh snapped.

"Borrowing all that money. Still, it's only business," she added with an airy wave of the hand.

"Imagine holding a grudge all these years."

"Well, ma'am," said Joe Ray, "we're not folks to forget our grievances. We got long memories, the boy an' me, an' it looks like Travis here's been busy, mighty busy." He turned to Travis. "You shoulda tole me what you was up to. I shore wouldn't a give the game away, if—"

"But you did, Mr. Brock," said Penelope smugly, "and Travis must be terribly disappointed that he had so little luck against us—except for that silly cattle dip company. And of course, the wedding and Jessica's clothes. What a shame we spent all that money on—"

"No luck against us?" Hugh cried. "Do you realize what it cost me to buy Justin out? Do you realize what I've had to . . ." He clamped his mouth shut.

"Well, really, Hugh, you can recover from a few minor setbacks."

"You idiot!" Hugh shouted at his wife.

"Nice to see your enemies fallin' out, ain't it?" Joe Ray remarked to Travis.

Travis, badly worried about Jessica, had risen to leave.

"Going upstairs to try to mend your fences?" asked Penelope sweetly. "You'll never manage it. My poor daughter's no doubt vastly disappointed that you've made such a fool of her—"

"How very motherly of you to see it that way, Penelope," said Travis and turned to the stairs and a confrontation that was going to be hard, very hard.

"—but she has some pride," Penelope called after him. "She won't take you back. And now that we know what you've been up to, you'll have to leave the house, so you'll have no more use for her, will you?"

215

Her laughter followed him up the stairs. No more use for Jess? Travis shook his head. Somehow he had to square this with her. He had to make her understand.

Chapter Fourteen

Jessica was sitting in a straight-backed chair, hands folded precisely in her lap, eyes fastened bleakly on the glass doors that led now, in December, to a balcony lashed by cold winds and a few flakes of snow. It might well be a white Christmas, she thought, remembering how her father had read them stories on Christmas Eve about snow and crackling fires on hearths and presents and families that lived happily ever after—her father, from whom she had run away.

He and Anne had tried to protect her, but she'd been too stupid, too infatuated, and too much in need of love to see that she was being used. By Travis, with whom she had been so happy these last months, for whom she would have done just about anything. God! She *had* done just about anything. How amused he must have been when she'd fallen so deeply in love, how disdainful of her physical passion for him. With her heart as bleak as the winter night outside her windows, she turned to watch him enter their room.

"I think you should go along to the hotel with Mr. Brock," she said in a dull voice. "The charade is over, so there's no reason for you to stay."

"I'm not going anywhere without you, Jess," he replied quietly. "I realize this has come as a shock to you, but we are married and—"

"Not really," she interrupted. "All those vows we made—yours were perjured. Dr. Campbell said nothing about marrying for revenge, using your wife to retaliate for some imagined—"

"Nothing imagined," he retorted, looking surprised.

"I don't know what Hugh did, Travis. I didn't even know Hugh back then—or Penelope, but whatever happened, I don't see how that excuses what you've done to me."

"What have I done to you?" he asked reasonably.

"You must really hate me to—"

"Jess, I don't hate you!" He looked at her somberly. Since Joe Ray had brought all this to a head, Travis decided that he might as well tell her everything. One way or another, they weren't going to be staying here, and he was tired of living a lie. "Do you recall my saying that my father died when I was eight?"

Jessica nodded, her face drawn with misery as he began the story of the confrontation in Gresham's office and his father's suicide. Travis described how he himself had found the body and then been shuffled aside by the hotel employees and the police, ending up on the street, grief-stricken and frightened; how he'd slept in an alley that night and returned the next morning to the hotel, where he had been called a "dirty little beggar" and turned away; how the Greshams, although they had seen him with his father, had claimed what was left of the estate for the bank, citing absence of heirs—evidently never mentioning him or making any effort to find him.

When he finished his tale, Jessica said, "You were eight years old. It's possible that you remembered that scene in the office incorrectly. After all, you thought Penelope had shot him, and that was wrong. Children—"

"Penelope's never been that good to you, Jessica," snapped Travis resentfully. He hadn't expected that she wouldn't believe him. "I see no justification for this sudden loyalty to her."

"Maybe you're right," said Jessica. "Maybe there's no reason for me to trust her, but at least her hostility has been right out where I could see it, while yours—I had no idea you blamed me for your childhood."

"I don't."

"Of course you do. Why else would you—" She shook her head and looked away from him, unable to go on. Those four years he had spent homeless in Fort Worth must have been terrible, worse than she had ever imagined, but she wasn't responsible! She hadn't done anything to him but offer her love, so very much love, so much love that knowing he rejected it and always had was like a stake driven into her heart.

All this time he'd cared for nothing but his revenge —not truth, not his wife, certainly not her feelings. How could he do that? "You're quite right, Travis," she said. "Thank you for the advice. I won't trust Penelope. Or you. You, least of all. Who could trust a man who marries for vengeance?"

"Jessica, no matter what my motives were," said Travis as persuasively as he could, "we've had a good marriage. We've been happy together."

"No, we haven't!" she cried indignantly. "It's been a sham—a meaningless—hopeless . . ." Her mouth closed in a tight line.

"How can you say that? Have you been *un*happy with me? Have I treated you badly?"

"Of course not. You wanted something. You wanted to get even with Penelope and Hugh. I was your means of doing it."

"Jessica, the truth is I haven't made a move against Hugh in months, not since—"

"—not since the last time you had a chance? Well, I'm sure if Mr. Brock hadn't given you away, you'd have found something else to do to him. In fact, considering the financial problems he seems to be having, I don't even believe you. You haven't stopped, have you?"

Travis realized with a pang that there was some truth in what she'd said. Because of Hartwig and Hamlet Arleigh—did he want to tell her about that? No. His best argument was their personal relationship. "In what way have I been a bad husband?" he persisted. She was a logical woman; she'd have to perceive the sense of what he was saying. "What more could I have done to make you happy?" He saw no softening of her expression, which was unlike Jessie; he'd always been able to talk her around. "You're upset, sweetheart," he continued gently, "so you're not looking at this clearheadedly."

"Oh, but I am, Travis, and for the first time—and please don't call me sweetheart. I always wondered why you married me, but I believed what I wanted to believe." Looking back, she wondered how she could have been so gullible. "I should have listened to my head instead of my heart; I should have remembered that you've never once said you loved me."

Hadn't he? Travis, for the first time since entering the room, felt real fear.

"Because you couldn't say that, could you, Travis?"

"You've never said that to me either, Jess," he temporized.

"But I did," she cried, tears welling helplessly in her eyes. "I did love you."

"Jess." He stepped toward her, but Jessica quickly turned her back. Why had he never said it? he asked himself. God! She'd never believe him now.

"Go away, Travis. You can't live here anymore. I won't let you use me to cause more trouble. Penelope—"

"Jess, believe me, Penelope can take care of herself," he protested. This was becoming a disaster. Had he lost Jessica's loyalty, only to have her transfer it to Penelope, of all people? "Think about it, Jessica. You know what she's like. She can't be trusted."

"If you knew that, why did you bring me here? You're the one who can't be—"

"Jessie, I don't want to leave you here alone," he cried.

"Why? Who here's likely to hurt me more than you have?"

Thinking of the story Justin had told, he felt a surge of fear. Had his reasons for rejecting that story about Penelope been a self-serving rationalization? It hadn't mattered then because he expected to be at Jessica's side to protect her should she need it, but if she insisted that he leave, if she wouldn't come with him—maybe that was the key; she herself had wanted to leave several months ago. "You wanted us to get a place of our own. Remember?"

"And now I know why you wouldn't."

221

Damn Hamlet Arleigh, he thought bitterly. "But I will. We'll start looking right away. Tomorrow."

"Tomorrow," she echoed, her face flushing. "I understand. You think you can take me to bed, and by tomorrow morning you'll have convinced me . . ." She stopped, confused. "Of what, Travis? That you never really meant anyone any harm?"

"Jess, I admit—"

"I should hope you do. Mr. Brock made it all perfectly clear. Only God knows which of Penelope and Hugh's problems you're responsible for."

Not enough, he thought angrily.

"Do you think I'm so lovesick that I'd do anything to keep from losing you? I don't even understand why you want to stay. What possible use can you make of me now, Travis?" she asked wearily. "Unless it satisfies your hatred of my mother to torture me."

"Jess, for God's sake, I don't want to hurt you. I never have. I want to protect you—from Penelope."

"Oh, of course," she said sarcastically. "Now I understand. To protect me from my mother, you have to live here, where you can continue your vendetta. Well, I wouldn't count on Hugh allowing it." She glared at him, hands on hips. "In fact, if you don't leave this minute, I'll call Hugh and ask him to throw you out."

Travis stared at his furious wife, his thoughts tumbling desperately. Maybe he should leave—for now. Travis couldn't believe that, when Jessica was calmer, he wouldn't be able to make her see reason. She still loved him; she'd have to forgive him sooner or later. But to let her stay behind, in this house . . .

"Jessica, I know you're upset," he began gently.

She turned her back on him.

Frowning, he approached and curved his hands

over her shoulders. "So I'll do what you ask."

"Don't touch me." She pulled violently away.

Travis suppressed the impulse to spin her around and kiss her senseless. "But this is not a permanent separation, Jessie, and you have to promise me that you'll be wary of Penelope. Don't—trust—her." His voice was low and emphatic.

She whirled to face him, eyes shining with tears. "Oh, you don't have to worry about my trusting the wrong people anymore," she cried, backing away from him step by step as if he were the danger she feared most. "I'm not likely to trust anyone from now on."

Travis's heart contracted. He'd never meant to hurt her. "I'll come back tomorrow morning, and—"

"Don't. I never want to see you again."

"You'll change your mind, Jessie. You need time to—"

"Go away. Just go away, Travis."

The tears were streaming down her face as she continued to retreat. Travis could have wept himself. Should he try to tell her how much he loved her? No, it wouldn't do any good. Not now.

But why in God's name hadn't he told her before? As he left the house, he realized that since his father's death, he'd gotten out of the habit of thinking in terms of love. Survival? Yes. Revenge? Yes. Love? He sighed bitterly. For seventeen years he hadn't even believed in it. Until Jess. And now he'd lost it again—but not for good, he promised himself. Unlike his father, she was alive, and he'd get her back! Penelope and Hugh wouldn't take Jess away from him. And the baby. Oh, God, if she was carrying his child, the shock of all this might hurt them both.

Of course, the idea of a child might be wishful

thinking. Maybe the idea that she'd forgive him and come back was wishful thinking too. Travis hunched his shoulders against the falling snow and walked away from the Greshams' house on West Seventh Street as he'd once walked away from their bank seventeen years ago.

Chapter Fifteen

Jessica awoke with swollen eyes and an aching head, confused for a moment as to what had caused this feeling of black gloom. Then she turned to the smooth pillow beside her and remembered: Travis was gone. She closed her eyes tight against the sting of returning tears; she would not cry again for him, not when she had been such a fool to love him in the first place. In two weeks, only two weeks, he had weaned her from her family, won her love, and delivered her to Penelope, a woman he hated and despised. Then for four long months she had allowed herself to be duped by him and browbeaten by Penelope—all because she was befuddled by love. Well, no more!

Jessica clenched her fists and rose to dress. She had work to do—no, to supervise. She didn't want to handle Travis's belongings herself, didn't want to touch clothes that had been on his body. The maids

would have to do the actual packing. With her chin
held at a resolute angle, she oversaw the whole
project, hiding her shame as they cast sidelong
glances at her.

Under the brave front, she wondered what would
happen to her now. She certainly wouldn't succumb
to Travis's importunities, if he bothered to make any
more. She couldn't imagine why he had wanted her
to leave Penelope's with him, unless it had been guilty
conscience speaking. If so, he'd get over that soon
enough. As for her mother, no doubt Penelope, who
had taken Jessica in only to spite Justin Harte, would
now delight in sending her back. Even if Penelope
didn't insist that Jessica leave, Hugh would. All those
financial troubles he seemed to be having—Travis
must have orchestrated them.

When they asked her to leave, where was she to go?
she wondered anxiously. Not home. She had deserted
her family for Travis, and although she had heard
from Anne, Frannie, and her brothers, there had
been no word from her father. Very likely he had
been glad to get rid of her once more. He'd hardly
want her back under his roof. She had no one to go
to, and she wasn't foolish enough to think she could
make her own way on what she earned writing for the
newspaper. Nor did she feel that she could demand
the inheritance left by her grandmother, the rendering of which would cause more financial problems
for her father, who had already lost money by selling
his bank shares because of her.

That left her legal training. Could she—no, Henry
Barnett had refused her once. He'd hardly want to
employ someone who'd shown such poor judgment,
who had been so easily tricked. How astute he had
been to refuse when she asked to work for him. She
could end up as destitute as Travis had been after his

father's death. He'd probably consider that poetic justice.

"Miz Jessica, what now?" asked Betty, pointing to the pile of suitcases, boxes, and parcels.

What indeed? Jessica wondered. She could not afford to hire a vehicle to take the things to his hotel. Part of her most recent payment from the newspaper had been spent on gifts for Penelope and Hugh because she had been convinced by her mother that homemade gifts would not do. With the rest she had bought an additional gift for Travis, a handsome cowhide money belt with four different compartments. It was such an ingenious item that at the time she had been unable to resist, thinking how useful it would be when he traveled. Now she wished that she could get back what she had spent on it.

"Don't look like that, miss," said Betty sympathetically. "I could ask Tommy. The missus ain't due back till afternoon. No reason he couldn't run your errand."

Jessica, weak with relief that Travis would have no excuse to come to the house, could only nod.

"You just lie down, miss. You do look pale. Me an' Lulu, we'll see to this. Where you want it sent?"

The maids would know that Travis had left the house, but now she had to acknowledge the end of her marriage. "To Mr. Travis at the Worth Hotel. If he's not there—" a flash of bitterness suggested that he might have gone to Fannie Porter's "—have it delivered to Mr. Joe Ray Brock. He *is* there."

"Don't hover at the door like a frightened rabbit, Jessica. Come in."

Jessica knew she hadn't been doing any such thing. She might be worried about her future, but she was no longer afraid of Penelope. She did, however, dislike her mother. By now Jessica had resolved in her own mind the question of why Penelope hadn't kept her baby after the divorce. Penelope, no doubt, hadn't cared one way or another what happened to Jessica.

"Travis certainly had you fooled, didn't he, dear?" trilled Penelope.

"No more than you," Jessica replied.

"Me? Why, he's always been charming to me. I rather suspect he finds me attractive."

"He hates you as much as he does Hugh," said Jessica flatly. Had Penelope really imagined Travis a bit in love with her? Obviously her mother had been almost as big a fool about him as Jessica herself had. Shivering, Jessica wondered if Travis hated her the way he did Penelope. Had he been hating her when he proposed, during the wedding ceremony, while they made love? Had he felt revulsion every time he touched her?

"Really, Jessica, just because he used you doesn't mean—"

"You were evidently very nasty to him when he was a child and even worse to his father," said Jessica.

"Nasty?" exclaimed Penelope. "What a word to use. I'm never—"

"Did he tell you what else he's done against us?" asked Hugh urgently.

"No," said Jessica. Hugh at least seemed to have some grasp of reality. Her mother had none.

"He was a very dirty little boy," said Penelope disdainfully. "I remember him."

"Are you sure he didn't give you any idea of what else he's been up to?" Hugh demanded.

Jessica shook her head.

"For heaven's sake, Hugh," said Penelope impatiently, "what else could he have done?"

"Nothing," Hugh muttered, but to Jessica he looked frightened.

"You might feel sorry for poor Jessica," said Penelope. "Think of how humiliated she's feeling— courted and married by a man whose only interest was revenge." She slanted a condescending glance at Jessica. "Now she'll have to go crawling back to her father, and you can be sure Justin won't be very sympathetic. Naturally, Travis won't have any further use for her now that his secret is out. I don't want to make you feel bad, Jessica, but it's always best to face the truth, no matter how unpleasant."

"Actually, Travis wanted me to go with him," said Jessica.

"You mean he wanted to stay here with you?" Penelope was frowning, two sharp pleats in her smooth forehead.

"No, he wanted me to leave with him. He insisted that we had a good marriage," said Jessica drearily.

"Well, you're not going off with him," snapped Penelope. "You'll stay right here."

"Penelope!" Hugh protested.

"Don't say a word, Hugh. He's not going to have it all his own way. *We'll* keep Jessica."

Jessica was momentarily confused at the about-face. Just a minute before, Penelope had intended to send Jessica back to a dubious welcome from her father. Now she evidently wanted to spite Travis by keeping his wife away from him. Well, why not? thought Jessica bitterly. She might as well take the free room and board until she got on her feet. It would help make up for all the unpleasantness she'd suffered at Penelope's hands, and if Travis was worried about her staying here, all the better.

"Do stop fretting, Hugh," Penelope was saying. "He'll have to support her. In fact, I think he should support her lavishly. You can handle the money."

Jessica shook her head and suppressed a wry smile. Penelope was going to be disappointed, because Jessica had no intention of asking for or accepting a penny from her treacherous husband. She could make enough money writing to pay for her food here, she had plenty of clothes, and she'd look for ways to make more money, enough to leave before Penelope got tired of her and demanded her departure.

Jessica sat on the straight-backed chair in her bedroom and stared broodingly at the Remington typewriter, her Christmas present from Travis. They had opened gifts that morning after breakfast, many for Penelope, a few for Jessica and Hugh. Of course, Jessica had received presents from her family in Weatherford, things she treasured, but she had opened those discreetly in her own room the night before while Penelope was entertaining downstairs.

Interestingly, Jessica was no longer required to attend Penelope's parties. Perhaps a married daughter with no husband on the premises was a social embarrassment, or perhaps Penelope saw Jessica's exclusion as a punishment. Whatever the reasons, Jessica had no quarrel with the situation; she was not feeling sociable. In fact, she would have valued the free time to write, but some days she was so depressed that she could hardly force herself to the all-important task of earning money to tide her over when Penelope asked her to leave. Soon enough Penelope would discover that Travis had left town and realize that her support of Jessica had become an empty gesture. Jessica herself had discovered his absence within the last hour.

Her mother and stepfather had departed to make holiday calls as soon as the last ribbon was removed from the last gift. As she prepared to leave, Penelope had said, "Oh, Jessica, there's another gift for you in the seat of the hat rack, a huge, unwieldy thing. I believe it's from your husband." She was in front of the hall mirror adjusting a hat as big as a tea tray with a whole bird, among other decorations, perched on its brim. "Travis brought it in the very night we all discovered just why he'd married you." Penelope had smiled sweetly and allowed Hugh to help her into a fashionable coat trimmed in fur. "You might as well have it since you've nothing else to show for your *very* brief marriage."

With that, Penelope and Hugh had left, and Jessica, torn between bitterness and curiosity, had peeked under the hinged seat. Curiosity won, and she undid enough of the paper to reveal the typewriter. She was overwhelmed by a tide of conflicting emotions.

Made forceful by anger, she had interrupted the Christmas festivities of the servants and insisted that Penelope's driver return the typewriter to Mr. Parnell at the Worth Hotel. Grumbling, Tommy had tried to do so, but he'd been told that Mr. Travis Parnell had checked out, leaving no indication that he might return and no forwarding address.

Somehow the news had seemed more than Jessica could bear, and, close to tears, she realized that she had been secretly hoping for a reconciliation, hoping that he would convince her of his good intentions as he had at the time of their elopement.

"Shall I take it upstairs, miss?" asked Tommy, the driver.

"You might as well," Jessica muttered. She trailed him to her room and stared at the machine with more hostility than any mere object warranted. Then she sat down in front of it and set about learning its operation. As Penelope had said, Jessica might as well get *something* out of her marriage. Three hours later, having read a booklet enclosed with the machine, she had her eyes tightly closed while she attempted to depress the proper keys with the proper fingers. It seemed to her that they might have made the whole process easier by lettering the keys in order instead of at random as they seemed to be.

"Miss Jessica, Mr. Duplessis is downstairs," said Lulu from the door to the bedroom.

Jessica opened her eyes. "Lulu, I don't want to see anyone."

"Miss Jessica, I ain't gonna tell Miz Gresham's papa no one wants to see him on Christmas day. He looked fit to be tied when he heard you was here an' them wasn't. He said you was to git your warmest wrap an' git on downstairs, or he'd come up an' git you hisself, an' Mr. Duplessis, he don't like stairs. He has to climb them stairs after you, well, I ain't gonna be around to hear what he says. I'm goin' straight down the back way to the kitchen, an' I'm stayin' there, 'cause if you think your mama's mean, you ain't seen Mr. Duplessis when he's done been crossed. Some folks say he ain't smiled in twenny years; that's what some folks say. Here's your wrap, an' Merry Christmas to you, Miss Jessica." With that Lulu left and closed the door firmly behind her. Jessica, seeing no escape, tied her mantle and descended the stairs with feet dragging.

"Where's your husband, girl?" was Oliver Duplessis' greeting.

Oh, Lord, no one had told him.

"Not dead is he?"

"No, sir," said Jessica, and once they were tucked into her grandfather's buggy, she allowed him to drag the story out of her.

"Not surprised to hear Hugh's business practices

have caught up with him," muttered the old man. "Still, there's no reason for you to break up your marriage over it. Travis doesn't blame you, does he?"

"I guess not, but he only married me because he planned to use me."

"Pride? Is that what's hurting you? Doesn't beat you, does he? Doesn't speak hard to you as far as I can see."

"No, but—"

"It would take a pretty angry man to marry a woman he didn't like at all."

"I'd never be able to trust him," whispered Jessica miserably.

"He strikes me as a smart boy—and reliable," said Oliver. "I'm an old man and a good judge of people. Hugh Gresham I wouldn't trust."

Jessica turned surprised eyes to her grandfather.

"Never have. Now, Travis Parnell—I'm inclined to trust that boy. Of course, I'll have to see. I'm not a man to go off half-cocked, but you should give him the benefit of the doubt."

Jessica shook her head. How could she ever put any faith in Travis again?

"He supporting you?"

"He's left town," said Jessica.

"He'll be back."

"It doesn't matter. I don't want anything from him."

"So what are your plans? Going back to Justin? No? Going to let Hugh and Penelope take care of you? I'm not sure I'd bank on those two. Oh, Hugh will keep you as long as my daughter tells him to, but Penelope's too changeable to count on."

"I'm trying to write and sell more articles," said Jessica, her pride stung. "And I'm—I'm going to look for work."

"Doing what?"

"Something to put my education to use."

"What, embroidery and piano playing? You're no great shakes as a musician, girl."

"Law," said Jessica shortly. When her grandfather looked puzzled, she told him about her education.

"Never heard of such a thing," Oliver muttered. "You studied law? Any other girls doing that? No, I thought not. Well, there's something to think about. You'll have your Christmas dinner with me since your mother saw fit to go off and leave you. Here, Bull, help me out." They had come to a stop in front of his large, gloomy house overlooking the river on Samuels Avenue.

They ate dinner in silence. Occasionally Jessica wondered what her grandfather was thinking about as he sat at the other end of the long table frowning at his plate. Mostly, however, she thought about her own problems and her grandfather's surprising opinion that she should return to her husband—as if she could if she wanted to. Travis, seeing no profit in hanging around Fort Worth, was long gone.

"Know anything about business?" Oliver Duplessis asked abruptly.

"Only as it concerns law, plus what I've learned from listening to men."

"I'm getting old," said her grandfather. "No sons, no grandsons. Just you, girl."

Jessica's lips thinned. No doubt a granddaughter was a disappointment to a wealthy man.

"So you'll come to work for me."

Jessica's heart plunged. She knew the lot of unmarried daughters and deserted wives. They became fixtures in the homes of wealthy relatives, keeping house and caring for the children, the sick, and the elderly, unpaid domestics on the periphery of family life. The least they could hope for a kind word now and then or a small bequest in someone's will to tide them over in their own old age. Was this what her grandfather had in mind when he said she was to work for him? Was this to be the end of all her studies and her dreams? "Doing what?" she whispered.

"Conducting business. What else?"

Jessica's eyes flew open.

"I told you I've no sons. You're a smart girl; we'll see how you take to business."

"Will you—will you pay me?" she stammered. She didn't want to seem greedy, but female relatives were often expected to work for nothing. She would need money.

Her grandfather was grinning. He was actually grinning at her. And Lulu said he hadn't smiled in twenty years.

"You just asked the right question, girl. Don't give anything away—even in your own family. That's been my motto for years, and I'm glad to see you learned it earlier than I did."

Jessica looked at him in some confusion.

"The answer is yes, I'll pay you. You do a good job for me, girl, and you won't want for money."

Jessica felt faint with relief. She would no longer be dependent on Penelope's erratic good will. She'd have a job! A salary! And she'd earn every penny of it. Never would her grandfather come to regret his generosity. Eyes shining, she tried to express her thanks, but he waved the words aside.

"Get Bull," Oliver instructed the maid. "Miss Jessica's going home now." Then he turned back to Jessica. "Be at my offices tomorrow morning at eight. Know where they are? Good. Be on time. I can't abide lateness."

He never asked, Jessica reflected, only commanded. Her grandfather wasn't going to be an easy man to work for, but still she felt as if someone had lifted a dark drapery aside to let a thin ray of light into the room of her life.

Travis leaned his head back against the upholstery of the train seat and closed his eyes, thinking, thinking. Once he left Jessica alone in the Greshams' house, he couldn't get out of his mind the accusation Justin Harte had made against his first wife. It had sounded so unbelievable at the time—that Penelope had tried to smother her own baby. Why would she have done such a thing? How had it escaped the gossip mill then and later? Yet, Justin hadn't expected him to take the story on faith; he'd said to ask Calliope.

Jessica too had spoken of Calliope, whom she had known since babyhood, whom she loved and trusted. The colored woman had been her nurse. Calliope still lived out at the Rocking T, Anne Harte's ranch in Parker County. Finally, on Christmas day when he couldn't get Jessica off his mind—Jessica by herself with those two vipers, unprotected from possible harm and separated from the family she loved— Travis decided to follow up that accusation. He'd gone to Weatherford, stayed the night in the hotel, rented a horse the next day, and ridden to the ranch, much relieved to find the family elsewhere. He would not like to explain to Justin Harte why he wasn't with Jessica during the holiday season. Fortunately, his luck was holding in this one matter; old Calliope had been there.

"So you Jessie's young man," she had said, looking him over with wise, ancient eyes. "She's mah baby, that one. More'n any the others. Ah birthed her.

236

Course, Ah birthed Miss Penelope too, but Ah turned mah back on that one."

"Why?" asked Travis.

"Never you mind. Old, sad tales, they best forgotten. Mistah Justin right about that."

"Justin told me to come to you. To ask you about why he took Jessica away from her mother."

"Why Mistah Justin want me to tell you somethin' he don't want no one to know?" she asked, her wrinkled eyelids lowering suspiciously over sharp eyes.

"Because Jessica and I have been living with Penelope Gresham, and—"

"Livin' with Miss Penelope? Mah baby livin' in harm's path?"

"So Mr. Harte said. He told me a story I couldn't believe, and when I didn't, he said to ask you."

"Oh, mah." Calliope rocked agitatedly. "Don' let her stay in that house. Miss Penelope, she got a devil in her. Ah seen it once, an' Ah don' wanna hear it riz agin."

"What did you see?" asked Travis.

"The pilla," said Calliope. "I seen her press the pilla on the baby's face. Fo' months an' months we 'fraid, Miss Anne an' me an' Mistah Justin, we scart Miss Penelope mighta killed that baby or make her simple. Din' happen. Miss Jessie, she smarter'n all them, but Miss Penelope, she try to kill that baby."

Travis had felt a surge of horror and fear. "Why?" he asked.

"No reason atall. Jus' pure selfishness. Mistah Justin, he 'spected her to be a mothah to her chile, an' she din' wanna. She wanna go inta Fort Worth to her papa an' buy fancy clothes an' go dancin' an' flirtin' like she allus done. Some folks got God in them, an' it keeps them folks good, but some ain't got nothin', an' that's Miss Penelope. She ain't got nothin' in her but wantin'. She wants ever'thin', don't give nothin'."

It was too accurate an assessment of Penelope's character for Travis to ignore. He returned to Fort Worth desperate to convince Jessica that she must follow him away from that house. In just a few days the Hamils and their crew would start drilling again outside Beaumont, and the Lucas well would come in. Travis knew it in his bones. When that happened, he'd have to go, and Jessica would have to go with him. It was the only safe option for her.

Chapter Sixteen

Jessica ran down the stairs as fast as she could, a large muff that held various necessities clutched in one hand, her warmest hooded mantle slung over the other arm. She barely had time for breakfast and the walk downtown to her grandfather's place of business, but when she glanced up from the gleaming oak steps, Travis confronted her at the bottom. What was he doing in Penelope's entrance hall? She jerked to a halt and stared at him helplessly, swallowing back a wave of regret. He looked so wonderful, his face ruddy from the cold December air, his black hair ruffled by the biting wind she would soon have to face herself.

"Jess," he said softly.

She forced her mouth to close in a tight line. This was the man who had betrayed her love; she had nothing to say to him.

"We have to talk."

Jessica shook her head, and Travis's gentle expression hardened. He closed long fingers on the soft blue wool of her sleeve and hauled her abruptly through the double doors of the drawing room. "Sit down," he ordered. Having little choice without making an embarrassing scene, she sat, choosing the least comfortable chair in the room. Travis towered over her for a minute, then turned restlessly.

"Jessica, I know you're very upset, although it seems to me that you've been better off since we married than before."

"You think living here in Penelope's house has been pleasant?" she snapped, then silently berated herself for answering at all.

"You're still here, aren't you?" he retorted.

Jessica closed her mouth and turned her head.

"Damn it, Jess," he muttered, recognizing that look. Then he took a deep, calming breath. "Jessica, you can't stay here."

"Really? Where do you expect me to go?" she asked.

"With me."

"No."

"Look, there's something about Penelope that you should know."

Jessica gave him a cynical look.

"You wondered why, when they divorced, you went with your father instead of with her."

Although her curiosity was piqued, Jessica remained stubbornly silent.

"Justin wouldn't let her near you again because she tried to suffocate you." He caught her look of outrage and sighed with relief. Now she'd go with him, and he wouldn't have to be terrified for her safety. "So you see, you can't stay here; you've got to leave with me."

"Travis, that is really contemptible, to make up

240

such a story. I realize that my mother is not the most agreeable person in the world, but to say—to expect me to believe such a—such a . . ."

"It's the truth," he insisted.

"Is it indeed? And how long have you known this?"

"Your father told me shortly after we were married," Travis admitted reluctantly.

"Then why have I been living here four months if you're so concerned for my safety?"

"I didn't believe him." What had seemed an irrefutable argument for reclaiming his wife was going awry.

"I see. As long as it served *your* interests to live here, my father was a liar. Now when, for whatever underhanded reasons, you don't want me here anymore—"

"Jessica, I don't want you here because it's dangerous."

"It was dangerous before, if you're telling the truth—not that I think you are. First you separated me from my father and stepmother. Now you want to separate me from my mother too," she accused bitterly. "Well, you're wasting your efforts this time, Travis. I seriously doubt that you'd be causing Penelope any grief if you managed to come between us."

"Jessica, I'm not here to make trouble for Penelope."

"You don't think accusing her of attempted murder is making trouble?"

"I can't protect you here."

Jessica sighed. "You're the one I need protection from."

Had she looked up, she would have seen her husband's face twist with pain. "Jess, if you won't come with me, at least go home to your mother and father in Weatherford."

241

"You've made that impossible."

"You know they'd take you back."

"I wouldn't ask them—not after flouting their wishes the way I did. And why?" she asked bitterly, then answered her own question. "Because I was so stupid as to believe you wanted to marry me for myself. I should have known better. I should have known your proposal had something to do with money."

"Jess, don't do this, sweetheart. We had a happy marriage. We still could if you'd only—"

"I'm going to tell the servants you're not to be allowed in this house."

Travis searched his mind desperately for some way to protect her. At the very least he had to get her away from Penelope. "How about this, Jess? I'll get you a house of your own and give you an allowance so that you'll be able to buy whatever you need."

"And where will you be," she asked cynically, "while I'm living in that house and spending your money?"

He sighed. "In Beaumont most likely." A flash of anguish shone briefly in her eyes, and he took heart. "I won't say I don't hope to end our separation, Jessica."

So that was it. He wasn't worried about her safety. He still thought he could use her against her family somehow.

"I mean to have you back, but I understand that you need time. This way I can give it to you and keep you out of Penelope's clutches."

"Go away, Travis," she said wearily.

"Do you really want to be beholden to Penelope?" he demanded desperately.

"I'm independent now," she said with some pride.

"Oh?" Travis frowned. "Did your father give you

242

that money you inherited from your grandmother?"

Money and revenge, she thought despondently. Those were the forces that turned his wheels. He wanted Cassandra's money. How had he found out about it? There seemed to be no end to his treachery. "My grandfather gave me a job." Let Travis try to profit from that.

"Wonderful!" he exclaimed, much relieved. "Why don't you move in with him?"

"Because he hasn't asked me," snapped Jessica. Did Travis hope to get something from her grandfather?

"Suggest it."

"I won't." The knock at the drawing-room door came as a great relief. Rescue was at hand. "Come in," she called.

"Miss, Cook says your breakfast is ready," Lulu announced.

"Oh, thank you, Lulu. Would you show Mr. Parnell to the door? He was just going." Jessica rose immediately, skirted around the maid, and hastened out into the hall without even saying good-bye to her husband. She couldn't; her eyes were full of tears, and she didn't want him to see.

"Jessica, did you really allow Travis Parnell in this house?" Penelope asked that evening.

Jessica looked up from the material she had been reading on the lumber business. "No, he was in the entrance hall when I came downstairs to breakfast. I don't know who let him in," Jessica replied calmly.

"You know what I mean, and take those dreadful glasses off your nose, young lady."

"I can't read without them," said Jessica, "and Grandfather expects me to become conversant with this material."

"What did Travis want?" Penelope demanded.

"He wanted me to move out of your house."

"Where?"

"With him, or back with my father, or into a house of my own. He even suggested that I ask Grandfather to take me in. He seems to think I'm in danger here." Jessica studied her mother for some sign.

"Danger?" Penelope's fingers interlaced nervously. "Whatever could that mean?" Penelope stared at Jessica, an aggressive light gleaming in her eyes. "You know the man's a liar. You're not to believe anything he says."

Jessica knew that she could no longer trust her husband, that in essence he *had* lied to her, but Penelope sounded almost threatening. Jessica shivered, then told herself that she was being silly. Penelope was just angry that Travis had returned. No mother would—would try to hurt her own baby. Not even Penelope. That story had to be a lie.

"You're not to see him again. I'll tell the servants."

"I already have," said Jessica, once again facing a future from which her husband would be absent. During the days, she managed to stay so busy with her grandfather's concerns that she could forget how much she missed Travis. However, at night when there was no more work to be done, when she lay alone in their bed, her body restless with longing, she missed him dreadfully. In sleep she dreamed of him, sometimes disturbingly erotic dreams. How could she still want a man who had used her so cold-bloodedly?

"We'll put an end to his hopes," said Penelope, her eyes narrowed in calculation. "Tomorrow. I have a party to attend tonight. New Year's Eve. Are you going anywhere?"

Jessica stared, astonished, at her mother. Where would she be going?

"You really didn't make any friends of your own, did you?" Penelope smiled. "Pity. Well, I'll have to take a hand. We can't have Mr. Parnell thinking he can get you back. No, if that's what he wants, I'll have to do something about him—and you."

Jessica thought her mother seemed stranger than usual. Penelope, who often stayed in her room until noon, had waylaid Jessica in the hall before she went off to work and demanded that she go back upstairs to the tub room. It took Jessica five minutes to convince Penelope that she really had to be at her grandfather's offices.

"You'll never get a husband that way," Penelope muttered darkly.

"In the eyes of the law I already have a husband," Jessica replied. Could her mother have forgotten Travis already? Had she been dosing herself at this hour with that tonic that made one feel so peculiar? Jessica literally tore herself from Penelope's grip and escaped, only to find her mother waiting for her when she got home, demanding again that they go upstairs immediately. Too tired to argue, Jessica followed with Betty, who had been commandeered to come as well.

"First, we're going to fix your hair," said Penelope.

"What do you mean?"

"The color. Get out of your dress. Betty, have you made up the rinse?"

"Yes, ma'am."

"Dreadful color," muttered Penelope, staring at Jessica's hair, "but we'll fix it."

Jessica was beginning to feel alarmed.

"Nothing to worry about, miss," said Betty soothingly. "It's just a lemon rinse. Used it for years on Miz Gresham's hair afore it turned gray."

"Shut up, Betty," snapped Penelope.

"But I don't want—" Jessica got no further. Between her mother and the maid, she found herself stripped to her petticoat and having her hair washed with some shampoo of her mother's, then rinsed in Betty's rinse, and finally brushed dry. As tired as she was, the attention was a luxury under which she could have fallen asleep if she hadn't been receiving a series of lectures on beauty care from her mother— lotions she must rub into her skin on various occasions, perfumed soap and shampoo to make her smell enticing, and, when her hair was dry, lessons on how to put it up. Penelope produced rats and switches; Betty showed her how to use them to produce a stylish pompadour that flattered her face and emphasized her large blue eyes.

"Keep your eyes open, Jessica," her mother ordered. "They're your best feature. You'll never attract suitors if you don't use them."

"Mother, I can't have suitors."

"Don't contradict me," said Penelope.

Betty and Jessica looked at one another, and Betty shrugged as if to say, *What can you expect?*

"Well, the color's better," said Penelope, inspecting Jessica's hair critically, "and it will continue to get better as long as you use the rinse."

Jessica looked closely herself and thought that her hair did look blonder, which could be rather embarrassing. What if someone noticed and asked what she had been doing to it? She'd be humiliated to have anyone think she dyed her hair.

"It ain't dye, you know," Betty whispered. "Most blonde ladies do it."

"They do? But I'm not blonde."

"Enough chatter. Take the hair down. Jessica has to learn to do it herself since *my* hair is your primary responsibility, Betty."

Jessica had to reassemble the style three times herself, drawing her hair up over the rats, placing the tortoiseshell and amber combs to hold it in place, making curls on the sides around her face. Only when she had mastered the technique did Penelope allow her to go to bed, and no one offered her any dinner. Penelope drank hers, muttering all the while that her life was extremely difficult, more difficult than she deserved, the difficulties being the imposition of having to improve someone else's looks, someone with absolutely no concept of the responsibilities entailed in maintaining an attractive appearance; personal ill health, which Penelope combated with alarming quantities of medicine, rendering herself largely incoherent by bedtime; and the disappointment about which she talked the most, the proposed change of *Harper's Bazaar*, a magazine which Penelope read devotedly, from a weekly to a monthly. Since Jessica never read the magazine, she couldn't quite see the change as a major tragedy.

Travis had received the word he had been expecting for ten days. The Lucas well had come in at Spindletop, a monster well, bigger than anything anyone had ever seen. His source had been wild with excitement, babbling about an explosion as soon as the drill went down on the morning of the tenth—a huge fountain of mud, rocks, gas, tons of pipe, and finally oil, shooting hundreds of feet into the sky, nearly drowning the Hamils and their crew, stampeding cattle for miles around, thousands of barrels a day flowing up from one well, so much they couldn't even

247

estimate the flow, had never seen such a well, couldn't cap it.

Travis knew he had to get down there. He wanted to, but he had unfinished business, and he couldn't get in to see Jessica, either at the Greshams' or at her grandfather's place of business. Finally Travis decided that he'd have to settle for seeing her grandfather, who would be interested in the news from Beaumont. On that pretext he managed to talk his way into the old man's house.

"The well came in," he announced abruptly to Duplessis.

Oliver's eyes lit up with interest.

"Bigger than anything this country's ever seen—some say five times, some ten. Spindletop's going to be a very important field, but if I'm any judge of where the oil is, it's going to be on the hill, not on the land surrounding it."

"Which means?"

"It means you want to sell off the surrounding stuff at the highest price you can get while oil fever's still high but before people begin to notice the dry wells on the plain. Hang onto your land on the hill. Sour Lake might be good too if you own anything out there. The water smells bad enough to turn your stomach, and there's oil seep and gas in the area."

"And why should I trust your advice?" Oliver asked. "The way I hear it, you've got a grudge against my family. Might be you want to see me take a big loss."

Travis stretched his boots out in front of his chair and gave the old man a straight glance. "Told you to hang onto the land, didn't I? If I'd wanted to do you an ill turn, I'd have offered to buy it myself or advised you to sell to Lucas when he was trying to fill in their holdings on the mound."

"I still don't know why you'd do me a good turn when you want to do my daughter ill."

"I've no quarrel with you; I do with her. Anyway, I want a favor from you."

The old man laughed. "Forward young fella, aren't you? What favor?"

"I have to go to Beaumont. I want you to look after Jessica for me. By the way, I appreciate your giving her a job since she won't accept support from me."

"What did you offer her?" asked Duplessis curiously.

"I wanted to take her with me, but she hasn't got over thinking I used her."

"Didn't you?"

"I was a good husband and had every intention of continuing to be. Anyway, that's neither here nor there. She won't have anything to do with me—yet."

"Think she'll change her mind?"

"Maybe. In the meantime, I offered to get her a house here and make her a generous allowance. She wouldn't have it, so I'm grateful that she has a salary coming in from you and a job to take her mind off her—" he sighed, looking troubled "—her unhappiness. But I don't want her living in your daughter's house."

"Not surprising," said Oliver. "Penelope's not liable to advance your cause with Jessica, that is if you're serious about getting the girl back."

"Oh, I'm serious. Jessica and I had a good marriage, and we will again. Nor am I worried about Penelope influencing her. I'm worried about Penelope hurting her."

"Hurting her how?" asked Oliver, frowning.

"Maybe like she did before."

"Don't know what you mean," said the old man

"You must have known why Justin Harte divorced

her," said Travis. Was the old man really ignorant of the story Calliope had told?

"They didn't get along. Chalk and cheese, those two. My daughter hated ranch life. Justin hated—"

"There was more to it than that. I'm only asking you to protect your granddaughter. She could live here with you."

The old man grunted.

"She's a smart girl, kind, good-tempered. You'd enjoy her company."

"Doubt she'd want to stay with an old man," said Oliver.

"She's not that happy with her mother, I can tell you. She was after me to move out before we separated."

"And you didn't. Doesn't it strike you as hypocritical to be asking me to protect her? If you really believe what you've been saying, you kept her in a place you thought was dangerous."

Travis flushed. "At least think it over."

"You think it over. You're the one who's leaving your wife to go chasing after oil wells."

"It's my business," said Travis.

"I've always thought husbands and wives were each other's business."

"Then tell her to come with me to Spindletop."

"We'll see," said Oliver. "We'll see."

"We haven't heard from you in a month." Hamlet Arleigh had caught Travis at the Worth just before his departure.

"And you won't," Travis replied with satisfaction. The only good thing to come out of his problems with Jess was that Hamlet Arleigh could no longer blackmail him.

"You know what's going to happen if you don't

cooperate," said the Pinkerton man threateningly.

"Sure. You're going to tell my wife something she already knows."

Hartwig whistled between his teeth. "How'd that happen?"

"Joe Ray Brock came to dinner," said Travis grimly.

"Damn." The lieutenant looked sincerely distressed. "Sorry about that, amigo. She kick you out?" Travis nodded. "Guess you liked her pretty well, after all."

"Guess I did," said Travis. "Anyway, you're on your own, Abe, and I'm on my way to Beaumont."

"Double damn," said Hartwig. "Not that you ever turned up much of anything."

Travis grinned. The lieutenant had once been his friend. In fact, the man had led him to Jessica, even if it had been for the wrong reasons. "Good luck with Gresham, Abe," said Travis. "Oh, and you might keep your eye on the depositors' accounts at Cattleman's."

"You know something?" asked Hamlet Arleigh. "It's your duty—"

"Go to hell!" Travis snapped. Then he turned to Hartwig. "It's just a hunch, but I'd keep it in mind if I were you."

Chapter Seventeen

Travis was gone. He'd left town to follow the lure of a new oil field in Beaumont, which was hundreds of miles away. Although Jessica knew that she might never see him again and that she had to forget him, she thought of her husband constantly. The memory of her misguided happiness with him was a cloud of anguish overhanging all other concerns. She rode the streetcars from one end of town to the other, calling on her grandfather's customers, taking and expediting their lumber and hardware orders. She had noticed, with a rush of cynicism, that her sales had doubled since Penelope had taken charge of her appearance. Unfortunately, neither her improved appearance nor her business success was any consolation.

The weather in January and February turned as cold and gloomy as her heart. Every day she watched the unfortunate motormen shivering on their frigid open platforms and jumping off to run alongside the slow-moving cars for the warmth the exertion gave them, and she remembered Travis and the happy Labor Day they'd had—telling stories with the electric-car drivers and the police and firemen. Some of the drivers remembered her and asked after her husband. What could she say? He was gone.

In the evenings when she came home, tired from her long working day, she had to dress in elaborate new clothes and poke fashionable ornaments into the new hair style Penelope insisted upon. She wondered what Travis would have thought of her hair with its golden highlights and chic coiffure and of the new gowns Penelope insisted on buying. Then when her mother dragged her off to dinners, dances, and theater performances and introduced her to dozens of eligible young men, Jessica compared them to Travis, who was so much more interesting and so much handsomer, and she wondered why Penelope insisted on all this social activity.

When Jessica dropped into bed at night, too exhausted to think of him any more, she fell asleep and dreamed of him, dreamed of his hands and mouth and body on hers. Sometimes she awoke weeping in the middle of the night, wondering if he had found a woman in Beaumont, but she never cried when she was awake. Pride kept her stoic.

One evening Jessica protested her inclusion in yet another social occasion, pointing out that all the introductions to eligible bachelors were futile since she was a married woman.

"But, Jessica," said Penelope, "you're going to divorce Travis. When I've found a suitable second husband for you, we'll see to it. I anticipate that Mr. Parnell will be *very* upset to find himself cast aside by an heiress, especially one who is now reasonably attractive. In fact, I'd love to see his face when he gets the news that he's been discarded, without half accomplishing his purpose in marrying you."

Penelope looked gleefully smug. Jessica felt sick. Divorce Travis? As long as they were still married, there was the hope that some miracle might reunite them. But she couldn't think that way. No woman of pride would want to hold on to a man who had used her and discarded her as Travis had. He hadn't even sent a note when he left town. As for Penelope, let her spin as many fantasy webs as she pleased; Jessica had no intention of remarrying—ever.

"And speaking of your inheritance, you should let Hugh invest it for you. Gracious, who'd have thought that dreadful Cassandra Harte would ever do anything to benefit me?"

Jessica looked at her mother in astonishment. Penelope knew about the legacy from Grandmother Harte? And how did Cassandra's having left Jessica that portion of land in Palo Pinto benefit Penelope?

"Lord, I hated that woman. I knew what she thought of me—sneering at the house Justin built for me, the furniture we ordered from Chicago, my gowns and furs. She expected me to stay out on his dreadful ranch in a log cabin having babies, cooking for cowboys, making soap and quilts. Just because she was some leathery old pioneer-woman type—"

"I loved my grandmother very much," said Jessica, unwilling to hear Cassandra vilified.

"Very astute of you, dear. Look how well you did because of it. I never managed to get an inch of their precious land. But now is the time to put your money into something more lucrative. Hugh will be happy to—"

"I don't have any money."

"Then insist that Justin give it to you. And, Jessica,

you must make a will. What if something happened to you? Travis would inherit, and you don't want that. Name me as your heir. That would be best."

Jessica watched her mother, now so agitated, pawing through a drawer for her medicine bottle and the pretty quassia cup from which she sipped the potions. Penelope wanted to be named Jessica's heir? Travis's warnings flashed through her mind, and she shivered.

Travis was gone. His absence came home most powerfully when her father arrived one morning before she went to work. Because he looked so grim, she anticipated some very serious complaint or disaster. Otherwise he wouldn't have come to see her at all. "Is something wrong?" she asked anxiously. "Mother's not ill, is she? Or Frannie? Or the boys? Are they all—"

"Fine," said Justin. "I'm not bringing bad news. We—we've heard that you and your husband are separated."

Jessica nodded unhappily. Had he come to say *I told you so?*

"I don't know what your financial situation is, but if you need the inheritance from your grandmother . . ." He paused, spreading his hands in a wordless offer.

Surprised, Jessica remembered Penelope's demand that she get the money and turn it over to Hugh and that she make a will in Penelope's favor. "I'd rather you kept it for me, Papa," she said hastily. If she didn't have the money from Cassandra, Penelope couldn't—couldn't what? Jessica wasn't sure what she was afraid of. Goodness, Penelope wasn't going to try to kill her. Jessica certainly didn't believe that story.

Elizabeth Chadwick

"I just don't want you dependent on your—ah—mother," said Justin, his voice gruff. "With you living here, I was afraid—"

"I'm working for my grandfather," Jessica interrupted. "He pays me well, enough for me to move out if I—if I should want to."

"I see. Good." Justin frowned. "Parnell's not supporting you?"

"I wouldn't take anything from him," said Jessica.

"What happened?" her father asked.

She swallowed hard and said, her voice low and pained, "I found out why he married me."

"For money?" Justin guessed.

"Not exactly." Here was another humiliation she had to suffer. "He married me for revenge on Penelope and Hugh."

"Revenge?" Justin looked astounded. "Why?"

"He says they caused his father's death."

Justin frowned. "Parnell?" He thought for a moment. "I knew a Will Parnell years ago, rode with him during the war when we were boys." He leaned back in his chair, remembering. "I think he committed suicide—got into serious financial trouble and killed himself. In the early '80s it was. I remember wondering why the hell he hadn't come to me if he had problems. I'd have helped him. Is Travis related to Will?"

Jessica nodded. "His son. Hugh called Mr. Parnell's loans, and when he shot himself, Travis found his father's body."

"My God!" muttered Justin. "Travis couldn't have been more than a child when it happened, and he's hated Hugh all these years?" He shook his head. "Will Parnell's son. It's a sad story, but why the hell did he drag you into it?" Justin Harte stared at his daughter for a moment, his face softening. "You're

256

looking pretty, Jessie," he said.

"Thank you," she replied, touched by the compliment. "I'm very sorry for the damage my foolishness has cost you. I understand you sold out at the bank because of my marriage."

"If that's the way Hugh runs it, driving good men to suicide when they need help, I reckon I'm well out of it. Besides that, I got a good price, although the scheme didn't accomplish what I'd hoped," he muttered.

Jessica wanted to ask her father what his aim had been but was afraid to in case it was, as Penelope had said, anger over his daughter's defection.

"I am sorry you've been hurt by all this, Jessica. You know if you need help, Anne and I want to give it." He cleared his throat and added gruffly, "We love you."

"Thank you, Papa," said Jessica in a small voice, and she forgot all about bank shares and family feuds. Her father loved her! If he said it, it was true. Unlike her husband, he never lied. Jessica's impulse was to throw herself into Justin Harte's arms and ask to come home, but she was a grown woman, a married woman, for all Travis was gone. She had to stand on her own feet. "I'm—I'm doing very well with Grandfather. He says I have a head for business."

"I'm not surprised," said Justin. "I reckon you're the smartest of my children. The boys are good ranchers, but they've yet to settle down. Maybe you take after Oliver. We had our differences, but he was always a canny businessman."

"So are you, Papa."

"Fair," her father admitted, "but I'm a better rancher. Your mother says you take after Cassandra. I reckon the important thing, and it's something I should have recognized years ago, is that you don't take after Penelope. Does she treat you decently?''

Jessica studied his face. According to Travis, it was her father who had first told him that incredible story of attempted murder. Would Justin warn her too, or had Travis made it up? Her father did look worried, but then Justin knew better than most how difficult Penelope could be, which would worry any parent whose child was subjected to her company. "Penelope is—in ill health," said Jessica slowly. "And difficult."

"I remember," said Justin. "You can come home, you know."

"Thank you, but—but I chose to leave. I think I must stick with it, put what talents I have to good use."

Her father nodded.

"Will you give my love to Mother and the family?" she asked wistfully.

"I will, and they send theirs to you. Your mother wants you to know how much she appreciates your letters. We all do."

Jessica nodded. She loved theirs too. If only—but there would be no letters from Travis.

"You let him in my house?" Penelope's outrage bordered on hysteria. "What has he been saying about me?"

"Very little," said Jessica. "He asked if I wanted to come home."

"You're not going back to Justin. You're going to stay here and make an advantageous marriage."

"Penelope, I'm already—"

"Did you ask about the money? Don't look blank. The money from Cassandra."

"It's tied up in land."

"That Buell boy would do," Penelope mumbled. "What was I saying? Oh. I won't have Justin Harte in my house. Why did you let him in?"

"The maid let him in."

"I'll fire her."

"Good help is hard to find."

"Yes, yes it is. Where's my medicine?"

To Jessica, Penelope seemed unsteady on her feet.

Oliver Duplessis dropped in unexpectedly on one of Penelope's Sunday afternoon soirees, during which Jessica always found herself coupled with one young man or another. Her grandfather sat there, bolt upright by the hearth, glowering at the proceedings. Jessica wasn't quite sure what his objections were, but the young men, unused to such grim disapproval in her mother's house, left early. Even friends of Penelope's age scattered as soon as politeness allowed. Jessica had to swallow back her laughter at the sight of so many fashionable people slinking away under the glares of one old man. It was seldom these days she found cause for mirth, and she rather enjoyed the afternoon until her mother and her grandfather confronted one another at the end of the less than successful social gathering.

"Maybe you'd like to explain what you thought you were doing this afternoon," said Oliver as soon as the last guest had turned tail.

"I have no idea what you mean, Father," Penelope replied breezily. She had slipped away for medicine three or four times to Jessica's knowledge and seemed to be feeling somewhat euphoric. "I'd like to know what *you* were doing. You certainly ruined my party."

"You're acting like a woman with an eligible

daughter you want to marry off," said Oliver Duplessis.

"That's just what I plan to do."

"Your daughter is already married."

"That's easily undone and no more than Travis Parnell deserves."

"Them whom God hath joined, let no man put asunder," roared Oliver.

"Oh, *really*, Father, don't quote scripture to *me*."

"Are you planning to divorce your husband, Jessica?" Oliver asked.

"No, sir," she replied. Jessica expected to live out the rest of her life alone, which was no different from the life she had anticipated before she met Travis, just an unhappier prospect now.

"I'm glad to hear that you, at least, have the decency to honor your vows." He nodded to Jessica, then gave his daughter a hostile look.

"Jessica will change her mind," Penelope assured him smugly.

"Jessica is coming to live with me," said Oliver. "Get your things together, girl. You're moving today."

"She is not!" cried Penelope angrily.

"I'm an old man. I need someone to look after me." Oliver slanted his daughter a wily glance. "Either Jessica moves in with me and does her duty, or I'll move in with you, Penelope."

Given that choice, Jessica knew what her mother would decide.

"You, girl," said Oliver to Lulu, who had come in to remove the teacups. "Get Bull in here to fetch and carry for Miss Jessica. She's moving out."

Living in her grandfather's house gave Jessica a measure of peace and contentment. Now her thoughts of Travis were often pleasant, memories of happy times together, memories that sometimes made her wonder how he could have given her so much joy when his motives were so black. Well, she'd had four wonderfully happy months. Perhaps a sojourn in fool's paradise was better than never having been in paradise at all.

As for her grandfather, he could be an interesting companion when he chose to talk. He spoke mostly of business, occasionally of his wife, who had died years ago and whom he had loved deeply. He never spoke of Penelope, which Jessica found curious. He must have loved his daughter, yet now he seemed to ignore her existence unless it was forced on his notice.

He did, however, speak from time to time of the sanctity of marriage, not overtly criticizing Penelope's aims, nor even offering Jessica advice. She wasn't quite sure what he meant to convey. He didn't mention Travis at all; he simply said now and then that married people belonged together.

In this fashion they lived companionably in the same house. Oliver seemed satisfied with her work, although she began to see that he did not need her. His own health and vigor, despite his advanced age, were quite adequate to the needs of his wide business interests. He had done her a kindness in giving her a job, and he was a patient teacher. Jessica came to feel much surer of herself than she had ever felt in her life, convinced of her own intelligence and her competence to function successfully in a sphere where women were seldom admitted as anything but onlookers.

Then in early March Oliver called her in and told her that he had bad news. Jessica began to tremble.

Something must have happened to one of the family in Weatherford. Her brothers—had one of them been injured?

"You know your husband is in Beaumont?" Oliver asked.

Travis? Something had happened to Travis? Jessica swallowed hard and nodded.

"I've just had word of a disaster there," he continued somberly. "Dangerous places, those oil fields."

Jessica looked at him with wide, frightened eyes.

"Seems there was a lake of oil. Sparks from an engine set it afire, millions of gallons. Then some fellow set a counterfire on the other side of the lake, and there was an explosion that rained burning oil everywhere. Hundreds killed according to the paper." Oliver waved his hand, and Jessica's eyes fastened on the horrifying headlines in the *Gazette*. "I haven't heard from Travis and can't get hold of him."

"You've kept in touch?" she asked, astonished. He'd never given a hint that he heard from Travis.

"Of course. He's been advising me on my holdings in Beaumont."

"But—but how could you trust him?"

"Do you take me for a fool, girl? I trust him because his advice is good."

"Oh." Jessica didn't know what to say. Her grandfather trusted Travis although—although—but what did it matter now? Travis was among the missing. She squeezed her eyes shut. Fire. He might have been caught in that huge, terrible fire her grandfather had described.

"If you want to go, I can arrange it for you."

"Go?" she asked blankly.

"Yes, go to see if he survived. Go to see if he needs help. The man's your husband. He could be injured instead of dead."

"Yes, of course. When can I leave?" Panic sent an icy tide through her body. If he were alive, how would she find him among the dead and dying? How would she manage to care for him in a strange place where disaster reigned?

"I'll put you on the train in an hour. You can change in Houston to a sleeper and get into Beaumont day after tomorrow."

"Yes. All right."

"I have a lot of business interests in Beaumont, and I've heard nothing from the fellow who manages them."

"You think he's been hurt?"

"He stopped reporting long before the fire," said Oliver dryly. "I'll want you to see what's happening there. Protect my holdings. Your law training should be helpful. The courts are full of suits over property leases and deeds, some of mine among them. You can look out for my interests."

Jessica nodded. How long did he expect her to stay there? It was hard to think of anything but Travis.

"I'll make some notes for you while you're packing."

Jessica nodded and hurried from the room without putting to him any of the questions she would ordinarily have asked about the business portion of her mission. She had to get to Beaumont and find her husband. Surely he wasn't dead. If he were, she would have known it, feeling the way she did about him.

Book III

Spindletop
March, 1901, to
August, 1901

Chapter Eighteen

Too anxious to sleep during the eighty-five-mile, overnight trip from Houston, Jessica rose before dawn to sit staring out at the featureless coastal plain that stretched away into the distance. Now and then a clump of trees, ghostly with shrouds of trailing moss, loomed up outside her window, then faded away again in the dim light where low-hanging clouds became indistinguishable from flat horizons. It was an empty, ominous landscape in which Jessica herself seemed the only sentient being, and she wondered if this feeling of bleak isolation could be a warning that Travis had indeed died. She shuddered and stared down at her fingers, clenched in protest on the navy serge of her traveling suit.

Then, before six when the train was scheduled to arrive in Beaumont, the other passengers began to stir, lights came on, and men bustled up and down the aisles eyeing her curiously and talking among themselves of money, land, and oil. A few voices, like dimly heard messages from an alien world, became many; whispers from the far ends of the car grew into an alarming din as the train pulled into the station under a smoke-blackened sky and the passengers pushed and jostled their way off the car.

Jessica stayed seated, waiting until the aisle cleared and the conductor came back to assist her. She carried little luggage since she planned to stay only a few days. If Travis was alive—and surely she hadn't come all this way to bury him, she assured herself, hope renewed—she could go home, taking him with her if he needed nursing. As for her grandfather's elusive Beaumont manager, a Mr. André Malliol, she would find him and urge him to take up his responsibilities. If he was not to be found, she'd hire a replacement.

As she walked from the train, carrying her own carpetbag, she was stunned by the scene that met her eyes. The station was mobbed with people, the street with buggies, surreys, hacks, and wagons. On the board sidewalks ragged boys tried to sell her crude maps and souvenir whiskey flasks filled with Spindletop oil—"Just twenty-five cents, miss." Hack drivers wanted twenty dollars to take her to the fabulous Lucas well. Men waving greenbacks in denominations she hadn't known existed wanted to lease or buy land from her—"You own land, lady? I'm buyin', anywhere within a hundred miles." Others with placards in their hats offered to sell or lease land that would "make your fortune, ma'am; I got a fifteen-acre lease on the Humboldt tract."

A man in a black frock coat stood on a barrel not twenty feet from her haranguing the crowd with dire predictions—"The end of the world is at hand, brothers; fire shall sweep the earth, set by Satan in the guise of an oil driller." Another predicted that the whole coast would collapse if the drilling were allowed to continue.

Across the street, where her grandfather had advised her to lodge, stood the Crosby House, a frame structure with tall windows and long galleries thronged with gesticulating men, the lovely gardens of which Oliver had spoken nowhere in evidence. They had been replaced by six-foot squares, crudely partitioned with boards and used as offices by swarms of frantic bargainers. Added to all this confusion, the horrendous clamor of bells and whistles assaulted her ears. Bedlam could not have been worse, and somehow Jessica had to find her husband in this frantic mass of humanity.

She picked her way across the street to the hotel, thinking to secure a room before she began her search for Travis, but once she had pushed and elbowed a path through the mob in the lobby, the clerk informed her that they had no rooms. In fact, he knew of no rooms anywhere in Beaumont. He advised her to take the next train out, if she could get a seat. Nor did he know a Mr. William Travis Parnell, although he assured her that his ignorance didn't mean there might not be such a man here among the thousands of newcomers who had crowded in since Captain Lucas's well had drenched the county in oil and oil boomers.

"Ah know Travis, ma'am," said a Stetson-hatted man with an elbow on the desk.

"He's alive, then?" asked Jessica eagerly.

"Last Ah heard," drawled the man.

"He wasn't killed in the fire?"

"Warn't no one killed in the fire—exceptin' livestock."

Jessica felt her whole body wilt with relief. No one

had been killed? The papers had said thousands. Her own paper had said that; she'd have to send them a story. "Could you tell me where to find him?"

The man grinned and asked, "Wouldn't Ah do instead?"

"I'm Mrs. Parnell," said Jessica stiffly and gave him her best quelling look, a look the girls had practiced at the Mount Vernon Seminary, a look one of the mistresses had called "as good a protection as a sturdy escort, girls, if you execute it properly." Jessica was a master of execution when it came to *the look*. Her admirer in the Stetson backed up a full foot, which was as far as the mob around him allowed.

"Travis got a room down to the Ervin Boardin' House on Calder Avenue. That's right across from Cap'n William Weiss's house. Under the big magnolia trees. He's married? Travis?"

The last was added with great astonishment and made Jessica feel very peevish. Why was the man so surprised? Had Travis been conducting himself in an unmarried fashion?

"He might be out to the hill. He's drillin'. Got a rotary rig he freighted in from Corsicana. Out east a Cap'n Lucas's well." With each additional dab of information, the man backed a little further away, the well location taking him through a gap in the crowd and out of Jessica's sight.

Then Jessica herself squirmed through the mob in the Crosby lobby, clutching with one hand her navy blue taffeta hat with its voluminous burden of blue and white ribbons and bows, in the other hand her carpetbag. No one offered to help. No one even got out of her way. On the street, a hack driver wanted five dollars to take her to Calder Avenue and the Ervin Boarding House, which she gathered was in the very same town. She gave him a contemptuous refusal and

270

got, for twenty-five cents, directions from one of the map-peddling street urchins, also a look at his map, which was a crude thing and vastly overpriced. He assured her that men who wanted to locate leases they had bought or hoped to buy were begging to obtain the maps for three dollars each.

Jessica felt that the world had gone mad as she began her walk to the Ervin Boarding House. What would she do if Travis had already left? She had no intention of paying the outrageous price of twenty dollars for a hack ride out to his well on Spindletop hill. If his landlady or landlord could assure her of Travis's good health, perhaps she'd just leave him a note and take the next train home. No, she had business to conduct for her grandfather. But no place to spend the night. Lord, how was she to manage?

Once Jessica got away from the maelstrom around the depot and Crosby House, she began to relax. Calder Avenue was actually a pleasant surprise; large houses sat back on spacious lawns shaded by old oaks and luxuriant magnolia trees. As she walked along, switching her bag from hand to hand as comfort required, she wished she had asked the whereabouts of her grandfather's man as well. Perhaps André Malliol had been injured in the fire; he might be in a hospital here in town, which she could visit as soon as she had seen her husband. She located the boardinghouse just where the map seller had said it would be and shifted the bag yet again as she waited for an answer to her knock.

"May I speak to Mr. William Travis Parnell?" she asked when a weary-looking woman answered.

The woman frowned at her and announced brusquely, "No females allowed here."

Jessica frowned back and replied, "I'm not looking for accommodations." Certainly not in the same house with Travis. "I simply wish to speak to Mr. Parnell."

The woman disappeared inside without another word, leaving Jessica to wonder if she had gone for Travis or just gone. Setting her bag down, Jessica faced the closed door and waited, mouth set in an uncompromising line.

That was how Travis found her a few minutes later, looking grim but, to him, very beautiful. Had she always been so lovely, he wondered, or was he simply starved for the sight of her? He took a giant step out onto the porch and swept her into his arms. "Jess, love," he groaned into her ear, "thank God, you're here at last."

Before she could protest what was obviously some misunderstanding on his part, he caught her mouth with his and overwhelmed her in a devouring hunger, or so it seemed to her dazed senses.

"Mr. Parnell!" came a shocked voice from behind them.

Slowly, and with obvious reluctance, Travis loosened his hold on Jessica a fraction and lifted his mouth a bare inch from hers. "Molly," he said, his warm breath bathing Jessica's trembling lips, "this is my wife."

"Oh. Well." The voice sounded a trifle less shocked. "Well, I don't think the missus be goin' to let her stay here. We don't take no ladies."

Travis wasn't listening. He had returned his mouth to Jessica's, and she had to struggle away from him, mumbling shakily about misunderstandings.

"I know, love," he replied soothingly as he ducked under her tilted hat again and nuzzled her neck, "but now that you're here, we can work out any misunderstandings we may have—"

"Travis, I'm here on business for my grandfather,"

she interrupted desperately. She could hardly admit that she had come primarily out of concern for Travis's life and thus feed his evident expectation that they would be reconciled. "His—his manager has simply dropped out of contact. I thought—" ah, she had an inspiration "—I thought you might be able to give me news of the man. André Malliol?" She gave her husband a bright, hopeful look.

He stared back with puzzled disappointment, no doubt because, for a minute there, she had forgotten their differences and kissed him back with fervor. But her suspicions had swiftly returned. Did Travis's warm welcome mean that he still foresaw possibilities of using her against her family? "Mr. Malliol handled Grandfather's lumber interests here, not to mention Duplessis land holdings and the wholesale hardware business."

"Your grandfather has a house out in Spindletop Heights. Seems to me I heard Malliol's living there," said Travis brusquely.

"What?" Here was very disturbing news indeed. From Oliver's notes to her, she had learned that among Mr. Malliol's derelictions of duty was a failure to collect rent on the house. She'd certainly have to look into that. "Would you by any chance be able to suggest the name of some respectable woman who could rent me a room for the night?" she asked stiffly. Straightening out the matter of Mr. André Malliol might take another day.

"There are none," said Travis. "The only bed in town that might be open to you is mine."

Jessica flushed. "That's quite impossible. Not only are women boarders not allowed here, but I have no intention of—of—"

"Enjoying my company to that extent?" he asked dryly. "Well, if you won't share my bed, perhaps I can offer you breakfast. If you came in on the night train from Houston, I doubt you've had any."

"I haven't," Jessica admitted, and she was very hungry, having been too anxious to eat much of what had been served her in a Houston restaurant the night before. She had never eaten by herself in public and hadn't relished the experience at all, although she supposed she might have to accustom herself to such unusual situations if she continued to do business for her grandfather.

"Come along then," said Travis.

"The Queen of the Neches!" exclaimed Jessica. "This place is dreadful, certainly not the queen of anything."

Travis laughed. "Beaumont was a nice little timber and rice marketing town before the Lucas well came in. Now—well, I'll have to admit it's a bit hectic, but then that's Texas for you. Corsicana was bad in its time; so was Fort Worth when the railroad first came in and the cattle drives were still roaring through. You must have heard about those days from your parents."

Jessica nodded. Her father had been a force in the big cattle drives of the '70s before she was born.

"Every boom town's a hell hole until it catches up with its growth and becomes respectable—especially Texas towns. You know what General Phil Sheridan said about Texas? He said if he owned both Texas and hell, he'd rent out Texas and live in hell."

Jessica couldn't help laughing. No matter how reprehensible his behavior had been, talking to Travis, after so many evenings spent with her mother's friends, was like opening a window to let a fresh breeze sweep through a room filled with cigar smoke —which this crowded, noisy restaurant was. Didn't any of these men know that no gentleman smoked in a lady's presence? Not only was the air unbreathable, but the service was dreadful as well.

"How good it is to hear your laughter, Jess," said Travis, "and I must say you're looking exceedingly beautiful."

The compliments should go to Penelope, thought Jessica wryly. She herself felt like a fraud, for even after moving to her grandfather's, she had continued to use the lemon rinse on her hair, which was what must have impressed Travis.

When Jessica failed to respond, Travis returned to the subject of Beaumont. "No matter what else you say about Beaumont, it's the most exciting place in Texas right now, the most exciting place in the whole country, I reckon. That Lucas well is producing six to eight times more than any well I ever heard of, maybe somewhere between fifty and eighty thousand barrels a day. Back in Corsicana all the wells in the whole field only put out around twenty-three hundred barrels a day. We're going to break the Standard Oil monopoly right here at Spindletop."

Travis's smug pleasure in making that prediction reminded her of his remarks early in their acquaintance about Pierce, Waters and Senator Bailey. How impressed she had been with him then. How little she had understood his motives for pursuing her.

"Hell, even the Russians can't compete," he continued proudly. "They've got a big field, but they're six hundred miles from the ocean, and there's a forty-six-cent tariff on their oil. When a few more wells come in here at Spindletop, and they will, we'll rule the world," he exclaimed enthusiastically. "There'll be a boom like nothing anyone has ever seen, and all of us from Corsicana who know how to work the rotary drills and have the equipment and experience—" he smiled a slow, satisfied smile "—we're going to do *real* well."

"Have you moved your drilling business here?" she asked curiously.

"I have. Brought a rig and crew down, and I've got more coming. Just to drill someone else's well, I get around five thousand dollars."

"Good heavens."

"And I've my own land and leases here. I'm going to be a very rich man, Jessie. Doesn't that interest you?"

Her face closed. Did he really think money would make her forgive what he had done, make her expose her family any further to his plotting? As he became more powerful, he could only become more dangerous.

"I guess money *doesn't* interest you," he decided bitterly. "Reckon that comes of always having had it. Hey, Turner!" He had turned away from her to hail someone at another table. "Where's André Malliol living?"

"Oh, he's got him a house out in Spindletop Heights. He's tradin' land and leases an' rentin' ever' room in his place to three or four boomers for as much as the traffic will bear."

The man laughed, but Jessica gasped in indignation. Obviously Malliol was working only for himself and ignoring his responsibilities to her grandfather while he used her grandfather's house as his base and a source of personal profit.

"There you are," said Travis. "That what you wanted to know? I have to get out to my crew, but I'll see if I can find you a train ticket back to Fort Worth. Tell Oliver if he wants me to deal with Malliol for him, I'll do it." He waved the waiter over and paid the two dollars for their plates of ham and eggs, plus a four-dollar tip.

"Travis," exclaimed Jessica, "have you gone mad? You overtipped that waiter outrageously."

"You either tip four or five dollars, or the next time you come for a meal, the service takes forever and they've just run out of most everything on the menu you order. Now do you want me to go to the railroad station with you?"

"No, I'll take care of it myself," said Jessica absently. She had already decided to find the sheriff and have Mr. Malliol and his boarders removed from her grandfather's property. If they weren't paying rent, they'd have to go. Then she could stay in the house while she interviewed people to take over Mr. Malliol's neglected duties. With all the men milling around town, it shouldn't be too hard to hire a replacement. She'd have to find a telephone and call Oliver long distance to tell him her plans. "Good-bye, Travis. Thank you for breakfast," she said with cool politeness as they emerged from the restaurant.

He gave her an angry look and strode away.

André Malliol, a weasely looking fellow, short and slender with dark, lank hair, found it inordinately amusing that a strange young woman would expect him and his paying guests to vacate the house in which they were living. His amusement disappeared when the sheriff, at Jessica's request, arrived with the proper legal papers and the weaponry to effect an eviction.

Ras Landry made so impressive an appearance that Jessica could hardly keep from grinning. He had a face suitably stern that could be transformed by an amiable smile if he were so inclined. He had a soft

Louisiana accent, but otherwise seemed the quintessential Westerner with his wide-brimmed white hat, his beautifully tooled boots, and his two pearl-handled revolvers with which, one of his deputies had told her in a voice hushed with reverence, the sheriff was "very handy." Mr. Malliol too must have heard of the sheriff's talent with his fancy guns, for her grandfather's ex-business manager left without further argument, he and two other men then in the house.

Having cleared the place of occupants, the sheriff advised her not to think too badly of Mr. Malliol. "Everyone's gone oil mad, Miz Parnell," he said. "No one wants to work for regular wages when they think they can strike it rich an easier way. Now, I'll just tack up this notice on your door that the owner has repossessed the house. We got the belongings of the boarders who haven't come in yet out on the porch, and here's a shotgun for you to keep a few days till those who lived here are convinced they can't come back. You know how to use a shotgun?"

Jessica had no intention of using the shotgun, but she thanked the sheriff for his concern and, bidding him good-bye, turned to the pigsty in which she would have to spend a night or two. It was disgusting; Malliol and his boarders had left the house grimy and littered. Putting water on to boil, she considered which room to attack first. Even the water was disgusting. It smelled bad. And the sheriff had warned her not to drink it unboiled, lest she contract "the Beaumonts," evidently a virulent form of diarrhea which Ras Landry was too gentlemanly to explain with any clarity.

General Phil Sheridan had been quite right about Texas, thought Jessica, at least as his comments applied to Beaumont. She too would rent it out. Hell could hardly be worse. In fact, she intended to rent out this particular part of Beaumont once she had cleaned it up. She ought to be able to get a fortune for a decent house even if it was surrounded with oily muck and assaulted by revolting smells and noises.

Tomorrow she'd have to walk into town since she was not about to spend twenty dollars of her grandfather's money on a hack ride. Should she be unable to hire a man immediately, perhaps she could rent a bicycle. Yes, that was a cheering thought, the only one she'd had since finding Travis still alive. It would be a joy to ride a bicycle again.

The thought of pleasure immediately brought to mind Travis's kiss. Oh Lord, how vulnerable she still was! Swallowing back the pain of her hopeless love for him, she took up a mop she'd found unused in a corner, lifted the hot water from the stove, and set to work.

Jessica faced the morning bleary-eyed. After three attempted intrusions by Malliol's former boarders, she had been too nervous to sleep again. Each time in the night when anxiety or intruders awakened her, she rose, lit an oil lamp, and added another paragraph or two to her article for the *Gazette* on her impressions of Beaumont and Spindletop. Once in town she planned to post the material, but she hoped fervently that the day would see a reliable man hired to replace Malliol so that she could leave.

She donned the other outfit she had brought with her, a walking skirt, a smart blouse with a choker collar, a jacket, and sturdy boots. Then she set out on the three- or four-mile walk. Jessica was dusty and tired by the time she arrived, only to discover that she must share her breakfast table with three drummers from east Texas who had come to sell various prod-

Elizabeth Chadwick

ucts and stayed to make their fortunes, although none
had yet achieved that aim.

As soon as the first finished his breakfast, another
man, tall and broad with a full mustache and a slight
Germanic accent, dropped into the chair and introduced himself as Captain Anthony Lucas. Jessica's
eyes went wide. "The Captain Lucas who brought in
the first well?" she asked.

"Yes, madam," he replied with formal courtesy.
"Do I understand that you represent the Duplessis
lumber interests?"

Jessica nodded doubtfully. If he had some complaint, she didn't know how she could answer it,
being totally unacquainted with the state of her
grandfather's business in Beaumont. She assumed
that it must be chaotic after Malliol's defection.

"Thank the gut Lord," murmured Captain Lucas.
"You may have heard of the fire on the oil lake below
my vell."

Again Jessica nodded.

"Ve haf lost three carloads of lumber as vell as a
frame building that housed eighty men."

Jessica tried to look sympathetic while wondering
why the man was interrupting her breakfast with his
tale of woe.

"Ve need lumber."

So that was it. "I'm hoping to hire a man today to
run my grandfather's business here in Beaumont.
Shall I send him to you as soon as—"

"You haf the power to act for your grandfather?"

"Well, yes, but—"

He made an offer on enough board feet to replace
his losses, a good offer. Jessica smiled pleasantly and
reiterated that she would be glad to send her grandfather's manager to conclude the deal as soon as she
had hired a manager. The captain looked impatient

280

and made a better offer. Jessica sighed, put down her fork, and said, "Since I have just arrived in town, Captain Lucas, and have no idea what the market price is—" He made an offer that Jessica considered ludicrously high, too high to pass up. "Very well, sir," she replied, "I shall arrange for delivery by week's end, provided that, after inquiry, I do not find your offer under the market."

"Madam, you vill not," the captain assured her and, beaming, shook her hand. "By veek's end," he repeated happily as he went away. The remaining salesmen looked at her with respect as she consumed her last piece of ham, took her last sip of coffee, and tipped the waiter what she considered to be a more ludicrous amount than Captain Lucas had offered for her grandfather's timber. Then she went to the Crosby House and posted a notice of the job as Duplessis manager, to the post office to mail her newspaper article to Fort Worth, and to various stores in search of a rental bicycle so that she would not have to walk home.

As it happened, there were only two bicycles not privately owned in Beaumont, both the property of a merchant who desperately wanted to rid himself of a product for which there was no market. He refused to rent one of his machines to Jessica, although it had the drop frame devised specifically for ladies. Instead he offered her a very good price to induce her to buy. Sighing, Jessica agreed, although she would have to take it back on the train and would then own two bicycles.

She walked her new machine back to the Crosby House, not an easy feat with so many people on the sidewalks, and was disappointed to discover that no job hunters had applied for the position. Jessica went to the newspaper to put in an advertisement and then to visit the mayor, a round man dressed to the nines but absolutely discouraging about her prospects of finding a man, any man, to take the job.

By late afternoon, thoroughly disheartened and unwilling to take another meal in one of Beaumont's overcrowded, understaffed restaurants, she purchased groceries and pedaled the three or four miles back to her house, where she found and gave short shrift to yet another Malliol boarder. She spent the evening washing sheets in an iron kettle and writing an article on boom towns where well-paid jobs went begging while fools pursued will-o'-the-wisp dreams of wealth and power.

Chapter Nineteen

Jessica interviewed two men in the next two days. One was drunk; the second offered to take the job in return for a lease on some property Oliver owned west of Spindletop. Thoroughly discouraged, she secured Captain Lucas's lumber herself, although she had to travel east by train and hack, staying overnight in another strange town, to set up increased shipping from her grandfather's sources. When she returned to Beaumont she was glad of her foresight, because other drillers approached her with orders. Evidently the local lumber king, a Mr. Carroll, could not meet the demand, which made Jessica wonder how much business her grandfather had lost because of his manager's defection.

A message from a Mr. Tolliver also awaited her on her return, and she hoped fervently that he would be an acceptable candidate for the job she was now doing. Instead he proved to be a bluff, fast-talking man who claimed to own the land on which her Spindletop Heights house stood. To Jessica that was the last straw. She was exhausted from her long journey, from having had little sleep in a strange bed, and from the strain of trying to do business with lumbermen who thought women belonged in the nursery with the babies, not on the road issuing instructions to their betters. In one case, it had taken an irate telegram from her grandfather to move a stubborn employee to cooperate.

And now some shifty-eyed cheat thought he was going to claim her house, the house she had scrubbed herself, the very bed where she planned to drop as soon as possible for twelve, maybe fourteen hours of sleep. She rounded on an astonished Mr. Tolliver and snapped, "I suppose you're going to tell me you have ownership papers to the icebox I cleaned out before I left, to the sheets I washed, to the—"

"Lady," interrupted Mr. Tolliver, "I ain't interested in your household goods. I just want to hire a drillin' rig an'—"

"Well, let me tell you, Mr. Tolliver, I can cite the deed history of that piece of land back to the days of the Republic of Texas, back to Spanish land grant times."

Mr. Tolliver looked taken aback. "Now, ma'am, I got this conveyance—" he fumbled in his coat pocket and brought out a wrinkled piece of paper "—from John Jack Placerman."

"What is that?" Jessica snatched the paper from his hand.

"Like I said, it's a conveyance."

"This is not a legal document."

"No, ma'am. It's—well, it was an inside wrapper from some Mail Pouch chewing tobacco."

"You're claiming my grandfather's land on the basis of something scribbled on a chewing-tobacco wrapper?"

"Well, you bein' a lady, ma'am, you probably don't realize—"

"Mr. Tolliver," said Jessica haughtily, "I studied law for three years at Columbian University in Washington City, the capital of our country, so do not try to tell me what is and is not legal."

"You're a lawyer?" Had she declared herself a brown bear, Mr. Tolliver could not have been more surprised.

"*If* anyone actually took your money for that chewing-tobacco wrapper, Mr. Tolliver, you'd best take *him* to court, for you won't have a prayer against my grandfather and me. Our title to that land is unassailable."

"Maybe we could strike a deal on the mineral rights," said Mr. Tolliver. "It ain't like I care about the house. We could each put up—"

"Good day, sir." Jessica slapped the tobacco wrapper into his hand, stalked away to retrieve her bicycle from the merchant who had sold it to her, purchased groceries, and went home. Mr. Tolliver, she reflected with satisfaction, had undoubtedly thought he could hornswoggle her because she was a woman. Realizing that she would probably be the object of further such efforts, she resolved to research her grandfather's land holdings at the county courthouse.

On subsequent days she rode her bicycle into Beaumont, carried out her studies at the courthouse, took several more substantial lumber orders, saw to the early delivery of Captain Lucas's order, established a bank account with his payment, and fended off men who wanted to lease the land on the hill. She always smiled sweetly and said, "I am not interested in disposing of the drilling rights at this time."

The answer usually prompted a higher offer. In fact, the whole process intrigued her, and she became quite curious as to how high a bid would ultimately be made. Of course, she did not plan to accept. Jessica didn't want an oil derrick in her front yard and had no intention of entering a lease agreement as long as she had to live in the house. Her grandfather seemed to think that might be for some time, or so she surmised when he sent her law books and most of her clothes after she informed him of the additional lumber orders she had negotiated. However, though she did not want to lease her yard, she was learning a lot about how the agreements worked. Beaumont and Spindletop might be unsavory, but they were fascinating.

Because of her courthouse researches, she could now drive off people who made bogus claims on her grandfather's land by treating them to extensive discussions of deed history and land law. Although she knew the court dockets to be crowded with suits, none had been filed against her grandfather since her arrival. In fact, she had been so successful in fending off would-be claimants that two suits were dropped and several men had asked legal advice of her, which was flattering. Would they pay her? she wondered. Would it be legal for her to accept fees? She'd have to find out.

In the meantime, she needed to call her grandfather about wholesaling hardware here in Beaumont. The orders were to be had, and the prices being charged were phenomenal. She herself had bought a hammer to nail down a loose shutter at her house and been astonished at the cost. After making her purchase, she talked to the store owner about the possibility of buying from Duplessis Hardware. The man expressed an interest, although he was more interested in rumors about the latest lease offer she'd refused.

"Good for you, little lady," he'd said admiringly. "Wish I had some land up there, although I don't know if I could hold out the way you've been doing." Jessica gave him an enigmatic smile, but wondered if she should tell her grandfather of the offers. She might be depriving him of good money because of her own selfish desire to avoid oil raining down on her roof or a well catching fire in her front yard. Jessica shuddered at the thought and decided to court local admiration a while longer, at least until someone took over for her.

She had reached the point of suggesting that her grandfather send a manager from Fort Worth, but he insisted during their last telephone conversation that he had no one to send, certainly no one who could do as competent a job as she. His praise was welcome, but would he feel so pleased if he knew of the offers she had refused?

"Jessica?"

She looked up into the eyes of her husband. Now she knew why he had stayed away. He hadn't heard that she was still in town, not if his surprise and indignation were any indication. "Goodness, Travis, you're just the man I needed to see," she improvised quickly.

Travis frowned. "You mean you came back to town to see me?"

"Well, no. Actually, I haven't left—except for a quick trip to east Texas. I just have one question." She'd ask him whether her latest offer on the Spindletop land was a good one, for she really did want to know, not that she could be sure Travis would give her reliable advice. Oliver might trust him; she

didn't. Still, this way she could talk to him imperson-
ally for a few minutes, then make her escape. How
wonderful he looked in his flat-crowned hat, jeans,
and boots, but wearing only a plaid wool shirt and a
leather vest against the nippy March weather.

"Where are you staying?" he demanded.

"My grandfather's house on Spindletop Heights."

"My God, you're not up there by yourself?"

"Yes, Travis, I am. Now my question—"

"I'll see you home and have a look at the place."

He sounded extremely irritated as he took her
elbow in one large, rather grimy hand and turned her
down the street. "I'm not finished with my business,"
Jessica protested. She did not want Travis coming
home with her.

"I don't know what Oliver's thinking of, letting you
stay here in Beaumont by yourself."

"Let go of me, Travis. My bicycle is back there
at—"

"You're riding a bicycle around here? I'm surprised I haven't heard of it." He kept hustling her
down the street. "Reckon I'm spending too much
time out at the well."

"Travis!"

"This man botherin' you, ma'am?" asked one of
Sheriff Landry's deputies.

"This man is her husband," said Travis.

"That right, ma'am?"

"We're separated," said Jessica stiffly, her cheeks
flushed.

"Married is married," the deputy decided after a
minute's thought, and he took himself off.

"I suppose if you'd been pulling a gun to shoot me,
he'd have said 'married is married' and left," said
Jessica bitterly.

"You didn't have to tell him we're separated,"

Travis muttered. After an argument, they compromised. Travis rode his horse. Jessica rode her bicycle and ignored him, the more so because he had grumbled that her short cycling shirt showed her ankles. She told him that her ankles were no longer his concern. They made a very mismatched pair on the road and elicited humorous comments from men coming into town from the drilling sites.

Once at the house, Travis prowled around, checking windows, doors, and locks, usually remarking that they wouldn't keep out a six-year-old. Jessica knew that but hadn't wanted to be reminded. Then Travis discovered her tin bathtub. "You've got to let me use it," he pleaded.

Jessica glared at him.

"Do you have any idea of how few tubs there are in Beaumont? Not above twelve, I'd guess, most of them in barber shops and so filthy you'd rather go dirty than put your body in one."

Travis had always been a fastidious man, but now he looked scruffy. Not just his clothes—Travis himself. Jessica could understand how much that would bother him.

"I'll make you a deal, Jessie. Dinner and a bath, and I'll fix up your doors and windows. How about it?"

He was giving her such an appealing smile, and there *were* things that needed to be done around the house, things she herself did poorly or couldn't do at all. "Very well," she said grudgingly, "but dinner won't be much. I hadn't planned on company."

Travis gave her a merry grin and scooped up some tools piled on the kitchen table. "You start heating the water. I'll start on the front door. No, I'll pump the water for you first." She watched him jumping energetically off the back stoop, a bucket in either hand, and bit her lip hard, the pain a reminder that he was not to be trusted, that what he wanted from her was not the love she had wanted to give him.

Travis was as good as his word. He effected an amazing number of repairs while his bath water was heating. Then he had his bath while she cooked dinner and thought about him, wet and naked in the small tin tub they had moved to her sitting room since she would not allow him to take his bath in the kitchen while she worked there.

She stood at the stove, absently stirring a pot of stew and staring into the night. There were still men out there on the hill boring down into the earth. She could hear them, their shouts and the sound of their equipment. Travis probably had a crew working tonight. He might be going back to them after he'd had his dinner, or he might be going into town—to one of those girls at Deep Crockett, as they called the sporting district.

She could remember when she had worried about his visits to Fannie Porter's. Then he had assured her that he was happy at home, but now he had no home, so he probably—Lord, she was still jealous, jealous of a man she'd never live with again. He had betrayed her and—

Her thoughts were cut off when two brown, bare arms encircled her from behind, pulling her back. "Two months, Jess," he whispered against her ear, his warm breath stirring the fair, fine hair. "For two months I've been thinking about you, wishing I had you in my arms, wanting to share the excitement of things here with you, and then when I thought you'd come back to me—" He sighed. "Ah, love, that was cruel. I thought—"

"Travis, let go of me." Instead of letting go, his arms tightened, pressing her hard against his body.

Virgin Fire

"I don't want to, honey." His desire to kiss her neck frustrated by her high collar, he nipped her earlobe instead. "I don't want you living here by yourself." He pressed one forearm across her waist while with the other hand he released the hooks of her collar and kissed her neck, then her shoulder. "I don't want you living anywhere but with me."

Jessica was virtually immobilized, by his arm which held both of hers helpless, by the realization that he had started to undress her, and by the wave of passion that swamped her as he first nuzzled her bared shoulder, then closed his free hand over her breast. Through the fabric of her shirtwaist, he stroked the tip with his thumb. In response the nipple tightened, and an old ache bloomed low in her body, weakening her resolve, firing the passion she had tried so hard to bank since she had thrust him from her life.

"I want you back, Jessie. I just plain want you." His voice was low and urgent.

Jessica tried to detach herself from what he was doing to her. Once, knowing she might be hurt, she had let herself love him, and she *had* been hurt—in a way she never anticipated. Now, she didn't want to take any more chances. Now, she understood him better. He probably did want to make love to her, but there would be other, more pressing motivations. She could guess at them. "Maybe what you really want is this land," she replied. "What did you have in mind, Travis, besides moving in with me? A lease in your name? A well in the front yard?"

She had made her voice scathing. His hands fell away, and he stepped back.

"When's dinner?" he asked coolly.

"Ten minutes," she replied. His passion was highly controllable it would seem, fueled by greed,

291

quenched by the frustration of that greed.

"You've got a bad step out back. I'll mend it." He went into the sitting room for his shirt, threw out the bath water, and was soon pounding nails into the loose step that led up to her back stoop. When he came in for dinner, he brought her two more buckets of water for which she thanked him politely.

Over dinner he advised her to keep holding out against offers on Oliver's property. He said the boom hadn't even begun, that by the end of the month more wells would have come in and prices would shoot out of sight. For the next few months she would be able to sell Oliver's off-hill land for huge amounts; it would bring prices far in excess of its value because people would not yet realize that little or no oil lay beneath that flat plain. He advised her to sell, not lease, the off-hill land for as much as she could get and do it before too many dry holes had been drilled there.

Why not lease it? she asked. Because the lease would guarantee to drill within a given period of time and promise her a percentage of the potential oil revenues, but there would be none, he explained. Then the lease would lapse, and the land would be worth considerably less because by then everyone would realize that the oil was on the hill. At that time she could make up her mind to sell or lease the hill property.

Jessica understood his reasoning. Her only problem with his advice was the possibility that it might be deliberately misleading. After all, Oliver was Penelope's father; Travis might hold a grudge against him. On the other hand, Travis's advice might be well meant, but that didn't guarantee that he was right. People were buying up that flat land surrounding Spindletop even now because they expected to become rich. Wells were being drilled.

Travis watched her frowning and said with a lazy smile, "Distrust is written all over your face, Jess, but I can tell you, Oliver won't appreciate it if you lose him a lot of money."

"I imagine you're really enjoying it—putting me in this position," she replied angrily.

"I'm not enjoying anything about my problems with you, Jess," he said sharply. "I don't want to cheat you or quarrel with you. What I want is to stay here tonight and make love to you, tonight and tomorrow night and . . ."

Jessica rose hurriedly and left the room. Behind her she heard him swear, then stamp to the door and slam it behind him.

Jessica had been in Beaumont three weeks when she acquired a housekeeper. She always remembered the date, March twenty-sixth, because it was the day the Beatty well came in, blowing the driller, Jim Sturm of Corsicana, right off the derrick floor and gassing Lige Adams, the farmer who had leased the land to Beatty and taken a job as a cook at the well site. She knew both of them.

When she heard the news, her first thought was of Travis, and she wanted to find him, to be sure he hadn't been hurt. Then she realized that the first of his predictions had come true. Oil had been found again on the hill and before the end of the month. Just as he had said, prices skyrocketed and pressure increased on her to sell or lease her grandfather's land. She was offered dozens of deals, but all she could think of was that Travis's well would come in soon and he might be injured or killed.

She hired the woman who appeared at her door that morning for several reasons. First, Jessica liked her on sight, even though she had never seen anyone like her new housekeeper, who was tall, taller than Jessica herself, with dark red-brown skin and wide, high cheekbones. She seemed to be around Jessica's own age, but regal and exotic in appearance, forceful if somewhat taciturn in personality.

When Jessica opened the door to her, the woman simply announced that Jessica needed a housekeeper, a statement with which Jessica had to agree. As her business activities multiplied in Beaumont and on the hill, it became obvious that she would have to let her domestic arrangements go entirely if she were to keep writing articles for the Fort Worth newspapers, articles for which she was now being well paid. Papers competed to buy them because of their popularity with readers. She'd even had offers from out-of-town newspapers and often sold the same article two or three times, but she couldn't continue to write and keep her clothes and bedding clean and her table set each day. Therefore, she agreed when told that she needed a housekeeper. She needed one and could afford to pay the price the woman asked.

In addition, another person in the house would act as a barrier between herself and Travis, should he decide to call. Some days she ached to see him and had the disconcerting suspicion that she would throw her arms around him should he appear at her door—but not if there were a housekeeper standing by. In fact, even if he never came again, others did, and another person in the house would offer a measure of protection.

Only after they had settled on terms did Jessica realize that her new housekeeper was married and expected to go home to her husband at night. Rainee lived in "South Africa," a neighborhood populated by Negroes and Mexicans. Perhaps, if the woman's husband proved to be a reliable man, Jessica would later invite the couple to move in with her here on Spindletop Heights. She had the room and would welcome the company. Maybe if they became friendly, the woman would tell her story. She had introduced herself simply as Rainee, but the name didn't fit her. Jessica was sure she was part Indian, as well as part black. Rainee Beeker, who said so little and worked so hard, piqued Jessica's curiosity and gave her something to think about in the evening hours, something besides Travis, who usually occupied her mind as she was falling asleep.

"That girl's going to make me another fortune," said Oliver Duplessis.

"Really, Papa?" asked Penelope. "And how could my little daughter make you a fortune? Is she dividing her newspaper earnings with you?" Penelope laughed musically to cover her irritation over the fact that Oliver kept returning the conversation to Jessica.

"Don't be a bigger fool than you usually are, Penelope," snapped her father. "Fortunes are being made at Spindletop. Land prices are going up, and they'll go higher still, and I own land there." He looked very self-satisfied, and Penelope was interested for once.

"What has Jessica to do with it?" she asked.

"She's handling sales and leases for me."

"Really? And you say the prices are going up?"

"They are. There are millions to be made in that market," said Oliver firmly.

"Millions?"

"Fool girl wants to come home, but I've told her she's to stay. She's doing too good a job to be replaced by some fella I can't trust."

"Oh, I quite agree, Papa. I think you should leave Jessica right where she is," said Penelope.

"Why?" asked her father, the many folds of his bulldog face quivering with suspicion. Then he chuckled, remembering that Penelope had hoped to effect a divorce between Travis and Jessica so that she could marry Jessica off—with some advantage to herself and Hugh, no doubt. Well, she was bound to be disappointed. She obviously didn't know that Travis Parnell was in Beaumont.

No, Oliver wasn't bringing his granddaughter home. He'd keep her right there on Spindletop until she and her husband reconciled. Travis wanted that; he and Oliver kept in touch, and Travis was keeping his eye on the girl, giving her advice when she needed it. So far she'd been smart enough to overcome her suspicions and take that advice. Smart girl, Jessica. Deserved a smart husband, and Oliver intended to see that she kept the one she had.

Chapter Twenty

"It's called the Easy Washing Machine," said Jessica as she demonstrated its operation to her housekeeper. "See. You turn this handle to stir the clothes around, and this is the wringer. It rolls the water out."

"Does handle take smell from water?"

"'Fraid not." Jessica grinned at Rainee. "But it's better than washing clothes in a cold stream." The housekeeper went into the kitchen to fetch a large kettle of hot water. When she returned, Jessica resumed the conversation.

"Where are you from, Rainee?" Jessica knew her questions to be intrusive, but she couldn't resist asking.

"Comanche Reservation in Oklahoma," said the woman.

"Are you—ah—a full-blooded Comanche?"

"Grandmother was slave, then captive, then second wife of war chief."

"Really?"

"You not think war chief marry slave?"

"Oh, I didn't mean that," said Jessica, flushing.

"No soul inside black skin," said Rainee impassively.

"That's nonsense," cried Jessica, aghast.

"Comanche believe no soul in black skin. Never take scalp of slave."

"Well, that must have been a blessing of sorts," Jessica mumbled, wishing she'd controlled her curiosity.

"But war chief not interested in wife with soul, looking for tall sons." Rainee's voice was sardonic.

"I only asked because my grandmother was kidnapped by a band of Comanches," Jessica explained defensively. "Her first child was born while she was still a captive."

"Indian father?" asked Rainee, thawing somewhat.

Jessica shook her head. "No, she was already married. My grandfather rescued her. Very romantic, don't you think?" she added, laughing.

Rainee didn't laugh.

"They might have known each other—our grandmothers."

Rainee looked at her as if to ask, *How likely do you think that is*?

"I suppose not," Jessica mumbled. The two women, as they talked, had been stuffing clothes into the Easy Washer. "Is Rainee an Indian name?"

"Rain Woman. Comanche name. Rainee . . ." She shrugged. "Husband give."

"Rain Woman," said Jessica dreamily. "That's nice. Is your husband a Comanche?"

"Black man," said Rainee. "Worked for freighter

298

who supplied trading post. When much work open here, he move. I move."

Jessica nodded. "Since the Beatty well came in, the town is twice as crowded, lots of new people seeking jobs."

Rainee had gone back to ignoring her.

"Well, if you understand the machine, I'm off to town," said Jessica, embarrassed at having trespassed on her housekeeper's privacy. "I'm going into the map business today."

As she pedaled away, Jessica wondered how her grandfather was going to take the inclusion of an Easy Washing Machine among her business expenses. Would he understand that a businesswoman needed clean clothes, especially in a place as dirty as an oil field, most especially in April when it was beginning to rain more frequently, turning the streets to mud?

She smiled to herself. If he didn't like it, he could always fire her. Once she had her map business going, she wouldn't need the salary, not with her earnings from the newspaper articles and the fees she charged people who asked for legal advice. Jessica always explained carefully that she was not licensed to practice in Texas and could not represent them in court; still, people came to her. Travis did. How surprised he'd been when she told him what fee she planned to charge him. He'd said in that case he should charge for his financial advice. Jessica retorted that he could trust her legal advice; she couldn't trust anything he said. He had left in a huff.

"All right, boys," said Jessica to the small crowd of ragamuffins who clustered around her. "These maps are twice as accurate as anything now being sold in Beaumont. I commissioned them from a professional mapmaker, and you should tell your customers that.

A poor map can make a difference of several thousand feet in the property lines, and several thousand feet can be the difference between wealth and poverty. Does everyone understand what I'm saying?" A dozen unbarbered young heads nodded.

"You'll be selling a better map and charging more money for it. Also, you'll be getting a better cut of the profits, so I expect you to work hard. When you need more maps, go to Mr. Kelleher at the printing shop. He'll keep track of how many you've taken out and how much money you return." Then she eyed them sternly. "If you're careless with either the maps or the money, or, worse, if you're dishonest, you'll be out of business. On the other hand, the boy who does the most business in a given week gets a bonus."

The high young voices cheered, and Jessica looked at them fondly. She had screened the boys she chose with care, poor things; they were all orphans or sons of women without husbands. Had Travis looked like one of these boys when he was homeless in Fort Worth? Jessica stifled her softer feelings for him and sent the children off to launch the new business.

"Jessica, I've got to talk to you. Why don't I come to your house tonight?" ·

"No."

Travis gritted his teeth. "All right. We'll go out to dinner."

"Just tell me what it is. There's no reason—"

"This is too important to be discussed on the street. I'll meet you at Crosby House at six. Be there."

Torn with indecision, Jessica watched him stalk away. On the one hand, she resented his brusque "Be there." On the other, he had looked very serious, and Jessica was almost afraid to ignore his invitation. Curiosity and dread overcame her better judgment, and she stayed in town to meet him, although she usually made it a point to be home with her doors locked by nightfall. No doubt, Travis would offer to see her home, but she didn't want him at her house, nor did she want to pedal home after dark. Oh, bother!

"Hurry," said Travis. "I've got a table." He hustled her into the dining room and all but pushed her into a chair at a table occupied by a man who looked perfectly villainous.

"Thanks, Bart," said Travis and handed the fellow a bill.

Greatly relieved, Jessica watched Bart leave. At least Travis didn't expect her to eat a meal with that person. "All right," she said impatiently, once they had ordered the seventy-five-cent chicken pot pie, "what's this crisis you have to talk to me about?"

"That's the gamblers' favorite, you know," he replied, adding, "the chicken pot pie," when she looked confused.

"Travis!" she snapped. Jessica felt short-tempered because he looked so attractive, while she was sure she looked a fright after a day of doing business in a muddy, oil-smeared town full of people who probably couldn't have taken a bath if they wanted to. She'd just spent two hours tramping around, checking her map sellers. It wasn't that they weren't doing well. Her maps were highly sought after. But she believed in keeping her boys honest by letting them know she had her eye on them.

"All right, Jess, but I thought we might at least have a pleasant dinner before we got down to haggling."

Jessica glanced uneasily over her shoulder and whispered, "That man has his hand on my chair."

"He wants your seat as soon as you finish."

"I haven't even been served yet. And what haggling? Do you need more lumber? I suppose you're putting up another derrick."

"I am, as a matter of fact, and I do want to buy from you. You're very reliable."

"Thank you," said Jessica, pleased. In a town known for wild dealing and double-dealing, Jessica valued her reputation as an honest and dependable businesswoman.

"But I took it for granted that we could come to terms on business matters. It's your bathtub—"

"I won't sell it," said Jessica. "I've had offers before."

"I just want to rent it, Jess."

"No. I've had offers of that sort too."

"Who wants to take baths at your house?" demanded Travis angrily.

"It's hardly your concern—"

"It damned well is."

"—because no one uses my tub but me, and watch your language, please." Then she turned completely around and glared at the man hovering behind her. Unabashed, the rude fellow stared right back.

"What are you doing with your bicycle now that the rains have started?" Travis asked.

Momentarily disconcerted by the change of subject and the stranger breathing down her neck, she muttered, "It's a problem."

"All right, let's trade."

"Trade what?" she asked suspiciously.

"You can leave your bicycle at Ervin's every day you come into town. In return, I get to use your bathtub—"

"No!"

"—say, four times a week."

"If you're sellin' baths, lady, I could use one," said the man behind her.

"I noticed," Jessica snapped and then felt ashamed of her own rudeness.

"Just four times a week," Travis wheedled. "And you get space for your bicycle five times—seven times a week if you want it."

"No!"

"Have a heart, Jessie. How would you like to go dirty? And I know for a fact that last Wednesday you couldn't get your bicycle across the street at all."

"How did you hear about that?"

"Jim Hogg told me. He lives at the Oaks on Calder Avenue."

Jessica remembered all too well the day when she had stood on one sidewalk looking at the mud that separated her from her goal, the far sidewalk. Then suddenly she had been hailed by a preposterous figure wearing an eye-catching green rain slicker and carrying a yellow umbrella. The man was driving his buggy to the Crosby House and offered her a ride after introducing himself as James Hogg.

"The governor?" she had stammered.

"Former governor, ma'am," he'd replied. "Former governor."

"This is most kind of you, sir, but I have my bicycle, which I—"

"A ridiculous machine," Jim Hogg had interrupted, and he took both Jessica and her bicycle across the street to the hotel, all the while giving her a lecture, the gist of which was that only a monkey would make a suitable rider for such a contraption. He advised a pretty young lady like herself to find a more appropriate mode of transportation.

"You can't count on former governors of the state

of Texas to come to your rescue every time the streets are afloat in mud or water," said Travis, interrupting her thoughts, "but I think you can count on solid ground from your house to Calder Avenue, where you can leave your bicycle safely at my place. In return I'll only ask to use your bathtub, say, *three* times a week."

Jessica put her fork down and glared at him.

"This weather could go on all summer."

"Surely not!" she exclaimed.

"I wouldn't be at all surprised. Just three—"

"Once," said Jessica.

"Once a week? My God, Jess, who'll want to hire me as a driller if—"

"Once."

"Twice."

"Once." Jessica found she rather liked bargaining.

"Oh, all right," grumbled Travis. "Saturday night. Starting tonight."

"Next week."

He thrust his hand across the table. Gingerly she accepted the handshake. If she'd been smarter, could she have haggled him down to once a month? Now she was going to have him naked in her bathtub every single week, the thought of which made her stomach flutter disconcertingly.

"How about some pie?"

"No. I have to get home."

"Thank God," said the impatient aspirant to her chair.

"I'll take you," Travis offered, "and then I can have my first bath."

"No."

"Now, you know you don't want to ride home by yourself."

"I'll—I'll rent a hack."

"That'll cost you twenty dollars, honey."

"Hell, I'll pay for the hack if you'll just leave," said the man behind her.

"Done," said Jessica, rising with alacrity. The man passed her a twenty-dollar bill and dropped into her seat.

"Jessica, I'm surprised at you!" Travis exclaimed.

"Never be surprised at a woman, son," said the man as he consulted the menu.

Travis paid the bill and left the necessary generous tip, arriving outside in time to see his wife loading her bicycle into a hack. Damned stubborn woman, he thought, shaking his head, but he'd win her over yet. At least, now he had his foot in the door—or bathtub, which was even better. Bathtubs were a lot more intimate than doors. He remembered fondly an interlude with Jessica in Penelope's bathtub. Well, he and Jess would never be able to squeeze into hers together, but they'd make do.

"You heard my father bragging about the money to be made on his land, and you've read the papers. We can't afford to pass up the opportunity."

"You may be right about the profits," said Hugh, "but Oliver will never sell it to us, and I'd have to leave town to pull it off with Jessica."

"Of course," Penelope agreed. "We'll get a much better price from Jessica and make more money when we sell."

"But I can't leave, Penelope. Don't you understand? I'm being watched. I have to be here in case someone makes a move against me."

"Then I'll go," said Penelope.

"You? You don't know anything about business."

"Maybe not, but I know a lot about Jessica," said Penelope complacently. "I imagine I can talk her into

305

a more advantageous price than you could."

"Not if you don't know what to offer."

"You tell me how much, and you can be sure I'll get the land for half that much. She's *so* unsure of herself, poor thing. A few little criticisms, and she'll do anything I want her to."

"I don't know," muttered Hugh. "Let me think about it."

"We *need* the money. You're always saying so. This is our chance."

"It takes money to make money," said Hugh morosely. "I don't even have enough to pay for a lot here in Fort Worth."

"We'll give her a draft on the bank," said Penelope craftily. "Then we can take our time paying it."

"That's a thought," said Hugh. "Sometimes you seem almost intelligent, Penelope, instead of just being beautiful."

"*Just*?" she exclaimed angrily.

Jessica had begun to teach a Sunday-school class at the Mosso Saloon on Highland Avenue. Everyone thought the owner a saint because he had forgone his Sunday-morning profits to allow the classes. Jessica found it somewhat disconcerting to talk about God and heaven in a place that smelled of beer, hard spirits, and cigar smoke, that had sawdust on the floor, and that crowned religious instruction with a rush of saloon customers at noon. Their thirst threatened to trample her pupils.

Still, Mr. Mosso was the only person willing to accept her group of ragamuffins, and Jessica felt that she had to do something about the state of their souls. She had caught one of them smoking a cigarette behind the post office, and another using dreadfully unsuitable language. Also, her Sunday-school activities gave her an excuse to refuse her time to various philanthropic ladies' organizations. She had been approached by the Presbyterian church ladies, who served coffee and donuts to visitors, and by the Women's Christian Temperance Union, which gave away boiled water to keep thirsty men from drinking whiskey.

The only problem with her Sunday-school class was that the boys didn't want to attend. They said if they weren't going to sell maps, they could stand in line in front of the Crosby outhouses, then sell their places to men who hadn't the time or inclination to spend hours waiting a turn. A fellow could make ten dollars a day in an outhouse line, one boy assured her.

She had to lure them to the saloon with guest speakers like Patillo Higgins, a Baptist Sunday-school teacher himself and the discoverer of Spindletop. His combination of piety and potential wealth, for there were six wells being drilled on his lease, plus his missing arm and his reputation for having been a famous brawler in his time, all made him an acceptable hero to her young map sellers.

She had approached Travis too, suggesting that he could deliver a short talk on God and the rotary oil driller, but Travis had laughed uproariously and reminded her that he had a bath coming to him Saturday night, for which he would arrive promptly, bringing her a surprise. Jessica replied that she didn't need any surprises from Travis, thank you.

In the event, she couldn't find it in her heart to refuse the surprise, a fat puppy that looked astonishingly like Governor James Hogg. Travis swept into her house from a wild spring storm after she'd given up expecting him. She had even convinced herself that his absence was a relief. The wind howled around the corners of her house, and a cold rain out of the north pounded her windows and doors so loudly that she had not at first heard Travis when he did arrive, soaked to the skin and carrying a large, mysterious roll under his arm. He dumped the roll on her sitting-room floor before stepping outside once more to shake the water off his hat and begin to shed his dripping clothes.

"Travis, come in here," she ordered as she watched the heaving, squirming bundle suspiciously. "What is this you've brought?" Travis was down to his trousers by the time he reentered.

"It's a watchdog," he replied.

"It looks like a living carpet."

He laughed and unrolled the white sheepskin rug, which had been wool side in. "Not too wet," he decided and spread it in front of her fire. "And this little fellow isn't wet at all, although he didn't much enjoy the ride." The puppy had tumbled out of the final coil and immediately begun to lick Travis's ankles. "Stop that, dog," he ordered.

"Oh," said Jessica softly and knelt to run a delighted hand through the puppy's soft, white coat. "What kind of dog is he?"

"Damned if I know, love, but he's going to be a big one, which is what you need if you're not going to let me stay here to protect you. What are you going to call him?"

"James," she replied immediately.

"Jess, everyone's going to know who you named him after."

She started guiltily, surprised that Travis too had seen the resemblance to the governor. "Maybe no one else will notice as long as we don't let him wear a green slicker or carry a yellow umbrella," suggested Jessica, giggling.

"Or make speeches on platforms or tell stories in the Crosby Bar?" He had started to peel off his wet Levi's.

"Travis, you could at least wait until I get the hot water in the tub and retire to the kitchen."

"Don't be so proper, Jessie. We were still married last time I looked."

"Mind if I have a cigar?" asked Travis when he had had his bath and dinner.

"Of course not. Go right out on the porch."

"Jessica, it's still blowing a gale out there."

"You should stop smoking cigars. They're bad for your health."

"Nonsense."

"Anything that makes you cough has to be bad for your health."

"Cigars don't make me cough."

"Of course they do. They make me cough."

"I didn't know you smoked."

Jessica gave him a long-suffering look. "And around an oil field, they're doubly dangerous. I can't believe the foolishness of any man who would risk blowing himself up just to have a cigar. And they smell bad. What woman would want to kiss a man who's been smoking a cigar?"

"If you're willing to kiss me, I'm willing to give up cigars."

"Just the other day some shoestringer was trying to get me to invest in his lease. He was smoking a cigar, so naturally I—"

"—refused to kiss him, I hope."

"Refused to invest."

309

Elizabeth Chadwick

"Stay away from the shoestringers," he agreed. "The only way to get your money out of that sort of deal is through the oil, so you can't win. If he hits a dry hole, there won't be any, and even if he brings in a gusher, oil is cheap. You get more for a barrel of water these days, and there are dry holes everywhere."

"Galey and Guffey just brought in two gushers."

Travis shrugged. "That was on the hill. All right if we go into the sitting room? I think the dog's getting lonely."

Jessica nodded and preceded him from the table, remarking over her shoulder, "I'm going to advise my grandfather to invest in cigars and beer, for which there seem to be better markets than oil, at least around Beaumont."

Travis laughed and complimented her on her business acumen as he watched her drop down onto the sheepskin rug to play with the puppy. How lovely she looked with the fire highlighting blonde glints in her hair and her lacy shirtwaist hugging the tempting lines of her breasts. Travis ached for her and thought if she didn't let him stay, he might be reduced to visiting one of the Deep Crockett girls. Maybe he should tell Jess that. Or maybe he shouldn't. If she no longer cared, he wasn't sure he wanted to know it.

He sat down in her rocking chair to the left of the fire and said quietly, "Jess, look at me."

She glanced up from her game with the dog.

"Have you forgiven me yet?"

Jessica looked away.

"I can't change the past, you know, but I promise to do everything I can to make you happy in the future."

She picked up the puppy and held him tightly against her chest as if he could protect her from the

310

pain of decisions and commitments she was afraid to make.

"Don't squeeze the dog, Jess. He doesn't like it." Travis knelt on the sheepskin rug and took the puppy, putting him into a cozy box they'd made up by the hearth. Then he drew Jessica back against his chest, his arms crossed under her breasts. "Don't you know I want only good things and happy times for you, Jessie?" he asked softly. "I've never meant you any harm."

And he'd never mentioned love, she thought sadly as she stared into the fire. Well, at least he'd been honest in that respect. He didn't feel it, so he didn't say it. "I wish you'd go home, Travis. I really wish you would. You shouldn't have talked me into this bath arrangement, and I don't think you should hold me to it."

"Oh, but I will, Jessie—to this, to the marriage. If all I can have is Saturday nights, I'll take them." He released his hold and, hands on her upper arms, twisted her so that he could kiss her mouth in dozens of angled, fleeting touches. Finally when she trembled with frustration, Travis slid the last kiss off to her ear and whispered, "If I have to suffer this deprivation, sweet Jessie, I want to be sure you suffer the selfsame burden."

Before she could squirm away, he slid his lips back for a deep kiss, plunging his curled tongue into her mouth, then withdrawing before she was ready to give it up. "Remember how the real thing felt?" he asked her. "We could go into your room right now and do all the things we used to do in our bed at Penelope's."

Jessica pushed him away and blinked back tears as Travis stared at her with a set face. Then he shrugged and rose. "Next time," he said and bent to lift his damp coat from the chair where she had hung it to dry. Jessica dropped her face into her hands, and he was left with the vulnerable curve of her neck to tempt him. He knelt again behind her, taking her shoulders into his hands and kissing the soft down at her hairline. "Good night, love," he whispered. "Take care of yourself." Then he left her, and she was very close to tears, very close to calling him back.

Chapter Twenty-One

Rainee's disapproving stare communicated her opinion of Jessica's appearance. "Easy Washing Machine in bad trouble," she predicted.

Jessica had entered at the back door in the middle of the day, bedraggled and coated with greenish-black oil. "A well came in on the Higgins lease," said Jessica. "I was calling on Mr. Heywood about a lumber shipment when it happened." She held her hands away from her body, oil dripping off her fingers. "I just hope I can get the mess off my bicycle."

"After much rain, oil good for bicycle. Not good for clothes." Rainee turned away abruptly. "Great Cannibal Owl in parlor."

"What?" How had an owl got into the parlor? "Can't you drive it out with a broom or something?"

"Drive mother out with broom? Good idea."

Rainee grabbed a broom that was leaning against the wall beside the icebox.

"Wait!" cried Jessica. "My mother? Anne's here?" In her delight, Jessica completely forgot the lamentable state of her clothes and bicycle. "A red-headed woman?"

"Yellow hair. Speak with coyote tongue. Hard to believe that one your mother."

"Penelope," guessed Jessica, her enthusiasm waning. "I wonder what she's doing here."

"Treating Rainee like Tonkawa squaw," said Rainee ominously.

Assuming that it was an insult to be treated like a Tonkawa squaw, Jessica said, "Rainee, I am sorry."

"Uh-huh. I wash you off before you see Great Cannibal Owl."

"Great Cannibal Owl?" Jessica started to grin.

"Bad Comanche children eaten by Great Cannibal Owl unless change ways."

Jessica started to giggle at the idea of her beautiful, stylish mother being cast as the Great Cannibal Owl.

"No reason laugh. That one eat you alive. That one not act like mother."

"She actually is my mother," Jessica admitted, "but only by blood."

"Your servant is impudent, Jessica," said Penelope. "And goodness knows what racial stock she comes of. How could you hire such an unsuitable person?"

"Rainee suits me very well," snapped Jessica, furious that her mother would criticize Rainee, who had been a lot better friend to Jessica than Penelope ever had. And what was Penelope doing here, hundreds of miles from Fort Worth? The only travel that interested her involved the purchase of clothing, and Beaumont was hardly a fashion center.

"Is this a social call, Penelope? Perhaps you were worried about my welfare," Jessica suggested sarcastically. Jessica had written her several letters, but Penelope had not written back or communicated in any way.

"Well, I hardly think it my place to worry about you, Jessica," said Penelope, responding to the sarcasm. "It was, after all, your own decision to ignore my wishes and leave town. Goodness, you could have been married to any number of eligible young men by now if you'd let me arrange it."

"I'm already married. Did you want me to commit bigamy?"

"Are you living with Travis Parnell again?" demanded Penelope. "Have you no pride whatever? The man only married you because—"

"I am not living with Travis," Jessica interrupted. "I—I hardly ever see him."

"You should *never* see him." Penelope dropped petulantly into Jessica's best chair. "What a dreadful little house. Whatever possessed you to move in here? And I notice that you're wearing those tasteless short skirts again. In fact—" Penelope squinted at Jessica "—you haven't been rinsing your hair, have you? It's that mousy brown again."

Jessica gritted her teeth. Until now, she hadn't realized how much she enjoyed life in Beaumont. Here no one criticized her taste or appearance. Here she always had something interesting to occupy her time. And furthermore, she *was* rinsing her hair in the lemon preparation. From this moment forward she vowed to stop thinking about the drawbacks of Spindletop and appreciate what she had.

"Well, Mother, to take your objections in order, this dreadful little house belongs to Grandfather; I can tell him you object to it if you like." Jessica noted with satisfaction that her mother looked alarmed. "Then you mentioned my skirts. They're practical, given the mud and oil everywhere. Your skirts, I noticed, are soiled at the hem, and take my word for it, you'll not get the oil stains out. Then—what was it? Oh, my hair. Decent water is in short supply here. Also lemons. I do the best I can with what's available in the way of time and supplies. I think Grandfather might object if I spent more time on my hair than his business, but again, I can pass your complaint on to him." Jessica was feeling quite smug at the end of her counterattack because her mother looked absolutely stunned. What had Penelope expected? That Jessica would burst into tears?

"My goodness, Jessica, don't be so sensitive. If I seem critical, it's for your own good, and for heaven's sake, don't bother your grandfather." Penelope then flashed a brilliant smile and added, "Actually, my dear, I think you'll be delighted with the nature of my errand. I am here on business."

Jessica gave her mother a wry look. Business? What business could Penelope have here? And if she really did, why hadn't she let Grandfather Duplessis handle it for her instead of traveling all the way to Beaumont?

"Your grandfather has been telling us about the land he owns here, which he expects you to sell for him, so Hugh and I have decided to help you out, dear, by buying it. Hugh is . . . rather busy just now, so he asked me to handle the matter."

Jessica frowned at her.

"Aren't you pleased?" asked Penelope impatiently.

"All of it?"

"Well, that will depend on how good a price you make me," Penelope replied, smiling coyly.

Jessica had seen that particular smile directed at various men, even Travis, but never at herself. "Land speculation can be a risky venture," said Jessica.

"Nonsense," Penelope snapped, waving a dismissing hand. "The papers are full of the fortunes being made."

Her mother had oil fever, thought Jessica, astonished. "The land is terribly expensive," she murmured. "Especially on the hill where I guess it's ten times as much as acreage surrounding Spindletop."

"Well, since it's all in the family, and since I'm doing you a favor by—"

"Penelope, have you talked to Grandfather about this?"

"Your grandfather will be delighted to—"

"Yes, but have you *talked* to him?"

"Well, Jessica, I thought *you* were in charge. Of course, if you're just a little errand girl . . ." Penelope paused, obviously expecting to goad Jessica into an ill-considered reaction.

"I would certainly have to consult Grandfather before making any special prices—for you or anyone," said Jessica.

Penelope frowned. "How little family feeling you have—and after I took you in and paid for your wedding and your—well, no matter. I can see that such considerations mean nothing to you."

She waited, expecting Jessica to show some family feeling. Jessica remained silent. "How much do you expect me to pay for this land?" Penelope demanded angrily when it became obvious that Jessica was not going to respond to either bullying or appeals to sentiment.

After ascertaining that Penelope was interested in buying rather than leasing, Jessica quoted what she thought might be the going rates on various parcels owned by her grandfather. Presumably her mother and Hugh planned to resell later when the prices had risen.

"Well, it's obvious that getting more land for less money is better than less land for more money," said Penelope smugly.

"Not necessarily," warned Jessica, wanting to be fair. "Travis says the off-hill land will lose its value sooner or later because there'll be no oil there."

"You *have* been seeing him!" exclaimed Penelope. "Have you no shame, Jessica? Even if you're not very pretty, at least you could maintain your pride by staying away from a man who used you so abominably. And if you're too stupid to see that he's trying to do us damage again, I'm not. He obviously said that because he himself wants to get that lower-priced land cheap."

"No, he—"

"Don't be a fool, Jessica, and don't take me for one."

"Very well, Penelope," said Jessica grimly.

"This is certainly more than I expected to pay," said Penelope frowning, "but goodness gracious, we'll still make lots and lots of money." Her face lit up at the thought. "I'll write you a draft on Cattleman's this very minute."

"We only deal in cash."

"I'm your mother. I—"

"You made it clear to me months ago," Jessica cut in, "that I'm not to think of you that way."

"I said not to *call* me Mother. Of course you may think of me as your mother."

"It doesn't matter. When it comes to land, it's cash only," Jessica insisted.

"Why, you selfish little chit," snarled Penelope. "You and Travis probably plan to have that land for yourselves, but that's my father's land. I have a right to make the profit on it. Why, I've a mind to talk to Father about the way you've treated me."

"Do that," Jessica replied. "And keep in mind that the price goes up all the time."

"You just said it was going to fall."

Jessica shrugged. "Sooner or later, if Travis is right, it will."

Penelope rose, jabbing the tip of her parasol against the floor with a sharp click. "I'll be back," she announced threateningly. "See that you don't sell before I return."

"I'll make the best deal I can for Grandfather. After all, I'm his agent, not yours."

"Father does not need the money," said Penelope. "You're both being shockingly greedy, and I don't know how he can trust important matters to a stupid girl like you. If I don't buy the land, you'll probably manage to do the wrong thing with it, and then where will I be when Father dies and I inherit his estate?"

Jessica looked at her with distaste. Grandfather Duplessis was in excellent health for a man his age and had always been very generous with his daughter in the past, or so Jessica had heard. How could Penelope talk about his death with such indifference? Rainee's description of her as the Great Cannibal Owl no longer seemed so funny.

"And I want you to know how much I resent your forcing me to make this trip *twice*. Two days on a disgusting train to get here! Of course, the conductor and various gentlemen were very attentive—" Penelope had gathered up her parasol and reticule "—but I should be home seeing to my fall wardrobe. I had to

319

miss two appointments with my dressmaker." She left without even saying good-bye and climbed daintily into the waiting hack.

Jessica shook her head in amazement; Penelope had once again outdone herself in the contest for most selfish and insensitive mother of the year. After coming so far, she had criticized Jessica's housekeeper, home, and appearance, tried to interfere in her marriage, proposed to satisfy her greed at Jessica's expense—because Jessica was sure Grandfather Duplessis would not appreciate any financial losses negotiated for Penelope's sake—and then left—without showing the slightest interest in Jessica's welfare or activities. She hadn't even stayed to tea.

Jessica felt so depressed by the visit that she didn't do any more business that day. The idea that she might be handling her grandfather's interests badly nagged at her, making her feel uneasy and indecisive, hardly a frame of mind in which to be out making deals. Had Travis been giving her bad advice about the future of land values? Was he again trying to set someone in her family up for a loss? Everything he had said made sense to her, especially after she talked to knowledgeable oil men like Captain Lucas and Patillo Higgins and to other drillers like the Hamils and the Sturms. But then maybe they would back Travis up because he was one of their own. Maybe he had warned them to support him. Maybe they were all laughing about how gullible she was.

"Whatever coyote tongue say to you," Rainee advised, "you not listen."

Jessica had been rocking in her rocking chair, hands clenched in her lap, for over an hour when the housekeeper came in and gave her a stern look.

"Woman like that make bad medicine. She say not call her Mother?"

Jessica nodded unhappily.

"Then not think mother. Think Great Cannibal Owl want to eat you. Or maybe you not trust Rainee?"

"Rainee, you're about the only person in Beaumont I do trust." Jessica rose impulsively to clasp the woman's hands. "I do feel so alone here sometimes."

Rainee's severe face softened. "You give me protection. I give you good counsel."

They smiled at one another. Several days earlier Jessica had arrived home for the noon meal to find Rainee being harassed by a strange white man. Jessica had given him a sharp poke with her umbrella and, having got his attention, her best Mount Vernon Seminary look, after which she said, "If I ever see or hear it said that you have bothered my housekeeper again, sir, I shall have Sheriff Ras Landry arrest you, and if you should ever get out of jail, I have friends who would be glad, on my behalf, to shoot you."

The man had scuttled away, leaving Rainee looking surprised at Jessica's nerve and Jessica feeling rather pleased with herself. She had even offered to purchase a firearm for Rainee's protection, although she admitted that she herself abhorred them.

"Who shoot it?" Rainee asked dryly. "I shoot white man, I get hung. You maybe faint before you pull trigger." Jessica had giggled; Rainee ventured a half smile. "We do fine. You have cold eye of mother panther; I have claws." She lifted one side of her skirt to reveal an evil-looking knife in a sheath strapped to her thigh.

"Could you use that?" asked Jessica, greatly impressed.

Rainee shrugged. "Skin of man more tender than hide of buffalo."

"My goodness." Jessica hadn't known what to say,

but she felt safer after that. In a really tight spot, a knife was probably more potent protection than a cold eye.

"I go home now," said Rainee, bringing Jessica back to the present. "You all right?"

Jessica nodded reluctantly. She still hated being alone in the house, and her mother's unpleasant visit had left her feeling very vulnerable. Consequently, an hour later when there was a knock at her door, her fear tempted her to pretend the house was empty, although the lamps were lit. Hesitantly, she approached the window and peered out, convinced after a moment that the tall figure on her porch was Travis. Why had he come? she wondered. It wasn't Saturday. Had something terrible happened?

"Travis?" she called cautiously.

"Who else?"

He sounded so sure of himself that Jessica could have kicked him once she had the door open. He was grinning widely until he saw her face. Then he frowned and stepped in without asking. "What is it? Has someone been bothering you?" He looked absolutely fierce, and his very protectiveness made her feel less prickly, although at the back of her mind was the thought that relaxing in his presence was dangerous.

"Why are you here?" she asked. "You're only allowed on Saturday."

"I want you to cut my hair."

That request took her by surprise. "I don't know anything about hair cutting," she stammered. "Why would you ask me?"

"Because by the time I get back to town from the drilling site, my barber has already rented out all his chairs for the night. People sleep in them," he added

322

in answer to her puzzled look. "If I don't get a haircut soon, my hair will be as long as yours."

Jessica looked at him suspiciously. Was this some new ploy? she wondered. Maybe not. His hair was long. He looked rather like a shaggy frontiersman, maybe the way her father had looked as a young man driving cattle to Kansas, coming home to his mother's ranch in Palo Pinto County, which was still dangerous country in those days. As Spindletop was in these.

"Jessica, what is it, honey?" Travis asked.

"Nothing." She shook off her fantasy. "I guess I could cut your hair, but I've never done anything like that."

"I'm not fussy," Travis assured her. "I just want to get it off my shoulders."

She nodded and led him to a straight chair in the kitchen, draped a large cloth over his shoulders, and went to look for her comb and scissors. When she began to comb out the tangles the wind had blown in, Travis sighed and relaxed. Jessica tried not to notice how pleasant his hair felt in her hands, but its springy strength seemed to move with a life of its own, and its silkiness slipped across her skin, making her fingertips and palms tingle.

This had been a bad idea; any situation where she had to touch Travis was. Pressing her lips together firmly, she picked up the scissors and tentatively closed them on a lock toward the back of his neck. As she worked around toward his face, she asked him casual questions about land values, hoping to get some reassurance against her mother's accusations, hoping to find out that she wasn't a fool for beginning to believe him—and his colleagues. She hated being so unsure of herself.

Her lack of confidence must have shown in her voice, because after she had put the scissors down and carefully brushed away the bits of cut hair, Travis caught both of her hands in his and asked gently, "What is it, Jess? You seem so troubled tonight."

Jessica bit her lip and turned away defensively.

"No, don't shut me out, honey. Let me help."

Hesitant, she glanced to him. Could she trust him? "I'm never sure that—that I'm handling things properly. I'm so new to this."

"Why, Jess, you're doing wonderfully well. Your grandfather would be the first to complain if you weren't."

"Maybe he expects all sorts of stupid mistakes. Maybe he's just humoring me or—"

"Nonsense." Travis pulled her firmly down onto his lap. "Who's been criticizing you? Don't let some stupid man take advantage of you by saying a woman doesn't know what she's doing."

"It wasn't a man," she whispered miserably.

"Not a man?" He looked nonplused, then forced her chin up. "Have those church ladies been bothering you again? No, they wouldn't be talking about land speculation."

"Penelope was here." The whole story spilled out while Travis held her tight against his shoulder and stared grimly over her head.

"All right," he said when she was finished. "This is what you do, Jessie. Walk into the Crosby and say you've got land to sell. The offers will pour in, and you'll find out what top dollar is on those parcels off the hill. Then when she gets back with the cash, and she will because Penelope wants to make a quick killing at your expense and your grandfather's—"

"But why?"

"Because she's greedy. When she comes around

with the money, don't back down a penny on the price."

"But she could lose it all."

"Did you warn her?"

Jessica nodded unhappily.

"Then it's her lookout. Yours is to protect Oliver's interests. If you're still worried about this, get in touch with him. Tell him what's happening."

"I don't want to cause trouble between them."

"Oh, Jess, you're such a sweet thing." His arms tightened. "You don't deserve to be thrown in among the lions, and I include myself among them, honey," he admitted, tipping her chin up with one finger.

She tried to pull away, but Travis held on.

"I haven't had a cigar all day." He was smiling whimsically. "Decided this morning I couldn't wait till Saturday to see you, and I didn't want to come by smelling bad."

"Well, that's one more day you managed to survive without blowing yourself up at the well head," she mumbled, feeling warm and weak in the circle of his arms.

"If it matters to you, I'll quit smoking entirely," he murmured and bent his head slowly toward her mouth, giving her the opportunity to withdraw.

She didn't. By that time she yearned to feel the exciting pressure of his lips again and the hot certainty of his passion, which was the one thing she had never doubted in their relationship. Travis had continued to want her since the first time they'd made love, just as she continued to want him, more tonight than ever before. She reveled in the rough texture of his tongue when she allowed him access. In a whirl of confused excitement, his hands seemed to be everywhere, touching her back and breasts, loosening her clothes and his own until she found herself astride him, still on the straight chair in her kitchen, gasping as she reacted explosively to his initial entrance.

"Too long," he muttered. "I don't have any control when I can't have you in my bed all the time." He had followed her immediately over the peak. "But I'll do better." Travis lifted her with him as he rose and pushed their clothing carelessly into some semblance of order, then swung her up into his arms. "Which door to the bedroom?"

"We shouldn't."

"Yes, we damned well should, Jessica." He chose a door and carried her through to what was not actually her room. There were no sheets or blankets on that bed, but with Travis disrobing her, following his careful fingers with maddening lips, Jessica hadn't the breath or the desire to protest further or point out his mistake.

When he had unbuttoned her shirtwaist, brushing his fingertips repeatedly over her nipples as he did so, and disposed of her corset and camisole, he rubbed and rolled the tender, rosy nubs to aching excitement before unbuttoning her skirt and petticoat and dropping them to the floor. Since her drawers had been left in the kitchen, she was bare and vulnerable when, on his knees, he clasped her waist and buried his lips and tongue in her navel, then at the juncture of her thighs. Jessica's knees had begun to wobble and the moans to well in her throat when he took pity and lifted her to the bed and covered her.

A tiny whimper escaped from her arched throat as he took her once more, and he whispered, "We're all alone, sweetheart. We've no one to please but ourselves, and there'll be no one to complain in the morning."

Then he plunged into the warm haven of her body

and drove a cry of ecstasy from her that she had never been able to release before. Their lovemaking was fierce and anguished, prolonged to a point so savage and tender that Jessica sometimes found herself clinging precariously to consciousness, at other times painfully sensitive to each sensation and wildly exultant with the knowledge that she was driving Travis into excesses of feeling well beyond his own control.

They so exhausted one another that Rainee was in the house the next morning before Jessica even thought of how embarrassed she'd feel to be discovered by her housekeeper in the arms of a man never seen there before. Travis was quite unruffled. He introduced himself, ate a huge breakfast cooked by the housekeeper, kissed Jessica lingeringly, and went off, humming exuberantly, to his latest derrick.

Once he was out the door, Rainee gave Jessica a straight look and said, "Taking in strange man dangerous. Not like you."

"He's my husband," Jessica mumbled.

"Oh?" Rainee's brows rose. "Why husband not live here?"

"Because we're estranged."

"Estranged?" Rainee frowned at the unfamiliar word. "Now estranged husband move clothes into Jessica's lodge?"

"No," said Jessica.

"Why not? You need man. He looks like good one."

Jessica didn't know what to say. She could explain why Travis was not a good man, but then how could she explain why she had let him back into her bed? How could she explain that to herself, much less Rainee? Well, she'd have to give it some thought, since she'd need a defense by nightfall. Travis would be back, of that she was sure, and in the meantime she had business to conduct. Jessica intended to take Travis's advice by finding out exactly what her grandfather's land was worth, and that was what she'd charge Penelope, not a penny less. The Great Cannibal Owl could try to eat up someone else's profits; Jessica intended to protect her own.

Chapter Twenty-Two

"I'm afraid you misunderstood, Travis," said Jessica when he appeared at her door that evening.

"Honey, it would be hard to misunderstand what happened between us last night."

"True," she agreed, and Travis smiled at her. "You just misunderstood what it meant."

He felt his optimism begin to dissipate. Jessica was too cool. She hardly seemed the same woman who had moaned in his arms the night before. He had been distracted by the memory all day. Men from two different crews remarked on his carelessness, which made him uneasy. A driller who valued his hide kept his mind on his business when he was working in the oil fields. "Maybe you'd better tell me, Jess," he said. What the hell could it have meant? She still loved him, that's what; she was ready to take him back.

"Pleasure," said Jessica. "I enjoy your—ah—attentions, and since we are married, for all I meant little or nothing to you when you proposed to me—"

"Jess, that's not—"

"—relevant?" she interrupted sweetly. "Well, perhaps not, but misunderstandings do happen. I misunderstood the nature of your interest in me initially, and you misunderstood mine last night. Just because I enjoyed your visit doesn't mean you can move in with me, Travis. Goodness, I'd have to be on guard all the time." She shook her head, as if dismayed at the toll such vigilance would take. "I guess what it amounts to is that you used me initially; last night I returned the favor. And after all, why not? As I said, we are married—more or less."

The idea that a woman, particularly Jessica, who had been an innocent when he first married her, would use him for physical satisfaction seemed quite alien to Travis, and yet, as she said, why not? He'd taught her to enjoy the physical pleasures; she was just profiting from the lesson—and getting back at him in the bargain. "I guess if being used is all I'm allowed for now," he replied, trying to control his temper and salvage what he could from the situation, "I'll have to be happy with that, won't I? Are you in the mood tonight, or do I have to wait for Saturday?"

"I didn't say I wanted you on a regular basis," she snapped.

"Now *you* misunderstand, honey. I didn't mean just sex. We made a deal. Your bicycle; my bath. See you Saturday."

Jessica glared after him as he jumped off her porch. When she had plotted her defense, she had expected him to be at least somewhat offended, maybe even a little embarrassed or hurt at the idea that she viewed him as a sort of male sporting lady. Instead he'd hardly blinked an eye. Men! What pigs they were! It was just as that article in *Vogue* had said;

they didn't know a thing about romantic love.

Should she let him in Saturday? After all, last night had been . . . Jessica blushed at her own thoughts and sulkily headed into her house, telling herself she had better things to think about than Travis Parnell. Tomorrow she would visit the Crosby to see what offers she got on the land Penelope wanted. How furious Penelope would be if she knew Travis had spent the night. Too bad, thought Jessica angrily. She couldn't stand either of them.

Travis, for his part, was still trying to deal with his own amazement as he mounted his horse and set out for Calder Avenue. The little devil, he thought admiringly. Could she have decided she needed some loving and used him to get it? If so, she'd sure as hell better not consider getting it elsewhere.

Surprised, Travis pulled the horse up. Was he jealous? He'd never been jealous of a woman before, but then he'd never felt about any other woman the way he felt about Jessie. Travis wished that he could tell her, but she was still too angry. She'd never believe him. In fact, knowing Jessica, he assumed that any declarations of love from him at this point would only increase her distrust.

But in the meantime, he worried about her. This was a rough town for a girl on her own, a girl raised mostly in a fancy, sheltered boarding school. He didn't know what he'd do if anything bad happened to Jessica. She'd have been safe at home under Anne Harte's protective wing if it weren't for him. But if she was safe in Weatherford, he'd have no chance to win her back. Travis groaned. If only she'd forgive him so they could get on with their lives.

"She insists on cash," said Penelope.
"I don't have it," Hugh muttered.

"But we can't pass up this opportunity. People are making millions. They buy the land one day and sell it for twice as much the next. Even at the price she's asking, in only a few months we'd be millionaires— many times over. Think of it, Hugh. Rich beyond our wildest dreams."

Hugh Gresham, who had taken terrible chances to save his bank by buying Justin Harte's shares, wanted to invest in the Spindletop land as much as Penelope did. He too saw it as a chance to be wonderfully rich, rich at the expense of his father-in-law, who had always refused to trust him. However, Hugh saw no way to get the cash they'd need. He was being watched. He couldn't afford to take chances. He couldn't even leave town, because he had to be on hand to juggle the books when necessary and to take advantage of his connection with Cassidy when the opportunity arose.

"The bank is full of money," said Penelope.

"It's not ours."

"Borrow it. You've done it before, and we'll have it back in the accounts before anyone misses it."

"Penelope, for God's sake, I could be ruined. I'd—we'd—"

"Two months, Hugh. No one would ever know."

Travis awoke feeling gloomy and resentful. Damn her. She still didn't trust him. Within two hours his mood improved because a gusher came in on his own land, drenching him and his crew in black-green muck and bringing the usual crowd of excited gawkers. He took the strike as a good omen; most of the wells he drilled, those done on sites chosen by the owners or leasers, turned up dry holes. His own hadn't; still, given the price of oil, which was less per barrel than a bottle of water, he thought he'd sell the new well to someone with more money than sense. There were plenty of those around.

"Grandfather's here," said Jessica when Travis arrived for his Saturday bath.

Travis scowled; he'd been planning a passionate night of being used as the object of Jessica's pleasure. An evening of conversation with Oliver Duplessis might be interesting, but it wasn't what he'd had in mind. Did the old man plan to stay at the house with Jessica? Travis certainly hoped not.

"My boy," said Oliver expansively, "why haven't you and my granddaughter made up your differences?"

"I'm certainly willing," said Travis. Maybe Oliver's visit wasn't such a bad idea.

"I'd like to see some great-grandchildren before I die," boomed the old man.

Travis gave Jessica a long look, thinking of the time when he'd imagined her to be with child. How happy he'd been at the thought. Unfortunately, he'd been wrong about that, just as he'd been wrong to think he could keep his deception from her. He sighed, wondering if he'd ever win her back, if they'd ever have a child together.

Jessica turned away when she heard her grandfather's words. She had been reading an article by Dr. D. Abraham Jacob, who recommended what he called "scientific birth control." Jessica had decided that if she were so foolish as to give in again to her embarrassing passion for Travis, at least she'd better be sure not to get herself trapped by pregnancy. Unfortunately, Dr. D. Abraham Jacob hadn't been specific about how one went about practicing "scientific birth control."

"All my inquiries lead me to believe that your

advice to hold onto my land here was very good," Oliver continued.

"Has Jessica told you that your daughter wants to buy it?" Travis asked.

"Yes," said Oliver, "and I've told her to let Penelope have it at ten percent above market value."

"But, Grandfather, if Travis is right, Mother and Hugh stand to lose huge amounts of money."

"I don't doubt Travis *is* right, which means we want to be out of the market before the end of May. Let's see; it's the end of April now; if Penelope hasn't returned with the money by, say, the fifteenth, sell at the best price you can get."

"But not on the hill," Travis warned. "Those prices will skyrocket once everyone realizes how many dry holes there actually are elsewhere. I've drilled dozens myself. You can see the boiler smoke everywhere across the plain."

"Mother's going to be furious if she takes a loss," Jessica fretted.

Shrugging, Oliver snapped, "You warned her, didn't you? My daughter always was headstrong— not to mention greedy. She thinks she and Hugh are going to reap a profit from my foresight. When she loses, she'll learn a valuable lesson about the pitfalls of greed."

Jessica was surprised at how cold her grandfather sounded.

Travis listened with interest. What he had hoped for seemed to be happening. Oliver was turning away from his daughter and toward his granddaughter. Good. Jessica deserved the love and support of someone in her family. She had had it from Cassandra Harte, but Cassandra was dead. Oliver would make a good substitute. He was a gruff old man, not outwardly affectionate, but his good opinion was something to be valued, and Jessica had earned it, a fact she could be proud of. As for Penelope, if she became estranged from her father and his considerable fortune, good. Travis would be happy for her.

"And what do you plan to do with the land on Spindletop?" asked her grandfather.

Jessica, who had been clearing away the remains of dinner, paused and looked thoughtful. "I thought I might wait for a few more gushers to come in, then drill myself."

Both her grandfather and Travis frowned, for they knew that it was the landowners, not the operators, who were making money.

"Got oil fever, do you?" asked Oliver dryly.

"Heavens, no. I hate the idea of a derrick in my yard."

"So do I," said Travis. "An oil well's damned dangerous. I don't want you—"

"Who are you to talk?" she interrupted. "You're always around them."

"Now, now, children," Oliver intervened with a smug grin. "I'm pleased to see that you're concerned about each other—" they both gave him surprised looks "—but we're talking business. I want to hear Jessica's plans."

"If I strike oil on your hill land, Grandfather," Jessica continued, giving Travis a haughty what-business-is-it-of-yours look, "and the chances are good, according to Travis, that I will, then I'll probably sell the well to someone else. Goodness, a proven producer should bring lots of money. Why are you grinning, Travis?"

"Because you're absolutely right, sweetheart, and a man likes to know he's got a real smart wife."

Jessica flushed with pleasure, although he was wrong; most men would be furious to think they had smart wives, unless the wives kept that intelligence well hidden. Damn Travis Parnell anyway. Just when she thought she'd got the best of him, he said something that turned her stupid heart right over.

"Well, anyway," she mumbled, "if I can bring a producing well in and sell it at an absolutely sinful price, I'll cut the rest of the hill land up into the smallest parcels anyone can get a derrick on and sell or lease that too."

Oliver roared with laughter. "Girl, you're worth your weight in gold."

"I'm glad you think so, Grandfather," she replied promptly, "because from now on I want to work on commission."

"Do you now?" The old man sank his bulldog chin down onto his chest, creating several hundred more wrinkles.

"Yes," she said somewhat belligerently.

"You have that much confidence in yourself?"

"Yes." Jessica wondered if she was allowing herself to be prodded by the resentment she had felt when Penelope intimated that she was incompetent.

"Good," said the old man. "We'll draw up a contract."

"Wait a minute," Travis objected. "I don't want her living in the middle of a forest of oil derricks. Have you ever seen an oil-field fire?"

The two looked at him as if he were some interloper trying to interfere in matters that didn't concern him. "If you want to decide where she lives, boy," said Oliver, "you'll have to talk her into living with you."

Jessica scowled. "Isn't it time you were getting back to Beaumont, Travis?" she asked. "I'll show you to the door."

With her hands folded demurely at her waist and

336

her mouth set in the gracious lines the students had practiced at her school, Jessica glided through the sitting room ahead of her fuming husband. "Good night, Travis," she murmured, and she opened the door for him.

Travis grasped her wrist and yanked her out on the porch, pinning her between his own aroused body and the clapboard wall. Abandoning the lady-of-the-manor act, Jessica responded by pressing her hips forward and digging her fingers painfully into the hard muscles of his back as she lifted her mouth hungrily to his. When they broke apart, she murmured, "So nice of you to come by, Travis."

"When's Oliver leaving?" Travis snarled.

"Oh, Monday or Tuesday, I believe." Jessica leaned her head back against the wall, breasts rising in quick, shallow breaths.

"I'll be by then."

"That wasn't our agreement."

"I missed my bath." He had cupped two large hands over her bottom and lifted her against him. "My bath and more important things."

"Nothing of real importance," she murmured, airily deceitful. Her loins were melting with desire.

"Nothing important? Jessica, honey, about two more minutes of this, and I could take you right here against the wall with your grandfather in there wondering where the hell you were. Oh, and there's no way I'm going to let you live out here by yourself surrounded with derricks. There are a thousand dangerous things that could go wrong."

"Rainee, does your husband work in the oil field?" Jessica asked.

"They not want our kind on rigs. Easterners think colored can't do white man's job." Rainee smiled a slow, bitter smile. "White man not know colored think work on rig mean quick trip to land beyond sun."

A quick trip beyond the sun? Jessica took that to mean a quick death. "You mean from the fires?" Shivering, Jessica reminded herself that if she drilled in her own yard, she exposed herself to that danger, and Travis risked his life daily. One careless cigar, sparks from a train, and either or both of them could die.

"Not just fire," said Rainee. "Well blows in, workers breathe evil air, go blind, fall off platforms. Some drown in mud. Some knocked on head or killed when rocks and pipes fly like arrow from bow. White men every night fight, shoot, knife."

Jessica looked at Rainee with horror. She'd never realized how many dangers Travis exposed himself to.

"Jed, Rainee's husband, drive wagon, build derrick, house, store. White skins make more money. Dark skins live longer." Rainee smiled coldly. "Money make death."

"Are you sure you want to do this?" Jessica eyed her mother anxiously. Penelope was as fashionably dressed as always, wearing a beautifully cut yellow gown with diagonal panels of lace overlaid across the skirt and an immense black hat topped by two birds' wings dyed yellow to match the dress. Still, there were disturbing lapses in her appearance—a loose strand of hair, the color of which seemed wrong; a spot on the tucked front of her bodice; splashes of mud on the trailing flounces.

Admittedly, May had brought increasing rain and with it mud, but Penelope, who was usually so fastidious about her appearance, seemed unaware of the other lapses. Her hands had developed a fine tremor, her voice a tendency to rise out of control. She had always kept Jessica on edge with her critical remarks; now her whole demeanor was disturbing.

"Of course I do," Penelope replied, a note of near hysteria threading her voice. "You gave your word."

Jessica had done no such thing. "The price is fifty thousand an acre. That's a lot of money."

"I know that, and you see, I was right. It's rising all the time."

"But—"

"Don't try to cheat me. The money's been transferred here to the bank where you do business. We'll go immediately. I know you want the land for yourself, but I won't allow it. It's my right to—to—did you tell your grandfather? Is it his idea to keep me out?"

"Grandfather says you must do whatever you want," Jessica replied.

"See! See! Papa sided with me. He's always loved me best. He used to call me his little sweet pea. His beautiful little sweet pea. Isn't that ridiculous? Such a common flower. I'll show him. Hugh and I are going to be richer than—than anyone. No one will ever say I picked the wrong man." Penelope snapped her parasol open. "Let's go. Why are you stalling?"

"I'm quite ready, Penelope."

Jessica opened her own parasol, and as her palm slid over the carved ivory handle, she thought of Travis, who had given it to her as a birthday present, a very sensuous birthday present. He had said the carved woman reminded him of her, and then they had . . . Jessica took a deep breath, trying to control the wild acceleration of her heart and the heated flush that blossomed across her body. Tomorrow

Travis would come to her house. With trembling hands, she tilted the parasol behind her head.

"To the side, Jessica," snapped Penelope. "Tilt your parasol to the side. Can't you ever do anything right? The sun is touching your cheek and forehead."

To Jessica the sun felt good—wonderful—like the touch of a lover. "Turn left, Penelope," she instructed. "The bank is just a few doors down."

"Do you have the papers? I've hired a lawyer to be sure you're not trying to cheat me. Don't think you can—you can . . ." Penelope stopped right in the middle of the pushing, shoving throng on the sidewalk. "You've made me forget what I was going to say," she accused a complete stranger. The man ignored her.

Jessica wished the transaction was over. This sale would benefit her grandfather, but Penelope had not the slightest idea what she was doing. She seemed to be motivated by thoughtless greed and some frightening combination of unfounded resentment and suspicion.

Rainee had been gone for several hours, and Travis was late arriving. As always, Jessica worried about him and tried to tell herself she wasn't. To divert her anxieties, she had been making a pie of mayberries. Rainee had bought them that afternoon from a little girl who was selling baskets in Gladys City, the area for oil-field workers with families. So involved had Jessica become in trying to duplicate her mother's crust that she failed to hear Travis enter until he had pinned her hips against the work counter with his own.

"Do I get a hug?" he whispered into her ear.

"Don't be silly," she replied severely, trying to

ignore the exciting pressure of his loins against her backside. "My hands are covered with flour and pie dough. In fact, the whole front of me is. You'd better move away before you find yourself all messy too."

"I guess I'm safe as long as I keep you pinned here back to front," he laughed. "In fact—" He moved his hips provocatively against her. "In fact—" Keeping her in place with the weight of his body, he used his hands to work the back of her skirt up.

"Travis!" Jessica tried to struggle loose.

"That's having a very pronounced effect on me, sweetheart," he told her, having pulled both skirts and petticoats free. "Now let's see. What do we have here? Buttons? Tapes? Ladies' clothes are always so numerous and complicated—or maybe it just seems that way to a man who's been driven beyond discretion by a soft, squirming female bottom against his—"

"For heaven's sake, Travis, what are you doing?" Jessica wasn't sure what he had in mind, but she felt a panicky excitement.

"For heaven's sake, Jessica," he mimicked good-naturedly, "I'm about to satisfy your lusty if occasional desire to make use of me."

"But I don't—you can't—"

"Of course we can. Haven't you ever seen a stallion and a mare? We'll have a wonderful time trying out something new."

To her horror, he had loosened her drawers and boosted her upper body onto the table, at which point she began to struggle in earnest.

"Give me a minute, love, and you can wiggle all you want," he murmured, fitting himself as carefully into her as he could, given her lack of cooperation. "Ah-h. Wonderful, Jess, but just relax and let me get you

341

started." He was holding her hips firmly and moving in and out with slow deliberation. "That doesn't hurt, does it?"

Jessica was too deeply in shock to reply, but it didn't hurt. It felt—

"Relax," he crooned.

—different. She hadn't been as excited as she usually was when they got to this point. His strokes had been shallow. Now they became deeper.

"All right? Do you like it?"

Jessica wasn't sure.

"You don't want me to stop, do you?" He stayed deeply inserted and moved in short, sharp thrusts, his breathing starting to become audible.

He was getting very excited, she thought. She was, herself. A quivering had begun inside her, just the slightest tremors, nothing like the power of his drive toward satisfaction. "Don't stop," she begged, suddenly frightened that he would finish too soon.

"I won't." He began to move up and down.

"Please."

"It's going to be fine," he gasped. "Trust me."

"No, you'll—" She began to shudder.

"Now, Jess, now!" He thrust up powerfully as all her muscles clenched and released in a flood of rapture.

Somehow she found herself in her own bed, naked, Travis lying with one thigh sprawled across hers. She could never remember feeling so drained, so physically contented, or so embarrassed.

"Stop worrying about it," he said to her in a lazy, satisfied voice. "Anything we want to do is fine. It's our business, our marriage."

"What marriage?" Jessica mumbled, but with little conviction in her own protest.

"Ours. You and I are so good together we ought to make headlines from here to Fort Worth."

"Travis!" she protested.

"Want me to prove it to you again?"

"You couldn't," she laughed.

"You're probably right," he agreed ruefully. "I've never met a woman who does to me what you do."

"All I was doing was making a pie," she muttered, but in her heart she hoped that he was telling the truth. She wanted to be the woman he prized above all others.

Chapter Twenty-Three

April had been reasonably dry. During May heavy rains turned the streets of Beaumont into a bog, and Jessica had to cross on foot. As a result, she arrived late one Friday afternoon at Travis's boardinghouse with very muddy shoes and a short temper, which exploded when she found her bicycle gone from its accustomed place by the wash house in the back yard. She stamped up the front stairs and pounded at the door, demanding of Molly, the woman who had refused her admittance in March, that Travis be produced forthwith.

"Ain't here," said the woman.

"I'll wait," snapped Jessica, "inside." The drizzle had started up again, and she had no intention of being soaked before Travis returned. How like him! He had probably borrowed the bicycle himself.

"No ladies allowed inside," said the woman.

"This lady will be my dinner guest."

Jessica turned and stared at the stranger who had spoken as he mounted the steps.

"We allow no female dinner guests," Molly repeated. "You know that, Mr. Reavis."

"Ah, so we don't. An oversight that obviously needs rectification. Mrs. Parnell, so glad to meet you at last." He offered his hand. "Holland S. Reavis at your service. I've been wanting to interview you for some time." He bowed, held the door open, and ushered an astonished Jessica inside past the glaring woman, who looked as if she'd like to attack them both with her feather duster. In the dining room a number of men were already seated, passing around bowls of food at a long table.

"Gentlemen, may I present Mrs. Jessica Parnell, Travis's wife?" Jessica was introduced to, among others, a Mississippi lawyer; his partner, a young man who had been lured by oil away from his father's Louisiana coal company; Walter Fondren, a Corsicana driller who had his own business on Spindletop; and her host, Holland S. Reavis, a Saint Louis journalist covering the oil boom for his newspaper but talking of starting a journal for oil investors.

"There's enough land, lease, and stock fraud going on here in Beaumont to bankrupt the whole country," Reavis declared, helping Jessica to a slice of beef from a large roast, "and I hope to expose it. Would you care to go in with me on the journal, Mrs. Parnell?" he asked. "I've seen your articles on Beaumont in several newspapers—good stuff."

Jessica thanked him politely for his compliment, but privately she questioned his motives. Her writing was hardly investigative, and she doubted that a publication for oil investors would be long on local color, which was her forte. No, likely Mr. Holland Reavis wanted a partner with money to invest in his publishing venture. Half the people she met wanted her to invest in some scheme or other. Jessica admired his aim; the swindlers and fly-by-night oil companies needed to be exposed. However, she doubted that Grandfather Duplessis would be interested in financing the effort, and she had other plans for the money she had saved from her own earnings.

"Did you hear that Patillo Higgins has gone to court?" asked the Mississippi lawyer, addressing the table at large. "He's suing Lucas and Carroll."

"What for?" The lawsuits spawned by the oil boom fascinated Jessica.

"Higgins and the Gladys City Oil Company owned the hill, or most of it, but they hadn't the money to develop it after ten years of trying, so they sold out to Lucas. Higgins was promised ten percent of Lucas's interest, and Carroll—he's in lumber—"

"I know Mr. Carroll," said Jessica. "You might say he's a competitor of mine."

"Mrs. Parnell handles the Duplessis timber interests here in Beaumont," Reavis explained.

"No wonder she don't need poor old Travis," Fondren murmured to the coal-company heir. "Duplessis money must make Parnell look like small potatoes."

"You underestimate Travis," said the coal heir. "He's doing as well as anyone I know."

Jessica heard and gave them both a cold look. She resented having it thought that she'd left her husband for mercenary reasons. "You were saying, sir," she prompted the Mississippian.

"Well, Carroll was to match the ten percent Lucas promised Patillo Higgins, but then Lucas ran out of money and got Galey and Guffey—"

"They financed Corsicana," Walter Fondren added.

"Guffey's the money man, and Galey—that fella can *smell* oil, I swear."

"Better than Higgins?" asked the New Orleans coal heir. "I hear Higgins witched Spindletop with a peach limb."

"Nonsense," Jessica said firmly. "Mr. Higgins does not use peach limbs. He goes by more sensible signs—oil seepage, an odor like rotten eggs, that sort of thing."

"You know Higgins?" asked the Louisianian, abashed to be corrected by a woman more knowledgeable than he.

"Mr. Higgins gave a very interesting address to my Sunday school class at the Mosso Saloon," Jessica replied, helping herself to the mashed potatoes as the community bowl came her way.

Holland S. Reavis, chuckling, said, "Now I know I have to interview you, Mrs. Parnell. Canny businesswoman, lawyer, bicycle rider, saloon Sunday school teacher."

"It's very public-spirited of Mr. Mosso to forgo his illegal profits to accommodate the Lord's work," said Jessica stiffly.

"Lawyer?" echoed the Mississippian, looking astounded.

"I have the education," said Jessica grimly, "but because I'm a woman, I have neither the degree nor a license to practice."

"If I were Travis," said Fondren, "and I had me a lawyer wife, I'd sure try to get her back. Ain't a man owns land within a hundred and fifty miles of Beaumont don't need all the legal help he can get."

"What a romantic view of marriage you have, Mr. Fondren," muttered Jessica. Then she turned back to the Mississippi lawyer and prompted the continuation of his story about the Higgins lawsuit.

"Well, Lucas had to get financing from Galey and Guffey, which he did, and brought the well in, and others since, of course. Now Higgins wants his money, so he's gone to court to get it."

"So he should," murmured Jessica. "There's a wealth of cases with much less merit than that. In fact, some swindler tried to tell me he owned my grandfather's Spindletop Heights land by virtue of a few scratchings on a chewing-tobacco wrapper."

"You'll probably find yourself in court," predicted Reavis. "Your title could be in question for years, considering how overburdened the dockets are. Otherwise he'll try to get money or drilling rights from you in exchange for dropping the claim."

"Indeed he won't. My grandfather's title is well documented. When that bounder came back, I gave him the whole history and threatened to countersue, which I fully intend to do should he threaten me further."

"Good for you," said Walter Fondren admiringly. "You planning to drill on your land? Beatty just sold a proven well for a million and a quarter to a fella from New York named Pullen. You could probably do the same, ma'am, and I'd be glad to do your drilling, since you're on the outs with Travis."

Fondren was chuckling for no reason that Jessica could understand until she heard her husband's voice saying, "Walter, I never thought to see an old acquaintance from Corsicana trying to sweet-talk my wife."

"Just business, Travis, just business. If the lady needs a driller, I'm available."

"The lady doesn't need a driller. Would you want a wife of yours living in the shadow of a derrick?"

Virgin Fire

Jessica turned sharply and glared at Travis. "My bicycle's gone," she said accusingly.

"I know, sweetheart. I just got it back."

"You did?" she cried happily, then began to frown. "You took it off on some foolishness, didn't you?"

"Muddy Willie Hoberkamp took it off on some foolishness. I found him and the bicycle down on Crockett Street."

"Oh, now, Travis," roared Holland Reavis, "what were you doing on Crockett with all those ladies of easy virtue?"

Jessica felt her cheeks turn pink with embarrassment and anger.

"I was retrieving my wife's bicycle, Holland," said Travis. "Muddy Willie had it down there showing off for the ladies, and it was quite a scene, I must say. You'd have enjoyed it, Jessie."

"I doubt it," she muttered through clenched teeth.

"Well, maybe not," he admitted. "I'll swear every second one of those shady ladies had her gown or her hair covered with feathers, and I do know how you feel about feathers."

"Feathers?" asked the Louisiana coal heir, who had been blushing ever since prostitutes were mentioned in the presence of a lady.

"My wife deplores the slaughter of birds to decorate ladies' wear, but here now, I'm being distracted from my story. Muddy Willie had a bet on with some Pennsylvania driller that he could beat him in any race. Course, Willie thought they'd be running on foot or racing horses, but the Pennsylvania man picked bicycles."

"Just what I'd expect," said the coal heir. "Those Pennsylvanians don't know a thing about drilling or racing either."

349

"Course, Willie didn't have a bicycle," Travis continued, "but he'd seen you riding yours, Jessie, so he came over and borrowed it."

"I'm calling the sheriff," said Jessica angrily.

"No need. I got it back."

"What'd you do? Shoot him?" asked Reavis. "Muddy Willie's about as big and mean as any roughneck I know. I can't imagine he'd just hand over something he wanted to hang on to. Or had he already won the race?"

"Had to forfeit," said Travis. "We argued a little." Travis rubbed his jaw ruefully. "And then Willie had an accident, so he wasn't in any condition for racing."

Jessica was staring at her husband, aghast, having noticed for the first time the bruise and swelling on his chin. "Couldn't you have called in the authorities?" she asked.

"Jessie, Muddy Willie Hoberkamp is a big man with a mean temper, and he's never been on a bicycle in his life. I figured if I let him ride in that race, which he'd have done before the sheriff could get there, you wouldn't have a bicycle to get back. First time he fell off, fifty feathered ladies from Deep Crockett would have laughed themselves silly, and he'd likely have kicked your bicycle to pieces. He did that to a horse once that threw him. Knocked the horse out cold."

"Broke his own fist too," said Walter Fondren. "Couldn't have happened to a more deserving fella."

Travis took a seat beside Jessica and helped himself to meat and potatoes. "I realize you're here about your bicycle, Jess, but I must say I'm surprised to see you inside the house. How'd you manage that?"

"Mr. Holland Reavis invited me to dinner," she replied.

"Oh well, that explains it. Holland could probably

talk a Rockefeller into voting for James Hogg, the king of the Texas antitrust laws, which reminds me, I heard today that Guffey transferred that fifteen-acre J. M. Page lease to a syndicate the governor and Jim Swayne have formed. Swayne was Hogg's floor leader in the state senate when Hogg was governor," he added for Jessica's benefit.

"I know that," she muttered.

"What did he get for it?" asked Holland Reavis, whipping out a notebook.

"Hundred and eighty thousand is what I heard," Travis replied.

"I'd have held out for more if it were my land," said the Mississippi lawyer.

"Guffey may have wanted some political favors as well," Travis murmured. "Hogg still cuts a wide swath in this state."

"Besides which that title is clouded," said Jessica. "If I were a lawyer contesting it in a Texas court, I'd a lot rather do it for the governor than for some outlander."

"I told you she was one smart woman," Travis murmured to Holland Reavis. "You about ready to go, Jessica? I'll see you home, and don't bother to argue."

She didn't.

"I don't care what you say, Travis, I'm putting a well on this land. If you don't want to drill it for me, Mr. Fondren has offered."

Travis sighed. "Honey, it's just that I don't want any oil-well fires fifteen feet from your back porch."

"Then I'll have to see that the workers are careful, or I'll have to move."

"Move, hu-uh?" Travis looked thoughtful. "Well, if you're set on it."

"I am. If Mr. Beatty got a million two hundred and fifty thousand for his well, I really can't, in good conscience, forgo that kind of profit for Grandfather just to suit my own convenience."

Travis nodded. "Then I'll drill it. At least that way I can be sure it's being done with every precaution."

"Have you stopped smoking?" she demanded.

"Why? Do you want to kiss me?"

"I want you to drill my well without blowing me up," she snapped, flushing.

"No fear, love. I'm going to take good care of you. And I'll tell you another thing. Don't let a single tourist on your land. Those people are a bunch of damned fools, coming up here with women and children, smoking, turning on the valves so they can see a gusher. I heard there were fifteen thousand in town last Sunday. They seem to think this is some kind of sideshow."

"I know," Jessica agreed. "I thought I'd be jostled to death trying to get out of town from Mosso's last Sunday, and then the road was packed with men on horseback and families in every kind of vehicle. I saw women carrying babies and dragging toddlers out to see the hill." She shook her head disapprovingly. "This town is dreadful enough during the week with all the mud, oil, and boomers."

Travis laughed. "You think Beaumont's bad? You should try living out on the South Plains for a few years. Of all the ugly, flat—"

"It's ugly and flat here," Jessica interrupted.

"Here we got a few trees. In fact, Beaumont used to be a pretty town with all the oaks and magnolias. Why, the Crosby had roses and banana plants and those little purple flowers—what are they?—violets. Then the boomers trampled all over the shrubbery to put up outdoor offices on the grounds. But even now

352

we've got the river and the ocean not so far."

Jessica shrugged. She couldn't see much to like about Beaumont. "The streets are quagmires," she pointed out.

"What's a quagmire or two?" Travis grinned. "Out on the South Plains you've got the wind blowing night and day year round, leaving grit between your teeth and a prairie fire at your back. You're living in a sod house with a chimney made of sticks and clay that's likely to catch fire and take you with it any day of the year."

Jessica blanched at that picture, and Travis, looking smug, continued with relish, "If your cattle aren't stampeding, there's a plague of grasshoppers eating everything from your grass to your underwear on the wash line. There's drought in the summer and blizzards in the winter, tornadoes every spring blowing everything you own into the next county. God, I just purely hated that place."

"It does sound awful," Jessica had to admit, "but here, my goodness, our water isn't even drinkable."

"But we've got oil," said Travis. "No matter how bad things are, we've got the oil—and the excitement. Admit it, Jessie. You're having more fun than you've ever had in your life."

"Well, maybe." She had to laugh. "But it is wearing."

"You just need to get out of town for a day. What do you say we go on an excursion of our own Sunday while all the visitors are making life miserable for anyone stupid enough to stay around?"

"Where?" asked Jessica.

"Oh—how about the ocean? It's only a couple of miles south down the river. You can smell the salt air when the wind's right."

Jessica fought a losing battle with herself. Her

Elizabeth Chadwick

Sunday-school class had been canceled because Mr. Mosso caught the boys sneaking drinks behind the bar, and she did want to go with Travis. "I might consider it, but if I were to agree, you'd have to forgo your Saturday night visit here." She was interested to see what he'd decide, having always wondered whether it was herself or her bathtub that lured him to her house each week.

"Why?" he asked sharply.

Why? She could hardly tell him that she was testing him. "I'm beginning a new venture. I'll need the time to do my planning."

"What venture?"

"I've decided to go into the building business," said Jessica enthusiastically. "There's an immense demand for housing and offices, and at the rate things are burning down, the demand can only increase. Since I already have the timber supply at my command, it should be easy."

"You're right about the demand, but you know nothing about building, Jess, and getting workmen will be next to impossible. Every man who comes here wants the wages we pay in the oil field. You couldn't compete for labor."

"If I hire Nigrahs, I can."

"Now Jess, it takes a good man to get any work out of a Nigrah."

"Well, you're wrong about that, and besides, Rainee's husband's a good man, and he knows a lot about building, not to mention the fact that he's smart and ambitious. I think I'm going to make a lot of money at this."

Travis thought about her proposition, eyes narrowed. "Would that be Jedediah Beeker?" he asked.

Jessica nodded.

"Jed is a good worker," Travis admitted, "but it's

354

going to take a lot of money to get going. Still—well, if you need financing, I'll back you."

Jessica's mouth dropped open. She had thought he'd oppose the idea; instead he was offering to help. Once again she was forced to admit that Travis really did have confidence in her. "I—I do thank you for that offer," she stammered, "but I've already talked to Grandfather."

"That's fine, Jess, if you want to do this as an employee, but it's your idea. I'll help you do it on your own."

"So will Grandfather. He's lending me the money to get started. Also he said to use his name when I run across men who don't want to deal with a woman."

"You've already got a reputation for being dead reliable. I don't think you'll have too much trouble that way, and using Nigrahs, that just might put you ahead of the other builders who can't get people who'll stay on the job. Jed going to get the men for you?"

"Well, actually I still have to talk him into it. I thought I'd offer him a cut of the profits."

Travis leaned over and kissed her on the mouth.

"What was that for?" she asked, taken by surprise.

"For being as smart as you are pretty. Now are we going down to Sabine Pass come Sunday?"

Jessica lifted her face into the sharp salt breeze and savored the day. The sky was blue and sunny with cotton-boll clouds scudding across the horizon. Sometimes she thought she could see the flash of sunlight on water to the south, but the marshy plain across which they traveled was so flat that she couldn't be sure. Travis said, "Not yet," each time she asked. They were following the Neches down to the gulf, driving a rented buggy since Jessica had refused to ride horseback and Travis insisted that bicycles would have been impossible.

"Did you bring your bathing costume?" he asked.

Jessica looked at him in astonishment. "I did not."

"Well, why not? We're going to the ocean."

"Have you ever seen a proper bathing dress? A woman could drown in one of those things—unless she stayed out of the water."

"If no one's about, I suppose we can swim in the altogether," he suggested, grinning. "Do you know how to swim?"

"I do. Papa insisted that we all learn, but I have no intention of bathing without—without . . ."

Travis laughed. "Even if I promise not to peek?"

Jessica gave him a sour look which caused him to laugh harder and Jessica to change the subject quickly to the Heywood II well, which had come in just the day before. "It's bigger than anything I've ever seen," she remarked with awe.

"It's bigger than anything anyone's ever seen," said Travis, "but it's not the most important thing that's happened lately."

Jessica slanted him a questioning look.

"In the long run I reckon the Kiser Kelly dry hole will be more important. Heywood II just proved what we already knew, that there's oil on the hill. Kiser Kelly proves what no one wanted to believe—that the whole area's not floating on oil the way the government geologists said. Land prices on the plain have been falling since that one, and I reckon they'll keep falling."

"Oh, Lord," muttered Jessica. "Penelope's going to blame me."

"You warned her."

"It won't make any difference. My mother never

did function on logic, and she's stranger than ever." Jessica shivered. "She even *looks* . . . odd. Her eyes . . . and her hair. She doesn't seem to be taking care of herself, and she was always so—so—"

"Vain?" suggested Travis wryly. Again he remembered Justin Harte's warning that Penelope was dangerous. Well, let her be. Travis had plans for his wife, plans that would put her back under his protection. He'd buy her a house on Calder Avenue; he had already made the offer.

As soon as she discovered what it was like to have an oil-drilling crew in her backyard—he planned to move them in the next week—and saw the house, she'd come back to him. Then she would be safe from Penelope, for he had no doubt that the woman would be wild with fury when she found that her dreams of great wealth had metamorphosed into heavy losses.

Where had she got the money for that land? he wondered. Had Hugh collected it through his association with Butch Cassidy and the Wild Bunch, or was he raiding his own bank? Travis was glad he hadn't stayed in Fort Worth. He might have been tempted to get involved with Hugh's problems, see that the man got what was coming to him. But then maybe he wouldn't. He realized with surprise that he was free at last from that grinding desire for revenge. He'd never pass up the excitement of Spindletop or, more important, his chance to get Jessica back just to get even with Hugh and Penelope. He was free!

"There it is," cried Jessica excitedly. "It's the ocean!"

"Haven't you ever seen it?" asked Travis.

"Of course I have—the Atlantic, but I haven't seen the Gulf of Mexico, and I haven't seen any clean water in months, salt or fresh. I'd almost forgotten that it came without nasty smells and oil scum."

"Poor Jessica." Travis laughed and pulled the horses up. Within minutes they had removed their shoes and stockings, hiked up skirts and trousers, and waded into the gently lapping waves of the gulf, Jessica laughing with delight.

"The water's warm," she cried.

"Of course, honey. It's June."

"The ocean wasn't warm off the Maryland coast this time of year. Oh, it's glorious!" With one hand holding her straw hat in place, the other holding her skirt up almost to her knees, she splashed happily in the shallow waves.

Travis smiled at this picture of the girl she must have been before her touchy family situation sobered and saddened her and before he himself forced her to grow up entirely. Then he stepped forward and caught her around the waist as she began to lose her balance. "You're going to end up soaked through and through," he warned.

Jessica sighed, her laughter fading. "It's not much fun to be a girl," she said sadly. "If I weren't a girl, I could go swimming. I wouldn't have to wear a heavy wool monstrosity that would get wet and pull me under in two seconds flat."

"Who says you have to?" Travis countered. "There's not a soul here but us."

"I'm not going to take off all my clothes," she retorted stubbornly.

"Just strip down to your chemise and drawers," he suggested. "You'll be covered up enough to preserve your modesty, although why you should care with me, I don't know."

"You're not my husband anymore," she said gloomily. "It wouldn't be proper."

"Oh, Jess, what kind of nonsense is that? One week you're a shockingly modern woman, taking me to bed for the fun of it, and the next you're too modest to let me see you in your chemise. Does that make sense? Where's my hot-blooded little sensualist?"

"That's all men care about," she snapped defensively. "Pleasure. I read that men don't believe in romantic love at all—just sexual attraction."

"Nonsense!" he said sharply.

Jessica looked at him with surprise. Did he mean—

"What this man cares about at the moment is having a swim on a warm day, and I'm going to." He began to disrobe almost before he finished the sentence. "I'm going to swim straight out for about five minutes," he said to her hastily presented back. "During that time I suggest you peel off a few layers and come in after me."

"I can't put on my dress over wet undergarments," she protested wistfully.

"You'll dry out in no time. There's hardly a cloud in the sky. Now hurry up. Your five minutes start now."

Jessica peeked over her shoulder to see his naked backside disappearing into the water, and then he was swimming straight out as he had promised. Unable to resist the invitation, she quickly took his advice and stripped to her chemise and drawers, following him into the water within minutes.

When he had reached the first sandbar, Travis turned on his back and squinted at Jessica, now clad only in her sheer cotton undergarments, tentatively dipping a toe into the incoming tide. She seemed a young girl, slender and sweetly innocent, covered modestly in embroidered white drawers and chemise with ruffles around her fine-boned ankles and lacy straps over her delicate shoulders, but beneath the straps of the chemise, her breasts thrust out against the fabric, and beneath the narrow waist of her drawers, her hips swelled into a womanly curve.

Already her hair, catching golden glints from the sun, was coming loose around her shoulders and down her back. She quickly pulled the pins from it and extracted the rats and switches that puffed it out, turning gracefully to toss the lot back to the small pile of their clothes on the sand. Then turning again toward the water, she raised her arms to braid the tawny flow of hair as he watched the lift and fall of her breasts beneath her undergarment.

How could he ever have thought her plain? he wondered. Just the sight of Jessica braiding her hair with the sea swirling around her ankles stirred his body with desire. Now she shaded her eyes against the sun-blind water to search for him. Travis swam back to rejoin her, and they frolicked happily in the waves for an hour or more.

"All tired out?" he asked sympathetically when at last they dropped side by side at the water line, lying on their backs, gasping, propped on elbows to watch the tide coming in.

Turning her head slightly to smile at him, Jessica nodded.

"Good," said Travis and rolled on top of her.

"What do you think you're doing?" she demanded.

"I'm going to have my evil way with you."

"Here?" she asked, scandalized.

"You're supposed to say, 'Never, never, you cad,' or something like that, not quibble about the site."

Jessica giggled, then added, "Stop that!" as he fumbled with the tapes at her waist.

He not only failed to stop; he managed to hold her upper body against the sand while, under water, he pulled the drawers from her lower body.

"How am I supposed to get home in any kind of

proper condition if my undergarment washes out to sea?" she demanded.

In answer he tossed the drawers onto the sand and lowered himself between her thighs, which felt very pleasant to Jessica, even in their unprecedented position. "There," he said, smilingly pleased with himself. "All taken care of. Now wrap those lovely, long legs around me."

"No," said Jessica.

"Mulish woman," he muttered.

"I'm being taken against my will," she replied haughtily.

"Are you indeed?" Travis laughed and thrust into her, feeling great satisfaction as her involuntary response surrounded him. "The outside of you may think it's unwilling, but the inside doesn't," he advised her and thrust again.

"You're going to drown me," she protested as the tide washed up further around them.

"But you're going to enjoy it," he promised. The next wave and his next thrust left them both sputtering and doubly excited. "I think we'd better move above the high-water line."

"What if someone else arrives?"

"Then we'll move back and drown. You know you don't want me to stop at this point."

She didn't. Her body was already pulsing with excitement as they scooted further up the beach. "Hurry," she gasped as his driving thrust pushed her deep into the sand. She should have been terribly uncomfortable, she thought fuzzily, but her body was already rising on its own tide, dissolving into Travis and into the bubbling, swirling water around them. On the final wave of passion, her neck arched, and after that the whole curve of her body as she stared into the blue depths of the sky above. How she loved him!

Travis rolled onto his back in the sand, carrying her into a sprawl on top of him. When Jessica moved to detach herself, he protested. "Stay where you are, sweetheart. It feels so—friendly, and I've got something I want to talk to you about while you're feeling friendly."

Jessica was too tired to argue, although she wondered vaguely if she might not go home with a sunburned backside. Penelope had always been after her about the dangers of exposing one's skin to sunlight. How horrified she'd be to think that more than Jessica's face was in danger of dreaded, countrified brown skin.

"I'm going to buy us a house on Calder Avenue," Travis was saying. "I don't want you living by yourself alongside an oil rig."

"No," said Jessica.

"No what?"

"No, I'm not moving in with you," she replied stubbornly.

"So what was going on just now? And don't tell me you were being taken against your will. I know better."

"Just youthful hot-bloodedness," she replied, but she felt some compunction, for she could see that he was hurt by her answer. Had he really meant that men felt romantic love? That *he* did? If so, why hadn't he told her? He'd never even expressed remorse for using her in his schemes of revenge.

"Youthful hot-bloodedness? All right." He began to edge the wet chemise up from her waist.

"Now what are you doing?" she gasped.

"Throwing some more lace and ruffles up the beach to dry," he replied as he dragged the chemise over her head and tossed it toward the drawers. "Then we can get on with the youthful hot-bloodedness."

Jessica glared down at him. He was so damned adaptable, always ready to take whatever he could get. Obviously, he hadn't been serious about her moving into a house on Calder Avenue with him. Such a house would cost a fortune anyway. If they were going to live together again, it would be more practical—she caught herself at that point and decided that she too had better concentrate on their mutual hot-bloodedness, which was beginning to feel very good again. She surely hoped that no one turned up on this beach. Even if he was her husband, the scandal would be—

"Pay attention," Travis commanded.

After that she did. Making love on a beach might be wicked, but—well, maybe that's what made it so much fun, Jessica thought as the waves of heat began to pound through her. Cooler waves were coming up around them, but at least they weren't in danger of drowning yet, she thought vaguely, and maybe the tide would turn before they tired themselves out.

Chapter Twenty-Four

Rainee, gathering the week's wash, muttered, "Clothes full of sand."

"Travis and I went to the beach yesterday," said Jessica apologetically.

"Even find sand in drawers." After beating the grains out of the ankle ruffles, Rainee stuffed the garment into the machine. "Should share lodge, not make babies on beach."

"We weren't," Jessica protested. At least she hoped not.

Rainee's eyebrows rose expressively. "No one tell you how babies made? Only taking man on Saturday night and beach not stop baby. Babies made in tepees, in woods, on—"

"Oh, all *right!*"

"People talk bad about woman who see man on Saturday in bed and Sunday on beach."

"I thought your husband was suppposed to come by

to see me this morning. Didn't you tell him about my idea?"

"Jed come after deliver load for Mr. Carroll. You change subject. Babies—"

"Rainee!"

"Your man get tired of Saturday-night wife. Go get squaw in other lodge. Leave you with baby and no buffalo robe."

Jessica threw up her hands and stamped out of the kitchen. She wasn't sure which she was more anxious to do—get off the topic of Travis and their unusual marital situation or get on with her plan to enlist Rainee's husband, Jedediah Beeker, in a building venture. A whole new town was springing up on Spindletop around the Guffey Post Office and the Gladys City Depot—saloons, restaurants, stores, and bullpens, as oil men called the sleeping shacks they provided for their workers. Jessica wanted her share of that particular boom.

She peered out the window to look for Jed and saw, instead, Travis's crew. They had come to spud in on her grandfather's land, the value of which had become astronomically high in the last few weeks. Jessica hoped she had done the right thing in electing to drill instead of sell or lease. On June first the Gulf, Colorado, and Santa Fe had sponsored the demonstration run of an oil-burning locomotive. If all the railroads switched from coal to oil, that should certainly raise the price of oil, and why wouldn't they change over? The engine had gone over four hundred miles on forty-two barrels. A coal burner would have used twelve tons of coal, which she assumed was a lot of coal. Jessica couldn't even picture that much coal, whereas twelve barrels of oil was easy to picture. She'd seen a hundred times that much spewing out of one well in a single day. She'd probably had more than twelve barrels running off her parasol.

Besides, if she didn't want to keep the well, she could sell it to some Easterner as Mr. Beatty had done. It would only cost five thousand to drill, and Beatty had got over a million dollars for his! Jessica shook her head, aghast that she could even think in such terms, much less discount five thousand dollars as negligible.

Yes, her well, unless it turned up dry, would be a good investment. On the other hand, she knew her mother had done the wrong thing by investing money off the hill. Penelope and Hugh had bought at fifty thousand dollars an acre. During the time when two letters of warning from Jessica had gone unanswered, the going price had fallen to below five thousand, and Travis predicted it would go lower. Jessica shook her head. Perhaps Penelope had already sold. If so, she might have eased Jessica's mind by saying so.

Jessica patted the head of James Hogg, who was turning from a lively puppy into a huge, *fat*, lively puppy. He had been well named, for her dog would eat anything, even her own dinner if she didn't keep an eye on him. She doubted that he'd ever be a good watchdog, but he would roll over on command. Were anyone to threaten her, she could order James Hogg to roll over on the culprit, which would probably be fatal.

Her musings were stemmed by the arrival of Rainee's husband, a man even taller than his wife, with dark brown skin and a sober demeanor. Jed Beeker was slow to speak but knowledgeable when he did so. Jessica had met few men of late who inspired more confidence than her chosen partner in this building venture. She had already investigated work that he had done in South Africa, an area populated by Nigrahs and Mexicans where Rainee and Jed had a house of their own. It was a shanty town for the most part, but the small houses Jed built were solid and sturdy, as he himself was.

They came to a quick agreement once Jed discovered that Jessica planned to pay his men two to three dollars a day and him a generous and rising share of the profits when the business got off the ground. "If you can find customers for a company run by a woman an' manned by colored, Ah can promise you good workers an' good work," said Jed, "but Ah ain't quittin' my job with Mr. Carroll till you got a contract."

Jessica smiled. "I'll start today." She held out her hand, and although he looked somewhat surprised, Jedediah Beeker took it, his wife looking on expressionlessly.

"This idea work?" Rainee asked when her husband had driven off.

"I'm sure of it," Jessica replied, "and I have another suggestion to make." She had been thinking of Travis's plan to buy a house on Calder Avenue for the two of them. "Why don't you and Jed move in here with me?"

Rainee shook her head.

"There are all sorts of advantages." Jessica counted them off on her fingers. "Number one, you'd be more comfortable; number two, there's plenty of room; and number three, that way I wouldn't have to live here alone."

Rainee stared at Jessica a minute, then replied, "One, I not live by oil well; two, I like own house; three, you want company, you live with your man."

"I guess I'll go out and get a building contract," muttered Jessica, disgruntled. "I know someone who wants to build a saloon on the hill, and Mr. Carroll won't let them have one in Gladys City."

"Fine idea. Building saloon make good name for woman married on Saturday night and Sunday beach."

Jessica had to laugh. She then surprised Rainee by giving her a hug and exclaiming, "Why, Rainee, you made a joke!"

"Comanche very humorous people," Rainee replied solemnly.

"If you say so." Jessica grinned.

"I say."

Jessica giggled. Humorous? Her housekeeper hardly ever smiled, much less laughed.

"Jessica not serious person," said Rainee disapprovingly.

"Of course I am. It's only that you bring out the fool in me."

"How possible? *Rainee* serious person."

"That's what I said."

Rainee threw up her hands, but Jessica could have sworn there was a twinkle in the woman's eye. Thinking wistfully of how close she felt to Rainee, Jessica went out and climbed onto her bicycle. She had so wanted the Beekers to move in. It would have been like having family again—a sister.

Jessica loved Frannie, but with Rainee she felt comfortable. Basically they were the same sort of people, serious ones, she supposed, to whom laughter was only a sometime bit of comic relief in the arduous process of getting on with one's life. Jessica appreciated the fact that Rainee seemed to have her interests at heart. Rainee took the trouble to give advice, not that Jessica always followed it. In return, she wanted to make Rainee's life better, and this building company should do it. Jessica was determined to make a success of it for all their sakes.

"Damn," she muttered under her breath as rain began to fall again. Riding a bicycle while holding an umbrella was awkward. Maybe Jed could devise an umbrella holder for a bicycle.

Why hadn't Rainee wanted to live with her? Jessica wondered sadly. It wouldn't have meant more work—less probably, since she would have had only one house to tend—but she'd said she wanted her own house. Her grandmother, the Nigrah wife of a Comanche war chief, had been a slave before she was captured, but the Comanches had been a free-ranging people before they were confined to the reservation, where Rainee herself had grown up. Did Rainee, with her mixed heritage of absolute independence and absolute bondage, feel that living in Jessica's house would compromise her sense of freedom and dignity?

"I'd like an option to buy," said Travis.

"Option? People either buy a house or they don't. Are you an oil man?" The woman eyed him suspiciously.

"I have to show it to my wife," said Travis. "I'm sure she'll like it, but—"

"If you're an oil man, just be warned: You can't put any derricks on Calder Avenue."

"I want to *live* here, not—"

"The neighbors won't stand for it. Anyway, it's against the law."

"Actually, that law applies to property within the city limits. This is just the other side of the line, if I'm not mistaken."

"You do want to drill here."

"Ma'am, I *am* an oil man, but I assure you—"

"I knew it!" she exclaimed smugly. "Well, I don't object to taking your money, but you can't drill here."

"There's no oil here even if I wanted to drill, which I don't."

"Oh, you say that, but—"

"I want this house just so that my wife won't *have* to have an oil well in her yard."

"Don't say I didn't warn you. You oil men think you own the world, but folks on Calder Avenue won't stand for it."

Travis sighed. The things he put up with, trying to get his wife back.

Jessica could have screamed with frustration. Jed had provided her bicycle with a marvelous umbrella holder so that she could pedal along protected from the rain. However, today when she got to the Ervin Boarding House, she hadn't been able to get the umbrella out of its slot so was forced to take the bicycle into the business district or arrive soaking wet for her appointment with a timber customer. That meant walking the machine through the mobs of people on the board sidewalks, the street being too deep in mud for riding.

So far, half the days in June had been rainy, not a promising situation for a budding contractor. She had in progress a boardinghouse, a saloon, and a warehouse, but rain kept falling on her projects. Her wagons got stuck in the mud even though Jed knew and hired the best freighters. She had men putting up structures at night by lantern light, any time when the weather permitted; that way Jed could bring the crews indoors to work when the clouds opened up again.

Other contractors laughed at her methods, but

then they couldn't hire crews who would work odd hours—they often couldn't hire crews at all— whereas she and Jed were getting more contract offers than they could accept. They were both about to drop from exhaustion. In addition, Jessica had her grandfather's business to keep up with, although she'd finally managed to hire a salesman to take some of that load off her shoulders. As for her newspaper writing, she hardly had time for it anymore, and the editors who bought her articles had begun to hound her for more. Everyone wanted news of Spindletop; why she couldn't imagine. What a wretched place!

She stared bitterly at the river that had replaced the street she must cross to keep her appointment. What was she supposed to do? Swim? How long ago her day at the beach with Travis seemed, a day free from responsibilities and frustrations—and rain.

When Jessica heard the hearty guffaws, she knew they must be directed at her. It wouldn't be the first time some oaf had laughed at her umbrella-protected bicycle, but today she didn't feel like being the object of anyone's misplaced mirth and looked up with a cutting remark on her tongue. What she saw silenced her, for a skiff, manned by an elephantine figure in the same bright green rain slicker topped by the same brighter yellow umbrella, had beached at her section of the sidewalk.

"Miz Parnell, isn't it?" boomed Governor James Hogg. "You're lookin' mighty forlorn, ma'am. Can I give you and your contraption a ride across the street?"

Jessica giggled, thinking of her dog James, who had bade her good-bye that morning with her breakfast bacon dangling from his jaws and a resounding "woof," reminiscent of the governor's best speech-making volume. "My contraption and I wouldn't

371

want to swamp your skiff, Governor," she replied.

"No fear, Miz Parnell. If my weight hasn't sunk it, one little lady with her bicycle and umbrella won't either. Now, give me your hand." He helped Jessica in, pulling the bicycle after her. "Mighty ingenious, ma'am," he said as he shoved his skiff away from the sidewalk. "As you know, I don't think much of bicycles, but if you've got to ride one, a bicycle with an umbrella has its merits, at least during the Beaumont rainy season."

"I hear you have a fifteen-acre section on the hill now, Governor," said Jessica, knowing he loved to gossip, especially when the news concerned himself. "Are you going to start drilling soon?"

The governor laughed uproariously. "No, ma'am, the Hogg-Swayne Syndicate is going to cut it up into twenty-foot leases."

"Twenty *foot*?" Jessica's eyes went wide.

"That's enough for a derrick. Figure to see a heap of derricks rising there, and why not? We can get a hundred thousand a lease and make a lot of oil-hungry Texas voters happy. That's what Swayne tells me anyway."

Dazed, Jessica climbed out of the skiff at her destination. A hundred thousand dollars for a twenty-foot lease? "Thank you, Governor," she mumbled, taking possession of her bicycle again and returning the governor's wave as he set out toward the Crosby House across the river of brown water.

A hundred thousand dollars? She could do the same if she were willing to live in the middle of a hundred derricks. Would her grandfather want her to? Could she survive the experience? The whole tract could go up in a howling inferno, taking her with it. What would her percentage be if she arranged the deal? Jessica began to calculate as she wheeled her bicycle toward the office where her late morning appointment awaited her. How many twenty-foot leases were there in her grandfather's tract? It had been a while since she'd done any problems in geometry.

"Jessica, just the person I wanted to see. Have supper with me."

"Oh, Travis, I—" She couldn't finish her protest because he had already whisked her into a restaurant. At least, she thought, shaking out her napkin, she was out of the rain. "Take your hand off my chair," she ordered, glaring at a bearded fellow who had staked a claim to her place before she could order.

"Feeling a little touchy today, are you?" asked Travis cheerfully. "The rain will do that."

"Then why are you all smiles? I wouldn't think drilling a well in the rain would be any easier than building a saloon."

"Jessica Parnell, sure you're not building a saloon! Mr. Carroll isn't going to like that. He closed up the first one, had a clause in the Gladys City contract that he got the land back if anyone tried to sell alcohol on it."

"My saloon—and before you say it," she forestalled him, "I don't mean I'm going to own or run it."

"I should hope not."

"The saloon isn't on Gladys City land. I've no desire to bring Mr. Carroll's wrath down on my head."

"Smart girl. Well, Jessica, my love, I'm so cheerful because I've got an option to buy a house out on Calder Avenue."

Jessica's heart sank. She didn't want to have this argument with him.

"We'll go out to see it straight after we've eaten."

"I have neither the time nor the inclination." But she was thinking of how much nicer it would be to live on Calder Avenue with Travis than by herself on Spindletop Heights surrounded by oil derricks. If she leased that land, she might never get another night's sleep.

"Now, Jessica, the house is for you—for us."

"What scheme have you come up with that requires my cooperation, Travis? Maybe you're afraid you won't get the word quickly enough when my mother realizes how much money she's lost. Or maybe you want me around when it comes time to gloat."

"I can damn well gloat on my own," he snapped, "and my information from Fort Worth is just fine, thanks; I don't need your sources." Then he regretted letting his bitterness show, for Jessica looked distraught. Why couldn't she understand that he had good cause, the best, for the things he'd done? He'd loved his father, who had always treated him wonderfully. The Greshams had invited Will's trust and then betrayed him to his death. Still, nothing Travis had done to revenge that betrayal had been directed against Jessica, and he'd stopped entirely when he realized how much he cared for her. What did she want of him?

"Honey," he said reasonably, "you can't blame me for Penelope's stupidity. She'd have been in high clover if she'd taken my advice, which, incidentally, was meant for you and Oliver, not her."

To his horror, Jessica burst into tears. He was around the table, kneeling beside her in seconds, his arm encircling her shoulders. "Don't cry, love. What's the matter? Surely, you don't blame yourself because Penelope got greedy. Here, use my handkerchief. Look, I won't pressure you about the house. I've got a month's option on it; you can see it any time."

"I don't—"

"Sh-sh-sh. Don't say no. Take a look at it. It's a fine house—trees, grass. Don't you remember how much you wanted a house in Fort Worth?"

"Yes, I did, but you wanted to stay at my mother's, spying and making trouble."

"Jess, we're never going to reconcile if you don't forgive me."

"How can I forgive you when you're not sorry? You'd do the same things all over again, given the opportunity."

"No, I wouldn't."

Jessica sniffed and dabbed her eyes with his handkerchief. "I don't believe you."

Travis gritted his teeth. If she had an ounce of sense, she'd see that his enemies were no friends of hers, even if they were blood kin. Hugh Gresham wasn't even that.

"Lady, here's your dinner. Eat it, will you?" said the impatient man behind her chair to a weeping Jessica.

"Shut up and back off," snapped Travis. He rose and towered threateningly over the man, who backed up in alarm. Travis returned to his chair. "We'll talk about the house some other day," he muttered.

"No."

"All right, we won't." Mule-headed woman! How was he to convince her? An excursion might do it. The trip to Sabine Pass had been a success, and she looked more tired and worried now than she had then. What she needed was some fun, but he'd better not suggest an outing today. He'd bring it up Saturday night and spirit her away Sunday. Maybe if he could get her out of town, he could convince her to move in with him. He'd be damned if he was going to let a bitch like Penelope Gresham deprive him of his wife.

"Say, Jess, could you read over this lease I'm considering? I was out near Sour Lake a couple of days ago, and it looks real promising."

"Certainly," said Jessica, wiping her eyes. "That'll be five dollars, ten if I have to revise it, and I hope you realize that I'm giving you a family discount."

Well, at least she thought of him as family. Did she realize what she'd just said? Travis grinned to himself. Oh yes, he *was* going to get her back!

"What did I tell you?"

"All the signs of oil," Jessica agreed. They were taking a leisurely buggy ride from the hill toward Sour Lake.

"Walter Sharp and Ed Prather have been buying in this area. Walter missed out on Spindletop land—sick at the time, I heard—but he's got rigs drilling all over the hill. Ah, there's a farmhouse. You ready, little bride?"

"Oh, Travis, I'm never going to be convincing," she protested.

"Why not? You told me you'd been in plays at that fancy school in Washington. Just pretend you're in a play about a bride whose husband wants to buy her a nice, safe farmhouse away from the dangers and sins of Spindletop. Some of it's true. I am your husband, and I do want to get you away from the hill."

"Don't start that again. I'm not moving to Calder Avenue, and if I were looking for a nice place to live, it wouldn't be here." She stared disdainfully at the tumbledown target he'd chosen.

"Now, Jessica, don't be picky. Remember, you get

half the rights to this place if we buy it and if you want them."

She sighed. "It seems dishonest to me, tricking some poor farmer."

"Jessica, I'm going to offer the man more than he ever dreamed of getting for this miserable piece of land. Either he'll think I'm the original dumb tenderfoot sent by God for him to take advantage of, or he'll know what he's got and refuse to sell. If he sells, he'll have enough to buy a better farm somewhere nicer."

"Somewhere nicer is right," she agreed, half convinced.

"That old scoundrel," exclaimed Jessica as she laid out the lunch on the checkered tablecloth she had spread beneath a tree. "He could hardly stop snickering when he took your money."

"Well, if there's no oil, he'll have reason."

"And he pinched me."

"He pinched you? Where?"

"Never mind."

Although Travis looked incensed, Jessica was giggling at the thought of that aged lecher pinching her bottom; he must have been in his eighties. Of course, he hadn't had much strength in his fingers. If he had, she might have ignored his years and given him a slap. His was the second piece of land they'd scouted and bought that afternoon. Jessica was really beginning to enjoy the action, especially as it was evident that the sellers were every bit as underhanded as everyone else she met these days.

"You certainly have the talent for chicanery, Travis," she remarked, grinning. "It's a wonder you've never been arrested and sent to jail." Since she had made the remark lightheartedly, she was shocked when Travis's mouth compressed into a bitter line. *"Have* you been in jail?" she asked, wide-eyed.

"Yes," he snapped.

"Whatever for?"

"Something I didn't do," he muttered, "but I ended up on a road gang anyway."

"How did it happen?" She couldn't imagine Travis a prisoner; as independent as he was, he must have hated the subjugation.

He shrugged. "It's a long story, Jess—from back in '87 when I was a boy on the streets of Fort Worth. I'd had myself a fairly steady job for about six months delivering mail."

"I didn't know the government hired children."

"They didn't. I caught the mailman drunk and throwing the mail away, so I said I'd report him or he could pay me to deliver it for him—blackmail, in other words, but I made a little money, and the people got their mail. I wasn't too picky about how I kept eating."

"And that's what you were arrested for?"

"No, I was arrested for robbing and killing a drunken cowboy behind a saloon."

Jessica's face went pale.

"I told you I didn't do it," he snapped. "Seems the mailman had a deputy friend who was willing to say he saw the whole thing. Once they got me in jail, they said if I'd confess to the robbery, they'd ignore the fact that the man had been killed. That way I wouldn't hang. I was twelve years old—no family, no friends, no money, and scared to death. I confessed."

"Oh, Travis," said Jessica miserably, tears coming to her eyes. No wonder he hated her family. "I'm so sorry."

"Cheer up," he said dryly. "I could have hung."

"How long were you on the road gang?"

"Until Joe Ray came riding along a road in Tarrant County on his way to sell some land in Fort Worth. He recognized me—said I looked just like my dad. Somehow or other he got me pardoned—probably a combination of threats and bribes. Turns out they'd found who committed the murder, but they didn't bother to see that I got set free. Might have looked bad for the deputy who lied in the first place. Anyway, I owe Joe Ray a lot, even though I never could get along with him and purely hated it out on his ranch."

Impulsively Jessica leaned across the tablecloth and kissed him on the mouth. "I'm so sorry, Travis. I wish I could change the past for you."

"Don't let it worry you, honey. I'm not a poor scared child anymore." He shrugged off the gloomy memories and added, laughing, "If you want to change something, you could change my future."

She was tempted. His fingers curved around her ribs, palm to the side of her breast. She was tempted to scoot across into his arms, to do anything he wanted, including move into that house on Calder Avenue with him. But if she did, all the bitterness of his childhood would lie like poisoned water between them. She should stay away from him, maybe even get that divorce Penelope had tried to force on her. A divorce would set him free to find someone he could truly love, the way she loved him.

"For heaven's sake, Jessie. You're getting awfully teary lately. No reason to cry over a few weeks on a road gang. Hell, that work used to be done by ordinary citizens."

He gave her a wonderful, wry smile, and she knew it would be a while longer before she could give him up for good. The thought of another woman claiming Travis made her absolutely sick with jealousy. At least, as long as they were man and wife, he was still hers legally; she could have her Saturday-night marriage, as Rainee so disdainfully called it. Travis was always willing.

"Is that a lusty gleam I see in your eye?" he asked, laughing. "Are you about to spread a balm of kisses on my painful boyhood memories?"

"I am not," she replied and threw a biscuit at him.

"Hardhearted woman," Travis muttered and dove across the tablecloth, scattering the remains of their picnic while Jessica rolled into the marshy grass to escape his clutches.

Chapter Twenty-Five

Late one afternoon Jessica was talking to Al Hamil, the driller who brought in the first Lucas well. "I'm sure I can offer you a better price on lumber," she said. A huge roar cut off the bid she was about to make.

Hamil cried, "Oh, Lord, that's our well!" and pulled her under a wagon bed.

"What happened?" she shouted as, peeking out, she saw the rig topple while the derrick was blown into fragments and the pipe shot into the air. Closer to the well, men were dropping to the ground.

"Gas blowout!" Hamil shouted back. Tons of pipe had begun to rain down around them.

The roar continued; the pipe bombardment ceased eventually, and Hamil helped her out, telling her to get away as fast as she could. "Head into the wind and away from the gas."

"What about you?" she asked, even as he was pushing her in the right direction.

"Gotta drag my men away from the well," he replied and sprinted into the center of the destruction.

Jessica's first impulse was to help, but she realized that she hadn't the physical strength. She'd never be able to drag away even one inert male body. Then she thought of Travis. He might have been hurt by falling pipe if he had been at her well or closer. There might be a fire. Glancing apprehensively behind her, she hopped onto her bicycle and set off to warn her husband and her own people.

"Gas blowout!" she called to the crew at the building site. "Head into the wind and watch for fire." Jed and his men gathered their tools, piled into the wagons, and took off.

She met Travis halfway to her house on Spindletop Heights. He was shirtless, sweaty in the damp, hot air of late June, and pale with fear. When he saw her, he swept her up onto his horse and took off in the opposite direction, muttering, "Thank God, you're all right. Rainee said you had an appointment with Hamil. I thought—"

"My bicycle," she interrupted, for he had left it behind.

"The hell with the bicycle; that was a gas blowout. I'm getting you as far away as I can."

"But Rainee, is she—"

"Fine. Heading for home."

Travis carried her all the way into town, shouted so angrily at Molly that Jessica was allowed to stay in his room, kissed her with a brief, desperate intensity, and headed back to the field to offer whatever help he could.

Badly shaken both by the blowout and by her fear for Travis, Jessica sank onto his bed and tried to rationalize away the conviction that she was further from falling out of love with her husband than ever. She needed distraction. Glancing at his desk, she decided to write to Anne in Weatherford. Even as she began the letter, she realized that Anne was always the person she turned to at the best and worst times of her life.

A week later her stepmother replied in a letter full of anxiety, begging Jessica to come home, away from the dangers of Spindletop, offering to welcome Travis as well. How generous and loving Anne was, Jessica marveled, while Penelope . . . oh well, there was no use thinking about Penelope.

"I have to put the money back into the accounts," said Hugh desperately.

"I thought you had some other way of getting it."

"Yes, but it's more dangerous than what I did in the first place."

"Well, really, Hugh, it's your bank. You ought to be able to do whatever you want. If we sell the land now, we'll miss out on even bigger profits. Someone sold an oil well for over a million dollars—just one well."

"When was that?"

"I don't know," said Penelope vaguely. "Several months ago."

"You mean you haven't been keeping track of the investment?" he demanded.

"Me?" Penelope looked astounded. "You're the banker."

Hugh groaned. "It takes all my time just trying to keep things together here. I haven't even had time to read the papers lately."

"Well, as I told you, someone got a huge amount for just one well."

"Wonderful! Get down there and have Jessica sell our holdings before I'm caught and arrested."

Penelope laughed. "People of our sort do *not* get arrested. And it isn't as if you've done anything really wrong, after all."

"Shut up and do what you're told," he snapped.

Penelope's eyes narrowed. "Watch what you say to me, Hugh."

Travis had been leaning against the wall of the Guffey Post Office thinking about a message he'd had from Lieutenant Hartwig in Fort Worth. Wagoner, Montana? It seemed an unlikely area for Butch Cassidy and the Wild Bunch to be operating when their home base was Fannie Porter's brothel in Hell's Half Acre. Still, Hartwig was sure they were responsible for the June 3 raid on a Great Northern train and that Hugh Gresham would be useful to them if they came back to Fort Worth with the loot, forty thousand in nonnegotiable securities. But would they come back? Travis wondered. Last winter the Sundance Kid had been in love with one of Fannie's girls, Etta Place, so maybe they'd return; maybe they'd use Hugh.

Travis shook his head. If Hugh went outside the law now with Hartwig and Arleigh watching his every move, he'd be caught, and then it would be "Goodbye, Penelope." A husband broke and in jail wasn't going to enhance her social position, especially if Oliver realized that she had pushed Hugh into a life of crime. Long ago when Penelope had gotten herself in trouble, Oliver had stood by her, having no other heir except a baby granddaughter he had never seen. Now he had Jessica—full-grown, smart, honest, hard-working Jessica—a descendant to be proud of, unlike his bitch of a daughter.

"Parnell, I hear you've bought a place on Calder Avenue."

Startled, Travis confronted the man who would be his and Jessie's new neighbor. "That's right," he replied warily, for Captain Weiss was scowling.

"Then take fair warning. We won't put up with any oil derricks in the neighborhood."

"You haven't a thing to worry about," Travis assured him. "I want to move in, not drill for oil."

"You haven't moved in yet," said the owner of the house across the street from the Ervin. "When do you plan to do it?"

"Soon," said Travis, confident Jess was on the verge of coming back to him. Hadn't she looked for him first thing after the Guffey well blew out, just as frightened for his safety as he had been for hers?

"So we've decided we're ready to sell the land," said Penelope, unwinding the veils from her wide hat.

She had arrived unannounced at Jessica's house late in the afternoon of a very hot July day. To Jessica she looked worse than on her last visit; she was too thin, her face still beautiful but now gaunt and pale. Her eyes, strangely dilated, held a blank hostility in eerie contrast with her air of friendly nonchalance. Jessica shivered at the scene she anticipated when her mother realized how little the land was now worth.

"I've read such wonderful reports in the papers about land prices," said Penelope, becoming somewhat more animated. "Nine hundred thousand dollars an acre—over a million for one well."

"Penelope, I've been writing to you for two months."

"So sweet of you to take the trouble."

"But did you *read* the letters?" Jessica felt as if she were talking to someone who wasn't there.

"I have a very busy social schedule, Jessica," Penelope replied irritably. "But I do appreciate your writing. Now Hugh says you can take care of selling the property for us. Father speaks so highly of your business acumen—unsuitable in a young woman, to be sure, but since you haven't seen fit to follow any of my advice . . ."

"Penelope, the land you bought is worth less than three thousand an acre now. That's what I've been telling you in the letters. The price has been dropping since May."

"Jessica, if you think you can buy that land back from me at some ridiculously low price and reap all the profits for yourself—"

"I don't want to buy it."

Penelope at last began to look alarmed. "But the newspaper said—"

"The newspaper was talking about land on the hill. The price of off-hill land has been plummeting for several months. There's no oil on it."

"You mean you cheated me? You sold me worthless land and made me pay a fortune for it?"

Jessica sighed. "I told you before you bought in that Travis expected that land to lose its value."

"Well, really, Jessica, you can hardly expect me to follow the advice of an enemy. I'm not a complete fool. Now I expect to make a profit on my holdings." Her voice had risen hysterically. "You find me a buyer."

"I can't."

"Don't tell me you can't, you little cheat. You did it because you're jealous of me. Well, you won't get away with it. Hugh says we have to have the money; he'll blame me if I don't bring it back."

"Penelope, I can't—"

"You'll have to buy it back yourself."

"At two thousand dollars an acre," said Jessica, controlling her temper with difficulty.

"No. I want the price I expected to get."

"I warned you before you insisted on buying it, and I've been warning you ever since. I don't know what else I could have done. Grandfather said originally that if you insisted, I was to sell it to you. He didn't say he'd be willing to take a huge loss when you changed your mind."

"It's my money," said Penelope, a sly look replacing the hostility. "I'm his heir—just as I'm yours, am I not?"

"You'll have to talk to Grandfather," Jessica replied, her face hardening. "I couldn't knowingly take a financial loss of such magnitude without his authorization."

"Now you're trying to come between me and my father."

Jessica's mouth tightened.

"You have named me in your will, haven't you?" Penelope demanded.

"Are you expecting me to die?" Jessica snapped back.

"This is a dangerous place. Should anything happen to you, we wouldn't want your money to go to Travis Parnell, would we? Or have you gone crawling back to him?" Penelope's voice held an unpleasant sneer that brought a flush to Jessica's cheeks.

"I don't have time for making out wills or for trying

to rectify your mistakes, Penelope, especially when they were made by ignoring everything I tried to tell you. If you want to talk to Grandfather about this, by all means do it."

"Oh, I shall," said Penelope threateningly. "No doubt, when he hears what I have to say, you'll find yourself out of a job."

"I doubt it. Grandfather *does* read my letters. There isn't anything you can tell him about this or any other business I'm involved in that he doesn't already know."

Penelope, her face pale as she took in the full extent of her predicament, dropped into a chair and groped in her bag for the medicine she always carried with her. What had her mother planned to tell Oliver Duplessis? Jessica wondered. Some pack of lies?

"Do you know how much I dislike you?" Penelope's voice was venomous, her hands trembling as she poured a dram of bitters into a little cup, raised it to her lips, and drained it. "What an embarrassment to have such a plain, socially awkward daughter! I'd never have had a thing to do with you if I hadn't known how much my taking you in would infuriate your father. You're—"

"You're drunk," Jessica interrupted wearily. "Rainee!" Rainee appeared almost instantly. "Mrs. Gresham is leaving now. Would you see her out?"

Had Penelope not begun screeching imprecations, Jessica would have thought that her mother looked rather pathetic as Rainee ejected her from the house.

"Great Cannibal Owl hungry for prey," said Rainee when she came back several minutes later.

Jessica gave her a wan smile.

"You prey she hungry for," Rainee warned, her face grim.

"I know," said Jessica shivering.

"Watch back," advised Rainee.

"You're early," said Jessica, looking up in surprise when Travis entered her kitchen carrying a burlap bag. "Are those the chickens?"

"No."

"Travis," wailed Jessica, "you've ruined the surprise."

"What's so surprising about chickens? Unless it's that there wasn't an edible dead chicken in Beaumont this morning. I went out and shot some rabbits, though why you should need four I don't know. We couldn't have eaten four chickens if I could have got them."

"That's the surprise," she said brightly. "I've invited the Hamil brothers for dinner tonight—a sort of thank you for saving me from falling pipe when the well blew out. I knew you'd be pleased." Travis didn't look pleased. "You three being old friends from Corsicana and all."

"Wonderful," muttered Travis. "Guess I'll have to take my bath this afternoon."

"You do like the Hamils?" Jessica's eyes were twinkling.

"I do like them," he agreed. "I also, as you well know, look forward to having you to myself on Saturday since you have yet to succumb to my charms and move in with me."

Deciding a change of subject was in order, Jessica murmured, "I've never cooked a rabbit."

"Well, first you skin it," said Travis as he dragged out the bathtub.

"I'll do no such thing. You shot it; you skin it. Out on the back porch."

"Only if you come out to keep me company." He

picked up the rabbits and headed for the door, remarking over his shoulder, "Rainee said Penelope had been by."

Jessica followed him out onto the porch and sat down on the step. "She was furious. Evidently she and Hugh needed the money."

"Did they?" Travis turned away to hide his smile. He might not be actively pursuing them anymore, but he had no reason to wish them well.

"She blames me."

"Well, don't blame yourself."

"I think she plans to convince Grandfather that I tried to cheat her."

"Oliver's too smart to believe that."

Jessica had been watching him as he methodically and efficiently skinned the second of the four rabbits. There was a satisfaction shining in his eyes that she didn't like. "If she hadn't known it was your advice, she might have listened to me."

"If I hadn't given any advice, what would she have done?" he retorted.

"Don't look so smug. She wants me to make a will so you don't get my money if anything happens to me."

"Naming who?" he asked.

Jessica remained silent; the consternation that showed on his face hurt her.

"Naming who?" he demanded again. "Her?" Travis scowled and put down his knife. "Listen, Jess, you better go in tomorrow and see a lawyer, and don't, for God's sake, leave anything to Penelope."

She could have wept. He evidently did hope to inherit her money should anything happen to her.

"Name Anne."

"Anne?" Jessica's unhappy thoughts tumbled into confusion.

"Sure, Anne. You love her best, don't you? Name her; then write Penelope—no, telegraph her what you've done."

"Then you don't want the money?"

"I don't care about the money, Jess. I do care about keeping you healthy, so be sure she knows she has nothing to gain from your death."

"Really, Travis!"

"Or designate your brothers and your sister. I don't care who, but do it tomorrow," he added urgently.

"What about my father?"

"Fine. Name Justin. Just get that will made and the telegram sent," he ordered.

"I remember that mornin' as if it was yesterday," said Al Hamil as the four of them—Travis, Jessica, Al, and his brother Curt—sat at Jessica's table finishing their coffee after a rabbit stew of dubious quality and an excellent peach pie made from Anne Harte's recipe.

"It was cold."

Curt Hamil nodded his agreement.

"No clouds. The mornin' paper said diamonds had been discovered out near El Paso, an' I thought, 'What am I doin' here in Beaumont, freezin' to death over someone else's oil well when I could have been makin' a fortune down on the border?'"

Travis laughed. "Al, you got oil in your veins. You're never gonna turn diamond miner."

Al grinned and resumed his story. "There was just us three, Curt an' me an' Peck Bird. We'd put in a new fishtail bit, an' Curt was up on the double board steerin' the drill stem; that's forty feet above the derrick floor, ma'am."

"Long way to fall," muttered Curt.

Jessica had to agree with that.

"Mud started boilin' up over the rotary table, so me an' Peck backed up fast. Then it shot up the derrick an' got ole Curt all over mud an' gumbo."

"I slid down that ladder, an' we all run for our lives," said Curt. "Never seen nothin' like that at home in Corsicana. Six tons of four-inch pipe headin' up the derrick, right over the top an' then tryin' to spear us as it come down. Knocked off the crown block. Like to scared me to death, all slick an' slidin' around as I was."

"Well," Al resumed, "it got quiet then, so we went back an' started cleanin' about a foot of muck off the derrick floor when all of a sudden there was this here roar like nothin' I ever heard. Maybe if you was lyin' between the tracks with the train runnin' right over you, or someone set off a cannon in your ear; I don' know.

"Anyways, up come the mud again, an' then the gas, an' we all scattered. Poor Peck, he fell in the slush pit, an' then comes the oil—green-black an' beautiful, headin' for the sky, more oil than you ever seen in your life." Al Hamil shook his head. "Reckon there won't be nothin' that excitin' happen to me again, no matter how many gushers we bring in."

"Amen," said Travis.

"Peck went for the cap'n, an' he was so flustered when he got there, he fell down the hill tryin' to git outa his buggy. Then he just stood in the rain of oil. So did we all. Reckon ever'one in the county turned up an' stood under that rain of oil, 'cause we all knew it was gonna change our lives." Al sighed, then grinned at another memory. "Me an' Curt an' Peck even took a bow.

"Course ever'one wasn't happy. Farmers had their livestock stampedin' all over the place, an' some folks thought it was the end of the world—preachers an' such."

"I heard some of them when I first got to town," said Jessica.

"Jessica arrived a few days after the lake caught fire," Travis explained.

"Now that was somethin'," said Curt. "I lost a good jacket tryin' to put that fire out. An' you'd a thought it *was* the end of the world when we set the backfire an' the two met. That clap a thunder like to knocked me over, an' the smoke covered the whole sky an' drifted on down as far as Port Arthur, so they say. *That's* when the preachers started sayin' the whole world was goin' up in flames." He helped himself to another cup of coffee and grunted scornfully, "Didn't, though. Didn't even hurt the well."

"We may not always be so lucky," Travis muttered, still worrying about his wife living in the shadow of a well, for he had brought hers in just the day before.

"Well, the safety committee ought to help," said Al.

The conversation drifted on a while longer. Then the Hamil brothers thanked Jessica for a fine meal and left so abruptly that she had no chance to send Travis off with them as she had planned. Had he somehow engineered that? Piqued, she left him in the sitting room while she carried the dishes to the kitchen, where she poured hot water from a kettle into a pan and dumped the dishes in after.

She was washing them when Travis came up behind her and pinned her against the counter. "Do you remember what was happening this time last year?" he asked.

Jessica ignored him and went on with her dish-washing.

"Right about now I was kissing you on the veranda

at your parents' house and wishing I could drag you off into the shrubbery and seduce you."

Jessica maintained her silence as she lifted plates from the pan and dumped them, wet, onto the counter.

"Of course, I was too much of a gentleman to do it."

"Gentleman?" exclaimed Jessica, forgetting her determination to ignore him. "My mother caught us and sent you away. And anyway, I doubt that you were all that interested."

"Oh, I was definitely interested, and I think I should get a reward for my past restraint."

"Have another piece of pie," she suggested.

"I'd rather ravish you."

"In the kitchen?"

"The kitchen's a very sensuous place," he whispered into her ear. "Don't you remember the time I seduced you on the counter?"

Shivers ran from the touch of his breath in her ear.

"Course, I admit that bedrooms are more comfortable."

"I have dishes to do," she replied, trying to ignore the effect he was having in the pit of her stomach, just the sound of his voice and the pressure of his body against her back.

"Well, don't let me interrupt. I'll just—" He began to inch up the back of her skirt and petticoat. "Those rational-clothing people are right. Women wear too many clothes."

"Stop that," cried Jessica, whirling to face him.

"Caught you." He wrapped her in his arms and lifted her into the air. "Our first anniversary," he purred, burying his face against the soft swell of her breasts.

Jessica's eyes closed as she felt, even through the

layers of clothing, his mouth against a nipple. "You want to celebrate a night I got a lecture from my mother on what a danger you were to my reputation?" she mumbled.

"I want to celebrate the night I realized that if I didn't get you into bed pretty quick, I was going to go crazy with frustration."

"Is that true?" she asked. Had he really wanted *her* as well as revenge on Penelope and Hugh?

Travis had swept her into his arms and was heading for the bedroom. No matter what the answer, she knew that she was not going to stop him. As it happened, she got no answer, only a wonderful night of love.

Chapter Twenty-Six

Jessica stretched luxuriously. Beside her, Travis mumbled in his sleep and turned to pull her back into his arms. She relaxed against him, feeling wonderful. The cool morning drifted into her window on a light breeze that rustled the curtains and brushed over her body, which still held the languid pleasure of Travis's tenderness and passion. At times like this, when her flesh spoke more convincingly than her mind, she could hardly believe that he *didn't* love her.

On the other hand, if he did, why had he never said it, and when had it happened? But that was the mind speaking again. She didn't have to listen. For these few minutes before he awoke and left, she could pretend that they had an ordinary marriage—no, an extraordinary marriage. She nestled her face into the soft hair on his chest, inhaling the familiar scent of him. For a man who worked in an oil field and had access to a bathtub only once a week, he smelled unbelievably good, she thought.

"Anything I can do for you?" asked Travis, voice deep with laughter.

"When did you wake up?" she countered. She didn't want to open her eyes or talk.

"The minute you moved away," he replied. "Did anyone ever tell you you have beautiful breasts?" He ran a finger over the one most easily accessible. "And legs." He moved the finger to stroke lightly along her inner thigh, causing Jessica to shiver. "And a tummy a man could kill for." He leaned over to kiss it.

At that moment someone knocked at her front door, and Jessica shot upright in the bed. "Pretend you're not here," he whispered. She shook her head. "We're busy," Travis insisted, grinning. "Can't come to the door for at least an hour."

"Raince will be here by then," Jessica pointed out as she rose and wrapped a robe around herself. "Anyway, it must be something important."

"I thought what we were doing was important." Reluctantly he released her hand and closed his eyes again. When he next opened them, Jessica stood in the doorway, her face white and stricken, a piece of paper in her hand. "What is it, love?" he asked.

"Grandfather has died."

"Oh, sweetheart." Travis rose quickly and crossed the floor to hold her.

"I thought he was in good health," she whispered. "No one said he was sick."

"Oliver was an old man, Jess."

"But he was so—so vigorous." She was still staring incredulously at the telegram. "Maybe this is some cruel trick on Penelope's part. I just—just don't understand what she could gain by it."

"It's not from Penelope, Jess," he said softly as he took the wire from her and read it. "Do you want me to go to Fort Worth with you?"

"No," she replied, tears beginning to fall. "No. I'll have to go alone."

"You don't have to do anything alone, honey. I'm always—"

"You wouldn't be welcome, Travis. They know what you wanted to do to them."

"The only thing that matters is what you want, Jess. If you agree, I'll go with you."

She shook her head.

The doctor couldn't understand it himself. Oliver had had only a summer cold accompanied by a slight bit of chest congestion, hardly enough to keep him in bed. "Of course, he was old," said the doctor.

"But he was healthy," Jessica insisted.

"It could have been pneumonia." The man didn't sound as if he really thought so. "Some things defy explanation," he added.

On the plain outside Fort Worth the funeral cortege, with its hundreds of buggies, spread out in every direction from the graveyard. Throngs of black-clad mourners assembled to pay their respects to Oliver Duplessis. Initially, Penelope, who seemed more excited than grief-stricken, announced that she would not wear black. She said black was not a becoming color and sneered when she came down the stairs to find Jessica in formal mourning. "Your stepmother was always wearing black for someone or other in the days when I had to see her. Perhaps she thought she looked good in it, but she didn't, of course. Neither do you, Jessica."

"My stepmother," Jessica retorted angrily, "loved people besides herself. When they died, she mourned for them, as any decent person does."

"I suppose you mean I should be crying over

Father." Penelope studied herself in the mirrored wall. "Well, he's dead. What good will my tears do him? Not as much good as his money will do me." She smiled at her reflection.

Hugh had arrived in time to hear this remark and insisted that Penelope go upstairs and change into proper clothing. "And don't, for God's sake, take any more of that medicine until the funeral is over," he added. It was one of the few times Jessica could remember him forcing Penelope to do anything she didn't want to do.

As they were leaving the graveyard, Penelope murmured, "You can stop crying, Jessica. I'm not impressed at all." The hours without her medicine had shortened her temper considerably. "I suppose you're regretting that you tried to cheat me." She grasped Jessica's wrist to keep her from walking away. "And don't expect to continue your employment with Duplessis," she warned triumphantly. "As soon as the will has been read, I shall take great pleasure in dismissing you."

"I'm sure you will," Jessica replied, snatching her wrist from her mother's grasp and hurrying off in search of Henry Barnett. Penelope no longer even pretended to any family feeling, so Jessica felt no obligation to stay longer, especially in her mother's house. "Henry," she asked when she found him, "could you drop me at the station? I'm going straight back to Beaumont."

"You have to remain in town for the reading of the will," he reminded her.

"Oh, everyone knows what it will say."

"Nonetheless, you must be there. I too, although I can't imagine why; I've never handled business for Oliver Duplessis. Do you want to stay at my house, Jessica?"

She accepted with gratitude and moved her few belongings out before her mother got back to town. On the third day after the funeral, the reading of the will sent a shock wave through the few Duplessis heirs. Hugh turned gray, but Penelope, who had been well medicated for the event and looking complacent, almost up to her old standards of beauty, went into a screaming rage because Jessica had been named the primary heir. Oliver had left her everything but a trust fund set aside for Penelope, the principal of which she could not touch. The trust was to be handled by Henry Barnett.

"That's not my father's real will," Penelope shrieked. "I know what it said. She substituted some forgery."

"Mrs. Gresham, Mrs. Gresham," soothed Oliver's attorney, "I assure you that this will is legitimate. Your father dictated it to me personally less than a month ago. The document was witnessed by several well-respected business associates of Mr. Duplessis's." The man turned to Hugh for help as Penelope continued to scream abuse at the lawyer and at Jessica, to whose side Henry Barnett moved protectively. "Mr. Gresham, would you look at the signatures? These men are customers of your bank. You can assure Mrs. Gresham—"

Hugh turned and walked out, his shoulders sagging. Penelope, shaking with rage, demanded that he return and "Do something! After what I did for you, you—"

"Shut up!" he shouted at her. Penelope and all the others in the room stiffened with shock at his tone, which was heavy with loathing. "You've ruined me," he muttered, and he left.

"Why would he blame *me*?" she whimpered, tears making streaks in powder and rouge that Jessica hadn't realized her mother used. "Mr. Foley, you know I've always been a wonderful wife to Hugh." Penelope swayed in the direction of her father's lawyer and grasped his lapel. "You must do something about this terrible will. You, of all people, know that my father never meant to cut me off." She gave the embarrassed lawyer her sweetest tear-stained smile.

"Mrs. Gresham," Foley stammered, "your father didn't cut you off. He's provided you with a—a generous income."

"Generous!" screamed Penelope, helpless tears abandoned. "A washerwoman couldn't live on that money, especially dispensed by Henry Barnett. Everyone knows he hates me. He's Justin Harte's toady. They'll all be laughing, Justin and his sluttish wife and their cheat of a daughter. They've conspired to see me in poverty."

"You have a wealthy husband," Foley pointed out. "How can you say—"

"He's not as wealthy as Father was, and I was to be my father's heir. Everyone knew that. I'm the Duplessis heiress. My father never meant—why would he . . ." Penelope's eyes narrowed as they fell on Jessica, who sat in her straight-backed chair, frozen at the spectacle of her mother's mad harangue. "She did it! She must have poisoned his mind against me. She made him change his will. Get the police."

"Mrs. Gresham," cried Mr. Foley, shocked, "your daughter didn't influence Mr. Duplessis."

"She's not my daughter. I disown her."

"Nonetheless, Mrs. Parnell hasn't been in Fort Worth in months. One had only to look at her face to see that she was as surprised as you by this will, Mrs. Gresham. Truly, I think you do her an injustice." He smiled ingratiatingly at Jessica.

"Why didn't he name you to oversee my trust fund?" Penelope demanded. "Why name Henry Barnett? That was her doing. Hers and Justin's."

"Your father worried that you might not handle your money prudently," mumbled Foley.

"What money?"

"Any money," snapped the lawyer, then tried to look conciliatory.

Jessica suspected that he wanted to keep Hugh's business and feared to alienate Hugh's wife.

"Your father felt that I, having known you from childhood, might be too—too soft-hearted to handle your interests as he directed."

The lawyer looked so embarrassed that Jessica assumed her grandfather must have believed him too weak-kneed to stand up to Penelope. No doubt Grandfather Duplessis, who had never been one to mince words, had said as much to Mr. Foley.

"You'll be sorry for this," Penelope snarled at Jessica.

Jessica closed her eyes and wished herself elsewhere. Then she felt Henry's firm hand on her shoulder. "If there's nothing else, Foley," he said, "I shall see Mrs. Parnell out. She's had a grievous few days."

"Yes, yes, of course. My condolences, Mrs. Parnell," said Foley. "I'll be in touch with you concerning the provisions of the will."

"Get in touch with Mr. Barnett," Jessica advised, rising from her chair. "He will handle my interests."

"Jessica," snapped Penelope before Jessica could get out of the room. "I want to see a copy of your will. Be sure you've done what you were told to."

Jessica glanced over her shoulder with somber

disbelief. Penelope must be mad indeed if she still believed that Jessica would make a will in her favor.

"You all right?" asked Rainee. Jessica had left Spindletop to attend the funeral before Rainee arrived for work, so they had neither seen nor spoken to each other in a week.

"My grandfather died." Jessica's eyes filled with tears.

"Travis tell me." Rainee held out her arms, a first-time invitation that caused Jessica to weep helplessly against the Comanche woman's shoulder.

"He left me almost everything." Jessica cried harder.

"Much money bad medicine," agreed Rainee gloomily. "Now evil spirit in mother's body make bad medicine against daughter."

"There's nothing she can do." Jessica pulled away and took out a handkerchief to wipe away the last of her tears. "How are the building projects going?" she asked, deciding that the best escape from grief would be her work.

"No rain, house rise fast." Rainee frowned disapprovingly. "You work too much. Need time to weep for old man."

"I can't believe he's gone." Jessica sighed. "I'd come to love him so much."

"You got husband."

Jessica swallowed hard. She wanted to see Travis. Just the thought of him eased her grief. Only he and Rainee understood how much her grandfather had meant to her, how much she would miss him, and how little his generous treatment of her in the will was going to make any difference in her loneliness. Maybe she would run into Travis when she went over to check out her building projects on the hill.

Henry Barnett had thought she should move back to Fort Worth to handle Oliver's business interests, which centered there, but she just couldn't do it. She'd delegated responsibility to various of Oliver's lieutenants, even hired new managers, and then she'd come home, knowing that her attachment to Spindletop was an attachment to Travis. Soon she'd have to make up her mind about their marriage.

As Rainee had told her, Jed Beeker was performing miracles now that the heavy rain had stopped. Three strangers caught her on the street to ask that she submit bids on their building projects. Another wanted to buy lumber for a derrick, which she sold him on behalf of Duplessis—no, on behalf of herself; she was Duplessis now. Jessica blinked back tears and climbed onto her bicycle to pedal past the Log Cabin Saloon toward another appointment. Infectious laughter stopped her before she could set out.

"That's a bicycle, isn't it?"

Jessica looked up to see a giggling girl astride a horse, ruffled taffeta skirts hiked up, orange hair frizzed out in every direction around a pretty face. Jessica was sure God never made any hair that color and assumed that she had been accosted by one of the Deep Crockett girls. She'd heard they had taken to riding circuit and setting up assignations with hill workers. It was their way of meeting the competition from prostitutes who lived and worked on Spindletop.

"What's your name?" asked the girl, looking ingenuously friendly.

Jessica didn't know what to do. Society dictated that she and this person never speak to one another. "Jessica Parnell," she mumbled. Penelope would say

404

that her predicament was her own fault, the result of doing a job meant for men and frequenting places she had no business being. She glanced around surreptitiously to see if anyone was observing this encounter. She couldn't afford to have her reputation sullied, not when she had to do business with men every day. She wouldn't be safe on the streets were it thought that she consorted with women of ill repute.

The girl squealed, "Parnell? Do you know Travis? He's one of my very best friends. I just love Travis."

Jessica felt the color draining from her cheeks. Did that mean he . . . paid this girl for . . . for her favors?

"Can I have a ride on your bicycle? I ain't never tried one." She looked so eager that Jessica almost felt guilty at her own animosity, but this was a beautiful young woman, excepting her dreadful hair, and Travis evidently . . . visited her.

"Can I? Please?" the girl wheedled.

"Lissie, what are you *doin'*?" Another young female of the same ilk pulled up beside the orange-haired girl and grasped the reins. "Come away before you get yourself arrested, you fool. She don't know no better, ma'am." This remark was addressed to Jessica. "Don't make her no trouble; she din' mean nuthin'."

Jessica was left staring after them as the second girl forced the first to ride with her down the street. Penelope's allegations must have been true; he *had* patronized Fannie Porter's. All his talk about being happy at home had been lies, and here where they weren't even living together, he no doubt felt perfectly justified in pursuing his dirty pastime. How many more ways was he betraying her? The one thing they had, the one link between them that she had trusted, had been a lie. Jessica forgot her next appointment and went home.

Rainee assumed her tears were for her grandfather and plied her with tea, cookies, and platitudes about the good life he had had.

"With Penelope for a daughter?" Jessica asked sharply.

"Old man had you too," Rainee replied and poured more tea.

Jessica heard the murmur of voices at the back door and assumed some country woman had come to sell Rainee eggs, but minutes later she found herself in Travis's arms. Briefly she relaxed against him and laid her tear-stained face on his shoulder. Then she remembered and pulled away.

"You should have told me you were home, sweetheart," he said reproachfully. "I've been worried every minute about you, and then I had to hear from someone else that you were back."

"Who told you?" asked Jessica bitterly. "Your dear friend Lissie?"

Travis looked confused.

"The orange-haired girl riding the circuit on the hill. She assured me just this afternoon of what great friends you are and how much she loves you."

Travis grinned. "Lissie loves everyone."

"I'm sure, but she seems to feel that you're a special lover."

"Lover? Why, Jess, sweetheart, are you jealous? That's sure good news. All you have to do is come live with me in town, and you'll never have to worry about—"

"I don't intend to worry," she interrupted, her anger growing with each humorous evasion. "I don't intend to put up with an unfaithful, lying, deceiving—"

"Hold it," Travis snapped. "I don't know what

Lissie said to you, but I'm sure as hell not one of her customers, if that's what you're implying. I've been kind to the girl because I feel sorry for her; she's simpleminded. Maybe you were too busy thinking about yourself to notice anyone else's problems, but believe me, Jessica, your life looks like heaven compared to that poor child's."

Jessica flushed. How dare he attack her? Did he really think her so stupid that she didn't know what the orange-haired girl had been talking about? Did he imagine she was naïve enough to believe that a man could befriend a prostitute without expecting favors in return?

"Jess, I'm sorry you were upset when you'd just got back from Oliver's funeral," he said in a gentler tone. "This is no time for us to be arguing."

"Why not?" she snapped. "Oh, of course. You heard about the will and don't want to miss out on anything. I guess I'll be the target of every unprincipled scoundrel in the country, with you first in line."

Travis's face flushed with anger. "Maybe you'd like to explain that remark."

"Don't play the innocent with me, Travis. Penelope accused me of influencing him in some underhanded way, but if anyone did that, it would have been you."

"So he made you his heir," Travis mused. "Good. I hoped he would."

"I'm sure you did." Jessica felt almost sick with anger and betrayal. "Not only have you managed to destroy my mother—and Hugh as well, if his reaction was any indication—" Travis actually had the audacity to smile; he wasn't even trying to hide his triumph "—but I suppose you planned to get the money for yourself through me. Well, you won't, Travis. You—"

"You know damned well I don't want or need your money," he broke in. "I've made more out of this oil

407

field than you and Oliver put together, and I don't need a penny from any Harte, Gresham, or Duplessis.''

Jessica had never seen him so angry and backed away instinctively.

"I've made my own way. Nobody gave me a thing, and if I'm pleased to see ill luck befall people who did me ill, that's my own damned business. I wanted you to have Oliver's money because you deserved it, but I didn't do anything to bring it about. Hell, I'd have sworn the man would live another twenty or thirty years.''

For a moment Jessica was struck with the truth of what Travis said. She too could hardly believe her grandfather had died. On the other hand, she wouldn't allow herself to be taken in again. After that encounter with Travis's simpleminded little harlot— if she *was* simpleminded; the whole scene might have been a piece of trouble-making on the girl's part, an impulse designed to hurt Jessica, which it had. "I'm so glad you don't want anything from anyone in my family, Travis," said Jessica furiously, "because you're not going to get anything. Now, please leave my house.''

Travis gave her a hard look, swung on his heel, and left, slamming the door behind him. Jessica caught at the back of a chair as a wave of sick vertigo swept over her.

"Woman who tame stallion, then drive him away with tongue like whip spend life on foot,'' said Rainee from the doorway, her dark face severe and expressionless.

Jessica tried to look unconcerned. "I guess now he'll have to find somewhere else to have a bath," she replied with wobbly sarcasm.

"Travis lodge have metal pond. He come here for you, not bath."

"Well, I *have* been a fool then," said Jessica, giving up her pretense of indifference. "Everything he ever told me was a lie, and I believed it all at one time or another."

A week later Travis heard that Hugh Gresham had been arrested for handling nonnegotiable currency stolen from a Great Northern train in Wagoner, Montana. The train robbers had left town; their banker hadn't been so foresighted. Fort Worth was rife with rumors that accounts at Cattleman's Bank had been emptied. An investigation was in progress. Somehow, Travis didn't get as much pleasure from the news as he had expected.

Chapter Twenty-Seven

To combat the depression that threatened to over-whelm her, Jessica began to lease out small parcels of land surrounding her house. Night and day the derricks went up, and the drills ate into the earth, the noise so constant that it blanked her mind. Rainee grumbled. Jessica had to leave home to make business decisions, and she had many to make now that she was Duplessis Company. Wires and telephone calls from Fort Worth followed her as she pursued her Beaumont enterprises. Travis thought he was so successful—more successful than either she or Oliver. She'd show him.

Then one day in August she came home to find a furious housekeeper awaiting her return. Penelope was back. How did she have the nerve to show up after the things she had said at the reading of the will? Jessica hadn't expected to see her mother again—ever; she hadn't wanted to.

"Great Cannibal Owl as welcome to Rainee as skunk in tepee," fumed the Comanche woman. "I should tell her, 'Open mouth again, I scalp.'"

Jessica, who had been growing anxious at the thought of having to face her mother, started to grin.

"Why smile?" demanded Rainee. "You think Rainee not know how to take scalp? I more Comanche than black. I tell her that." Rainee's mouth twisted in a macabre smile that sent a shiver up Jessica's spine. "Comanche woman not usually count coup; maybe I start on her."

Jessica didn't know what *count coup* meant, but it didn't sound good; she decided that her housekeeper might not be joking and she'd best get Penelope out of the house as fast as possible. With that in mind, she hurried into the sitting room.

"That woman threatened me, that smart-mouthed Nigrah of yours. I'm going to the sheriff as soon as I—"

"Comanche," said Jessica.

"What?" Penelope paled.

"Her name is Rain Woman; she's Comanche, and I wouldn't go complaining to Ras Landry, who's a friend of ours. Rainee might take offense. Besides, who'd believe you anyway? You smell of spirits."

"Don't you talk to me that way."

"Why have you come here, Penelope?"

"I'm your mother; that's why. And you've treated me shamefully. Now that Hugh has been arrested—"

"What's that?"

"Oh, don't act as if you didn't know. You probably arranged it."

"What was he arrested for?"

Penelope looked at Jessica sharply, then shrugged. "What does it matter? It's very embarrassing, and of course I've left him, or I would have if he hadn't been taken away, but now there's the problem of money. It wouldn't have been a problem—"

"What happened to Hugh's money?" Even without Oliver's estate, they had always had all the money anyone could want. What could Hugh have done?

"How would I know?" muttered Penelope petulantly. "He's been whining about his financial problems for months. I tried to help, but you ruined that. Now, since you've stolen Father's estate, you'll just have to see that I'm taken care of properly. You should split the inheritance with me. I want you to see to it right away."

"You already have an income from Grandfather," Jessica pointed out.

No matter what Hugh had done, it seemed to Jessica that her mother should have stood by him. They had been married for over twenty years, and he had been generous to a fault where Penelope was concerned. On the other hand, Penelope had proved herself repeatedly a woman with no loyalty, no gratitude, no affection for others, and no sense when it came to money.

"That little bit Papa left me is nothing, and Henry Barnett controls it. He won't let me have it."

"Well, not the principal. If you spent that, you'd be left with nothing, which is evidently what Grandfather was worried about."

"Henry Barnett hates me. That's why he won't let me have the money to tide me over."

"Why would he hate you?"

"Because he was Justin's lawyer in the divorce," Penelope replied sullenly.

"Oh." Jessica thought about the story Travis had told her. "Then Henry must know about your trying to smother me when I was a baby," she said, as much to see her mother's reaction as for any other reason.

"Lies!" cried Penelope, turning pale. "Who told you that? Your father? Your husband? You owe me respect and—and support in my time of trial. I took you in when you needed help."

"Yes, you did," said Jessica, "and I intend to repay you. I'll estimate what you spent on me and send it to Henry to use in your behalf."

"What good would that do? That would be a pittance. I'm accustomed to wealth. I deserve—"

"I suppose it would be a pittance considering what you ordinarily spend on yourself, but then that means I'm not as much in your debt as you keep saying."

Penelope looked confused.

"The truth is you don't like me, Penelope, and you've treated me badly at every opportunity."

"I don't know what you're talking about."

Jessica sighed. "Go home. I'll send Henry some money for you, but I don't want to see you anymore. I'm tired of your criticism and your accusations. I've never been unkind to you, and I don't deserve your—your—contempt."

Penelope's eyes had turned mean when she realized that she wasn't going to be able to bully Jessica into splitting the inheritance. "You should do what you're told, Jessica, because if you don't, I'll have to take steps. I can't allow people to take advantage of me. I didn't let your father, and I won't let you."

James Hogg had shambled in and dropped with a thump beside Jessica's chair during the confrontation. He watched Penelope curiously as she railed at his mistress, then growled low in his throat and bared his teeth. Penelope drew back and stopped talking. Jessica was surprised. Her dog had never growled at a soul before. "Go home," said Jessica wearily. "We've nothing to say to one another."

"You'll do what I tell you," retorted Penelope

threateningly, "or you'll be very sorry." She rose and gathered her gloves and parasol. James Hogg, still growling, had risen as well, every hair on his spine bristling.

"You haven't moved in yet," said another of the Calder Avenue residents. "It's all over town you plan to drill on your land."

"I can't help what people are saying," snapped Travis. He didn't want to hear about the damned house. He turned his head when he rode past it, and he continued to live at the Ervin.

"We're willing to buy it from you," said the neighbor and named a figure twice what Travis had paid.

"Done," said Travis. Why should he keep the house he'd bought for a woman who wouldn't live with him?

"You'll take the offer?" asked the man, surprised.

"I'll take it."

"Oh." The fellow looked doubtful now that he'd achieved his purpose. He probably regretted having bid so much when he might have got the place for less, or so Travis surmised.

In August while a Heywood tank was being filled from a well, lightning set afire the gas venting from the top and sent a column of fire into the air. Although the fire was smothered with wet blankets brought by men from nearby wells, the potential for disaster in money and lives sent shock waves through the hill population, for the tank had been near a forest of derricks. Jessica looked at the towers sprouting around her house and shuddered, then went on with her daily routine, but the story was told in newspapers elsewhere and read by Anne Harte, who came swiftly to Spindletop.

"You can't stay here," said Anne after kissing and hugging Jessica. "It's too dangerous. Look at that." Anne waved at the vista from the sitting-room window. "What would happen to you if this whole place went up in flames?"

Jessica sighed. There was nowhere to go had she wanted to. "Mother—Anne—"

"I may not have borne you, Jessica," said Anne, "but I am your mother."

Jessica nodded humbly. Anne Harte was the only mother she'd ever known; Anne's love had been the most constant factor in Jessica's life, and it overwhelmed her as Anne put loving arms around her.

"You must come home, child. You simply can't stay here. You have no one in this dreadful, dangerous place now."

Jessica started to protest but was interrupted.

"I take it that you and Travis are still separated."

"You don't have to tell me that you warned me against him," said Jessica glumly.

"I'm not here to say I told you so. I wish it had worked out for you."

Jessica felt her heart twist. Anne hadn't trusted Travis, and rightly so; her instincts had been sound, and yet she had hoped for Jessica's happiness, something Penelope had never done.

"I realize that your housekeeper has your interests at heart," murmured Anne. "I had a long talk with that young woman, and I must say you've been lucky in her. Still, she's not family. . . ."

As Anne continued to talk, Jessica acknowledged another of the differences between her real mother and her stepmother. Penelope had hated Rainee; Anne saw her worth immediately.

". . . and we all want you to come home where you'll be safe and loved."

What a temptation it was. Jessica and her father had had the best talk of their lives before she left Fort Worth; if she went home, she could build on that understanding, and she could see her beloved brothers again and Frannie, who could probably use an older sister now that she was growing up. There were so many reasons to do what Anne wanted, but one overwhelming reason not to. Oliver Duplessis had offered Jessica the responsibilities of adulthood and then made sure she accepted them by leaving her his wealth. "I can't, Mother. I have too many obligations."

Anne sighed. "The inheritance," she guessed. "I could almost wish he'd passed you by, but I can understand why he didn't. Your grandfather was a brilliant man in his way; even Justin always said that, although they were usually at odds. I suppose Mr. Duplessis couldn't bear to see what he'd built squandered."

"I couldn't bear it either, Mother. It's a trust. You can see that."

"But you could go to Fort Worth. That's where the business is. At least you'd be closer to home that way, and safer."

"That's where Penelope is," Jessica muttered.

Anne's face paled. "She's an evil woman," Anne said urgently. "Always remember that."

Anne's vehemence made Jessica even more certain that she didn't want to go back to Fort Worth. "It's not so terrible here," she said reassuringly. "We've got a safety committee now, making and enforcing all sorts of rules we should have had long ago. Heavy fines for lighting matches in the field. Safe drainage from the wells—a lake of oil caused the first fire. No saloons within a thousand feet of a well."

"Jessica, I can see what sort of place this is. I've known rough frontier towns in my time, but this is worse. The men here—" She shook her head. "To be safe, you'd need to carry a gun."

"You're wrong about that, Mother. Gunfighters are ostracized on Spindletop, and anyway I could never shoot anyone. Could you?" Jessica thought she had come up with the unanswerable argument.

"I have," said Anne firmly. "Several—all of whom needed shooting."

Jessica's mouth fell open. "No one bothers me here," she stammered. "If that school Papa sent me to taught me anything, it was to freeze an improper advance in its tracks."

"Oh, my dear child, a cold look won't always suffice." She took both Jessica's hands in hers. "Is there no chance of your reconciling with Travis?"

"Mother!" exclaimed Jessica. "Surely you know what he was up to."

"Yes, your father told me, and I suppose he must have been very badly hurt as a boy."

"He was," Jessica admitted.

"I remember Will Parnell—a gay, reckless man— mostly reckless after his wife died. Your father thought a lot of Will; they were boys together in the war." Anne looked closely at Jessica. "Do you still love Travis?"

Tears welled in Jessica's eyes. "Yes," she admitted. "Isn't that pathetic?"

"There's nothing pathetic about love. Doesn't he want you back?"

"He did."

"Then go back to him. You're married, and you love him. The rest can be worked out. Surely by now you see that he had reason to hate Hugh and Penelope. Don't hurt yourself for their sakes."

"I doubt that he wants me anymore. We—we've quarreled badly."

"Listen to your heart, Jessica," Anne advised. "You'll be a happier woman for it. But if you don't go back to your husband, come home to us."

"I'll think about it, Mother." Jessica knew she wouldn't be going home; she was long past the stage of living as a dutiful daughter in her father's house.

Travis heard of Anne Harte's visit and decided that, no doubt, they'd had a fine time blackening his name. Anne must have been suspicious of him from the start. It was she who insisted on a year's engagement. Then he thought of his wife, unprotected in that field of derricks and gushers. Gritting his teeth, he took his mind off his worries by purchasing more land out toward Sour Lake. A man was better off with money than with a woman who gave him nothing but trouble, he told himself. Too bad she hadn't gone home to Daddy. No doubt that had been Anne Harte's mission.

Well, Jessica should have gone. He wasn't going to look out for her any longer, even if this was a place no sensible woman would live in by herself. Jessica had left *him*, so she was on her own—stupid, distrustful girl. She'd actually thought he was buying favors from a poor dimwit like Lissie, whose hair looked and felt like the back end of a mule, whereas Jess's hair was as silken as clear, clean water sliding through a man's fingers on a hot day. Damn. He was the fool for thinking that way.

"Why, Sheriff Landry." Jessica smiled to see the lawman on her doorstep. "What can I do for you?"

"Well, Miz Parnell, we—ah—need to talk to you."

Behind Ras Landry stood a man who looked familiar. "Of course. Come in, Sheriff. Rainee and I were about to have our midday meal. Will you join us?"

"No, ma'am."

Jessica thought Landry looked uncommonly nervous. Was it improper to invite a sheriff to one's table? The mistresses at the Mount Vernon Seminary probably wouldn't have known what to do with a sheriff, had they ever had the opportunity to interact with one socially. Jessica had to suppress a desire to giggle at the thought of Sheriff Ras Landry and the headmistress of the Mount Vernon Seminary trying to make conversation over cups of tea. Rainee had remarked several times in the last week that Jessica was getting silly. Perhaps it was true.

"This is Lieutenant Hartwig from Fort Worth, ma'am."

"Sir." Jessica nodded politely and invited the men to be seated. "Perhaps you'd care for a cool drink," she suggested hospitably.

"No thanks, ma'am." Ras Landry frowned, shifting uncomfortably in his chair. "We're here on business, as you might say. About your grandfather's death."

"Really?" Jessica was mystified.

"There's some thought that he might have been smothered in his sleep."

"Why—why would anyone think that?" asked Jessica, shocked.

"Because a maid in his house said she seen it," said Lieutenant Hartwig. "Matter of fact, she says she seen you smother him."

Jessica gaped at him. Rainee, who had been standing by the kitchen door at the edge of Jessica's vision, moved out of sight abruptly. "But—but—"

"Lieutenant Hartwig wants to take you back to Fort Worth, Miz Parnell. I told him you didn't strike me as a woman who'd be likely to harm a soul, but seein' as they got an eyewitness . . ."

"That's impossible," cried Jessica. "There couldn't be a witness to something that never happened."

"Your mother says as how no one had a better motive than you," added Hartwig.

"What motive? I loved my grandfather. I couldn't believe it when I received word that he had died."

"You inherited a pile of money, Miz Parnell," said Hartwig. "Greed's a mighty powerful motive."

Jessica shook her head helplessly. "No one knew he'd changed his will—well, his lawyer did, but the rest of us were shocked, especially me." The person who had expected to inherit was Penelope. And once upon a time Penelope had tried to smother Jessica—although who could say if that story was really true?

Jessica considered telling them, but she had no evidence that her mother had done anything all those years ago or at the time of Grandfather Duplessis's death. If she spoke up, they'd think she was trying to save herself by casting suspicion on her mother. Nor could she make an accusation with no proof.

"Even if I'd known that I was his heir," said Jessica earnestly, "I would never have—" She stopped because it seemed obvious that they wouldn't take her word, not with a witness accusing her. How could she clear herself? "Sheriff, except for my grandfather's funeral and an excursion to the beach some weeks before that, I haven't been off Spindletop or out of the Beaumont area since I came here in March."

"Is there anyone could swear to that—that you was here the night your grandfather died?" asked the sheriff. "Does your housekeeper live here?"

"No," said Jessica.

"Then no one knows where you were that night," Hartwig concluded.

"I know, Abe," said Travis.

The three of them looked up in surprise at the figure in the doorway.

"She spent the evening with me and the Hamil brothers, and she spent the night with me—in bed," Travis said, entering. "I was here when she got the telegram the next morning."

Flushing uncomfortably, Jessica looked from Travis to the Fort Worth officer. Travis had called the man by his first name. So she *had* seen Lieutenant Hartwig before, and she remembered where. At the Labor Day picnic.

"I thought you an' your missus was separated," remarked Hartwig suspiciously.

"Some of the time we are," Travis replied, his voice as cool as Jessica's face was hot. "Ask her housekeeper."

"He come here," Rainee confirmed. "Saturday night mostly. He here night old man died. After he take her to depot, he come back. Tell me she go to Fort Worth for funeral." Both the Jefferson County sheriff and the Tarrant County policeman looked intrigued at this information. Jessica thought she'd almost rather be accused of murder than have her unconventional marital arrangements revealed so bluntly.

"If you're looking for someone with a motive to kill Oliver Duplessis, it's his daughter, Penelope Gresham, you should be talking to," said Travis. "Everyone, including Penelope, thought she'd get his money."

"Travis, we got a witness who says your wife smothered the old man," said Hartwig.

"Then you got a witness who's lying, and you got a daughter of the victim, Mrs. Gresham, who tried to smother someone in the past."

The two lawmen stared at him.

"Ask Justin Harte," said Travis. "Better yet, ask an old black woman at the Rocking T Ranch in Parker County. She saw Penelope Gresham try to smother her own baby."

"Calliope saw it?" whispered Jessica.

"Thank you for your time, ma'am," said Lieutenant Hartwig. "Travis, if we could have a word with you."

Jessica watched them go. Travis hadn't said a thing to her, not even good-bye. He hadn't so much as glanced her way as he left. "How did he know to come?" she wondered out loud.

"He out back at derrick. I go get him," said Rainee.

Chapter Twenty-Eight

Jessica hung up the telephone with a trembling hand. She took business calls from Fort Worth each morning on the newly installed line to her house, but the most recent communication had not been about business.

"Whose voice walk on wire with bad news?" asked Rainee.

"Henry Barnett," Jessica replied. "My father's lawyer."

"Something happen to father?"

Jessica shook her head. "To my mother."

"Good mother or Great Cannibal Owl?"

"Penelope."

Rainee smiled. "So. Voice like arrow from bow carry news of enemy."

Jessica frowned at her housekeeper. "She's been arrested for Grandfather's murder."

Rainee looked unsurprised. "Travis right. Now you take him back?"

Jessica shifted uneasily. Had Travis's remarks to Lieutenant Hartwig been responsible for the investigation that led to Penelope's arrest? "The maid who implicated me—they brought her in again and put a lot of pressure on her. Now she says it was Penelope she saw holding a pillow over Grandfather's face, not me."

"Why she not tell truth before?"

"Who knows what the truth is?" murmured Jessica, deeply troubled. "The maid—her name is Grace—says Penelope had come over to take care of Grandfather when he was sick."

"Not sound like Great Cannibal Owl."

"I know," Jessica agreed. "I can't remember Penelope ever doing that before—for Grandfather or anyone else. In fact, she raised money for the hospital in Fort Worth but wouldn't go near the patients. Anyway, Grace claims Grandfather went to sleep much earlier than usual that night—right after he and Penelope had supper together in his room."

"Sleeping herb in coffee," guessed Rainee.

"He only had chicken broth."

"So. Sleeping herb in soup."

Jessica glanced at her, remembering how she herself had reacted to a small dose of Penelope's medicine; she'd been dizzy, then fallen into a deep sleep. Could Penelope have given him some of that nerve medicine? Of course, there was no proof, nor was there likely to be.

"When Grace went upstairs to check on him, Penelope was pressing a pillow over his face," Jessica went on. "Grace told the police she must have gasped when she saw it, because Penelope heard her and said if she didn't keep her mouth shut, Penelope would call in the police and accuse her of killing him. The poor girl was terrified and let herself be convinced that no one would believe the word of a servant over the word of Mrs. Hugh Gresham."

"Turkey magic," muttered Rainee.

Startled, Jessica looked at her questioningly.

"Turkey never fight, always run from enemies," she explained. "Why mother make turkey-spirit maid lie about you?"

"That was after I inherited instead of Penelope. Ironic, isn't it? If she hadn't wanted to get even with me, she'd never have been caught. No one but the maid thought his death was anything but natural."

"Not just for get even. If you hang, maybe mother think she get money."

Jessica sat down abruptly. It made a sort of crazy sense; Penelope must have killed Oliver for the money. Then when Jessica inherited instead and refused to share, Penelope had forced the maid into a false accusation. Her mother had been so strange in the last months; it was just possible she actually believed herself to be Jessica's heiress.

"Indian way better. Give away or kill dead person's horses and bury clothes. Then no reason for family kill each other."

Jessica smiled wryly at the idea of Penelope being forced by custom to give away or bury Oliver Duplessis' fortune. "Henry says she wants me to come to Fort Worth to stand by her."

Rainee grunted contemptuously. "Great Cannibal Owl still hungry. You stay here, not get eaten."

Jessica nodded. "I'm not going, but I can hardly believe she actually—her own father. How could she—"

"That one could do anything."

"But what if she didn't? What if everything the

425

maid said was a lie? I suppose I should at least send the money she spent on me when she took Travis and me into her house—the wedding she gave us and everything."

"They pay to get you husband?" asked Rainee, looking more disapproving than ever. "Foolish custom. How Travis know your value if not pay for you? Jed Beeker give my father many horses."

Jessica smiled weakly. "I'm sure you were worth every horse of it, Rainee."

"You speak truth. If Travis pay for you, he not let you go. Insist on wife or get horses back."

"I don't want to hear anything about Travis."

"Huh. Good you not go to mother. Why she think you would?"

"Penelope has a very selective memory," said Jessica wearily. "She remembers forever what she considers offenses against herself, but rarely the offenses she commits against others. She always considers those justified. In fact, I'm not sure that she remembers much of anything any longer. She—she has—"

"Too much firewater in belly?" Rainee suggested. Jessica nodded and closed her eyes.

"You all right?"

"Actually, I don't feel very well. Maybe I'll lie down for a bit before I go out on business."

"Good. You look like coyote who drinks from poison spring."

"I tell you sometime baby come from Saturday-night marriage."

"I don't know that I'm with child," said Jessica in a wobbly voice.

"I know. Tomorrow send for husband."

Jessica shook her head.

"Send!" Rainee commanded in her best no-nonsense voice. "Now you two share lodge. No more Saturday night—"

"He doesn't come on Saturdays anymore," Jessica interrupted drearily.

"—like you some loose woman in feathers," Rainee continued. "You tell husband baby come. He move back to your lodge."

"You're a very bossy woman," said Jessica sulkily. "Just because I feel that you're family doesn't mean you can treat me like a child."

"You act like child; Rainee treat like child," said Rainee, but her tone had softened considerably at Jessica's declaration that she regarded her housekeeper as family.

"Oh, Rainee, what am I going to do?"

"Send for husband."

"I doubt that he'd come," said Jessica unhappily. Then she straightened her shoulders. "And I wouldn't want him to. I can raise the child by myself. That would be better than giving him a father who can't be trusted."

"No trust?" exclaimed Rainee. "Why you say that? You need Travis, he come. He keep you from hanging for grandfather's death. Now you send for him."

"No, and you're not to either."

"What are you doing here?" asked Jessica, overcome with confusion and alarm. She looked around wildly for her housekeeper, but Rainee was nowhere in sight.

"I've come to make my peace with you, Jessica. I know we've had hard words, but it's wrong for a mother and daughter to be at odds."

427

"I thought you'd been arrested," said Jessica bluntly, too upset by her mother's unexpected appearance to observe any amenities.

"It was a mistake, dear. As you can see, they let me go." Penelope gave her a bright, nervous smile. "Surely you didn't believe that I killed my own father?"

"You told them I had," Jessica stammered defensively. The dog had slunk into the room and began to growl at Penelope from behind Jessica's skirts.

"I said no such thing. Why would I say you'd hurt Father? You weren't even in Fort Worth when he died." Penelope glanced down at the agitated dog. "I think that creature wants to go outside, Jessica. Why don't you—"

"The police officer from Fort Worth said you told them I was the one with the motive."

"He lied," snapped Penelope impatiently. "Now put your dog out."

"He doesn't like to go outside." Where was Rainee, for God's sake? Jessica wondered desperately.

"Mothers and daughters should be close," said Penelope. "I was so touched when you sent Henry the money for me."

Had Penelope really been touched? Jessica wondered. She had expected resentment because she hadn't sent more. "I was returning what you spent on me—for the wedding and everything," Jessica mumbled. The conversation seemed unreal. Penelope was talking almost like a normal mother.

"I've brought you a little gift," said Penelope. "It's not much, of course. My income is quite small."

Ah, now the demands and recriminations would start.

"But I did make these myself." Penelope smiled and produced a little package wrapped in gaily colored paper. Reluctantly, Jessica accepted it because it was thrust into her hands. "Open it," said Penelope eagerly.

Jessica did and found inside three little tea cakes of the kind her mother liked, except that these were misshapen and inexpertly frosted. Jessica realized with astonishment that her mother might actually have made them. "Th-thank you," she stammered.

"You're welcome." Penelope gave her another sweet smile. "Have one," she invited.

"Oh, I'll—I'll save them for later."

Penelope frowned. "It's not often I cook, Jessica."

Jessica hadn't known she ever did.

"I made them just for you."

"Thank you."

Penelope snatched one of the cakes from the open package and thrust it at Jessica. "The least you could do is show your appreciation by trying one."

Jessica backed away from the out-thrust hand, but James Hogg, always ready to accept offerings of food, didn't. He leapt up, jaws open and drooling, to snatch the cake from Penelope's hand with a loud and appreciative "woof."

"Bad dog," cried Jessica and then had to stifle a nervous giggle at the expression of alarm on her mother's face.

"Make him give it back," Penelope demanded.

"I'm afraid it's too late," said Jessica. The dog had swallowed the little cake whole and was eying the remaining lumps in the package with longing. "But I promise I'll eat the others myself. Cake isn't good for dogs."

"Yes, do have one now, Jessica. I certainly didn't make them for your—your animal."

Penelope was reaching for another sweet when Rainee burst in breathlessly, saying to the man behind her, "There is evil one." The man was Ras Landry.

Jessica looked from the sheriff to her mother. "She said she'd been freed," Jessica said.

"Only on bond," said the sheriff, "and she jumped it two days ago and disappeared. Had a telegram from Hartwig just this morning. They were afraid she might be heading this way."

James Hogg had begun to whine at Jessica's feet. Penelope was backing up, her eyes flicking apprehensively to the dog, whose whimpers and twitching increased. Jessica looked down at him too, then back at her mother. "What have you done?" she whispered.

"Nothing," said Penelope. "He shouldn't have been so greedy."

"Come along, Miz Gresham." The sheriff took her in a firm grip. "I'll be putting you on a train back to Fort Worth."

"Yes, yes," Penelope agreed. "I must go back. Don't forget your present, Jessica."

The dog had gone rigid, then limp. Rainee was staring at the cakes on the table. "Great Cannibal Owl make evil medicine," she muttered.

Penelope smiled flirtatiously at the sheriff. "I'm Jessica's heir, you know," she murmured to him. "The Duplessis heiress still." She produced her old trilling laughter.

"You're not," said Jessica, overcome with horror. How could her mother have thought that?

"Of course I am. Now, Sheriff, you realize that I have to travel first class."

"Yes, ma'am. I'll even provide an escort," he added dryly.

"Enjoy your cakes, Jessica," crooned Penelope.

The sheriff was urging her toward the door. "Wait, I must have some of my medicine." She rummaged in her bag as Ras Landry led her away.

"You all right?" Rainee asked into the silence that followed their departure.

Jessica nodded.

"I take dog away."

Jessica shook her head.

"You eat cake?" Rainee was looking worried.

Jessica shook her head again.

"You want sit by self?"

Jessica nodded.

Studying her for a moment longer, Rainee nodded as well and went into the kitchen.

Jessica was in the rocking chair, her fingers trailing through James Hogg's thick fur, when a sound at the front door attracted her attention. Travis stood on the threshold, his face cold and closed. "Rainee sent word that you wanted to see me."

"She shouldn't have," Jessica whispered, her heart aching. Travis looked at her as if she were a stranger.

Then his eyes sharpened, and he demanded, "What's wrong with you, Jessica?"

At his harsh tone, Jessica burst into tears. Had he been kind, she acknowledged to herself, she would probably have fallen into his arms in gratitude. As it was, his barely withheld anger toppled the last block in the wall of her self-control. "She killed James Hogg," Jessica mumbled incoherently, tears pouring down her cheeks.

Travis looked at the dog, who appeared to be sleeping by Jessica's chair. "He looks all right to me."

"Dog dead," Rainee declared. She stood in the kitchen doorway, hands on hips, scowling at both of them.

"What did you want me to do about it?" asked Travis warily. "You sent for me because the dog died?"

"If dog not die, Jessica die. Poison meant for her."

Travis's face turned white and grim. "Penelope," he guessed. "I thought she was in jail in Fort Worth."

"She escape. Come for father's money."

Travis's mouth twisted. "So you put her in your will, after all?" He stared at Jessica with contempt. "You do pick the damnedest people to trust," he added bitterly. "Anyone of your blood, is that it?"

"I not send for you to make her feel worse," snapped Rainee.

"Why then?" He wasn't giving an inch.

"I have evil crazy woman in house, need help. Sheriff come first."

"Well, then I'm *not* needed."

"You talk to wife. She have news for you." Rainee gave Jessica a compelling look.

"What?" Travis asked, studying Jessica in a way that made her want to run from the room.

"Nothing," she replied quickly.

"Only foolish man leave without news," said Rainee, "but then, you both fools." She whirled and slammed the kitchen door behind her.

"All right, what is it?"

"I didn't make Penelope my heir," Jessica replied, hoping that statement would divert him.

"Now, why don't I believe that's what Rainee was talking about?" he asked dryly. "Have you made a will at all?"

"No."

"Well, you'd best do it to be on the safe side, hadn't you? You wouldn't want all that Duplessis and Harte money to go to your worst enemy."

"You're not my worst enemy," she whispered.

"Since when? Do I look a little less reprehensible because I, at least, haven't tried to kill you?" he asked sarcastically. "But that's getting us off the subject of your will. Since you're young, maybe you can afford to put off making one. Not feeling poorly, are you?"

"N-no," Jessica stammered.

"Are you?" Travis looked at her more closely. "Jess, is something wrong with you?"

"No," she said, alarmed.

"Are you sick?"

Had Rainee told him about the attacks of nausea?

"Have you seen a doctor? Let me look at you." Travis pulled her abruptly from the rocking chair, and Jessica's hands flew protectively to her stomach, a gesture that he didn't miss.

"I'll be damned," he muttered, remembering how much he'd wanted her to be carrying his child last winter—the night Joe Ray had blown their relationship sky high. Now evidently she was, now when they were further apart than ever. "You weren't planning to tell me, were you?" he asked sadly.

Jessica turned her head away, tears rising again in her eyes.

"Were you?" he demanded. "Do you really hate me that much?"

"You know it's not that."

"Well then, you don't trust me." When she didn't reply, he pulled her roughly into his arms. "That's not fair, you know, not trusting me. I've always tried to make you happy. You were happy, damn it, until Joe Ray opened his big mouth. Look at me, Jessica." He forced her chin up and looked into blue eyes drowned with tears. "It's not as if you've been so happy since you kicked me out."

Her lips trembled, but she didn't answer.

"You agree? Good. Well, I've been patient long

enough. No matter how you feel about me, we're living together, same house, same bed, and you'll find I'm a damned good father to the child. I don't suppose you wanted it."

"I did too," she protested.

"Well, that's a start. Damn, I don't have a house."

"What happened to it?"

"I sold it. I was so mad at you that I sold it."

"Did you make a profit?"

Travis stared at her in astonishment. "Jessica, you are one unromantic woman! Did I make a profit? Here I bought you a house, and all you care about is if I sold it at a profit."

"I have no reason to be romantic about you, Travis. I wasn't married for romantic reasons. Our marriage came about because you hate my family."

"Look, Jessica, let's get something straight. I've known for months that Hugh was mixed up with thieves, and I didn't do anything about it. Not because I don't hate him. I do. I kept out of it for your sake."

"You did?"

"I did."

"But they're both in jail," she ventured uncertainly.

"I didn't put them there."

"But you're probably happy about it."

"Delighted," he agreed. "You should be too. Hugh's a thief, and Penelope's a murderer, several times over if she could have got away with it. For God's sake, you were an intended victim, Jess! As for the Harte side of your family, I probably like them better than they like me."

"Are you saying all this because of Grandfather's money?" she asked suspiciously.

"Don't be dense, Jessie. I'm rich too. I'm also hopelessly, head-over-heels in love with you."

Jessica's eyes widened. Her mouth rounded in an "O" of surprise. Her breath caught helplessly in her chest. Hopelessly, head-over-heels in love? Could that be the truth?

"At a certain point, in case it hasn't occurred to you, a few million extra doesn't make any difference," he continued.

If he really was so much in love with her, why had it taken him a year to tell her?

"And that's how I feel about your money. It's nice, but we hardly need it."

Except for the initial deception, he'd always been truthful—so maybe . . . just maybe . . .

"Jessica, are you listening to me?"

"You really mean it?"

"About the money?"

"No, not the money," she retorted impatiently. "About being in love with me."

"Yes." He looked wary again.

"Aren't you going to say anything else?" The brief glow ignited by his declaration was fading fast.

"Why?"

Although Jessica felt like an importunate fool, he was waiting for an answer, looking rather grim. "I just—just wanted to hear about—about your loving me."

"And then what? You're going to say you don't believe me? Or you don't care?"

She studied him with surprise. He was afraid of being rejected! He must have believed her when she told him she was using him for physical pleasure. Although he'd laughed at the time and seemed to accept the situation, perhaps he had been hurt. Had she been so protective of her own pride that she'd failed to realize his was at stake as well? "Travis, you know that I've always loved you."

"I haven't known it lately," he muttered, "but it doesn't matter. We're going to have a child, and I'm not letting you go through that alone. We'll just have to live together—somewhere. I shouldn't have sold that damn house."

"It doesn't matter about the house," she replied tenderly.

"Of course it matters. We're not living here; it's too dangerous, and you can't move into my room at the boardinghouse."

"Even though it does have a bathtub," she added, smiling mischievously at what had once seemed the ultimate betrayal.

"I never said it didn't," he replied defensively.

"I realize that. I forgive you."

"About the bathtub?"

"About everything."

"Everything?"

"Everything, Travis. I love you very much."

"Oh, sweetheart." His arms tightened around her. "I'm going to make you so happy."

Epilogue

Beaumont, Texas
April, 1902

"A gusher sold for as little as eight thousand dollars in January and February, but I got nine hundred thousand for mine before the prices crashed," said Jessica with great satisfaction.

"Nine hundred thousand dollars? Good grief!" exclaimed Anne Harte. She and Justin had come to Beaumont for the birth of their first grandchild.

"Jessica is as much responsible for the drop in well prices as Hogg and Swayne," said Travis, grinning at her.

"What nonsense!" she replied, grinning back. It was an old argument between them.

"Well, I'm not the one who let the derricks go up every twenty feet and drove the price of oil down to nothing," said Travis virtuously.

"I hope you have a good doctor, Jessica," said Anne.

"The man's an idiot," Travis complained. "I told

him she was to have ether for the delivery, and he told me it was a woman's lot to suffer in childbirth."

"Ether?" exclaimed Anne, alarmed.

"Oh, I know, Mother. I opposed it myself at first," said Jessica soothingly, "but when that stupid doctor started telling me about paying for the sins of Eve, it was really too much. I told him I agreed with Travis and asked if he was afraid people would accuse him of having his wicked way with me while I was unconscious." Jessica laughed merrily. "That shut him up. He was horrified."

"I should think so," said Justin.

"But ether?" Anne looked very dubious.

"If it's good enough for Queen Victoria, it's good enough for Jessie," said Travis. "I won't have her going through that sort of pain when it's unnecessary. Jessica controls the dosage herself—holds the bottle and the handkerchief. When she loses consciousness, her hand will fall away naturally. There's no danger whatever."

"Unless someone is smoking a cigar in the delivery room," Jessica added.

Mother and daughter, peeking at each other, started to grin. "Would you like me to be there, Jessie?" Anne asked, trying to control her laughter.

"I think you should, Mother. Someone has to keep an eye out for cigars and improper conduct on the part of the doctor."

"Jessica," said Justin, "childbirth is not a matter for humor. Your husband, at least, takes the situation seriously. Why, when your mother had Frannie . . ." Justin cut himself off because his wife had lost control of her enforced solemnity once more. "Anne, what are you laughing at?" he asked.

Anne wiped the smile from her face, but Jessica had started to giggle. Both of them remembered that

Justin had been frantic with worry during Frannie's birth, while Anne, who had already borne twin sons under the worst of circumstances, had taken her confinement with complete calm once the doctor insisted that Justin and his cigar leave the house and stop upsetting everyone.

Trying to look properly solemn, Anne murmured, "Travis, would you mind passing the lima beans?"

They were dining in the house on Calder Avenue, which Travis had repurchased from the neighborhood committee once he managed to convince them that he did not intend to let his pregnant wife live next to an oil well.

"Jessie told me you're Will Parnell's son," Justin remarked. Jessica had finally gone into labor. Anne, Rainee, and the reluctant doctor were with her in the large corner bedroom upstairs. Justin and Travis had been banished to Travis's study.

"That's right." Travis didn't want to talk about his father, who could now, he hoped, rest in peace.

"Will and I were friends," said Justin, "had been since we were boys."

Finally Travis remembered something that had hovered at the edge of his mind the first time he met Justin Harte, something obscured for years by the more vivid recollections of Hugh and Penelope. His father had said to Hugh Gresham, "Justin won't let you do this." So this was the man Will Parnell had hoped would save him from Hugh's plotting.

"I thought a lot of Will," said Justin, "although I didn't see much of him after Anne and I got married. He was ranching in Jack County by then. I still had land in Palo Pinto in the '80s, but I was spending most of my time in Weatherford and Mitchell County . . . even some time out of state." Justin leaned back in his chair and gave Travis a somber look. "I'd like to hear what happened to Will."

"He got caught between Cattleman's Bank and the fence cutters," said Travis.

"Well, I know about the fence cutting. Had some of my own cut in '83 when the drought got bad; cost a lot of money."

Travis nodded, remembering the fury of the open-range cattlemen, who cut fences to get their stock to water and left hanged effigies and roughly painted threats by the uprooted fence posts. "Then Gresham called his notes, most of them loans Hugh had talked him into. Pa just gave up when he heard that Cattleman's wouldn't stand by him."

"And then?"

"He shot himself." Travis felt the old bleakness settle over him once more. "I found him."

"Jessie told me. What happened after that?"

"The hotel owner took what money we'd brought with us to pay the bill, and I ended up on the street."

"There had to be something left besides what Will had in his pockets," said Justin, frowning. "His land must have been worth more than his notes. And there was bound to be stock."

"All I ever got was his rabies stone, and Joe Ray Brock gave me that four years later when he found me and took me back to Lubbock County."

"I remember that stone. Your father swore it saved his life when he was bit by a wild dog up on the Llano Estacado. But what happened to the rest of the property?"

"Joe Ray said the bank took it. Maybe you profited, being a shareholder. I never saw a penny."

"Your father's debts were paid off after his death. Nothing else showed on the books. I remember seeing that at the stockholders' meeting the end of

'83," mused Justin, his frown deepening.

"The whole idea of that bank, as far as I was concerned, was to carry ranchers through the bad years. Hugh didn't agree with me, but I usually got my way because I had a majority on the board. Still, I'll admit I didn't attend all the meetings in '83." Justin brooded over the story he had just heard. "So you were out for revenge and used Jessie to get it."

"I did," Travis admitted, "but I regretted it soon enough. For Jessie's sake, I'd stopped going after Hugh long before he was arrested."

"You must have loved my daughter pretty deeply to put aside that kind of hate."

"I did, and I do," said Travis. "She's a woman in a million."

"So was her mother," said Justin dryly.

Travis frowned, and his mouth tightened in anger.

"Oh, I don't mean Jessie's like Penelope, any more than sweet and smart is like stupid and vicious. Frankly, as far as I'm concerned, anything you managed to do to Penelope and Hugh was well deserved. Or were their troubles a matter of divine retribution?"

Travis laughed. "I can't take credit for everything that happened to them. In fact, your putting your bank shares on the market did a lot to bring him down. He had to raise the money to get them by—"

"Hugh bought my shares?" exclaimed Justin. "I didn't sell them to him."

"He used others to front for him, but he raised the money, and the way he did it brought them to grief—both him and Penelope." Travis watched his father-in-law's slow grin.

"That bitch," Justin muttered pleasantly. "It does my heart good to think she's in jail."

"Well, we agree on that," said Travis.

"You realize, of course, that she and Hugh may well have stolen your inheritance?"

"I know it," said Travis somberly, "but in the end I got something a lot more precious." He sighed and studied his father-in-law thoughtfully. "I have a favor to ask—not for myself, for Jessie."

Justin's eyebrows shot up. "What's that?"

"You're an influential man. You know lots of judges and lawyers, right?"

Justin nodded cautiously.

"All it takes to get licensed to practice law in this state is a favorable investigation by a committee of three lawyers and the approval of the judge who appointed them. Henry Barnett could be on the committee. You can choose the judge and the other two lawyers."

"Well, I don't know."

"It's her heart's desire."

"I thought you were her heart's desire."

Travis laughed. "She just tolerates me."

"You sounded like your father just then," said Justin. "I guess I can call in a few favors, since it's for Jessica."

At that moment Anne came down the stairs with a blanket-wrapped bundle in her arms.

"Jessica—is she all right?" Travis asked anxiously. He couldn't believe that for a few minutes there he'd forgotten that his wife was upstairs having his child.

"Of course," said Anne.

A smug expression spread over Travis's face. "We didn't hear a sound!" he exclaimed triumphantly as he peered down at the baby's face. "That means she felt no pain."

"The doctor felt no pain," corrected Anne. "Jessica drifted off after a few sniffs of ether, flung the handkerchief in the doctor's face, and dropped the bottle. The doctor was anesthetized, and I delivered the baby."

Travis looked astounded.

"You have a son," she informed him.

"So much for modern medicine," said Justin, grinning. "What are you going to call him?"

Travis looked at his father-in-law for a long minute. "Would you like to name him?" Travis asked.

"Yes, I would," said Justin. "How about Will Parnell?"

Pleased, Travis clapped Justin's shoulder warmly before taking young Will Parnell into his arms.

"I have a surprise for you," Travis told Jessica.

She smiled at him dreamily from the comfort of her bed as she cuddled the new baby.

"You're going to get your license."

"What license?"

"To practice law. Your father's going to arrange for the judge and the committee."

"Oh, that's nice."

Travis looked disappointed at the casual reception his gift had met.

"It's very thoughtful of you and Papa," she continued, "but I want a horseless carriage for my birthing present."

"Those things are dangerous!" Travis exclaimed.

"That's what you always say about oil wells," she retorted. "For goodness sake, Travis, it's the age of petroleum. We oilmen have to set an example." She shifted the baby and smiled down at him, then up at her husband. "You and I, love, are founding an oil dynasty here. We're no little shoestring outfit. We're going to make even Papa and the big cattle barons look like small potatoes."

Travis laughed delightedly. His father would have

adored Jessica. "Well, when you put it that way, sweetheart, how can I refuse you a motorcar?" He bent over to kiss her. "Lord, Jess, I do love you. It scares me to death when I think that you might have refused to forgive me—ever."

"Oh, I couldn't have done that, Travis," she replied, touching his mouth softly with a fingertip. "I fell in love with you at the dinner table the first night we met."

"Makes me a little slow, doesn't it?" Travis asked ruefully. "Do you forgive me?"

"Always," she replied.